The Rivals of
Sherlock Holmes

www.noexit.co.uk

About the Editor

Nick Rennison is a writer, editor and bookseller with a particular interest in the Victorian era and in crime fiction. He is the author of many books including *The Bloomsbury Good Reading Guide to Crime Fiction*, *100 Must-Read Crime Novels*, *Sherlock Holmes: An Unauthorised Biography* and *Peter Mark Roget – The Man who became a Book*. He is currently working on his own crime novel set in nineteenth century London.

Other books by Nick Rennison

100 Must-Read Crime Novels
The Bloomsbury Good Reading Guide to Crime Fiction
Sherlock Holmes: An Unauthorised Biography
Peter Mark Roget: The Man Who Became a Book

The Rivals of
Sherlock Holmes

An Anthology of Crime Stories 1890 – 1914

Edited by
NICK RENNISON

NO EXIT PRESS

First published in 2008 by No Exit Press
P.O. Box 394, Harpenden, Herts, AL5 1XJ

Editorial material © Nick Rennison 2008

The right of Nick Rennison to be identified as the author
of this work has been asserted in accordance with the
Copyright, Designs and Patents Act 1988.

A CIP catalogue record for this book is available from the British Library.

ISBN 978-1-84243-248-8

2 4 6 8 10 9 7 5 3 1

Typeset by Matrix Media Services, Chichester, West Sussex
Fingerprint/Magnifying Glass image © Shutterstock 2007
Printed and bound in Great Britain by Cox & Wyman, Reading

To Eve with love and thanks

Contents

Introduction

Sherlock Holmes is the most famous fictional detective ever created. The supremely rational sleuth and his dependable companion, Dr Watson, will forever be associated with the gaslit and smog-filled streets of late nineteenth and early twentieth-century London. Yet Holmes and Watson were not the only ones solving mysterious crimes and foiling the plans of villainous masterminds in Victorian and Edwardian England. The years between 1890 and 1914 were a golden age for English magazines and most of them published crime and detective fiction.

Of course, crime fiction had not been born with Holmes's first appearance in *A Study in Scarlet*, a novel-length story published in *Beeton's Christmas Annual* of 1887. Scholars of the genre still bicker over when exactly it did first emerge. Some, marshalling more enthusiasm than evidence, claim it has its origins in stories from biblical and Ancient Greek literature. Others point to late eighteenth century fiction like William Godwin's *Caleb Williams* which hinges on the investigation of a murder. Certainly crime fiction, in a form recognisable to readers today, had been around for most of the nineteenth century and writers as various as the American Edgar Allan Poe, the Englishman Wilkie Collins and the Frenchman Émile Gaboriau had practised it. But it was Conan Doyle who took the genre to new heights of popularity.

Holmes was not an entirely original creation (Doyle openly borrowed elements from earlier detectives like Poe's Dupin and Gaboriau's Lecoq) but he rapidly became the most famous of all fictional detectives, a position he has held ever since and is unlikely to relinquish as long as crime fiction continues to be read. He did so because he appeared in short stories published in a monthly magazine. The truth is that, if Sherlock Holmes had only been the leading character in the first two novels about him Doyle published, it is extremely unlikely that he would be remembered today by anyone but a specialist in late Victorian literature. *A Study in Scarlet*, for which Doyle was paid the princely sum of £25, was not a great success and *The Sign of Four*, a much better story published in 1890, did little more to set the Thames on fire. It was only when Sherlock Holmes short stories began to appear in a new magazine named *The Strand* that the character really seized the public imagination.

In his autobiography, with the benefit of hindsight, Doyle could claim that he had spotted the particular type of market that magazines like *The Strand* offered. 'Considering these various journals with their disconnected stories,' he wrote, 'it had struck me that a single character running through a series, if it only engaged the attention of the reader, would bind that reader to that particular magazine... Looking round for my central character, I felt that Sherlock Holmes, who I had already handled in two little books, would easily lend himself to a succession of short stories.' The result of Doyle's insight (and the perspicacity of *The Strand*'s editor Greenhough Smith who commissioned him) was the first set of Holmes short stories which began with 'A Scandal in Bohemia' in July 1891. Doyle went on to become probably *The Strand*'s most highly valued contributor and fifty-five more Holmes tales appeared in its pages in the next thirty-six years.

Not that Doyle was the first writer to publish fiction in *The Strand*. He was not even the first to write a detective story for it. That honour goes to Grant Allen whose story 'Jerry Stokes' appeared a couple of months before 'A Scandal in Bohemia'. He could, however, claim to be the first to spot the importance of 'a single character running through a series'. There had been earlier detectives who appeared in sequences of stories in magazines (tales of the Glaswegian detective Dick Donovan, for example, date from the late 1880s) but Sherlock Holmes was undoubtedly the first such character to make a massive impact on a magazine's circulation. One immediate consequence was that Greenhough Smith began to commission other writers to produce series of detective stories. He wanted rivals to Sherlock

Holmes if only because Doyle was unable (or unwilling) to write a Holmes story for every issue of *The Strand* in the 1890s. So characters like Martin Hewitt, the lawyer turned detective created by Arthur Morrison, and Lois Cayley, the feisty 'New Woman' whose adventures were recorded by Grant Allen, made their debut in the magazine. The Martin Hewitt stories were even illustrated by Sydney Paget, the same artist who brought Holmes to life. L. T. Meade, a veteran writer of romances and crime fiction, collaborated with a doctor named Clifford Halifax to write stories about a doctor named Clifford Halifax. (Clifford Halifax was actually the pseudonym of a medic called Edgar Beaumont who was presumably drafted into the partnership to provide professional expertise.) None of these characters attained even a tenth of the fame of Holmes but all did their bit to increase the popularity of crime fiction. For many years after 'A Scandal in Bohemia', nearly every monthly issue of *The Strand*, almost without exception, included a story of mystery and detection.

Although it was a dominant player in the market, *The Strand* was only one of dozens of similar magazines that were published in the late Victorian and Edwardian era. And, like *The Strand*, nearly every one of them wanted crime stories. Writers were only too happy to oblige. Some of these writers, like Arnold Bennett, are now famous for other work. Some, like Grant Allen and Guy Boothby, were famous in their day but are now almost forgotten. Some, like Victor Whitechurch and Headon Hill, were not particularly famous even in their own lifetimes. All, however, were prepared to supply the monthly magazines' insatiable demand for fiction, especially crime fiction. Bennett's stories of the mischievous millionaire Cecil Thorold appeared in *The Windsor Magazine*; Thorpe Hazell, the railway detective created by Victor Whitechurch, not only appeared (appropriately enough) in *Railway Magazine* but also in *The Royal Magazine* and *Pearson's Magazine*; the adventures of Headon Hill's exotically named sleuth Sebastian Zambra could be followed in a lesser known magazine named *The Million*. Robert Barr's tales of Eugène Valmont, a French investigator exiled to London, could be found in *The Windsor Magazine* and *Pearson's Magazine*. Barr himself, together with Jerome K. Jerome, was closely involved in the establishment of *The Idler*, one of *The Strand*'s most successful competitors. *The Idler* played host to detectives like William Hope Hodgson's unusual character, Carnacki the Ghost Finder. Conan Doyle, a friend of both Barr and Jerome, contributed tales of mystery and the supernatural to their magazine.

It was not just in Britain that writers created detective heroes for the magazines. Some American authors published their work in British magazines. Several stories by the South Carolina orthodontist and mystery writer Rodrigues Ottolengui, for instance, appeared in *The Idler* in the mid-1890s. And, over on the other side of the Atlantic, there were plenty of home-grown magazines which provided a market for American authors, from Jacques Futrelle, creator of 'The Thinking Machine', to Arthur B. Reeve, whose tales of the 'scientific' detective Craig Kennedy began to appear in the years just before the First World War and continued to be popular for decades. It would have been perfectly possible to compile an anthology that consisted entirely of stories by American writers but, in the end, I have contented myself with choosing three.

A vast treasure trove of crime fiction, then, was published on both sides of the Atlantic in the years between 1890 and 1914 and it is from this that I have chosen the fifteen stories in this book. Others before me have produced similar anthologies. In the 1970s, Graham Greene's brother Hugh produced four collections of crime short stories from the Victorian and Edwardian era. Rather cheekily, I have borrowed the title of my anthology from one of his. However, the archive of fiction from the magazines of the 1890s and 1900s is so extensive that it is always possible to venture into it again, both to resurrect stories published in previous anthologies and to look for others.

The question remains – how good were all these rivals of Sherlock Holmes? The problem for those following in the wake of Conan Doyle in the 1890s and 1900s was that they were trying to compete with what rapidly became a phenomenon. Sherlock Holmes became so startlingly popular that writers looking to create successful fictional detectives faced an immediate difficulty. How could they differentiate their creations from Holmes? Some didn't really bother. Many Holmes clones can be found lurking among the back numbers of late Victorian and Edwardian periodicals. Some openly advertised their resemblance to the great detective. Some were rapidly categorised as

Holmes lookalikes at the time they were first published. Sexton Blake, for instance, the creation of a prolific writer of stories for boys' papers named Harry Blyth, was soon dubbed 'the office boys' Sherlock Holmes'. And making your central character just like Holmes, only more so, was not necessarily a recipe for poor fiction. Jacques Futrelle's Professor S. F. X. Van Dusen, 'The Thinking Machine', clearly owes a great deal to the Baker Street sleuth – staggering, almost inhuman intelligence, detachment from mundane reality, arcane knowledge, impatience with lesser intelligences etc. – but he is none the less one of the most memorable characters of the period.

Other writers chose a different strategy. Instead of trying to make their characters even stranger and more intellectual than Holmes, they chose to emphasise their ordinariness. Unlike the eccentric genius of Baker Street, Arthur Morrison's Martin Hewitt, who appeared in stories published in *The Strand* only three years after Holmes's debut in the magazine, is a deliberately colourless character. Hewitt is no deductive superman but someone not too different from the reader who solves his cases by the determined application of common sense. The ultimate embodiment of this technique is Chesterton's Father Brown who made his debut some twenty years after Holmes's first appearance in *The Strand*. The Roman Catholic priest is so nondescript that other characters in the stories often overlook his presence, so straightforward that he often appears simple-minded to those that do notice him. The paradox (and Chesterton was keen on paradoxes) is that it is Father Brown who sees further and deeper into the human heart than those who seem to be more sophisticated and intelligent.

By far the most common technique writers used in competing with Holmes, however, and one that is still employed today, was to give their characters a Unique Selling Point which was emphasised in every story. Provide your detective with a particular characteristic or give him or her the kind of career and lifestyle that (you hoped) no other detective had and you were several steps on the path towards success. For this reason, the period offers (amongst others), a blind detective (Max Carrados in the stories of Ernest Bramah), a detective who is a Canadian woodsman and hunter (November Joe, created by Hesketh Prichard), a detective who solves crimes from a corner seat in a London teashop (Baroness Orczy's Old Man in the Corner), a gypsy who own a pawnshop (Fergus Hume's Hagar), a wise old Hindu who travels to London from a remote Indian village (Headon Hill's Kala Persad) and a strangely named Edwardian gentleman whose opponents are largely supernatural (William Hope Hodgson's Carnacki).

One possible USP which very rapidly became anything but unique was to make your detective a woman. A large number of female detectives can be found in the pages of the magazines, from George R. Sims's Dorcas Dene and Catherine Louisa Pirkis's Loveday Brooke to Grant Allen's Lois Cayley and Baroness Orczy's Lady Emma of Scotland Yard. This may seem surprising at first but the reason is not hard to find. The late 1880s and the 1890s were the years of the 'New Woman', the proto-feminist who challenged men in what had previously been exclusively masculine domains. 'New Women' could be found at the ancient universities, in professions like journalism and running their own businesses. They could be seen riding bicycles and smoking cigarettes. They made their presence felt in ways that previous generations of women had not done. It was only to be expected that they would become detectives as well, if only in the pages of the magazines.

In the pages of this anthology, readers will find all sorts of crime solvers – women detectives, Holmes clones, deliberately ordinary detectives and detectives whose creators are keen to emphasise their special, defining characteristics. One or two of the protagonists of the stories I have chosen, like Chesterton's Father Brown, are well-known. I was determined to include a Father Brown story because it seems to me that the meek Roman Catholic priest is one of the very few detectives of the period, indeed perhaps the only one, entirely to escape the shadow of Sherlock Holmes. There are other detectives – Morrison's Martin Hewitt, Baroness Orczy's Old Man in the Corner, R. Austin Freeman's Dr Thorndyke – who are nearly as familiar. I could have included stories featuring these sleuths but I have never found any of them as compelling as their reputations would suggest. Besides, I wanted very much for the anthology to dig more deeply into the mountain of crime fiction that is to be found in the magazines of the era. I wanted to include less familiar heroes and most of those in the anthology fit this description. In the final analysis, I make no apology for preferring November Joe, Thorpe Hazell and Miss Lois Cayley to detectives with greater fame.

Not all the stories in this anthology are of equal quality. By very nearly every standard known to man, G. K. Chesterton, Arnold Bennett and Grant Allen were better writers than, say, Headon Hill and Victor Whitechurch and it shows in the tales they wrote. None the less all of the stories in the anthology are, in my opinion, well worth reading. Hill and Whitechurch may not have been as sophisticated as Chesterton or Allen but their stories remain engaging yarns and they tell us as much, if not more, about the era in which they were written as those by their literary superiors. Arthur B. Reeve's Craig Kennedy stories are naive when compared to Bennett's witty tales of Cecil Thorold but they have a buoyant enthusiasm for the wonders of newly emerging sciences which makes them just as appealing. The quarter of a century from the beginning of the 1890s to the outbreak of the First World War was a golden age for detective fiction. Sherlock Holmes reigned over it as undisputed king but, as this anthology endeavours to demonstrate, there were plenty of rivals to his crown and many of them are worth rediscovering.

Professor Augustus S. F. X. Van Dusen (The Thinking Machine)

Created by Jacques Futrelle (1875 – 1912)

ONE OF THE MOST memorable crime-solvers in the fiction of the decade before the First World War was the magnificently named Professor Augustus S. F. X. Van Dusen, otherwise known as 'The Thinking Machine'. Arrogant, cantakerous and eccentric, the very model of the mad scientist, Van Dusen solved a series of apparently insoluble mysteries, usually brought to his attention by his associate, the journalist Hutchinson Hatch. 'The Thinking Machine' was the creation of Jacques Futrelle, an American journalist and novelist born in Georgia in 1875. Futrelle wrote around fifty stories featuring the professor with a brain the size of a planet and doubtless there would have been more if the author had not met an untimely end in one of the most famous disasters of the twentieth century. In 1912, Futrelle and his wife were visiting England and chose to return to New York as first-class passengers on the *Titanic*. When the ship struck the iceberg and sank, Futrelle's wife survived but he was amongst nearly 1,500 who drowned.

The Problem of Cell 13

I

PRACTICALLY ALL THOSE letters remaining in the alphabet after Augustus S. F. X. Van Dusen was named were afterward acquired by that gentleman in the course of a brilliant scientific career, and, being honorably acquired, were tacked on to the other end. His name, therefore, taken with all that belonged to it, was a wonderfully imposing structure. He was a Ph.D., an LL.D., an F.R.S., an M.D., and an M.D.S. He was also some other things – just what he himself couldn't say – through recognition of his ability by various foreign educational and scientific institutions.

In appearance he was no less striking than in nomenclature. He was slender with the droop of the student in his thin shoulders and the pallor of a close, sedentary life on his clean-shaven face. His eyes wore a perpetual, forbidding squint – the squint of a man who studies little things – and when they could be seen at all through his thick spectacles were mere slits of watery blue. But above his eyes was his most striking feature. This was a tall, broad brow, almost abnormal in height and width, crowned by a heavy shock of bushy, yellow hair. All these things conspired to give him a peculiar, almost grotesque, personality.

Professor Van Dusen was remotely German. For generations his ancestors had been noted in the sciences; he was the logical result, the master mind. First and above all he was a logician. At least thirty-five years of the half-century or so of his existence had been devoted exclusively to proving that two and two always equal four, except in unusual cases, where they equal three or five, as the case may be. He stood broadly on the general proposition that all things that start must go somewhere, and was able to bring the concentrated mental force of his forefathers to bear on a given problem. Incidentally it may be remarked that Professor Van Dusen wore a No. 8 hat.

The world at large had heard vaguely of Professor Van Dusen as The Thinking Machine. It was a newspaper catch-phrase applied to him at the time of a remarkable exhibition at chess; he had demonstrated then that a stranger to the game might, by the force of inevitable logic, defeat a champion who had devoted a lifetime to its study. The Thinking Machine! Perhaps that more nearly described him than all his honorary initials, for he spent week after week, month after month, in the seclusion of his small laboratory from which had gone forth thoughts that staggered scientific associates and deeply stirred the world at large.

It was only occasionally that The Thinking Machine had visitors, and these were usually men who, themselves high in the sciences, dropped in to argue a point and perhaps convince themselves. Two of these men, Dr Charles Ransome and Alfred Fielding, called one evening to discuss some theory which is not of consequence here.

'Such a thing is impossible,' declared Dr Ransome emphatically, in the course of the conversation.

'Nothing is impossible,' declared The Thinking Machine with equal emphasis. He always spoke petulantly. 'The mind is master of all things. When science fully recognizes that fact a great advance will have been made.'

'How about the airship?' asked Dr Ransome.

'That's not impossible at all,' asserted The Thinking Machine. 'It will be invented some time. I'd do it myself, but I'm busy.'

Dr Ransome laughed tolerantly.

'I've heard you say such things before,' he said. 'But they mean nothing. Mind may be master of matter, but it hasn't yet found a way to apply itself. There are some things that can't be thought out of existence, or rather which would not yield to any amount of thinking.'

'What, for instance?' demanded The Thinking Machine.

Dr Ransome was thoughtful for a moment as he smoked.

'Well, say prison walls,' he replied. 'No man can think himself out of a cell. If he could, there would be no prisoners.'

'A man can so apply his brain and ingenuity that he can leave a cell, which is the same thing,' snapped The Thinking Machine.

Dr Ransome was slightly amused.

'Let's suppose a case,' he said, after a moment. 'Take a cell where prisoners under sentence of death are confined – men who are desperate and, maddened by fear, would take any chance to escape – suppose you were locked in such a cell. Could you escape?'

'Certainly,' declared The Thinking Machine.

'Of course,' said Mr Fielding, who entered the conversation for the first time, 'you might wreck the cell with an explosive – but inside, a prisoner, you couldn't have that.'

'There would be nothing of that kind,' said The Thinking Machine. 'You might treat me precisely as you treated prisoners under sentence of death, and I would leave the cell.'

'Not unless you entered it with tools prepared to get out,' said Dr Ransome.

The Thinking Machine was visibly annoyed and his blue eyes snapped.

'Lock me in any cell in any prison anywhere at any time, wearing only what is necessary, and I'll escape in a week,' he declared, sharply.

Dr Ransome sat up straight in the chair, interested. Mr Fielding lighted a new cigar.

'You mean you could actually think yourself out?' asked Dr Ransome.

'I would get out,' was the response.

'Are you serious?'

'Certainly I am serious.'

Dr Ransome and Mr Fielding were silent for a long time.

'Would you be willing to try it?' asked Mr Fielding, finally.

'Certainly,' said Professor Van Dusen, and there was a trace of irony in his voice. 'I have done more asinine things than that to convince other men of less important truths.'

The tone was offensive and there was an undercurrent strongly resembling anger on both sides. Of course it was an absurd thing, but Professor Van Dusen reiterated his willingness to undertake the escape and it was decided upon.

'To begin now,' added Dr Ransome.

'I'd prefer that it begin to-morrow,' said The Thinking Machine, 'because – '

'No, now,' said Mr Fielding, flatly. 'You are arrested, figuratively, of course, without any warning locked in a cell with no chance to communicate with friends, and left there with identically the same care and attention that would be given to a man under sentence of death. Are you willing?'

'All right, now, then,' said The Thinking Machine, and he arose.

'Say, the death-cell in Chisholm Prison.'

'The death-cell in Chisholm Prison.'

'And what will you wear?'

'As little as possible,' said The Thinking Machine. 'Shoes, stockings, trousers and a shirt.'

'You will permit yourself to be searched, of course?'

'I am to be treated precisely as all prisoners are treated,' said The Thinking Machine. 'No more attention and no less.'

There were some preliminaries to be arranged in the matter of obtaining permission for the test, but all three were influential men and everything was done satisfactorily by telephone, albeit the prison commissioners, to whom the experiment was explained on purely scientific grounds, were sadly bewildered. Professor Van Dusen would be the most distinguished prisoner they had ever entertained.

When The Thinking Machine had donned those things which he was to wear during his incarceration he called the little old woman who was his housekeeper, cook and maid servant all in one.

'Martha,' he said, 'it is now twenty-seven minutes past nine o'clock. I am going away. One week from to-night, at half-past nine, these gentlemen and one, possibly two, others will take supper with me here. Remember Dr Ransome is very fond of artichokes.'

The three men were driven to Chisholm Prison, where the warden was awaiting them, having been informed of the matter by telephone. He understood merely that the eminent Professor Van Dusen was to be his prisoner, if he could keep him, for one week; that he had committed no crime, but that he was to be treated as all other prisoners were treated.

'Search him,' instructed Dr Ransome.

The Thinking Machine was searched. Nothing was found on him; the pockets of the trousers were empty; the white, stiff-bosomed shirt had no pocket. The shoes and stockings were removed, examined, then replaced. As he watched all these preliminaries – the rigid search and noted the pitiful, childlike physical weakness of the man, the colorless face, and the thin, white hands – Dr Ransome almost regretted his part in the affair.

'Are you sure you want to do this?' he asked.

'Would you be convinced if I did not?' inquired The Thinking Machine in turn.

'No.'

'All right. I'll do it.'

What sympathy Dr Ransome had was dissipated by the tone. It nettled him, and he resolved to see the experiment to the end; it would be a stinging reproof to egotism.

'It will be impossible for him to communicate with anyone outside?' he asked.

'Absolutely impossible,' replied the warden. 'He will not be permitted writing materials of any sort.'

'And your jailers, would they deliver a message from him?'

'Not one word, directly or indirectly,' said the warden. 'You may rest assured of that. They will report anything he might say or turn over to me anything he might give them.'

'That seems entirely satisfactory,' said Mr Fielding, who was frankly interested in the problem.

'Of course, in the event he fails,' said Dr Ransome, 'and asks for his liberty, you understand you are to set him free?'

'I understand,' replied the warden.

The Thinking Machine stood listening, but had nothing to say until this was all ended, then:

'I should like to make three small requests. You may grant them or not, as you wish.'

'No special favors, now,' warned Mr Fielding.

'I am asking none,' was the stiff response. 'I would like to have some tooth powder – buy it yourself to see that it is tooth powder – and I should like to have one five-dollar and two ten-dollar bills.'

Dr Ransome, Mr Fielding and the warden exchanged astonished glances. They were not surprised at the request for tooth powder, but were at the request for money.

'Is there any man with whom our friend would come in contact that he could bribe with twenty-five dollars?' asked Dr Ransome of the warden.

'Not for twenty-five hundred dollars,' was the positive reply.

'Well, let him have them,' said Mr Fielding. 'I think they are harmless enough.'

'And what is the third request?' asked Dr Ransome.

'I should like to have my shoes polished.'

Again the astonished glances were exchanged. This last request was the height of absurdity, so they agreed to it. These things all being attended to, The Thinking Machine was led back into the prison from which he had undertaken to escape.

'Here is Cell 13,' said the warden, stopping three doors down the steel corridor. 'This is where we keep condemned murderers. No one can leave it without my permission; and no one in it can communicate with the outside. I'll stake my reputation on that. It's only three doors back of my office and I can readily hear any unusual noise.'

'Will this cell do, gentlemen?' asked The Thinking Machine. There was a touch of irony in his voice.

'Admirably,' was the reply.

The heavy steel door was thrown open, there was a great scurrying and scampering of tiny feet, and The Thinking Machine passed into the gloom of the cell. Then the door was closed and double locked by the warden.

'What is that noise in there?' asked Dr Ransome, through the bars.

'Rats – dozens of them,' replied The Thinking Machine, tersely.

The three men, with final good-nights, were turning away when The Thinking Machine called:

'What time is it exactly, warden?'

'Eleven seventeen,' replied the warden.

'Thanks. I will join you gentlemen in your office at half-past eight o'clock one week from to-night,' said The Thinking Machine.

'And if you do not?'

'There is no "if" about it.'

II

CHISHOLM PRISON WAS a great, spreading structure of granite, four stories in all, which stood in the centre of acres of open space. It was surrounded by a wall of solid masonry eighteen feet high, and so smoothly finished inside and out as to offer no foothold to a climber, no matter how expert. Atop of this fence, as a further precaution, was a five-foot fence of steel rods, each terminating in a keen point. This fence in itself marked an absolute deadline between freedom and imprisonment, for, even if a man escaped from his cell, it would seem impossible for him to pass the wall.

The yard, which on all sides of the prison building was twenty-five feet wide, that being the distance from the building to the wall, was by day an exercise ground for those prisoners to whom was granted the boon of occasional semi-liberty. But that was not for those in Cell 13. At all times of the day there were armed guards in the yard, four of them, one patrolling each side of the prison building.

By night the yard was almost as brilliantly lighted as by day. On each of the four sides was a great arc light which rose above the prison wall and gave to the guards a clear sight. The lights, too, brightly illuminated the spiked top of the wall. The wires which fed the arc lights ran up the side of the prison building on insulators and from the top story led out to the poles supporting the arc lights.

All these things were seen and comprehended by The Thinking Machine, who was only enabled to see out his closely barred cell window by standing on his bed. This was on the morning following his incarceration. He gathered, too, that the river lay over there beyond the wall somewhere, because he heard faintly the pulsation of a motor boat and high up in the air saw a river bird. From that same direction came the shouts of boys at play and the occasional crack of a batted ball. He knew then that between the prison wall and the river was an open space, a playground.

Chisholm Prison was regarded as absolutely safe. No man had ever escaped from it. The Thinking Machine, from his perch on the bed, seeing what he saw, could readily understand why. The walls of the cell, though built he judged twenty years before, were perfectly solid, and the window bars of new iron had not a shadow of rust on them.

The window itself, even with the bars out, would be a difficult mode of egress because it was small.

Yet, seeing these things, The Thinking Machine was not discouraged. Instead, he thoughtfully squinted at the great arc light – there was bright sunlight now – and traced with his eyes the wire which led from it to the building. That electric wire, he reasoned, must come down the side of the building not a great distance from his cell. That might be worth knowing.

Cell 13 was on the same floor with the offices of the prison – that is, not in the basement, nor yet upstairs. There were only four steps up to the office floor, therefore the level of the floor must be only three or four feet above the ground. He couldn't see the ground directly beneath his window, but he could see it further out toward the wall. It would be an easy drop from the window. Well and good.

Then The Thinking Machine fell to remembering how he had come to the cell. First, there was the outside guard's booth, a part of the wall. There were two heavily barred gates there, both of steel. At this gate was one man always on guard. He admitted persons to the prison after much clanking of keys and locks, and let them out when ordered to do so. The warden's office was in the prison building, and in order to reach that official from the prison yard one had to pass a gate of solid steel with only a peep-hole in it. Then coming from that inner office to Cell 13, where he was now, one must pass a heavy wooden door and two steel doors into the corridors of the prison; and always there was the double-locked door of Cell 13 to reckon with.

There were then, The Thinking Machine recalled, seven doors to be overcome before one could pass from Cell 13 into the outer world, a free man. But against this was the fact that he was rarely interrupted. A jailer appeared at his cell door at six in the morning with a breakfast of prison fare; he would come again at noon, and again at six in the afternoon. At nine o'clock at night would come the inspection tour. That would be all.

'It's admirably arranged, this prison system,' was the mental tribute paid by The Thinking Machine. 'I'll have to study it a little when I get out. I had no idea there was such great care exercised in the prisons.'

There was nothing, positively nothing, in his cell, except his iron bed, so firmly put together that no man could tear it to pieces save with sledges or a file. He had neither of these. There was not even a chair, or a small table, or a bit of tin or crockery. Nothing! The jailer stood by when he ate, then took away the wooden spoon and bowl which he had used.

One by one these things sank into the brain of The Thinking Machine. When the last possibility had been considered he began an examination of his cell. From the roof, down the walls on all sides, he examined the stones and the cement between them. He stamped over the floor carefully time after time, but it was cement, perfectly solid. After the examination he sat on the edge of the iron bed and was lost in thought for a long time. For Professor Augustus S. F. X. Van Dusen, The Thinking Machine, had something to think about.

He was disturbed by a rat, which ran across his foot, then scampered away into a dark corner of the cell, frightened at its own daring. After a while The Thinking Machine, squinting steadily into the darkness of the corner where the rat had gone, was able to make out in the gloom many little beady eyes staring at him. He counted six pair, and there were perhaps others; he didn't see very well.

Then The Thinking Machine, from his seat on the bed, noticed for the first time the bottom of his cell door. There was an opening there of two inches between the steel bar and the floor. Still looking steadily at this opening, The Thinking Machine backed suddenly into the corner where he had seen the beady eyes. There was a great scampering of tiny feet, several squeaks of frightened rodents, and then silence.

None of the rats had gone out the door, yet there were none in the cell. Therefore there must be another way out of the cell, however small. The Thinking Machine, on hands and knees, started a search for this spot, feeling in the darkness with his long, slender fingers.

At last his search was rewarded. He came upon a small opening in the floor, level with the cement. It was perfectly round and somewhat larger than a silver dollar. This was the way the rats had gone. He put his fingers deep into the opening; it seemed to be a disused drainage pipe and was dry and dusty.

Having satisfied himself on this point, he sat on the bed again for an hour, then made another inspection of his surroundings through the small cell window. One of the outside guards stood directly opposite, beside the wall, and happened to be looking at the window of Cell 13 when the head of The Thinking Machine appeared. But the scientist didn't notice the guard.

Noon came and the jailer appeared with the prison dinner of repulsively plain food. At home The Thinking Machine merely ate to live; here he took what was offered without comment. Occasionally he spoke to the jailer who stood outside the door watching him.

'Any improvements made here in the last few years?' he asked.

'Nothing particularly,' replied the jailer. 'New wall was built four years ago.'

'Anything done to the prison proper?'

'Painted the woodwork outside, and I believe about seven years ago a new system of plumbing was put in.'

'Ah!' said the prisoner. 'How far is the river over there?'

'About three hundred feet. The boys have a baseball ground between the wall and the river.'

The Thinking Machine had nothing further to say just then, but when the jailer was ready to go he asked for some water.

'I get very thirsty here,' he explained. 'Would it be possible for you to leave a little water in a bowl for me?'

'I'll ask the warden,' replied the jailer, and he went away. Half an hour later he returned with water in a small earthen bowl.

'The warden says you may keep this bowl,' he informed the prisoner. 'But you must show it to me when I ask for it. If it is broken, it will be the last.'

'Thank you,' said The Thinking Machine. 'I shan't break it.'

The jailer went on about his duties. For just the fraction of a second it seemed that The Thinking Machine wanted to ask a question, but he didn't.

Two hours later this same jailer, in passing the door of Cell No. 13, heard a noise inside and stopped. The Thinking Machine was down on his hands and knees in a corner of the cell, and from that same corner came several frightened squeaks. The jailer looked on interestedly.

'Ah, I've got you,' he heard the prisoner say.

'Got what?' he asked, sharply.

'One of these rats,' was the reply. 'See?' And between the scientist's long fingers the jailer saw a small grey rat struggling. The prisoner brought it over to the light and looked at it closely. 'It's a water rat,' he said.

'Ain't you got anything better to do than to catch rats?' asked the jailer.

'It's disgraceful that they should be here at all,' was the irritated reply. 'Take this one away and kill it. There are dozens more where it came from.'

The jailer took the wriggling, squirmy rodent and flung it down on the floor violently. It gave one squeak and lay still. Later he reported the incident to the warden, who only smiled.

Still later that afternoon the outside armed guard on Cell 13 side of the prison looked up again at the window and saw the prisoner looking out. He saw a hand raised to the barred window and then something white fluttered to the ground, directly under the window of Cell 13. It was a little roll of linen, evidently of white shirting material, and tied around it was a five-dollar bill. The guard looked up at the window again, but the face had disappeared.

With a grim smile he took the little linen roll and the five-dollar bill to the warden's office. There together they deciphered something which was written on it with a queer sort of ink, frequently blurred. On the outside was this:

'Finder of this please deliver to Dr Charles Ransome.'

'Ah,' said the warden, with a chuckle. 'Plan of escape number one has gone wrong.' Then, as an afterthought: 'But why did he address it to Dr Ransome?'

'And where did he get the pen and ink to write with?' asked the guard.

The warden looked at the guard and the guard looked at the warden. There was no apparent solution of that mystery. The warden studied the writing carefully, then shook his head.

'Well, let's see what he was going to say to Dr Ransome,' he said at length, still puzzled, and he unrolled the inner piece of linen.

'Well, if that – what – what do you think of that?' he asked, dazed.

The guard took the bit of linen and read this:

'Epa cseot d'net niiy awe htto n'si sih. T.'

III

The warden spent an hour wondering what sort of a cipher it was, and half an hour wondering why his prisoner should attempt to communicate with Dr Ransome, who was the cause of him being there. After this the warden devoted some thought to the question of where the prisoner got writing materials, and what sort of writing materials he had. With the idea of illuminating this point, he examined the linen again. It was a torn part of a white shirt and had ragged edges.

Now it was possible to account for the linen, but what the prisoner had used to write with was another matter. The warden knew it would have been impossible for him to have either pen or pencil, and, besides, neither pen nor pencil had been used in this writing. What, then? The warden decided to personally investigate. The Thinking Machine was his prisoner; he had orders to hold his prisoners; if this one sought to escape by sending cipher messages to persons outside, he would stop it, as he would have stopped it in the case of any other prisoner.

The warden went back to Cell 13 and found The Thinking Machine on his hands and knees on the floor, engaged in nothing more alarming than catching rats. The prisoner heard the warden's step and turned to him quickly.

'It's disgraceful,' he snapped, 'these rats. There are scores of them.'

'Other men have been able to stand them,' said the warden. 'Here is another shirt for you – let me have the one you have on.'

'Why?' demanded The Thinking Machine, quickly. His tone was hardly natural, his manner suggested actual perturbation.

'You have attempted to communicate with Dr Ransome,' said the warden severely. 'As my prisoner, it is my duty to put a stop to it.'

The Thinking Machine was silent for a moment.

'All right,' he said, finally. 'Do your duty.'

The warden smiled grimly. The prisoner arose from the floor and removed the white shirt, putting on instead a striped convict shirt the warden had brought. The warden took the white shirt eagerly, and then and there compared the pieces of linen on which was written the cipher with certain torn places in the shirt. The Thinking Machine looked on curiously.

'The guard brought you those, then?' he asked.

'He certainly did,' replied the warden triumphantly. 'And that ends your first attempt to escape.'

The Thinking Machine watched the warden as he, by comparison, established to his own satisfaction that only two pieces of linen had been torn from the white shirt.

'What did you write this with?' demanded the warden.

'I should think it a part of your duty to find out,' said The Thinking Machine, irritably.

The warden started to say some harsh things, then restrained himself and made a minute search of the cell and of the prisoner instead. He found absolutely nothing; not even a match or toothpick which might have been used for a pen. The same mystery surrounded the fluid with which the cipher had been written. Although the warden left Cell 13 visibly annoyed, he took the torn shirt in triumph.

'Well, writing notes on a shirt won't get him out, that's certain,' he told himself with some complacency. He put the linen scraps into his desk to await developments. 'If that man escapes from that cell I'll – hang it – I'll resign.'

On the third day of his incarceration The Thinking Machine openly attempted to bribe his way out. The jailer had brought his dinner and was leaning against the barred door, waiting, when The Thinking Machine began the conversation.

'The drainage pipes of the prison lead to the river, don't they?' he asked.

'Yes,' said the jailer.

'I suppose they are very small?'

'Too small to crawl through, if that's what you're thinking about,' was the grinning response.

There was silence until The Thinking Machine finished his meal. Then:

'You know I'm not a criminal, don't you?'

'Yes.'

'And that I've a perfect right to be freed if I demand it?'

'Yes.'

'Well, I came here believing that I could make my escape,' said the prisoner, and his squint eyes studied the face of the jailer. 'Would you consider a financial reward for aiding me to escape?'

The jailer, who happened to be an honest man, looked at the slender, weak figure of the prisoner, at the large head with its mass of yellow hair, and was almost sorry.

'I guess prisons like these were not built for the likes of you to get out of,' he said, at last.

'But would you consider a proposition to help me get out?' the prisoner insisted, almost beseechingly.

'No,' said the jailer, shortly.

'Five hundred dollars,' urged The Thinking Machine. 'I am not a criminal.'

'No,' said the jailer.

'A thousand?'

'No,' again said the jailer, and he started away hurriedly to escape further temptation. Then he turned back. 'If you should give me ten thousand dollars I couldn't get you out. You'd have to pass through seven doors, and I only have the keys to two.'

Then he told the warden all about it.

'Plan number two fails,' said the warden, smiling grimly. 'First a cipher, then bribery.'

When the jailer was on his way to Cell 13 at six o'clock, again bearing food to The Thinking Machine, he paused, startled by the unmistakable scrape, scrape of steel against steel. It stopped at the sound of his steps, then craftily the jailer, who was beyond the prisoner's range of vision, resumed his tramping, the sound being apparently that of a man going away from Cell 13. As a matter of fact he was in the same spot.

After a moment there came again the steady scrape, scrape, and the jailer crept cautiously on tiptoes to the door and peered between the bars. The Thinking Machine was standing on the iron bed working at the bars of the little window. He was using a file, judging from the backward and forward swing of his arms.

Cautiously the jailer crept back to the office, summoned the warden in person, and they returned to Cell 13 on tiptoes. The steady scrape was still audible. The warden listened to satisfy himself and then suddenly appeared at the door.

'Well?' he demanded, and there was a smile on his face.

The Thinking Machine glanced back from his perch on the bed and leaped suddenly to the floor, making frantic efforts to hide something. The warden went in, with hand extended.

'Give it up,' he said.

'No,' said the prisoner, sharply.

'Come, give it up,' urged the warden. 'I don't want to have to search you again.'

'No,' repeated the prisoner.

'What was it, a file?' asked the warden.

The Thinking Machine was silent and stood squinting at the warden with something very nearly approaching disappointment on his face – nearly, but not quite. The warden was almost sympathetic.

'Plan number three fails, eh?' he asked, goodnaturedly. 'Too bad, isn't it?'

The prisoner didn't say.

'Search him,' instructed the warden.

The jailer searched the prisoner carefully. At last, artfully concealed in the waist band of the trousers, he found a piece of steel about two inches long, with one side curved like a half moon.

'Ah,' said the warden, as he received it from the jailer. 'From your shoe heel,' and he smiled pleasantly.

The jailer continued his search and on the other side of the trousers waist band found another piece of steel identical with the first. The edges showed where they had been worn against the bars of the window.

'You couldn't saw a way through those bars with these,' said the warden.

'I could have,' said The Thinking Machine firmly.

'In six months, perhaps,' said the warden, goodnaturedly.

The warden shook his head slowly as he gazed into the slightly flushed face of his prisoner.

'Ready to give it up?' he asked.

'I haven't started yet,' was the prompt reply.

Then came another exhaustive search of the cell. Carefully the two men went over it, finally turning out the bed and searching that. Nothing. The warden in person climbed upon the bed and examined the bars of the window where the prisoner had been sawing. When he looked he was amused.

'Just made it a little bright by hard rubbing,' he said to the prisoner, who stood looking on with a somewhat crestfallen air. The warden grasped the iron bars in his strong hands and tried to shake them. They were immovable, set firmly in the solid granite. He examined each in turn and found them all satisfactory. Finally he climbed down from the bed.

'Give it up, professor,' he advised.

The Thinking Machine shook his head and the warden and jailer passed on again. As they disappeared down the corridor The Thinking Machine sat on the edge of the bed with his head in his hands.

'He's crazy to try to get out of that cell,' commented the jailer.

'Of course he can't get out,' said the warden. 'But he's clever. I would like to know what he wrote that cipher with.'

It was four o'clock next morning when an awful, heart-racking shriek of terror resounded through the great prison. It came from a cell somewhere about the center, and its tone told a tale of horror, agony, terrible fear. The warden heard and with three of his men rushed into the long corridor leading to Cell 13.

IV

As they ran there came again that awful cry. It died away in a sort of wail. The white faces of prisoners appeared at cell doors upstairs and down, staring out wonderingly, frightened.

'It's that fool in Cell 13,' grumbled the warden.

He stopped and stared in as one of the jailers flashed a lantern. 'That fool in Cell 13' lay comfortably on his cot, flat on his back with his mouth open, snoring. Even as they looked there came again the piercing cry, from somewhere above. The warden's face blanched a little as he started up the stairs. There on the top floor he found a man in Cell 43, directly above Cell 13, but two floors higher, cowering in a corner of his cell.

'What's the matter?' demanded the warden.

'Thank God you've come,' exclaimed the prisoner, and he cast himself against the bars of his cell.

'What is it?' demanded the warden again.

He threw open the door and went in. The prisoner dropped on his knees and clasped the warden about the body. His face was white with terror, his eyes were widely distended, and he was shuddering. His hands, icy cold, clutched at the warden's.

'Take me out of this cell, please take me out,' he pleaded.

'What's the matter with you, anyhow?' insisted the warden, impatiently.

'I heard something – something,' said the prisoner, and his eyes roved nervously around the cell.

'What did you hear?'

'I – I can't tell you,' stammered the prisoner. Then, in a sudden burst of terror: 'Take me out of this cell – put me anywhere – but take me out of here.'

The warden and the three jailers exchanged glances.

'Who is this fellow? What's he accused of?' asked the warden.

'Joseph Ballard,' said one of the jailers. 'He's accused of throwing acid in a woman's face. She died from it.'

'But they can't prove it,' gasped the prisoner. 'They can't prove it. Please put me in some other cell.'

He was still clinging to the warden, and that official threw his arms off roughly. Then for a time he stood looking at the cowering wretch, who seemed possessed of all the wild, unreasoning terror of a child.

'Look here, Ballard,' said the warden, finally, 'if you heard anything, I want to know what it was. Now tell me.'

'I can't, I can't,' was the reply. He was sobbing.

'Where did it come from?'

'I don't know. Everywhere – nowhere. I just heard it.'

'What was it – a voice?'

'Please don't make me answer,' pleaded the prisoner.

'You must answer,' said the warden, sharply.

'It was a voice – but – but it wasn't human,' was the sobbing reply.

'Voice, but not human?' repeated the warden, puzzled.

'It sounded muffled and – and far away – and ghostly,' explained the man.

'Did it come from inside or outside the prison?'

'It didn't seem to come from anywhere – it was just here, here, everywhere. I heard it. I heard it.'

For an hour the warden tried to get the story, but Ballard had become suddenly obstinate and would say nothing – only pleaded to be placed in another cell, or to have one of the jailers remain near him until daylight. These requests were gruffly refused.

'And see here,' said the warden, in conclusion, 'if there's any more of this screaming, I'll put you in the padded cell.'

Then the warden went his way, a sadly puzzled man. Ballard sat at his cell door until daylight, his face, drawn and white with terror, pressed against the bars, and looked out into the prison with wide, staring eyes.

That day, the fourth since the incarceration of The Thinking Machine, was enlivened considerably by the volunteer prisoner, who spent most of his time at the little window of his cell. He began proceedings by throwing another piece of linen down to the guard, who picked it up dutifully and took it to the warden. On it was written:

'Only three days more.'

The warden was in no way surprised at what he read; he understood that The Thinking Machine meant only three days more of his imprisonment, and he regarded the note as a boast. But how was the thing written? Where had The Thinking Machine found this new piece of linen? Where? How? He carefully examined the linen. It was white, of fine texture, shirting material. He took the shirt which he had taken and carefully fitted the two original pieces of the linen to the torn places. This third piece was entirely superfluous; it didn't fit anywhere, and yet it was unmistakably the same goods.

'And where – where does he get anything to write with?' demanded the warden of the world at large.

Still later on the fourth day The Thinking Machine, through the window of his cell, spoke to the armed guard outside.

'What day of the month is it?' he asked.

'The fifteenth,' was the answer.

The Thinking Machine made a mental astronomical calculation and satisfied himself that the moon would not rise until after nine o'clock that night. Then he asked another question: 'Who attends to those arc lights?'

'Man from the company.'

'You have no electricians in the building?'

'No.'

'I should think you could save money if you had your own man.'

'None of my business,' replied the guard.

The guard noticed The Thinking Machine at the cell window frequently during that day, but always the face seemed listless and there was a certain wistfulness in the squint eyes behind the glasses. After a while he accepted the presence of the leonine head as a matter of course. He had seen other prisoners do the same thing; it was the longing for the outside world.

That afternoon, just before the day guard was relieved, the head appeared at the window again, and The Thinking Machine's hand held something out between the bars. It fluttered to the ground and the guard picked it up. It was a five-dollar bill.

'That's for you,' called the prisoner.

As usual, the guard, took it to the warden. That gentleman looked at it suspiciously; he looked at everything that came from Cell 13 with suspicion.

'He said it was for me,' explained the guard.

'It's a sort of a tip, I suppose,' said the warden. 'I see no particular reason why you shouldn't accept – '

Suddenly he stopped. He had remembered that The Thinking Machine had gone into Cell 13 with one five-dollar bill and two ten-dollar bills; twenty-five dollars in all. Now a five-dollar bill had been tied around the first pieces of linen that came from the cell. The warden still had it, and to convince himself he took it out and looked at it. It was five dollars; yet here was another five dollars, and The Thinking Machine had only had ten-dollar bills.

'Perhaps somebody changed one of the bills for him,' he thought at last, with a sigh of relief.

But then and there he made up his mind. He would search Cell 13 as a cell was never before searched in this world. When a man could write at will, and change money, and do other wholly inexplicable things, there was something radically wrong with his prison. He planned to enter the cell at night – three o'clock would be an excellent time. The Thinking Machine must do all the weird things he did sometime. Night seemed the most reasonable.

Thus it happened that the warden stealthily descended upon Cell 13 that night at three o'clock. He paused at the door and listened. There was no sound save the steady, regular breathing of the prisoner. The keys unfastened the double locks with scarcely a clank, and the warden entered, locking the door behind him. Suddenly he flashed his dark-lantern in the face of the recumbent figure.

If the warden had planned to startle The Thinking Machine he was mistaken, for that individual merely opened his eyes quietly, reached for his glasses and inquired, in a most matter-of-fact tone:

'Who is it?'

It would be useless to describe the search that the warden made. It was minute. Not one inch of the cell or the bed was overlooked. He found the round hole in the floor, and with a flash of inspiration thrust his thick fingers into it. After a moment of fumbling there he drew up something and looked at it in the light of his lantern.

'Ugh!' he exclaimed.

The thing he had taken out was a rat – a dead rat. His inspiration fled as a mist before the sun. But he continued the search. The Thinking Machine, without a word, arose and kicked the rat out of the cell into the corridor.

The warden climbed on the bed and tried the steel bars in the tiny window. They were perfectly rigid; every bar of the door was the same.

Then the warden searched the prisoner's clothing, beginning at the shoes. Nothing hidden in them! Then the trousers waist band. Still nothing! Then the pockets of the trousers. From one side he drew out some paper money and examined it.

'Five one-dollar bills,' he gasped.

'That's right,' said the prisoner.

'But the – you had two tens and a five – what the – how do you do it?'

'That's my business,' said the Thinking Machine.

'Did any of my men change this money for you – on your word of honour?'

The Thinking Machine paused just a fraction of a second.

'No,' he said.

'Well, do you make it?' asked the warden. He was prepared to believe anything.

'That's my business,' again said the prisoner.

The warden glared at the eminent scientist fiercely. He felt – he knew – that this man was making a fool of him, yet he didn't know how. If he were a real prisoner he would get the truth – but, then, perhaps, those inexplicable things which had happened would not have been brought before him so sharply. Neither of the men spoke for a long time, then suddenly the warden turned fiercely and left the cell, slamming the door behind him. He didn't dare to speak, then.

He glanced at the clock. It was ten minutes to four. He had hardly settled himself in bed when again came that heart-breaking shriek through the prison. With a few muttered words, which, while not elegant, were highly expressive, he relighted his lantern and rushed through the prison again to the cell on the upper floor.

Again Ballard was crushing himself against the steel door, shrieking, shrieking at the top of his voice. He stopped only when the warden flashed his lamp in the cell.

'Take me out, take me out,' he screamed. 'I did it, I did it, I killed her. Take it away.'

'Take what away?' asked the warden.

'I threw the acid in her face – I did it – I confess. Take me out of here.'

Ballard's condition was pitiable; it was only an act of mercy to let him out into the corridor. There he crouched in a corner, like an animal at bay, and clasped his hands to his ears. It took half an hour to calm him sufficiently for him to speak. Then he told incoherently what had happened. On the night before at four o'clock he had heard a voice – a sepulchral voice, muffled and wailing in tone.

'What did it say?' asked the warden, curiously.

'Acid – acid – acid!' gasped the prisoner. 'It accused me. Acid! I threw the acid, and the woman died. Oh!' It was a long, shuddering wail of terror.

'Acid?' echoed the warden, puzzled. The case was beyond him.

'Acid. That's all I heard – that one word, repeated several times. There were other things, too, but I didn't hear them.'

'That was last night, eh?' asked the warden. 'What happened to-night – what frightened you just now?'

'It was the same thing,' gasped the prisoner. 'Acid – acid – acid!' He covered his face with his hands and sat shivering. 'It was acid I used on her, but I didn't mean to kill her. I just heard the words. It was something accusing me – accusing me.' He mumbled, and was silent.

'Did you hear anything else?'

'Yes – but I couldn't understand – only a little bit – just a word or two.'

'Well, what was it?'

'I heard "acid" three times, then I heard a long, moaning sound, then – then – I heard "No. 8 hat." I heard that twice.'

'No. 8 hat,' repeated the warden. 'What the devil – No. 8 hat? Accusing voices of conscience have never talked about No. 8 hats, so far as I ever heard.'

'He's insane,' said one of the jailers, with an air of finality.

'I believe you,' said the warden. 'He must be. He probably heard something and got frightened. He's trembling now. No. 8 hat! What the – '

V

When the fifth day of The Thinking Machine's imprisonment rolled around the warden was wearing a hunted look. He was anxious for the end of the thing. He could not help but feel that his distinguished prisoner had been amusing himself. And if this were so, The Thinking Machine had lost none of his sense of humour. For on this fifth day he flung down another linen note to the outside guard, bearing the words:

'Only two days more.'

Also he flung down half a dollar.

Now the warden knew – he knew – that the man in Cell 13 didn't have any half dollars – he couldn't have any half dollars, no more than he could have pen and ink and linen, and yet he did have them. It was a condition, not a theory; that is one reason why the warden was wearing a hunted look.

That ghastly, uncanny thing, too, about 'Acid' and 'No. 8 hat' clung to him tenaciously. They didn't mean anything, of course, merely the ravings of an insane murderer who had been driven by fear to confess his crime, still there were so many things that 'didn't mean anything' happening in the prison now since The Thinking Machine was there.

On the sixth day the warden received a postal stating that Dr Ransome and Mr Fielding would be at Chisholm Prison on the following evening, Thursday, and in the event Professor Van Dusen had not yet escaped – and they presumed he had not because they had not heard from him – they would meet him there.

'In the event he had not yet escaped!' The warden smiled grimly. Escaped!

The Thinking Machine enlivened this day for the warden with three notes. They were on the usual linen and bore generally on the appointment at half-past eight o'clock Thursday night, which appointment the scientist had made at the time of his imprisonment.

On the afternoon of the seventh day the warden passed Cell 13 and glanced in. The Thinking Machine was lying on the iron bed, apparently sleeping lightly. The cell appeared precisely as it always did to a casual glance. The warden would swear that no man was going to leave it between that hour – it was then four o'clock – and half-past eight o'clock that evening.

On his way back past the cell the warden heard the steady breathing again, and coming close to the door looked in. He wouldn't have done so if The Thinking Machine had been looking, but now – well, it was different.

A ray of light came through the high window and fell on the face of the sleeping man. It occurred to the warden for the first time that his prisoner appeared haggard and weary. Just then The Thinking Machine stirred slightly and the warden hurried on up the corridor guiltily. That evening after six o'clock he saw the jailer.

'Everything all right in Cell 13?' he asked.

'Yes, sir,' replied the jailer. 'He didn't eat much, though.'

It was with a feeling of having done his duty that the warden received Dr Ransome and Mr Fielding shortly after seven o'clock. He intended to show them the linen notes and lay before them the full story of his woes, which was a long one. But before this came to pass, the guard from the river side of the prison yard entered the office.

'The arc light in my side of the yard won't light,' he informed the warden.

'Confound it, that man's a hoodoo,' thundered the official. 'Everything has happened since he's been here.'

The guard went back to his post in the darkness, and the warden 'phoned to the electric light company.

'This is Chisholm Prison,' he said through the 'phone. 'Send three or four men down here quick, to fix an arc light.'

The reply was evidently satisfactory, for the warden hung up the receiver and passed out into the yard. While Dr Ransome and Mr Fielding sat waiting the guard at the outer gate came in with a special delivery letter. Dr Ransome happened to notice the address, and, when the guard went out, looked at the letter more closely.

'By George!' he exclaimed.

'What is it?' asked Mr Fielding.

Silently the doctor offered the letter. Mr Fielding examined it closely.

'Coincidence,' he said. 'It must be.'

It was nearly eight o'clock when the warden returned to his office. The electricians had arrived in a wagon, and were now at work. The warden pressed the buzz-button communicating with the man at the outer gate in the wall.

'How many electricians came in?' he asked, over the short 'phone. 'Four? Three workmen in jumpers and overalls and the manager? Frock coat and silk hat? All right. Be certain that only four go out. That's all.'

He turned to Dr Ransome and Mr Fielding. 'We have to be careful here – particularly,' and there was broad sarcasm in his tone, 'since we have scientists locked up.'

The warden picked up the special delivery letter carelessly, and then began to open it.

'When I read this I want to tell you gentlemen something about how – Great Caesar!' he ended, suddenly, as he glanced at the letter. He sat with mouth open, motionless, from astonishment.

'What is it?' asked Mr Fielding.

'A special delivery from Cell 13,' gasped the warden. 'An invitation to supper.'

'What?' and the two others arose, unanimously.

The warden sat dazed, staring at the letter for a moment, then called sharply to a guard outside in the corridor.

'Run down to Cell 13 and see if that man's in there.'

The guard went as directed, while Dr Ransome and Mr Fielding examined the letter.

'It's Van Dusen's handwriting; there's no question of that,' said Dr Ransome. 'I've seen too much of it.'

Just then the buzz on the telephone from the outer gate sounded, and the warden, in a semi-trance, picked up the receiver.

'Hello! Two reporters, eh? Let 'em come in.' He turned suddenly to the doctor and Mr Fielding. 'Why, the man can't be out. He must be in his cell.'

Just at that moment the guard returned.

'He's still in his cell, sir,' he reported. 'I saw him. He's lying down.'

'There, I told you so,' said the warden, and he breathed freely again. 'But how did he mail that letter?'

There was a rap on the steel door which led from the jail yard into the warden's office.

'It's the reporters,' said the warden. 'Let them in,' he instructed the guard; then to the two other gentlemen: 'Don't say anything about this before them, because I'd never hear the last of it.'

The door opened, and the two men from the front gate entered.

'Good-evening, gentlemen,' said one. That was Hutchinson Hatch; the warden knew him well.

'Well?' demanded the other, irritably. 'I'm here.'

That was The Thinking Machine.

He squinted belligerently at the warden, who sat with mouth agape. For the moment that official had nothing to say. Dr Ransome and Mr Fielding were amazed, but they didn't know what the warden knew. They were only amazed; he was paralyzed. Hutchinson Hatch, the reporter, took in the scene with greedy eyes.

'How – how – how did you do it?' gasped the warden, finally.

'Come back to the cell,' said The Thinking Machine, in the irritated voice which his scientific associates knew so well.

The warden, still in a condition bordering on trance, led the way.

'Flash your light in there,' directed The Thinking Machine.

The warden did so. There was nothing unusual in the appearance of the cell, and there – there on the bed lay the figure of The Thinking Machine. Certainly! There was the yellow hair! Again the warden looked at the man beside him and wondered at the strangeness of his own dreams.

With trembling hands he unlocked the cell door and The Thinking Machine passed inside.

'See here,' he said.

He kicked at the steel bars in the bottom of the cell door and three of them were pushed out of place. A fourth broke off and rolled away in the corridor.

'And here, too,' directed the erstwhile prisoner as he stood on the bed to reach the small window. He swept his hand across the opening and every bar came out.

'What's this in the bed?' demanded the warden, who was slowly recovering.

'A wig,' was the reply. 'Turn down the cover.'

The warden did so. Beneath it lay a large coil of strong rope, thirty feet or more, a dagger, three files, ten feet of electric wire, a thin, powerful pair of steel pliers, a small tack hammer with its handle, and – and a Derringer pistol.

'How did you do it?' demanded the warden.

'You gentlemen have an engagement to supper with me at half past nine o'clock,' said The Thinking Machine. 'Come on, or we shall be late.'

'But how did you do it?' insisted the warden.

'Don't ever think you can hold any man who can use his brain,' said The Thinking Machine. 'Come on; we shall be late.'

VI

It was an impatient supper party in the rooms of Professor Van Dusen and a somewhat silent one. The guests were Dr Ransome, Albert Fielding, the warden, and Hutchinson Hatch, reporter. The meal was served to the minute, in accordance with Professor Van Dusen's instructions of one week before; Dr Ransome found the artichokes delicious. At last the supper was finished and The Thinking Machine turned full on Dr Ransome and squinted at him fiercely.

'Do you believe it now?' he demanded.

'I do,' replied Dr Ransome.

'Do you admit that it was a fair test?'

'I do.'

With the others, particularly the warden, he was waiting anxiously for the explanation.

'Suppose you tell us how – ' , began Mr Fielding.

'Yes, tell us how,' said the warden.

The Thinking Machine readjusted his glasses, took a couple of preparatory squints at his audience, and began the story. He told it from the beginning logically; and no man ever talked to more interested listeners.

'My agreement was,' he began, 'to go into a cell, carrying nothing except what was necessary to wear, and to leave that cell within a week. I had never seen Chisholm Prison. When I went into the cell I asked for tooth powder, two ten and one five-dollar bills, and also to have my shoes blacked. Even if these requests had been refused it would not have mattered seriously. But you agreed to them.

'I knew there would be nothing in the cell which you thought I might use to advantage. So when the warden locked the door on me I was apparently helpless, unless I could turn three seemingly innocent things to use. They were things which would have been permitted any prisoner under sentence of death, were they not, warden?'

'Tooth powder and polished shoes, yes, but not money,' replied the warden.

'Anything is dangerous in the hands of a man who knows how to use it,' went on The Thinking Machine. 'I did nothing that first night but sleep and chase rats.' He glared at the warden. 'When the matter was broached I knew I could do nothing that night, so suggested next day. You gentlemen thought I wanted time to arrange an escape with outside assistance, but this was not true. I knew I could communicate with whom I pleased, when I pleased.'

The warden stared at him a moment, then went on smoking solemnly.

'I was aroused next morning at six o'clock by the jailer with my breakfast,' continued the scientist. 'He told me dinner was at twelve and supper at six. Between these times, I gathered, I would be pretty much to myself. So immediately after breakfast I examined my outside surroundings from my cell window. One look told me it would be useless to try to scale the wall, even should I decide to leave my cell by the window, for my purpose was to leave not only the cell, but the prison. Of course, I could have gone over the wall, but it would have taken me longer to lay my plans that way. Therefore, for the moment, I dismissed all idea of that.

'From this first observation I knew the river was on that side of the prison, and that there was also a playground there. Subsequently these surmises were verified by a keeper. I knew then one important thing – that anyone might approach the prison wall from that side if necessary without attracting any particular attention. That was well to remember. I remembered it.

'But the outside thing which most attracted my attention was the feed wire to the arc light which ran within a few feet – probably three or four – of my cell window. I knew that would be valuable in the event I found it necessary to cut off that arc light.'

'Oh, you shut it off to-night, then?' asked the warden.

'Having learned all I could from that window,' resumed The Thinking Machine, without heeding the interruption, 'I considered the idea of escaping through the prison proper. I recalled just how I had come into the cell, which I knew would be the only way. Seven doors lay between me and the outside. So, also for the time being I gave up the idea of escaping that way. And I couldn't go through the solid granite walls of the cell.'

The Thinking Machine paused for a moment and Dr Ransome lighted a new cigar. For several minutes there was silence, then the scientific jail-breaker went on:

'While I was thinking about these things a rat ran across my foot. It suggested a new line of thought. There were at least half a dozen rats in the cell – I could see their beady eyes. Yet I had noticed none come under the cell door. I frightened them purposely and watched the cell door to see if they went out that way. They did not, but they were gone. Obviously they went another way. Another way meant another opening.

'I searched for this opening and found it. It was an old drain pipe, long unused and partly choked with dirt and dust. But this was the way the rats had come. They came from somewhere. Where? Drain pipes usually lead outside prison grounds. This one probably led to the river, or near it. The rats must therefore come from that direction. If they came a part of the way, I reasoned that they came all the way, because it was extremely unlikely that a solid iron or lead pipe would have any hole in it except at the exit.

'When the jailer came with my luncheon he told me two important things, although he didn't know it. One was that a new system of plumbing had been put in the prison seven years before; another that the river was only three hundred feet away. Then I knew positively that the pipe was a part of an old system; I knew, too, that it slanted generally toward the river. But did the pipe end in the water or on land?

'This was the next question to be decided. I decided it by catching several of the rats in the cell. My jailer was surprised to see me engaged in this work. I examined at least a dozen of them. They were perfectly dry; they had come through the pipe, and, most important of all, they were not house rats, but field rats. The other end of the pipe was on land, then, outside the prison walls. So far, so good.

'Then, I knew that if I worked freely from this point I must attract the warden's attention in another direction. You see, by telling the warden that I had come there to escape you made the test more severe, because I had to trick him by false scents.'

The warden looked up with a sad expression in his eyes.

'The first thing was to make him think I was trying to communicate with you, Dr Ransome. So I wrote a note on a piece of linen I tore from my shirt, addressed it to Dr Ransome, tied a five-dollar bill around it and threw it out of the window. I knew the guard would take it to the warden, but I rather hoped the warden would send it as addressed. Have you that first linen note, warden?'

The warden produced the cipher.

'What the deuce does it mean, anyhow?' he asked.

'Read it backward, beginning with the 'T' signature and disregard the division into words,' instructed The Thinking Machine.

The warden did so.

'T – h – i – s, this,' he spelled, studied it a moment, then read it off, grinning:

'This is not the way I intend to escape.'

'Well, now what do you think o' that?' he demanded, still grinning.

'I knew that would attract your attention, just as it did,' said The Thinking Machine, 'and if you really found out what it was, it would be a sort of gentle rebuke.'

'What did you write it with?' asked Dr Ransome, after he had examined the linen and passed it to Mr Fielding.

'This,' said the erstwhile prisoner, and he extended his foot. On it was the shoe he had worn in prison, though the polish was gone – scraped off clean. 'The shoe blacking, moistened with water, was my ink; the metal tip of the shoe lace made a fairly good pen.'

The warden looked up and suddenly burst into a laugh, half of relief, half of amusement.

'You're a wonder,' he said, admiringly. 'Go on.'

'That precipitated a search of my cell by the warden, as I had intended,' continued The Thinking Machine. 'I was anxious to get the warden into the habit of searching my cell, so that finally, constantly finding nothing, he would get disgusted and quit. This at last happened, practically.'

The warden blushed.

'He then took my white shirt away and gave me a prison shirt. He was satisfied that those two pieces of the shirt were all that was missing. But while he was searching my cell I had another piece of that same shirt, about nine inches square, rolled into a small ball in my mouth.'

'Nine inches off that shirt?' demanded the warden. 'Where did it come from?'

'The bosoms of all stiff white shirts are of triple thickness,' was the explanation. 'I tore out the inside thickness, leaving the bosom only two thicknesses. I knew you wouldn't see it. So much for that.'

There was a little pause, and the warden looked from one to another of the men with a sheepish grin.

'Having disposed of the warden for the time being by giving him something else to think about, I took my first serious step toward freedom,' said Professor Van Dusen. 'I knew, within reason, that the pipe led somewhere to the playground outside; I knew a great many boys played there; I knew that rats came into my cell from out there. Could I communicate with someone outside with these things at hand?

'First was necessary, I saw, a long and fairly reliable thread, so – but here,' he pulled up his trousers legs and showed that the tops of both stockings, of fine, strong lisle, were gone. 'I unraveled those – after I got them started it wasn't difficult – and I had easily a quarter of a mile of thread that I could depend on.

'Then on half of my remaining linen I wrote, laboriously enough I assure you, a letter explaining my situation to this gentleman here,' and he indicated Hutchinson Hatch. 'I knew he would assist me for the value of the newspaper story. I tied firmly to this linen letter a ten-dollar bill – there is no surer way of attracting the eye of anyone – and wrote on the linen: "Finder of this deliver to Hutchinson Hatch, Daily American, who will give another ten dollars for the information."

'The next thing was to get this note outside on that playground where a boy might find it. There were two ways, but I chose the best. I took one of the rats – I became adept in catching them – tied the linen and money firmly to one leg, fastened my lisle thread to another, and turned him loose in the drain pipe. I reasoned that the natural fright of the rodent would make him run until he was outside the pipe and then out on earth he would probably stop to gnaw off the linen and money.

'From the moment the rat disappeared into that dusty pipe I became anxious. I was taking so many chances. The rat might gnaw the string, of which I held one end; other rats might gnaw it; the rat might run out of the pipe and leave the linen and money where they would never be found; a thousand other things might have happened. So began some nervous hours, but the fact that the rat ran on until only a few feet of the string remained in my cell made me think he was outside the pipe. I had carefully instructed Mr Hatch what to do in case the note reached him. The question was: Would it reach him?

'This done, I could only wait and make other plans in case this one failed. I openly attempted to bribe my jailer, and learned from him that he held the keys to only two of seven doors between me and freedom. Then I did something else to make the warden nervous.

I took the steel supports out of the heels of my shoes and made a pretense of sawing the bars of my cell window. The warden raised a pretty row about that. He developed, too, the habit of shaking the bars of my cell window to see if they were solid. They were – then.'

Again the warden grinned. He had ceased being astonished.

'With this one plan I had done all I could and could only wait to see what happened,' the scientist went on. 'I couldn't know whether my note had been delivered or even found, or whether the rat had gnawed it up. And I didn't dare to draw back through the pipe that one slender thread which connected me with the outside.

'When I went to bed that night I didn't sleep, for fear there would come the slight signal twitch at the thread which was to tell me that Mr Hatch had received the note. At half-past three o'clock, I judge, I felt this twitch, and no prisoner actually under sentence of death ever welcomed a thing more heartily.'

The Thinking Machine stopped and turned to the reporter.

'You'd better explain just what you did,' he said.

'The linen note was brought to me by a small boy who had been playing baseball,' said Mr Hatch. 'I immediately saw a big story in it, so I gave the boy another ten dollars, and got several spools of silk, some twine, and a roll of light, pliable wire. The professor's note suggested that I have the finder of the note show me just where it was picked up, and told me to make my search from there, beginning at two o'clock in the morning. If I found the other end of the thread I was to twitch it gently three times, then a fourth.

'I began the search with a small bulb electric light. It was an hour and twenty minutes before I found the end of the drain pipe, half hidden in weeds. The pipe was very large there, say twelve inches across. Then I found the end of the lisle thread, twitched it as directed and immediately I got an answering twitch.

'Then I fastened the silk to this and Professor Van Dusen began to pull it into his cell. I nearly had heart disease for fear the string would break. To the end of the silk I fastened the twine, and when that had been pulled in, I tied on the wire. Then that was drawn into the pipe and we had a substantial line, which rats couldn't gnaw, from the mouth of the drain into the cell.'

The Thinking Machine raised his hand and Hatch stopped.

'All this was done in absolute silence,' said the scientist. 'But when the wire reached my hand I could have shouted. Then we tried another experiment, which Mr Hatch was prepared for. I tested the pipe as a speaking tube. Neither of us could hear very clearly, but I dared not speak loud for fear of attracting attention in the prison. At last I made him understand what I wanted immediately. He seemed to have great difficulty in understanding when I asked for nitric acid, and I repeated the word "acid" several times.

'Then I heard a shriek from a cell above me. I knew instantly that some one had overheard, and when I heard you coming, Mr Warden, I feigned sleep. If you had entered my cell at that moment that whole plan of escape would have ended there. But you passed on. That was the nearest I ever came to being caught.

'Having established this improvised trolley it is easy to see how I got things in the cell and made them disappear at will. I merely dropped them back into the pipe. You, Mr Warden, could not have reached the connecting wire with your fingers; they are too large. My fingers, you see, are longer and more slender. In addition I guarded the top of that pipe with a rat – you remember how.'

'I remember,' said the warden, with a grimace.

'I thought that if any one were tempted to investigate that hole the rat would dampen his ardour. Mr Hatch could not send me anything useful through the pipe until next night, although he did send me change for ten dollars as a test, so I proceeded with other parts of my plan. Then I evolved the method of escape, which I finally employed.

'In order to carry this out successfully it was necessary for the guard in the yard to get accustomed to seeing me at the cell window. I arranged this by dropping linen notes to him, boastful in tone, to make the warden believe, if possible, one of his assistants was communicating with the outside for me. I would stand at my window for hours gazing out, so the guard could see, and occasionally I spoke to him. In that way I learned that the prison had no electricians of its own, but was dependent upon the lighting company if anything should go wrong.

'That cleared the way to freedom perfectly. Early in the evening of the last day of my imprisonment, when it was dark, I planned to cut the feed wire which was only a few feet from my window, reaching it with an acid-tipped wire I had. That would make that side of the prison perfectly dark while the electricians were searching for the break. That would also bring Mr Hatch into the prison yard.

'There was only one more thing to do before I actually began the work of setting myself free. This was to arrange final details with Mr Hatch through our speaking tube. I did this within half an hour after the warden left my cell on the fourth night of my imprisonment. Mr Hatch again had serious difficulty in understanding me, and I repeated the word "acid" to him several times, and later the words: "Number eight hat" – that's my size – and these were the things which made a prisoner upstairs confess to murder, so one of the jailers told me next day. This prisoner heard our voices, confused of course, through the pipe, which also went to his cell. The cell directly over me was not occupied, hence no one else heard.

'Of course the actual work of cutting the steel bars out of the window and door was comparatively easy with nitric acid, which I got through the pipe in thin bottles, but it took time. Hour after hour on the fifth and sixth and seven days the guard below was looking at me as I worked on the bars of the window with the acid on a piece of wire. I used the tooth powder to prevent the acid spreading. I looked away abstractedly as I worked and each minute the acid cut deeper into the metal. I noticed that the jailers always tried the door by shaking the upper part, never the lower bars, therefore I cut the lower bars, leaving them hanging in place by thin strips of metal. But that was a bit of dare-deviltry. I could not have gone that way so easily.'

The Thinking Machine sat silent for several minutes.

'I think that makes everything clear,' he went on. 'Whatever points I have not explained were merely to confuse the warden and jailers. These things in my bed I brought in to please Mr Hatch, who wanted to improve the story. Of course, the wig was necessary in my plan. The special delivery letter I wrote and directed in my cell with Mr Hatch's fountain pen, then sent it out to him and he mailed it. That's all, I think.'

'But your actually leaving the prison grounds and then coming in through the outer gate to my office?' asked the warden.

'Perfectly simple,' said the scientist. 'I cut the electric light wire with acid, as I said, when the current was off. Therefore when the current was turned on, the arc light didn't light. I knew it would take some time to find out what was the matter and make repairs. When the guard went to report to you the yard was dark, I crept out the window – it was a tight fit, too – replaced the bars by standing on a narrow ledge and remained in a shadow until the force of electricians arrived. Mr Hatch was one of them.

'When I saw him I spoke and he handed me a cap, a jumper and overalls, which I put on within ten feet of you, Mr Warden, while you were in the yard. Later Mr Hatch called me, presumably as a workman, and together we went out the gate to get something out of the wagon. The gate guard let us pass out readily as two workmen who had just passed in. We changed our clothing and reappeared, asking to see you. We saw you. That's all.'

There was silence for several minutes. Dr Ransome was first to speak.

'Wonderful!' he exclaimed. 'Perfectly amazing.'

'How did Mr Hatch happen to come with the electricians?' asked Mr Fielding.

'His father is manager of the company,' replied The Thinking Machine.

'But what if there had been no Mr Hatch outside to help?'

'Every prisoner has one friend outside who would help him escape if he could.'

'Suppose – just suppose – there had been no old plumbing system there?' asked the warden, curiously.

'There were two other ways out,' said The Thinking Machine, enigmatically.

Ten minutes later the telephone bell rang. It was a request for the warden.

'Light all right, eh?' the warden asked, through the 'phone. 'Good. Wire cut beside Cell 13? Yes, I know. One electrician too many? What's that? Two came out?'

The warden turned to the others with a puzzled expression.

'He only let in four electricians, he has let out two and says there are three left.'

'I was the odd one,' said The Thinking Machine.

'Oh,' said the warden. 'I see.' Then through the 'phone: 'Let the fifth man go. He's all right.'

Loveday Brooke

Created by Catherine Louisa Pirkis (1841 – 1910)

CATHERINE LOUISA PIRKIS began writing fiction in the 1870s and the majority of her novels are melodramatic romances in the loose tradition established by Wilkie Collins and other 'sensation' novelists of the previous generation. *The Experiences of Loveday Brooke*, a collection of stories which first appeared in *The Ludgate Monthly* in 1893, was not only her only venture into the detective genre but also her last published fiction. In the mid-1890s, she gave up writing to devote her time to charitable work. She and her husband became leading activists in the anti-vivisection movement and in the National Canine Defence League, of which they had been founding members in 1891. Loveday Brooke is one of the earliest and most interesting of the female detectives of the period. A professional who works for a Fleet Street Detective Agency, she shows resourcefulness when she is sent under cover (as she is in several of the stories) and confidence in her own ability to discover the truth about the crimes she is investigating. The adventures in which she is embroiled often share some of the melodramatic plot contrivances common in the kind of novels Pirkis wrote in her earlier career but they remain well worth reading for their depictions of a woman making her way successfully in a world usually the preserve of men.

The Murder at Troyte's Hill

'GRIFFITHS, OF THE Newcastle Constabulary, has the case in hand,' said Mr Dyer; 'those Newcastle men are keen-witted, shrewd fellows, and very jealous of outside interference. They only sent to me under protest, as it were, because they wanted your sharp wits at work inside the house.'

'I suppose throughout I am to work with Griffiths, not with you?' said Miss Brooke.

'Yes; when I have given you in outline the facts of the case, I simply have nothing more to do with it, and you must depend on Griffiths for any assistance of any sort that you may require.'

Here, with a swing, Mr Dyer opened his big ledger and turned rapidly over its leaves till he came to the heading 'Troyte's Hill' and the date 'September 6th'.

'I'm all attention,' said Loveday, leaning back in her chair in the attitude of a listener.

'The murdered man,' resumed Mr Dyer, 'is a certain Alexander Henderson – usually known as old Sandy – lodge-keeper to Mr Craven, of Troyte's Hill, Cumberland. The lodge consists merely of two rooms on the ground floor, a bedroom and a sitting-room; these Sandy occupied alone, having neither kith nor kin of any degree. On the morning of September 6th, some children going up to the house with milk from the farm, noticed that Sandy's bed-room window stood wide open. Curiosity prompted them to peep in; and then, to their horror, they saw old Sandy, in his night-shirt, lying dead on the floor, as if he had fallen backwards from the window. They raised an alarm; and on examination, it was found that death had ensued from a heavy blow on the temple, given either by a strong fist or some blunt instrument. The room, on being entered, presented a curious appearance. It was as if a herd of monkeys had been turned into it and allowed to work their impish will. Not an article of furniture remained in its place: the bed-clothes had been rolled into a bundle and stuffed into the chimney; the bedstead – a small iron one – lay on its side; the one chair in the room stood on the top of the table; fender and fire-irons lay across the washstand, whose basin was to be found in a farther corner, holding bolster and pillow. The clock stood on its head in the middle of the mantelpiece; and the small vases and ornaments, which flanked it on either side, were walking, as it were, in a straight line towards the door. The old man's clothes had been rolled into a ball and thrown on the top of a high cupboard in which he kept his savings and whatever valuables he had. This cupboard, however, had not been meddled with, and its contents remained intact, so it was evident that robbery was not the motive for the crime. At the inquest, subsequently held, a verdict of "wilful murder" against some person or persons unknown was returned. The local police are diligently investigating the affair, but, as yet, no arrests have been made. The opinion that at present prevails in the neighbourhood is that the crime has been perpetrated by some lunatic, escaped or otherwise, and enquiries are being made at the local asylums as to missing or lately released inmates. Griffiths, however, tells me that his suspicions set in another direction.'

'Did anything of importance transpire at the inquest?'

'Nothing specially important. Mr Craven broke down in giving his evidence when he alluded to the confidential relations that had always subsisted between Sandy and himself, and spoke of the last time that he had seen him alive. The evidence of the butler, and one or two of the female servants, seems clear enough, and they let fall something of a hint that Sandy was not altogether a favourite among them, on account of the overbearing manner in which he used his influence with his master. Young Mr Craven, a youth of about nineteen, home from Oxford for the long vacation, was not present at the inquest; a doctor's certificate was put in stating that he was suffering from typhoid fever, and could not leave his bed without risk to his life. Now this young man is a thoroughly bad sort, and as much a gentleman-blackleg as it is possible for such a young fellow to be. It seems to Griffiths that there is something suspicious about this illness of his.

He came back from Oxford on the verge of *delirium tremens*, pulled round from that, and then suddenly, on the day after the murder, Mrs Craven rings the bell, announces that he has developed typhoid fever and orders a doctor to be sent for.'

'What sort of man is Mr Craven senior?'

'He seems to be a quiet old fellow, a scholar and learned philologist. Neither his neighbours nor his family see much of him; he almost lives in his study, writing a treatise, in seven or eight volumes, on comparative philology. He is not a rich man. Troyte's Hill, though it carries position in the county, is not a paying property, and Mr Craven is unable to keep it up properly. I am told he has had to cut down expenses in all directions in order to send his son to college, and his daughter from first to last, has been entirely educated by her mother. Mr Craven was originally intended for the church, but for some reason or other, when his college career came to an end, he did not present himself for ordination – went out to Natal instead, where he obtained some civil appointment and where he remained for about fifteen years. Henderson was his servant during the latter portion of his Oxford career, and must have been greatly respected by him, for although the remuneration derived from his appointment at Natal was small, he paid Sandy a regular yearly allowance out of it. When, about ten years ago, he succeeded to Troyte's Hill, on the death of his elder brother, and returned home with his family, Sandy was immediately installed as lodge-keeper, and at so high a rate of pay that the butler's wages were cut down to meet it.'

'Ah, that wouldn't improve the butler's feelings towards him,' ejaculated Loveday.

Mr Dyer went on: 'But, in spite of his high wages, he doesn't appear to have troubled much about his duties as lodge-keeper, for they were performed, as a rule, by the gardener's boy, while he took his meals and passed his time at the house, and, speaking generally, put his finger into every pie. You know the old adage respecting the servant of twenty-one years' standing: "Seven years my servant, seven years my equal, seven years my master". Well, it appears to have held good in the case of Mr Craven and Sandy. The old gentleman, absorbed in his philological studies, evidently let the reins slip through his fingers, and Sandy seems to have taken easy possession of them. The servants frequently had to go to him for orders, and he carried things, as a rule, with a high hand.'

'Did Mrs Craven never have a word to say on the matter?'

'I've not heard much about her. She seems to be a quiet sort of person. She is a Scotch missionary's daughter; perhaps she spends her time working for the Cape mission and that sort of thing.'

'And young Mr Craven: did he knock under to Sandy's rule?'

'Ah, now you're hitting the bull's eye and we come to Griffiths' theory. The young man and Sandy appear to have been at loggerheads ever since the Cravens took possession of Troyte's Hill. As a schoolboy Master Harry defied Sandy and threatened him with his hunting crop; and subsequently, as a young man, has used strenuous endeavours to put the old servant in his place. On the day before the murder, Griffiths says, there was a terrible scene between the two, in which the young gentleman, in the presence of several witnesses, made use of strong language and threatened the old man's life. Now, Miss Brooke, I have told you all the circumstances of the case so far as I know them. For fuller particulars I must refer you to Griffiths. He, no doubt, will meet you at Grenfell – the nearest station to Troyte's Hill – and tell you in what capacity he has procured for you an entrance into the house. By-the-way, he has wired to me this morning that he hopes you will be able to save the Scotch express to-night.'

Loveday expressed her readiness to comply with Mr Griffiths' wishes.

'I shall be glad,' said Mr Dyer, as he shook hands with her at the office door, 'to see you immediately on your return – that, however, I suppose, will not be yet awhile. This promises, I fancy, to be a longish affair?' This was said interrogatively.

'I haven't the least idea on the matter,' answered Loveday. 'I start on my work without theory of any sort – in fact, I may say, with my mind a perfect blank.'

And anyone who had caught a glimpse of her blank, expressionless features, as she said this, would have taken her at her word.

Grenfell, the nearest post-town to Troyte's Hill is a fairly busy, populous little town – looking south towards the black country, and northwards to low, barren hills. Pre-eminent among these stands Troyte's Hill, famed in the old days as a border keep, and possibly at a still earlier date as a Druid stronghold.

At a small inn at Grenfell, dignified by the title of 'The Station Hotel', Mr Griffiths, of the Newcastle constabulary, met Loveday and still further initiated her into the mysteries of the Troyte's Hill murder.

'A little of the first excitement has subsided,' he said, after preliminary greetings had been exchanged, 'but still the wildest rumours are flying about and repeated as solemnly as if they were Gospel truths. My chief here and my colleagues generally adhere to their first conviction, that the criminal is some suddenly crazed tramp or else an escaped lunatic, and they are confident that sooner or later we shall come upon his traces. Their theory is that Sandy, hearing some strange noise at the Park Gates, put his head out of the window to ascertain the cause and immediately had his death blow dealt him; then they suppose that the lunatic scrambled into the room through the window and exhausted his frenzy by turning things generally upside down. They refuse altogether to share my suspicions respecting young Mr Craven.'

Mr Griffiths was a tall, thin-featured man, with iron-grey hair, cut so close to his head that it refused to do anything but stand on end. This gave a somewhat comic expression of the upper portion of his face and clashed oddly with the melancholy look that his mouth habitually wore.

'I have made all smooth for you at Troyte's Hill,' he presently went on. 'Mr Craven is not wealthy enough to allow himself the luxury of a family lawyer, so he occasionally employs the services of Messrs. Wells and Sugden, lawyers in this place, and who, as it happens, have, off and on, done a good deal of business for me. It was through them I heard that Mr Craven was anxious to secure the assistance of an amanuensis. I immediately offered your services, stating that you were a friend of mine, a lady of impoverished means, who would gladly undertake the duties for the munificent sum of a guinea a month, with board and lodging. The old gentleman at once jumped at the offer, and is anxious for you to be at Troyte's Hill at once.'

Loveday expressed satisfaction with the programme that Mr Griffiths had sketched for her, then she had a few questions to ask.

'Tell me,' she said, 'what led you, in the first instance, to suspect young Mr Craven of the crime?'

'The footing on which he and Sandy stood towards each other, and the terrible scene that occurred between them only the day before the murder,' answered Griffiths, promptly. 'Nothing of this, however, was elicited at the inquest, where a very fair face was put on Sandy's relations with the whole of the Craven family. I have subsequently unearthed a good deal respecting the private life of Mr Harry Craven, and, among other things, I have found out that on the night of the murder he left the house shortly after ten o'clock, and no one, so far as I have been able to ascertain, knows at what hour he returned. Now I must draw your attention, Miss Brooke, to the fact that at the inquest the medical evidence went to prove that the murder had been committed between ten and eleven at night.'

'Do you surmise, then, that the murder was a planned thing on the part of this young man?'

'I do. I believe that he wandered about the grounds until Sandy shut himself in for the night, then aroused him by some outside noise, and, when the old man looked out to ascertain the cause, dealt him a blow with the bludgeon or loaded stick, that caused his death.'

'A cold-blooded crime that, for a boy of nineteen?'

'Yes. He's a good-looking, gentlemanly youngster, too, with manner as mild as milk, but from all accounts is as full of wickedness as an egg is full of meat. Now, to come to another point – if, in connection with these ugly facts, you take into consideration the suddenness of his illness, I think you'll admit that it bears a suspicious appearance and might reasonably give rise to the surmise that it was a plant on his part, in order to get out of the inquest.'

'Who is the doctor attending him?'

'A man called Waters; not much of a practitioner, from all accounts, and no doubt he feels himself highly honoured in being summoned to Troyte's Hill. The Cravens, it seems, have no family doctor. Mrs Craven, with her missionary experience, is half a doctor herself, and never calls in one except in a serious emergency.'

'The certificate was in order, I suppose?'

'Undoubtedly. And, as if to give colour to the gravity of the case, Mrs Craven sent a message down to the servants, that if any of them were afraid of the infection they could at once go to their homes. Several of the maids, I believe, took advantage of her permission, and packed their boxes. Miss Craven, who is a delicate girl, was sent away with her maid to stay with friends at Newcastle, and Mrs Craven isolated herself with her patient in one of the disused wings of the house.'

'Has anyone ascertained whether Miss Craven arrived at her destination at Newcastle?'

Griffiths drew his brows together in thought.

'I did not see any necessity for such a thing,' he answered. 'I don't quite follow you. What do you mean to imply?'

'Oh, nothing. I don't suppose it matters much: it might have been interesting as a side-issue.' She broke off for a moment, then added:

'Now tell me a little about the butler, the man whose wages were cut down to increase Sandy's pay.'

'Old John Hales? He's a thoroughly worthy, respectable man; he was butler for five or six years to Mr Craven's brother, when he was master of Troyte's Hill, and then took duty under this Mr Craven. There's no ground for suspicion in that quarter. Hales's exclamation when he heard of the murder is quite enough to stamp him as an innocent man: "Serve the old idiot right," he cried: "I couldn't pump up a tear for him if I tried for a month of Sundays!" Now I take it, Miss Brooke, a guilty man wouldn't dare make such a speech as that!'

'You think not?'

Griffiths stared at her. 'I'm a little disappointed in her,' he thought. 'I'm afraid her powers have been slightly exaggerated if she can't see such a straightforward thing as that.'

Aloud he said, a little sharply, 'Well, I don't stand alone in my thinking. No one yet has breathed a word against Hales, and if they did I've no doubt he could prove an alibi without any trouble, for he lives in the house, and everyone has a good word for him.'

'I suppose Sandy's lodge has been put into order by this time?'

'Yes; after the inquest, and when all possible evidence had been taken, everything was put straight.'

'At the inquest it was stated that no marks of footsteps could be traced in any direction?'

'The long drought we've had would render such a thing impossible, let alone the fact that Sandy's lodge stands right on the gravelled drive, without flower-beds or grass borders of any sort around it. But look here, Miss Brooke, don't you be wasting your time over the lodge and its surroundings. Every iota of fact on that matter has been gone through over and over again by me and my chief. What we want you to do is to go straight into the house and concentrate attention on Master Harry's sick-room, and find out what's going on there. What he did outside the house on the night of the 6th, I've no doubt I shall be able to find out for myself. Now, Miss Brooke, you've asked me no end of questions, to which I have replied as fully as it was in my power to do; will you be good enough to answer one question that I wish to put, as straightforwardly as I have answered yours? You have had fullest particulars given you of the condition of Sandy's room when the police entered it on the morning after the murder. No doubt, at the present moment, you can see it all in your mind's eye – the bedstead on its side, the clock on its head, the bed-clothes half-way up the chimney, the little vases and ornaments walking in a straight line towards the door?'

Loveday bowed her head.

'Very well. Now will you be good enough to tell me what this scene of confusion recalls to your mind before anything else?'

'The room of an unpopular Oxford freshman after a raid upon it by under-grads,' answered Loveday promptly.

Mr Griffiths rubbed his hands.

'Quite so!' he ejaculated. 'I see, after all, we are one at heart in this matter, in spite of a little surface disagreement of ideas. Depend upon it, by-and-bye, like the engineers tunnelling from different quarters under the Alps, we shall meet at the same point and shake hands. By-the-way, I have arranged for daily communication between us through the postboy who takes the letters to Troyte's Hill. He is trustworthy, and any letter you give him for me will find its way into my hands within the hour.'

It was about three o'clock in the afternoon when Loveday drove in through the park gates of Troyte's Hill, past the lodge where old

Sandy had met with his death. It was a pretty little cottage, covered with Virginia creeper and wild honeysuckle, and showing no outward sign of the tragedy that had been enacted within.

The park and pleasure-grounds of Troyte's Hill were extensive, and the house itself was a somewhat imposing red-brick structure, built, possibly, at the time when Dutch William's taste had grown popular in the country. Its frontage presented a somewhat forlorn appearance, its centre windows – a square of eight – alone seeming to show signs of occupation. With the exception of two windows at the extreme end of the bedroom floor of the north wing, where, possibly, the invalid and his mother were located, and two windows at the extreme end of the ground floor of the south wing, which Loveday ascertained subsequently were those of Mr Craven's study, not a single window in either wing owned blind or curtain. The wings were extensive, and it was easy to understand that at the extreme end of the one the fever patient would be isolated from the rest of the household, and that at the extreme end of the other Mr Craven could secure the quiet and freedom from interruption which, no doubt, were essential to the due prosecution of his philological studies.

Alike on the house and ill-kept grounds were present the stamp of the smallness of the income of the master and owner of the place. The terrace, which ran the length of the house in front, and on to which every window on the ground floor opened, was miserably out of repair: not a lintel or door-post, window-ledge or balcony but what seemed to cry aloud for the touch of the painter. 'Pity me! I have seen better days,' Loveday could fancy written as a legend across the red-brick porch that gave entrance to the old house.

The butler, John Hales, admitted Loveday, shouldered her portmanteau and told her he would show her to her room. He was a tall, powerfully-built man, with a ruddy face and dogged expression of countenance. It was easy to understand that, off and on, there must have been many a sharp encounter between him and old Sandy. He treated Loveday in an easy, familiar fashion, evidently considering that an amanuensis took much the same rank as a nursery governess – that is to say, a little below a lady's maid and a little above a house-maid.

'We're short of hands, just now,' he said, in broad Cumberland dialect, as he led the way up the wide staircase. 'Some of the lasses downstairs took fright at the fever and went home. Cook and I are single-handed, for Moggie, the only maid left, has been told off to wait on Madam and Master Harry. I hope you're not afeared of fever?'

Loveday explained that she was not, and asked if the room at the extreme end of the north wing was the one assigned to 'Madam and Master Harry'.

'Yes,' said the man, 'it's convenient for sick nursing; there's a flight of stairs runs straight down from it to the kitchen quarters. We put all Madam wants at the foot of these stairs and Moggie comes down and fetches it. Moggie herself never enters the sick-room. I take it you'll not be seeing Madam for many a day, yet awhile.'

'When shall I see Mr Craven? At dinner to-night?'

'That's what naebody could say,' answered Hales. 'He may not come out of his study till past midnight; sometimes he sits there till two or three in the morning. Shouldn't advise you to wait till he wants his dinner – better have a cup of tea and a chop sent up to you. Madam never waits for him at any meal.'

As he finished speaking he deposited the portmanteau outside one of the many doors opening into the gallery.

'This is Miss Craven's room,' he went on; 'cook and me thought you'd better have it, as it would want less getting ready than the other rooms, and work is work when there are so few hands to do it. Oh, my stars! I do declare there is cook putting it straight for you now.'

The last sentence was added as the opened door laid bare to view, the cook, with a duster in her hand, polishing a mirror; the bed had been made, it is true, but otherwise the room must have been much as Miss Craven left it, after a hurried packing up.

To the surprise of the two servants Loveday took the matter very lightly.

'I have a special talent for arranging rooms and would prefer getting this one straight for myself,' she said. 'Now, if you will go and get ready that chop and cup of tea we were talking about just now, I shall think it much kinder than if you stayed here doing what I can so easily do for myself.'

When, however, the cook and butler had departed in company, Loveday showed no disposition to exercise the 'special talent' of which she had boasted.

She first carefully turned the key in the lock and then proceeded to make a thorough and minute investigation of every corner of the room. Not an article of furniture, not an ornament or toilet accessory, but what was lifted from its place and carefully scrutinised. Even the ashes in the grate, the debris of the last fire made there, were raked over and well looked through.

This careful investigation of Miss Craven's late surroundings occupied in all about three quarters of an hour, and Loveday, with her hat in her hand, descended the stairs to see Hales crossing the hall to the dining-room with the promised cup of tea and chop.

In silence and solitude she partook of the simple repast in a dining-hall that could with ease have banqueted a hundred and fifty guests.

'Now for the grounds before it gets dark,' she said to herself, as she noted that already the outside shadows were beginning to slant.

The dining-hall was at the back of the house; and here, as in the front, the windows, reaching to the ground, presented easy means of egress. The flower-garden was on this side of the house and sloped downhill to a pretty stretch of well-wooded country.

Loveday did not linger here even to admire, but passed at once round the south corner of the house to the windows which she had ascertained, by a careless question to the butler, were those of Mr Craven's study.

Very cautiously she drew near them, for the blinds were up, the curtains drawn back. A side glance, however, relieved her apprehensions, for it showed her the occupant of the room, seated in an easy-chair, with his back to the windows. From the length of his outstretched limbs he was evidently a tall man. His hair was silvery and curly, the lower part of his face was hidden from her view by the chair, but she could see one hand was pressed tightly across his eyes and brows. The whole attitude was that of a man absorbed in deep thought. The room was comfortably furnished, but presented an appearance of disorder from the books and manuscripts scattered in all directions. A whole pile of torn fragments of foolscap sheets, overflowing from a waste-paper basket beside the writing-table, seemed to proclaim the fact that the scholar had of late grown weary of, or else dissatisfied with his work, and had condemned it freely.

Although Loveday stood looking in at this window for over five minutes, not the faintest sign of life did that tall, reclining figure give, and it would have been as easy to believe him locked in sleep as in thought.

From here she turned her steps in the direction of Sandy's lodge. As Griffiths had said, it was gravelled up to its doorstep. The blinds were closely drawn, and it presented the ordinary appearance of a disused cottage.

A narrow path beneath the over-arching boughs of cherry-laurel and arbutus, immediately facing the lodge, caught her eye, and down this she at once turned her footsteps.

This path led, with many a wind and turn, through a belt of shrubbery that skirted the frontage of Mr Craven's grounds, and eventually, after much zig-zagging, ended in close proximity to the stables. As Loveday entered it, she seemed literally to leave daylight behind her.

'I feel as if I were following the course of a circuitous mind,' she said to herself as the shadows closed around her. 'I could not fancy Sir Isaac Newton or Bacon planning or delighting in such a wind-about-alley as this!'

The path showed greyly in front of her out of the dimness. On and on she followed it; here and there the roots of the old laurels, struggling out of the ground, threatened to trip her up. Her eyes, however, had now grown accustomed to the half-gloom, and not a detail of her surroundings escaped her as she went along.

A bird flew out the thicket on her right hand with a startled cry. A dainty little frog leaped out of her way into the shrivelled leaves lying below the laurels. Following the movements of this frog, her eye was caught by something black and solid among those leaves. What was it? A bundle – a shiny black coat? Loveday knelt down, and using her hands to assist her eyes, found that they came into contact with the dead, stiffened body of a beautiful black retriever. She parted, as well as she was able, the lower boughs of the evergreens, and minutely examined the poor animal. Its eyes were still open, though glazed and bleared, and its death had, undoubtedly, been caused by the blow of some blunt, heavy instrument, for on one side its skull was almost battered in.

'Exactly the death that was dealt to Sandy,' she thought, as she groped hither and thither beneath the trees in hopes of lighting upon the weapon of destruction.

She searched until increasing darkness warned her that search was useless. Then, still following the zig-zagging path, she made her way out by the stables and thence back to the house.

She went to bed that night without having spoken to a soul beyond the cook and butler. The next morning, however, Mr Craven introduced himself to her across the breakfast table. He was a man of really handsome personal appearance, with a fine carriage of the head and shoulders, and eyes that had a forlorn, appealing look in them. He entered the room with an air of great energy, apologized to Loveday for the absence of his wife, and for his own remissness in not being in the way to receive her on the previous day. Then he bade her make herself at home at the breakfast-table, and expressed his delight in having found a coadjutor in his work.

'I hope you understand what a great – a stupendous work it is?' he added, as he sank into a chair. 'It is a work that will leave its impress upon thought in all the ages to come. Only a man who has studied comparative philology as I have for the past thirty years, could gauge the magnitude of the task I have set myself.'

With the last remark, his energy seemed spent, and he sank back in his chair, covering his eyes with his hand in precisely the same attitude as that in which Loveday had seen him over-night, and utterly oblivious of the fact that breakfast was before him and a stranger-guest seated at table. The butler entered with another dish. 'Better go on with your breakfast,' he whispered to Loveday, 'he may sit like that for another hour.'

He placed his dish in front of his master.

'Captain hasn't come back yet, sir,' he said, making an effort to arouse him from his reverie.

'Eh, what?' said Mr Craven, for a moment lifting his hand from his eyes.

'Captain, sir – the black retriever,' repeated the man.

The pathetic look in Mr Craven's eyes deepened.

'Ah, poor Captain!' he murmured; 'the best dog I ever had.'

Then he again sank back in his chair, putting his hand to his forehead.

The butler made one more effort to arouse him.

'Madam sent you down a newspaper, sir, that she thought you might like to see,' he shouted almost into his master's ear, and at the same time laid the morning's paper on the table beside his plate.

'Confound you! Leave it there,' said Mr Craven irritably. 'Fools! Dolts that you all are! With your trivialities and interruptions you are sending me out of the world with my work undone!'

And again he sank back in his chair, closed his eyes and became lost to his surroundings.

Loveday went on with her breakfast. She changed her place at table to one on Mr Craven's right hand, so that the newspaper sent down for his perusal lay between his plate and hers. It was folded into an oblong shape, as if it were wished to direct attention to a certain portion of a certain column.

A clock in a corner of the room struck the hour with a loud, resonant stroke. Mr Craven gave a start and rubbed his eyes.

'Eh, what's this?' he said. 'What meal are we at?' He looked around with a bewildered air. 'Eh! – who are you?' he went on, staring hard at Loveday. 'What are you doing here? Where's Nina? Where's Harry?'

Loveday began to explain, and gradually recollection seemed to come back to him.

'Ah, yes, yes,' he said. 'I remember; you've come to assist me with my great work. You promised, you know, to help me out of the hole I've got into. Very enthusiastic, I remember they said you were, on certain abstruse points in comparative philology. Now, Miss – Miss – I've forgotten your name – tell me a little of what you know about the elemental sounds of speech that are common to all languages. Now, to how many would you reduce those elemental sounds – to six, eight, nine? No, we won't discuss the matter here, the cups and saucers distract me. Come into my den at the other end of the house; we'll have perfect quiet there.'

And utterly ignoring the fact that he had not as yet broken his fast, he rose from the table, seized Loveday by the wrist, and led her out of the room and down the long corridor that led through the south wing to his study.

But seated in that study his energy once more speedily exhausted itself.

He placed Loveday in a comfortable chair at his writing-table, consulted her taste as to pens, and spread a sheet of foolscap before her. Then he settled himself in his easy-chair, with his back to the light, as if he were about to dictate folios to her.

In a loud, distinct voice he repeated the title of his learned work, then its subdivision, then the number and heading of the chapter that was at present engaging his attention. Then he put his hand to his head. 'It's the elemental sounds that are my stumbling-block,' he said. 'Now, how on earth is it possible to get a notion of a sound of agony that is not in part a sound of terror? Or a sound of surprise that is not in part a sound of either joy or sorrow?'

With this his energies were spent, and although Loveday remained seated in that study from early morning till daylight began to fade, she had not ten sentences to show for her day's work as amanuensis.

Loveday in all spent only two clear days at Troyte's Hill.

On the evening of the first of those days Detective Griffiths received, through the trustworthy post-boy, the following brief note from her:

I have found out that Hales owed Sandy close upon a hundred pounds, which he had borrowed at various times. I don't know whether you will think this fact of any importance.
L.B.

Mr Griffiths repeated the last sentence blankly. 'If Harry Craven were put upon his defence, his counsel, I take it, would consider the fact of first importance,' he muttered. And for the remainder of that day Mr Griffiths went about his work in a perturbed state of mind, doubtful whether to hold or to let go his theory concerning Harry Craven's guilt.

The next morning there came another brief note from Loveday which ran thus:

As a matter of collateral interest, find out if a person, calling himself Harold Cousins, sailed two days ago from London Docks for Natal in the Bonnie Dundee?'

To this missive, Loveday received, in reply, the following somewhat lengthy despatch:

I do not quite see the drift of your last note, but have wired to our agents in London to carry out its suggestion. On my part, I have important news to communicate. I have found out what Harry Craven's business out of doors was on the night of the murder, and at my instance a warrant has been issued for his arrest. This warrant it will be my duty to serve on him in the course of today. Things are beginning to look very black against him, and I am convinced his illness is all a sham. I have seen Waters, the man who is supposed to be attending him, and have driven him into a corner and made him admit that he has only seen young Craven once – on the first day of his illness – and that he gave his certificate entirely on the strength of what Mrs Craven told him of her son's condition. On the occasion of this, his first and only visit, the lady, it seems, also told him that it would not be necessary for him to continue his attendance, as she quite felt herself competent to treat the case, having had so much experience in fever cases among the blacks at Natal.

As I left Waters' house, after eliciting this important information, I was accosted by a man who keeps a low-class inn in the place, McQueen by name. He said that he wished to speak to me on a matter of importance. To make a long story short, this McQueen stated that on the night of the sixth, shortly after eleven o'clock, Harry Craven came to his house, bringing with him a valuable piece of plate – a handsome epergne – and requested him to lend him a hundred pounds on it, as he hadn't a penny in his pocket. McQueen complied with his request to the extent of ten sovereigns, and now, in a fit of nervous terror, comes to me to confess himself a receiver of stolen goods and play the honest man! He says he noticed that the young gentleman was very much agitated as he made the request, and he also begged him to mention his visit to no one. Now, I am curious to learn how Master Harry will get over the fact that he passed the lodge at the hour at which the murder was most probably committed; or how he will get out of the dilemma of having repassed the lodge on his way back to the house, and not noticed the wide-open window with the full moon shining down on

it? Another word! Keep out of the way when I arrive at the house, somewhere between two and three in the afternoon, to serve the warrant. I do not wish your professional capacity to get wind, for you will most likely yet be of some use to us in the house.
S.G.

Loveday read this note, seated at Mr Craven's writing-table, with the old gentleman himself reclining motionless beside her in his easy-chair. A little smile played about the corners of her mouth as she read over again the words – 'for you will most likely yet be of some use to us in the house'.

Loveday's second day in Mr Craven's study promised to be as unfruitful as the first. For fully an hour after she had received Griffiths' note, she sat at the writing-table with her pen in her hand, ready to transcribe Mr Craven's inspirations. Beyond, however, the phrase, muttered with closed eyes – 'It's all here, in my brain, but I can't put it into words' – not a half-syllable escaped his lips.

At the end of that hour the sound of footsteps on the outside gravel made her turn her head towards the windows. It was Griffiths approaching with two constables. She heard the hall door opened to admit them, but, beyond that, not a sound reached her ear, and she realised how fully she was cut off from communication with the rest of the household at the farther end of this unoccupied wing.

Mr Craven, still reclining in his semi-trance, evidently had not the faintest suspicion that so important an event as the arrest of his only son on a charge of murder was about to be enacted in the house.

Meantime, Griffiths and his constables had mounted the stairs leading to the north wing, and were being guided through the corridors to the sick-room by the flying figure of Moggie, the maid.

'Hoot, mistress!' cried the girl, 'here are three men coming up the stairs – policemen, every one of them – will ye come and ask them what they be wanting?'

Outside the door of the sick-room stood Mrs Craven – a tall, sharp-featured woman with sandy hair going rapidly grey.

'What is the meaning of this? What is your business here?' she said haughtily, addressing Griffiths, who headed the party.

Griffiths respectfully explained what his business was, and requested her to stand on one side that he might enter her son's room.

'This is my daughter's room; satisfy yourself of the fact,' said the lady, throwing back the door as she spoke.

And Griffiths and his confreres entered, to find pretty Miss Craven, looking very white and scared, seated beside a fire in a long flowing *robe de chambre*.

Griffiths departed in haste and confusion, without the chance of a professional talk with Loveday. That afternoon saw him telegraphing wildly in all directions, and despatching messengers in all quarters. Finally he spent over an hour drawing up an elaborate report to his chief at Newcastle, assuring him of the identity of one Harold Cousins, who had sailed in the *Bonnie Dundee* for Natal, with Harry Craven, of Troyte's Hill, and advising that the police authorities in that far-away district should be immediately communicated with.

The ink had not dried on the pen with which this report was written before a note, in Loveday's writing, was put into his hand.

Loveday evidently had had some difficulty in finding a messenger for this note, for it was brought by a gardener's boy, who informed Griffiths that the lady had said he would receive a gold sovereign if he delivered the letter all right.

Griffiths paid the boy and dismissed him, and then proceeded to read Loveday's communication.

It was written hurriedly in pencil, and ran as follows:

Things are getting critical here. Directly you receive this, come up to the house with two of your men, and post yourselves anywhere in the grounds where you can see and not be seen. There will be no difficulty in this, for it will be dark by the time you are able to get there. I am not sure whether I shall want your aid to-night, but you had better keep in the grounds until morning, in case of need; and above all, never once lose sight of the study window. [This was underscored.] *If I put a lamp with a green shade in one of those windows, do not lose a moment in entering by that window, which I will contrive to keep unlocked.*

Detective Griffiths rubbed his forehead – rubbed his eyes, as he finished reading this.

'Well, I daresay it's all right,' he said, 'but I'm bothered, that's all, and for the life of me I can't see one step of the way she is going.'

He looked at his watch; the hands pointed to a quarter past six. The short September day was drawing rapidly to a close. A good five miles lay between him and Troyte's Hill – there was evidently not a moment to lose.

At the very moment that Griffiths, with his two constables, were once more starting along the Grenfell High Road behind the best horse they could procure, Mr Craven was rousing himself from his long slumber, and beginning to look around him. That slumber, however, though long, had not been a peaceful one, and it was sundry of the old gentleman's muttered exclamations, as he had started uneasily in his sleep, that had caused Loveday to pen, and then to creep out of the room to despatch, her hurried note.

What effect the occurrence of the morning had had upon the household generally, Loveday, in her isolated corner of the house, had no means of ascertaining. She only noted that when Hales brought in her tea, as he did precisely at five o'clock, he wore a particularly ill-tempered expression of countenance, and she heard him mutter, as he set down the tea-tray with a clatter, something about being a respectable man, and not used to such 'goings on'.

It was not until nearly an hour and a half after this that Mr Craven had awakened with a sudden start, and, looking wildly around him, had questioned Loveday who had entered the room.

Loveday explained that the butler had brought in lunch at one, and tea at five, but that since then no one had come in.

'Now that's false,' said Mr Craven, in a sharp, unnatural sort of voice; 'I saw him sneaking round the room, the whining, canting hypocrite, and you must have seen him, too! Didn't you hear him say, in his squeaky old voice: "Master, I knows your secret – ."' He broke off abruptly, looking wildly round. 'Eh, what's this?' he cried. 'No, no, I'm all wrong – Sandy is dead and buried – they held an inquest on him, and we all praised him up as if he were a saint.'

'He must have been a bad man, that old Sandy,' said Loveday sympathetically.

'You're right! you're right!' cried Mr Craven, springing up excitedly from his chair and seizing her by the hand. 'If ever a man deserved his death, he did. For thirty years he held that rod over my head, and then – ah where was I?'

He put his hand to his head and again sank, as if exhausted, into his chair.

'I suppose it was some early indiscretion of yours at college that he knew of?' said Loveday, eager to get at as much of the truth as possible while the mood for confidence held sway in the feeble brain.

'That was it! I was fool enough to marry a disreputable girl – a barmaid in the town – and Sandy was present at the wedding, and then – .' Here his eyes closed again and his mutterings became incoherent.

For ten minutes he lay back in his chair, muttering thus; 'A yelp – a groan,' were the only words Loveday could distinguish among those mutterings, then, suddenly, slowly and distinctly, he said, as if answering some plainly-put question: 'A good blow with the hammer and the thing was done.'

'I should like amazingly to see that hammer,' said Loveday; 'do you keep it anywhere at hand?'

His eyes opened with a wild, cunning look in them.

'Who's talking about a hammer? I did not say I had one. If anyone says I did it with a hammer, they're telling a lie.'

'Oh, you've spoken to me about the hammer two or three times,' said Loveday calmly; 'the one that killed your dog, Captain, and I should like to see it, that's all.'

The look of cunning died out of the old man's eye – 'Ah, poor Captain! Splendid dog that! Well, now, where were we? Where did we leave off? Ah, I remember, it was the elemental sounds of speech that bothered me so that night. Were you here then? Ah, no! I remember. I had been trying all day to assimilate a dog's yelp of pain to a human groan, and I couldn't do it. The idea haunted me – followed me about wherever I went. If they were both elemental sounds, they must have something in common, but the link between them I could not find; then it occurred to me, would a well-bred, well-trained dog like my Captain in the stables, there, at the moment of death give an unmitigated currish yelp; would there not be something of a human note in his death-cry? The thing was worth putting to the test. If I could hand down in my treatise a fragment of fact on the matter, it would be worth a dozen dogs' lives. So I went out into the moonlight – ah, but you know all about it – now, don't you?'

'Yes. Poor Captain! Did he yelp or groan?'

'Why, he gave one loud, long, hideous yelp, just as if he had been a common cur. I might just as well have let him alone; it only set that other brute opening his window and spying out on me, and saying in his cracked old voice: "Master, what are you doing out here at this time of night?"'

Again he sank back in his chair, muttering incoherently with half-closed eyes.

Loveday let him alone for a minute or so; then she had another question to ask.

'And that other brute – did he yelp or groan when you dealt him his blow?'

'What, old Sandy – the brute? He fell back – Ah, I remember, you said you would like to see the hammer that stopped his babbling old tongue – now, didn't you?'

He rose a little unsteadily from his chair, and seemed to drag his long limbs with an effort across the room to a cabinet at the farther end. Opening a drawer in this cabinet, he produced, from amidst some specimens of strata and fossils, a large-sized geological hammer.

He brandished it for a moment over his head, then paused with his finger on his lip.

'Hush!' he said, 'we shall have the fools creeping in to peep at us if we don't take care.' And to Loveday's horror he suddenly made for the door, turned the key in the lock, withdrew it and put it into his pocket.

She looked at the clock; the hands pointed to half-past seven. Had Griffiths received her note at the proper time, and were the men now in the grounds? She could only pray that they were.

'The light is too strong for my eyes,' she said, and rising from her chair, she lifted the green-shaded lamp and placed it on a table that stood at the window.

'No, no, that won't do,' said Mr Craven; 'that would show everyone outside what we're doing in here.' He crossed to the window as he spoke and removed the lamp thence to the mantelpiece.

Loveday could only hope that in the few seconds it had remained in the window it had caught the eye of the outside watchers.

The old man beckoned to Loveday to come near and examine his deadly weapon. 'Give it a good swing round,' he said, suiting the action to the word, 'and down it comes with a splendid crash.' He brought the hammer round within an inch of Loveday's forehead.

She started back.

'Ha, ha,' he laughed harshly and unnaturally, with the light of madness dancing in his eyes now; 'did I frighten you? I wonder what sort of sound you would make if I were to give you a little tap just there.' Here he lightly touched her forehead with the hammer. 'Elemental, of course, it would be, and – .'

Loveday steadied her nerves with difficulty. Locked in with this lunatic, her only chance lay in gaining time for the detectives to reach the house and enter through the window.

'Wait a minute,' she said, striving to divert his attention; 'you have not yet told me what sort of an elemental sound old Sandy made when he fell. If you'll give me pen and ink, I'll write down a full account of it all, and you can incorporate it afterwards in your treatise.'

For a moment a look of real pleasure flitted across the old man's face, then it faded. 'The brute fell dead without a sound,' he answered; 'it was all for nothing, that night's work; yet not altogether for nothing. No, I don't mind owning I would do it all over again to get the wild thrill of joy at my heart that I had when I looked down into that old man's dead face and felt myself free at last! Free at last!' His voice rang out excitedly – once more he brought his hammer round with an ugly swing.

'For a moment I was a young man again; I leaped into his room – the moon was shining full in through the window – I thought of my old college days, and the fun we used to have at Pembroke – topsy turvey I turned everything – .' He broke off abruptly, and drew a step nearer to Loveday. 'The pity of it all was,' he said, suddenly dropping from his high, excited tone to a low, pathetic one, 'that he fell without a sound of any sort.' Here he drew another step nearer. 'I wonder – ' he said, then broke off again, and came close to Loveday's side. 'It has only this moment occurred to me,' he said, now with his lips close to Loveday's ear, 'that a woman, in her death agony, would be much more likely to give utterance to an elemental sound than a man.'

He raised his hammer, and Loveday fled to the window, and was lifted from the outside by three strong pairs of arms.

******

'I thought I was conducting my very last case – I never had such a narrow escape before!' said Loveday, as she stood talking with Mr Griffiths on the Grenfell platform, awaiting the train to carry her back to London. 'It seems strange that no one before suspected the old gentleman's sanity – I suppose, however, people were so used to his eccentricities that they did not notice how they had deepened into positive lunacy. His cunning evidently stood him in good stead at the inquest.'

'It is possible,' said Griffiths thoughtfully, 'that he did not absolutely cross the very slender line that divides eccentricity from madness until after the murder. The excitement consequent upon the discovery of the crime may just have pushed him over the border. Now, Miss Brooke, we have exactly ten minutes before your train comes in. I should feel greatly obliged to you if you would explain one or two things that have a professional interest for me.'

'With pleasure,' said Loveday. 'Put your questions in categorical order and I will answer them.'

'Well, then, in the first place, what suggested to your mind the old man's guilt?'

'The relations that subsisted between him and Sandy seemed to me to savour too much of fear on the one side and power on the other. Also the income paid to Sandy during Mr Craven's absence in Natal bore, to my mind, an unpleasant resemblance to hush-money.'

'Poor wretched being! And I hear that, after all, the woman he married in his wild young days died soon afterwards of drink. I have no doubt, however, that Sandy sedulously kept up the fiction of her existence, even after his master's second marriage. Now for another question: how was it you knew that Miss Craven had taken her brother's place in the sick-room?'

'On the evening of my arrival I discovered a rather long lock of fair hair in the unswept fireplace of my room, which, as it happened, was usually occupied by Miss Craven. It at once occurred to me that the young lady had been cutting off her hair and that there must be some powerful motive to induce such a sacrifice. The suspicious circumstances attending her brother's illness soon supplied me with such a motive.'

'Ah! that typhoid fever business was very cleverly done. Not a servant in the house, I verily believe, but who thought Master Harry was upstairs, ill in bed, and Miss Craven away at her friends' in Newcastle. The young fellow must have got a clear start off within an hour of the murder. His sister, sent away the next day to Newcastle, dismissed her maid there, I hear, on the plea of no accommodation at her friends' house – sent the girl to her own home for a holiday and herself returned to Troyte's Hill in the middle of the night, having walked the five miles from Grenfell. No doubt her mother admitted her through one of those easily-opened front windows, cut her hair and put her to bed to personate her brother without delay. With Miss Craven's strong likeness to Master Harry, and in a darkened room, it is easy to understand that the eyes of a doctor, personally unacquainted with the family, might easily be deceived. Now, Miss Brooke, you must admit that with all this elaborate chicanery and double dealing going on, it was only natural that my suspicions should set in strongly in that quarter.'

'I read it all in another light, you see,' said Loveday. 'It seemed to me that the mother, knowing her son's evil proclivities, believed in his guilt, in spite, possibly, of his assertion of innocence. The son, most likely, on his way back to the house after pledging the family plate, had met old Mr Craven with the hammer in his hand. Seeing, no doubt, how impossible it would be for him to clear himself without incriminating his father, he preferred flight to Natal to giving evidence at the inquest.'

'Now about his alias?' said Mr Griffiths briskly, for the train was at that moment steaming into the station. 'How did you know that Harold Cousins was identical with Harry Craven, and had sailed in the *Bonnie Dundee*?'

'Oh, that was easy enough,' said Loveday, as she stepped into the train; 'a newspaper sent down to Mr Craven by his wife, was folded so as to direct his attention to the shipping list. In it I saw that the *Bonnie Dundee* had sailed two days previously for Natal. Now it was only natural to connect Natal with Mrs Craven, who had passed the greater part of her life there; and it was easy to understand her wish to get her scapegrace son among her early friends. The alias under which he sailed came readily enough to light. I found it scribbled all over one of Mr Craven's writing pads in his study; evidently it had been drummed into his ears by his wife as his son's alias, and the old gentleman had taken this method of fixing it in his memory. We'll hope that the young fellow, under his new name, will make a new reputation for himself – at any rate, he'll have a better chance of doing so with the ocean between him and his evil companions. Now it's good-bye, I think.'

'No,' said Mr Griffiths; 'it's *au revoir*, for you'll have to come back again for the assizes, and give the evidence that will shut old Mr Craven in an asylum for the rest of his life.'

Dr Halifax

Created by L.T. Meade (1854 – 1914) and Clifford Halifax (1860 – 1921)

L. T. MEADE WAS the pseudonym of Elizabeth Thomasina Meade Smith, an almost impossibly productive writer of the late Victorian and Edwardian eras who made her first appearance in print in the 1870s and went on to publish close to 300 books. At one stage in her career she was writing ten novels a year. In her lifetime she was best-known as the author of stories for girls, often with a school setting, but she also wrote many crime stories, sometimes in collaboration with other writers. With Robert Eustace, for example, she created a remarkable *femme fatale* and supervillain in Madame Sara who appeared in a series of stories in *The Strand Magazine* in 1902-3, later collected in a volume entitled *The Sorceress of the Strand*. 'Stories from the Diary of a Doctor' also appeared in *The Strand* but they were written eight years earlier and accredited to Meade and Clifford Halifax, the pseudonym of a writer and doctor named Edgar Beaumont. The central character is a medical man who finds himself involved in cases where medicine and crime come together. The stories are archetypally late Victorian in their values and are often melodramatic and stilted but many of them are also vividly memorable. 'The Horror of Studley Grange', with its central character driven to the brink of madness by what seem to be supernatural apparitions, is one of the best.

The Horror of Studley Grange

I WAS IN my consulting-room one morning, and had just said good-bye to the last of my patients, when my servant came in and told me that a lady had called who pressed very earnestly for an interview with me.

'I told her that you were just going out, sir,' said the man, 'and she saw the carriage at the door; but she begged to see you, if only for two minutes. This is her card.'

I read the words, 'Lady Studley'.

'Show her in,' I said, hastily, and the next moment a tall, slightly-made, fair-haired girl entered the room.

She looked very young, scarcely more than twenty, and I could hardly believe that she was, what her card indicated, a married woman.

The colour rushed into her cheeks as she held out her hand to me. I motioned her to a chair, and then asked her what I could do for her.

'Oh, you can help me,' she said, clasping her hands and speaking in a slightly theatrical manner. 'My husband, Sir Henry Studley, is very unwell, and I want you to come to see him – can you? – will you?'

'With pleasure,' I replied. 'Where do you live?'

'At Studley Grange, in Wiltshire. Don't you know our place?'

'I daresay I ought to know it,' I replied, 'although at the present moment I can't recall the name. You want me to come to see your husband. I presume you wish me to have a consultation with his medical attendant?'

'No, no, not at all. The fact is, Sir Henry has not got a medical attendant. He dislikes doctors, and won't see one. I want you to come and stay with us for a week or so. I have heard of you through mutual friends – the Onslows. I know you can effect remarkable cures, and you have a great deal of tact. But you can't possibly do anything for my husband unless you are willing to stay in the house and to notice his symptoms.'

Lady Studley spoke with great emphasis and earnestness. Her long, slender hands were clasped tightly together. She had drawn off her gloves and was bending forward in her chair. Her big, childish, and somewhat restless blue eyes were fixed imploringly on my face.

'I love my husband,' she said, tears suddenly filling them – 'and it is dreadful, dreadful, to see him suffer as he does. He will die unless someone comes to his aid. Oh, I know I am asking an immense thing, when I beg of you to leave all your patients and come to the country. But we can pay. Money is no object whatever to us. We can, we will, gladly pay you for your services.'

'I must think the matter over,' I said. 'You flatter me by wishing for me, and by believing that I can render you assistance, but I cannot take a step of this kind in a hurry. I will write to you by to-night's post if you will give me your address. In the meantime, kindly tell me some of the symptoms of Sir Henry's malady.'

'I fear it is a malady of the mind,' she answered immediately, 'but it is of so vivid and so startling a character, that unless relief is soon obtained, the body must give way under the strain. You see that I am very young, Dr Halifax. Perhaps I look younger than I am – my age is twenty-two. My husband is twenty years my senior. He would, however, be considered by most people still a young man. He is a great scholar, and has always had more or less the habits of a recluse. He is fond of living in his library, and likes nothing better than to be surrounded by books of all sorts. Every modern book worth reading is forwarded to him by its publisher. He is a very interesting man and a brilliant conversationalist. Perhaps I ought to put all this in the past tense, for now he scarcely ever speaks – he reads next to nothing – it is difficult to persuade him to eat – he will not leave the house – he used to have a rather ruddy complexion – he is now deadly pale and terribly emaciated. He sighs in the most heartrending manner, and seems to be in a state of extreme nervous tension. In short, he is very ill, and yet he seems to have no bodily disease. His eyes have a terribly startled expression in them – his hand trembles so that he can scarcely raise a cup of tea to his lips. In short, he looks like a man who has seen a ghost.'

'When did these symptoms begin to appear?' I asked.

'It is mid-winter now,' said Lady Studley. 'The queer symptoms began to show themselves in my husband in October. They have been growing worse and worse. In short, I can stand them no longer,' she continued, giving way to a short, hysterical sob. 'I felt I must come to someone – I have heard of you. Do, do come and save us. Do come and find out what is the matter with my wretched husband.'

'I will write to you to-night,' I said, in as kind a voice as I could muster, for the pretty, anxious wife interested me already. 'It may not be possible for me to stay at Studley Grange for a week, but in any case I can promise to come and see the patient. One visit will probably be sufficient – what your husband wants is, no doubt, complete change.'

'Oh, yes, yes,' she replied, standing up now. 'I have said so scores of times, but Sir Henry won't stir from Studley – nothing will induce him to go away. He won't even leave his own special bedroom, although I expect he has dreadful nights.' Two hectic spots burnt in her cheeks as she spoke. I looked at her attentively.

'You will forgive me for speaking,' I said, 'but you do not look at all well yourself. I should like to prescribe for you as well as your husband.'

'Thank you,' she answered, 'I am not very strong. I never have been, but that is nothing – I mean that my health is not a thing of consequence at present. Well, I must not take up any more of your time. I shall expect to get a letter from you to-morrow morning. Please address it to Lady Studley, Grosvenor Hotel, Victoria.'

She touched my hand with fingers that burnt like a living coal and left the room.

I thought her very ill, and was sure that if I could see my way to spending a week at Studley Grange, I should have two patients instead of one. It is always difficult for a busy doctor to leave home, but after carefully thinking matters over, I resolved to comply with Lady Studley's request.

Accordingly, two days later saw me on my way to Wiltshire, and to Studley Grange. A brougham with two smart horses was waiting at the station. To my surprise I saw that Lady Studley had come herself to fetch me.

'I don't know how to thank you,' she said, giving me a feverish clasp of her hand. 'Your visit fills me with hope – I believe that you will discover what is really wrong. Home!' she said, giving a quick, imperious direction to the footman who appeared at the window of the carriage.

We bowled forward at a rapid pace, and she continued:-

'I came to meet you to-day to tell you that I have used a little guile with regard to your visit. I have not told Sir Henry that you are coming here in the capacity of a doctor.'

Here she paused and gave me one of her restless glances.

'Do you mind?' she asked.

'What have you said about me to Sir Henry?' I inquired.

'That you are a great friend of the Onslows, and that I have asked you here for a week's change,' she answered immediately.

'As a guest, my husband will be polite and delightful to you – as a doctor, he would treat you with scant civility, and would probably give you little or none of his confidence.'

I was quite silent for a moment after Lady Studley had told me this. Then I said:-

'Had I known that I was not to come to your house in the capacity of a medical man, I might have re-considered my earnest desire to help you.'

She turned very pale when I said this, and tears filled her eyes.

'Never mind,' I said now, for I could not but be touched by her extremely pathetic and suffering face, by the look of great illness which was manifested in every glance. 'Never mind now; I am glad you have told me exactly the terms on which you wish me to approach your husband; but I think that I can so put matters to Sir Henry that he will be glad to consult me in my medical capacity.'

'Oh, but he does not even know that I suspect his illness. It would never do for him to know. I suspect! I see! I fear! but I say nothing. Sir Henry would be much more miserable than he is now, if he thought that I guessed that there is anything wrong with him.'

'It is impossible for me to come to the Grange except as a medical man,' I answered, firmly. 'I will tell Sir Henry that you have seen some changes in him, and have asked me to visit him as a doctor. Please trust me. Nothing will be said to your husband that can make matters at all uncomfortable for you.'

Lady Studley did not venture any further remonstrance, and we now approached the old Grange. It was an irregular pile, built evidently according to the wants of the different families who had lived in it. The building was long and rambling, with rows of windows filled up with panes of latticed glass. In front of the house was a sweeping lawn, which, even at this time of the year, presented a velvety and well-kept appearance. We drove rapidly round to the entrance door, and a moment later I found myself in the presence of my host and patient. Sir Henry Studley was a tall man with a very slight stoop, and an aquiline and rather noble face. His eyes were dark, and his forehead inclined to be bald. There was a courtly, old-world sort of look about him. He greeted me with extreme friendliness, and we went into the hall, a very large and lofty apartment, to tea.

Lady Studley was vivacious and lively in the extreme. While she talked, the hectic spots came out again on her cheeks. My uneasiness about her increased as I noticed these symptoms. I felt certain that she was not only consumptive, but in all probability she was even now the victim of an advanced stage of phthisis. I felt far more anxious about her than about her husband, who appeared to me at that moment to be nothing more than a somewhat nervous and hypochondriacal person. This state of things seemed easy to account for in a scholar and a man of sedentary habits.

I remarked about the age of the house, and my host became interested, and told me one or two stories of the old inhabitants of the Grange. He said that to-morrow he would have much pleasure in taking me over the building.

'Have you a ghost here?' I asked, with a laugh.

I don't know what prompted me to ask the question. The moment I did so, Sir Henry turned white to his lips, and Lady Studley held up a warning finger to me to intimate that I was on dangerous ground. I felt that I was, and hastened to divert the conversation into safer channels. Inadvertently I had touched on a sore spot. I scarcely regretted having done so, as the flash in the baronet's troubled eyes, and the extreme agitation of his face, showed me plainly that Lady

Studley was right when she spoke of his nerves being in a very irritable condition. Of course, I did not believe in ghosts, and wondered that a man of Sir Henry's calibre could be at all under the influence of this old-world fear.

'I am sorry that we have no one to meet you,' he said, after a few remarks of a commonplace character had divided us from the ghost question. 'But to-morrow several friends are coming, and we hope you will have a pleasant time. Are you fond of hunting?'

I answered that I used to be in the old days, before medicine and patients occupied all my thoughts.

'If this open weather continues, I can probably give you some of your favourite pastime,' rejoined Sir Henry; 'and now perhaps you would like to be shown to your room.'

My bedroom was in a modern wing of the house, and looked as cheerful and as unghostlike as it was possible for a room to be. I did not rejoin my host and hostess until dinner-time. We had a sociable little meal, at which nothing of any importance occurred, and shortly after the servants withdrew, Lady Studley left Sir Henry and me to ourselves. She gave me another warning glance as she left the room. I had already quite made up my mind, however, to tell Sir Henry the motive of my visit.

The moment the door closed behind his wife, he started up and asked me if I would mind coming with him into his library.

'The fact is,' he said, 'I am particularly glad you have come down. I want to have a talk with you about my wife. She is extremely unwell.'

I signified my willingness to listen to anything Sir Henry might say, and in a few minutes we found ourselves comfortably established in a splendid old room, completely clothed with books from ceiling to floor.

'These are my treasures,' said the baronet, waving his hand in the direction of an old bookcase, which contained, I saw at a glance, some very rare and precious first editions.

'These are my friends, the companions of my hours of solitude. Now sit down, Dr Halifax; make yourself at home. You have come here as a guest, but I have heard of you before, and am inclined to confide in you. I must frankly say that I hate your profession as a rule.

I don't believe in the omniscience of medical men, but moments come in the lives of all men when it is necessary to unburden the mind to another. May I give you my confidence?'

'One moment first,' I said. 'I can't deceive you, Sir Henry. I have come here, not in the capacity of a guest, but as your wife's medical man. She has been anxious about you, and she begged of me to come and stay here for a few days in order to render you any medical assistance within my power. I only knew, on my way here to-day, that she had not acquainted you with the nature of my visit.'

While I was speaking, Sir Henry's face became extremely watchful, eager, and tense.

'This is remarkable,' he said. 'So Lucilla is anxious about me? I was not aware that I ever gave her the least clue to the fact that I am not – in perfect health. This is very strange – it troubles me.'

He looked agitated. He placed one long, thin hand on the little table which stood near, and pouring out a glass of wine, drank it off. I noticed as he did so the nervous trembling of his hand. I glanced at his face, and saw that it was thin to emaciation.

'Well,' he said, 'I am obliged to you for being perfectly frank with me. My wife scarcely did well to conceal the object of your visit. But now that you have come, I shall make use of you both for myself and for her.'

'Then you are not well?' I asked.

'Well!' he answered, with almost a shout. 'Good God, no! I think that I am going mad. I know – I know that unless relief soon comes I shall die or become a raving maniac.'

'No, nothing of the kind,' I answered, soothingly; 'you probably want change. This is a fine old house, but dull, no doubt, in winter. Why don't you go away? – to the Riviera, or some other place where there is plenty of sunshine? Why do you stay here? The air of this place is too damp to be good for either you or your wife.'

Sir Henry sat silent for a moment, then he said, in a terse voice:-

'Perhaps you will advise me what to do after you know the nature of the malady which afflicts me. First of all, however, I wish to speak of my wife.'

'I am ready to listen,' I replied.

'You see,' he continued, 'that she is very delicate?'

'Yes,' I replied; 'to be frank with you, I should say that Lady Studley was consumptive.'

He started when I said this, and pressed his lips firmly together. After a moment he spoke.

'You are right,' he replied. 'I had her examined by a medical man – Sir Joseph Dunbar – when I was last in London; he said her lungs were considerably affected, and that, in short, she was far from well.'

'Did he not order you to winter abroad?'

'He did, but Lady Studley opposed the idea so strenuously that I was obliged to yield to her entreaties. Consumption does not seem to take quite the ordinary form with her. She is restless, she longs for cool air, she goes out on quite cold days, in a closed carriage, it is true. Still, except at night, she does not regard herself in any sense as an invalid. She has immense spirit – I think she will keep up until she dies.'

'You speak of her being an invalid at night,' I replied. 'What are her symptoms?'

Sir Henry shuddered quite visibly.

'Oh, those awful nights!' he answered. 'How happy would many poor mortals be, but for the terrible time of darkness. Lady Studley has had dreadful nights for some time: perspirations, cough, restlessness, bad dreams, and all the rest of it. But I must hasten to tell you my story quite briefly. In the beginning of October we saw Sir Joseph Dunbar. I should then, by his advice, have taken Lady Studley to the Riviera, but she opposed the idea with such passion and distress, that I abandoned it.'

Sir Henry paused here, and I looked at him attentively. I remembered at that moment what Lady Studley had said about her husband refusing to leave the Grange under any circumstances. What a strange game of cross-purposes these two were playing. How was it possible for me to get at the truth?

'At my wife's earnest request,' continued Sir Henry, 'we returned to the Grange. She declared her firm intention of remaining here until she died.

'Soon after our return she suggested that we should occupy separate rooms at night, reminding me, when she made the request, of the infectious nature of consumption. I complied with her wish on condition that I slept in the room next hers, and that on the smallest emergency I should be summoned to her aid. This arrangement was made, and her room opens into mine. I have sometimes heard her moving about at night – I have often heard her cough, and I have often heard her sigh. But she has never once sent for me, or given me to understand that she required my aid. She does not think herself very ill, and nothing worries her more than to have her malady spoken about. That is the part of the story which relates to my wife.'

'She is very ill,' I said. 'But I will speak of that presently. Now will you favour me with an account of your own symptoms, Sir Henry?'

He started again when I said this, and going across the room, locked the door and put the key in his pocket.

'Perhaps you will laugh at me,' he said, 'but it is no laughing matter, I assure you. The most terrible, the most awful affliction has come to me. In short, I am visited nightly by an appalling apparition. You don't believe in ghosts, I judge that by your face. Few scientific men do.'

'Frankly, I do not,' I replied. 'So-called ghosts can generally be accounted for. At the most they are only the figments of an over-excited or diseased brain.'

'Be that as it may,' said Sir Henry, 'the diseased brain can give such torture to its victim that death is preferable. All my life I have been what I consider a healthy minded man. I have plenty of money, and have never been troubled with the cares which torture men of commerce, or of small means. When I married, three years ago, I considered myself the most lucky and the happiest of mortals.'

'Forgive a personal question,' I interrupted. 'Has your marriage disappointed you?'

'No, no; far from it,' he replied with fervour. 'I love my dear wife better and more deeply even than the day when I took her as a bride to my arms. It is true that I am weighed down with sorrow about her, but that is entirely owing to the state of her health.'

'It is strange,' I said, 'that she should be weighed down with sorrow about you for the same cause. Have you told her of the thing which terrifies you?'

'Never, never. I have never spoken of it to mortal. It is remarkable that my wife should have told you that I looked like a man who has seen a ghost. Alas! alas! But let me tell you the cause of my shattered nerves, my agony, and failing health.'

'Pray do, I shall listen attentively,' I replied.

'Oh, doctor, that I could make you feel the horror of it!' said Sir Henry, bending forward and looking into my eyes. 'Three months ago I no more believed in visitations, in apparitions, in so-called ghosts, than you do. Were you tried as I am, your scepticism would receive a severe shock. Now let me tell you what occurs. Night after night Lady Studley and I retire to rest at the same hour. We say good-night, and lay our heads on our separate pillows. The door of communication between us is shut. She has a night-light in her room – I prefer darkness. I close my eyes and prepare for slumber. As a rule I fall asleep. My sleep is of short duration. I awake with beads of perspiration standing on my forehead, with my heart thumping heavily and with every nerve wide awake, and waiting for the horror which will come. Sometimes I wait half an hour – sometimes longer. Then I know by a faint, ticking sound in the darkness that the Thing, for I can clothe it with no name, is about to visit me. In a certain spot of the room, always in the same spot, a bright light suddenly flashes; out of its midst there gleams a preternaturally large eye, which looks fixedly at me with a diabolical expression. As time goes, it does not remain long; but as agony counts, it seems to take years of my life away with it. It fades as suddenly into grey mist and nothingness as it comes, and, wet with perspiration, and struggling to keep back screams of mad terror, I bury my head in the bed-clothes.'

'But have you never tried to investigate this thing?' I said.

'I did at first. The first night I saw it, I rushed out of bed and made for the spot. It disappeared at once. I struck a light – there was nothing whatever in the room.'

'Why do you sleep in that room?'

'I must not go away from Lady Studley. My terror is that she should know anything of this – my greater terror is that the apparition, failing me, may visit her. I daresay you think I'm a fool, Halifax; but the fact is, this thing is killing me, brave man as I consider myself.'

'Do you see it every night?' I asked.

'Not quite every night, but sometimes on the same night it comes twice. Sometimes it will not come at all for two nights, or even three.

It is the most ghastly, the most horrible form of torture that could hurry a sane man into his grave or into a madhouse.'

'I have not the least shadow of doubt,' I said, after a pause, 'that the thing can be accounted for.'

Sir Henry shook his head. 'No, no,' he replied, 'it is either as you suggest, a figment of my own diseased brain, and therefore just as horrible as a real apparition; or it is a supernatural visitation. Whether it exists or not, it is reality to me and in no way a dream. The full horror of it is present with me in my waking moments.'

'Do you think anyone is playing an awful practical joke?' I suggested.

'Certainly not. What object can anyone have in scaring me to death? Besides, there is no one in the room, that I can swear. My outer door is locked, Lady Studley's outer door is locked. It is impossible that there can be any trickery in the matter.'

I said nothing for a moment. I no more believed in ghosts than I ever did, but I felt certain that there was grave mischief at work. Sir Henry must be the victim of a hallucination. This might only be caused by functional disturbance of the brain, but it was quite serious enough to call for immediate attention. The first thing to do was to find out whether the apparition could be accounted for in any material way, or if it were due to the state of Sir Henry's nerves. I began to ask him certain questions, going fully into the case in all its bearings. I then examined his eyes with the ophthalmoscope. The result of all this was to assure me beyond doubt that Sir Henry Studley was in a highly nervous condition, although I could detect no trace of brain disease.

'Do you mind taking me to your room?' I said.

'Not to-night,' he answered. 'It is late, and Lady Studley might express surprise. The object of my life is to conceal this horror from her. When she is out to-morrow you shall come to the room and judge for yourself.'

'Well,' I said, 'I shall have an interview with your wife to-morrow, and urge her most strongly to consent to leave the Grange and go away with you.'

Shortly afterwards we retired to rest, or what went by the name of rest in that sad house, with its troubled inmates. I must confess that, comfortable as my room was, I slept very little. Sir Henry's story stayed with me all through the hours of darkness. I am neither nervous nor imaginative, but I could not help seeing that terrible eye, even in my dreams.

I met my host and hostess at an early breakfast. Sir Henry proposed that as the day was warm and fine, I should ride to a neighbouring meet. I was not in the humour for this, however, and said frankly that I should prefer remaining at the Grange. One glance into the faces of my host and hostess told me only too plainly that I had two very serious patients on my hands. Lady Studley looked terribly weak and excited – the hectic spots on her cheeks, the gleaming glitter of her eyes, the parched lips, the long, white, emaciated hands, all showed only too plainly the strides the malady under which she was suffering was making.

'After all, I cannot urge that poor girl to go abroad,' I said to myself. 'She is hastening rapidly to her grave, and no power on earth can save her. She looks as if there were extensive disease of the lungs. How restless her eyes are, too! I would much rather testify to Sir Henry's sanity than to hers.'

Sir Henry Studley also bore traces of a sleepless night – his face was bloodless; he averted his eyes from mine; he ate next to nothing.

Immediately after breakfast, I followed Lady Studley into her morning-room. I had already made up my mind how to act. Her husband should have my full confidence – she only my partial view of the situation.

'Well,' I said, 'I have seen your husband and talked to him. I hope he will soon be better. I don't think you need be seriously alarmed about him. Now for yourself, Lady Studley. I am anxious to examine your lungs. Will you allow me to do so?'

'I suppose Henry has told you I am consumptive?'

'He says you are not well,' I answered. 'I don't need his word to assure me of that fact – I can see it with my own eyes. Please let me examine your chest with my stethoscope.'

She hesitated for a moment, looking something like a wild creature brought to bay. Then she sank into a chair, and with trembling fingers unfastened her dress. Poor soul, she was almost a walking skeleton – her beautiful face was all that was beautiful about her. A brief examination told me that she was in the last stage of phthisis – in short, that her days were numbered.

'What do you think of me?' she asked, when the brief examination was over.

'You are ill,' I replied.

'How soon shall I die?'

'God only knows that, my dear lady,' I answered.

'Oh, you needn't hide your thoughts,' she said. 'I know that my days are very few. Oh, if only, if only my husband could come with me! I am so afraid to go alone, and I am fond of him, very fond of him.'

I soothed her as well as I could.

'You ought to have someone to sleep in your room at night,' I said. 'You ought not to be left by yourself.'

'Henry is near me – in the next room,' she replied. 'I would not have a nurse for the world – I hate and detest nurses.'

Soon afterwards she left me. She was very erratic, and before she left the room she had quite got over her depression. The sun shone out, and with the gleam of brightness her volatile spirits rose.

'I am going for a drive,' she said. 'Will you come with me?'

'Not this morning,' I replied. 'If you ask me to-morrow, I shall be pleased to accompany you.'

'Well, go to Henry,' she answered. 'Talk to him – find out what ails him, order tonics for him. Cheer him in every way in your power. You say he is not ill – not seriously ill – I know better. My impression is that if my days are numbered, so are his.'

She went away, and I sought her husband. As soon as the wheels of her brougham were heard bowling away over the gravel sweep, we went up together to his room.

'That eye came twice last night,' he said in an awestruck whisper to me. 'I am a doomed man – a doomed man. I cannot bear this any longer.'

We were standing in the room as he said the words. Even in broad daylight, I could see that he glanced round him with apprehension. He was shaking quite visibly. The room was decidedly old-fashioned, but the greater part of the furniture was modern. The bed was an

Albert one with a spring mattress, and light, cheerful dimity hangings. The windows were French – they were wide open, and let in the soft, pleasant air, for the day was truly a spring one in winter. The paper on the walls was light.

'This is a quaint old wardrobe,' I said. 'It looks out of place with the rest of the furniture. Why don't you have it removed?'

'Hush,' he said, with a gasp. 'Don't go near it – I dread it, I have locked it. It is always in that direction that the apparition appears. The apparition seems to grow out of the glass of the wardrobe. It always appears in that one spot.'

'I see,' I answered. 'The wardrobe is built into the wall. That is the reason it cannot be removed. Have you got the key about you?'

He fumbled in his pocket, and presently produced a bunch of keys.

'I wish you wouldn't open the wardrobe,' he said. 'I frankly admit that I dislike having it touched.'

'All right,' I replied. 'I will not examine it while you are in the room. You will perhaps allow me to keep the key?'

'Certainly! You can take it from the bunch, if you wish. This is it. I shall be only too glad to have it well out of my own keeping.'

'We will go downstairs,' I said.

We returned to Sir Henry's library. It was my turn now to lock the door.

'Why do you do that?' he asked.

'Because I wish to be quite certain that no one overhears our conversation.'

'What have you got to say?'

'I have a plan to propose to you.'

'What is it?'

'I want you to change bedrooms with me to-night.'

'What can you mean? – what will Lady Studley say?'

'Lady Studley must know nothing whatever about the arrangement. I think it very likely that the apparition which troubles you will be discovered to have a material foundation. In short, I am determined to get to the bottom of this horror. You have seen it often, and your nerves are much shattered. I have never seen it, and my nerves are, I think, in tolerable order. If I sleep in your room to-night – '

'It may not visit you.'

'It may not, but on the other hand it may. I have a curiosity to lie on that bed and to face that wardrobe in the wall. You must yield to my wishes, Sir Henry.'

'But how can the knowledge of this arrangement be kept from my wife?'

'Easily enough. You will both go to your rooms as usual. You will bid her good-night as usual, and after the doors of communication are closed I will enter the room and you will go to mine, or to any other that you like to occupy. You say your wife never comes into your room during the hours of the night?'

'She has never yet done so.'

'She will not to-night. Should she by any chance call for assistance, I will immediately summon you.'

It was very evident that Sir Henry did not like this arrangement. He yielded, however, to my very strong persuasions, which almost took the form of commands, for I saw that I could do nothing unless I got complete mastery over the man.

Lady Studley returned from her drive just as our arrangements were fully made. I had not a moment during all the day to examine the interior of the wardrobe. The sick woman's restlessness grew greater as the hours advanced. She did not care to leave her husband's side. She sat with him as he examined his books. She followed him from room to room. In the afternoon, to the relief of everyone, some fresh guests arrived. In consequence we had a cheerful evening. Lady Studley came down to dinner in white from top to toe. Her dress was ethereal in texture and largely composed of lace. I cannot describe woman's dress, but with her shadowy figure and worn, but still lovely face, she looked spiritual. The gleam in her large blue eyes was pathetic. Her love for her husband was touching to behold. How soon, how very soon, they must part from each other! Only I as a doctor knew how impossible it was to keep the lamp of life much longer burning in the poor girl's frame.

We retired as usual to rest. Sir Henry bade me a cheerful good-night. Lady Studley nodded to me as she left the room.

'Sleep well,' she said, in a gay voice.

It was late the next morning when we all met round the breakfast table. Sir Henry looked better, but Lady Studley many degrees worse, than the night before. I wondered at her courage in retaining her post at the head of her table. The visitors, who came in at intervals and took their seats at the table, looked at her with wonder and compassion.

'Surely my hostess is very ill?' said a guest who sat next my side.

'Yes, but take no notice of it,' I answered.

Soon after breakfast I sought Sir Henry.

'Well – well?' he said, as he grasped my hand. 'Halifax, you have seen it. I know you have by the expression of your face.'

'Yes,' I replied, 'I have.'

'How quietly you speak. Has not the horror of the thing seized you?'

'No,' I said, with a brief laugh. 'I told you yesterday that my nerves were in tolerable order. I think my surmise was correct, and that the apparition has tangible form and can be traced to its foundation.'

An unbelieving look swept over Sir Henry's face.

'Ah,' he said, 'doctors are very hard to convince. Everything must be brought down to a cold material level to satisfy them; but several nights in that room would shatter even your nerves, my friend.'

'You are quite right,' I answered. 'I should be very sorry to spend several nights in that room. Now I will tell you briefly what occurred.'

We were standing in the library. Sir Henry went to the door, locked it, and put the key in his pocket.

'Can I come in?' said a voice outside.

The voice was Lady Studley's.

'In a minute, my darling,' answered her husband. 'I am engaged with Halifax just at present.'

'Medically, I suppose?' she answered.

'Yes, medically,' he responded.

She went away at once, and Sir Henry returned to my side.

'Now speak,' he said. 'Be quick. She is sure to return, and I don't like her to fancy that we are talking secrets.'

'This is my story,' I said. 'I went into your room, put out all the lights, and sat on the edge of the bed.'

'You did not get into bed, then?'

'No, I preferred to be up and to be ready for immediate action should the apparition, the horror, or whatever you call it, appear.'

'Good God, it is a horror, Halifax!'

'It is, Sir Henry. A more diabolical contrivance for frightening a man into his grave could scarcely have been contrived. I can comfort you on one point, however. The terrible thing you saw is not a figment of your brain. There is no likelihood of a lunatic asylum in your case. Someone is playing you a trick.'

'I cannot agree with you – but proceed,' said the baronet, impatiently.

'I sat for about an hour on the edge of the bed,' I continued. 'When I entered the room it was twelve o'clock – one had sounded before there was the least stir or appearance of anything, then the ticking noise you have described was distinctly audible. This was followed by a sudden bright light, which seemed to proceed out of the recesses of the wardrobe.'

'What did you feel when you saw that light?'

'Too excited to be nervous,' I answered, briefly. 'Out of the circle of light the horrible eye looked at me.'

'What did you do then? Did you faint?'

'No, I went noiselessly across the carpet up to the door of the wardrobe and looked in.'

'Heavens! you are daring. I wonder you are alive to tell this tale.'

'I saw a shadowy form,' I replied – 'dark and tall – the one brilliant eye kept on looking past me, straight into the room. I made a very slight noise; it immediately disappeared. I waited for some time – nothing more happened. I got into your bed, Sir Henry, and slept. I can't say that I had a comfortable night, but I slept, and was not disturbed by anything extraordinary for the remaining hours of the night.'

'Now what do you mean to do? You say you can trace this thing to its foundation. It seems to me that all you have seen only supports my firm belief that a horrible apparition visits that room.'

'A material one,' I responded. 'The shadowy form had substance, of that I am convinced. Sir Henry, I intend to sleep in that room again to-night.'

'Lady Studley will find out.'

'She will not. I sleep in the haunted room again to-night, and during the day you must so contrive matters that I have plenty of time to examine the wardrobe. I did not do so yesterday because I had not an opportunity. You must contrive to get Lady Studley out of the way, either this morning or afternoon, and so manage matters for me that I can be some little time alone in your room.'

'Henry, Henry, how awestruck you look!' said a gay voice at the window. Lady Studley had come out, had come round to the library window, and, holding up her long, dark-blue velvet dress, was looking at us with a peculiar smile.

'Well, my love,' replied the baronet. He went to the window and flung it open. 'Lucilla,' he exclaimed, 'you are mad to stand on the damp grass.'

'Oh, no, not mad,' she answered. 'I have come to that stage when nothing matters. Is not that so, Dr Halifax?'

'You are very imprudent,' I replied.

She shook her finger at me playfully, and turned to her husband.

'Henry,' she said, 'have you taken my keys? I cannot find them anywhere.'

'I will go up and look for them,' said Sir Henry. He left the room, and Lady Studley entered the library through one of the French windows.

'What do you think of my husband this morning?' she asked.

'He is a little better,' I replied. 'I am confident that he will soon be quite well again.'

She gave a deep sigh when I said this, her lips trembled, and she turned away. I thought my news would make her happy, and her depression surprised me.

At this moment Sir Henry came into the room.

'Here are your keys,' he said to his wife. He gave her the same bunch he had given me the night before. I hoped she would not notice that the key of the wardrobe was missing.

'And now I want you to come for a drive with me,' said Sir Henry.

He did not often accompany her, and the pleasure of this unlooked-for indulgence evidently tempted her.

'Very well,' she answered. 'Is Dr Halifax coming?'

'No, he wants to have a ride.'

'If he rides, can he not follow the carriage?'

'Will you do that, Halifax?' asked my host.

'No, thank you,' I answered; 'I must write some letters before I go anywhere. I will ride to the nearest town and post them presently, if I may.' I left the room as I spoke.

Shortly afterwards I saw from a window Sir Henry and his wife drive away. They drove in a large open landau, and two girls who were staying in the house accompanied them. My hour had come, and I went up at once to Sir Henry's bedroom. Lady Studley's room opened directly into that of her husband, but both rooms had separate entrances.

I locked the two outer doors now, and then began my investigations. I had the key of the wardrobe in my pocket.

It was troublesome to unlock, because the key was a little rusty, and it was more than evident that the heavy doors had not been opened for some time. Both these doors were made of glass. When shut, they resembled in shape and appearance an ordinary old-fashioned window. The glass was set in deep mullions. It was thick, was of a peculiar shade of light blue, and was evidently of great antiquity. I opened the doors and went inside. The wardrobe was so roomy that I could stand upright with perfect comfort. It was empty, and was lined through and through with solid oak. I struck a light and began to examine the interior with care. After a great deal of patient investigation I came across a notch in the wood. I pressed my finger on this, and immediately a little panel slid back, which revealed underneath a small button. I turned the button and a door at the back of the wardrobe flew open. A flood of sunlight poured in, and stepping out, I found myself in another room. I looked around me in astonishment. This was a lady's chamber. Good heavens! what had happened? I was in Lady Studley's room. Shutting the mysterious door of the wardrobe very carefully, I found that all trace of its existence immediately vanished.

There was no furniture against this part of the wall. It looked absolutely bare and smooth. No picture ornamented it. The light paper which covered it gave the appearance of a perfectly unbroken pattern. Of course, there must be a concealed spring somewhere, and I lost no time in feeling for it. I pressed my hand and the tips of my fingers in every direction along the wall. Try as I would, however, I could not find the spring, and I had at last to leave Lady Studley's room and go back to the one occupied by her husband, by the ordinary door.

Once more I re-entered the wardrobe and deliberately broke off the button which opened the secret door from within. Anyone who now entered the wardrobe by this door, and shut it behind him, would find it impossible to retreat. The apparition, if it had material foundation, would thus find itself trapped in its own net.

What could this thing portend?

I had already convinced myself that if Sir Henry were the subject of a hallucination, I also shared it. As this was impossible, I felt certain that the apparition had a material foundation. Who was the person who glided night after night into Lady Studley's room, who knew the trick of the secret spring in the wall, who entered the old wardrobe, and performed this ghastly, this appalling trick on Sir Henry Studley? I resolved that I would say nothing to Sir Henry of my fresh discovery until after I had spent another night in the haunted room.

Accordingly, I slipped the key of the wardrobe once more into my pocket and went downstairs.

I had my way again that night. Once more I found myself the sole occupant of the haunted room. I put out the light, sat on the edge of the bed, and waited the issue of events. At first there was silence and complete darkness, but soon after one o'clock I heard the very slight but unmistakable tick-tick, which told me that the apparition was about to appear. The ticking noise resembled the quaint sound made by the death spider. There was no other noise of any sort, but a quickening of my pulses, a sensation which I could not call fear, but which was exciting to the point of pain, braced me up for an unusual and horrible sight. The light appeared in the dim recess of the wardrobe. It grew clear and steady, and quickly resolved itself into one intensely bright circle. Out of this circle the eye looked at me. The eye was unnaturally large – it was clear, almost transparent, its expression was full of menace and warning. Into the circle of light presently a shadowy and ethereal hand intruded itself. The fingers beckoned me to approach, while the eye looked fixedly at me. I sat motionless on the side of the bed. I am stoical by nature and my nerves are well seasoned, but I am not ashamed to say that I should be very sorry to be often subjected to that menace and that invitation. The look in that eye, the beckoning power in those long, shadowy fingers would soon work havoc even in the stoutest nerves. My heart beat uncomfortably fast, and I had to say over and over to myself, 'This is nothing more than a ghastly trick'. I had also to remind myself that I in my turn had prepared a trap for the apparition. The time while the eye looked and the hand beckoned might in reality have been counted by seconds; to me it seemed like eternity. I felt the cold dew on my forehead before the rapidly waning light assured me that the apparition was about to vanish. Making an effort I now left the bed and approached the wardrobe. I listened intently. For a moment there was perfect silence. Then a fumbling noise was distinctly audible. It was followed by a muffled cry, a crash, and a heavy fall. I struck a light instantly, and taking the key of the wardrobe from my pocket, opened it. Never shall I forget the sight that met my gaze.

There, huddled up on the floor, lay the prostrate and unconscious form of Lady Studley. A black cloak in which she had wrapped herself partly covered her face, but I knew her by her long, fair hair. I pulled back the cloak, and saw that the unhappy girl had broken a blood-vessel, and even as I lifted her up I knew that she was in a dying condition.

I carried her at once into her own room and laid her on the bed. I then returned and shut the wardrobe door, and slipped the key into my pocket. My next deed was to summon Sir Henry.

'What is it?' he asked, springing upright in bed.

'Come at once,' I said, 'your wife is very ill.'

'Dying?' he asked, in an agonized whisper.

I nodded my head. I could not speak.

My one effort now was to keep the knowledge of the ghastly discovery I had made from the unhappy husband.

He followed me to his wife's room. He forgot even to question me about the apparition, so horrified was he at the sight which met his view.

I administered restoratives to the dying woman, and did what I could to check the haemorrhage. After a time Lady Studley opened her dim eyes.

'Oh, Henry!' she said, stretching out a feeble hand to him, 'come with me, come with me. I am afraid to go alone.'

'My poor Lucilla,' he said. He smoothed her cold forehead, and tried to comfort her by every means in his power.

After a time he left the room. When he did so she beckoned me to approach. 'I have failed,' she said, in the most thrilling voice of horror I have ever listened to. 'I must go alone. He will not come with me.'

'What do you mean?' I asked.

She could scarcely speak, but at intervals the following words dropped slowly from her lips: –

'I was the apparition. I did not want my husband to live after me. Perhaps I was a little insane. I cannot quite say. When I was told by Sir Joseph Dunbar that there was no hope of my life, a most appalling and frightful jealousy took possession of me. I pictured my husband with another wife. Stoop down.'

Her voice was very faint. I could scarcely hear her muttered words. Her eyes were glazing fast, death was claiming her, and yet hatred against some unknown person thrilled in her feeble voice.

'Before my husband married me, he loved another woman,' she continued. 'That woman is now a widow. I felt certain that immediately after my death he would seek her out and marry her. I could not bear the thought – it possessed me day and night. That, and the terror of dying alone, worked such a havoc within me that I believe I was scarcely responsible for my own actions. A mad desire took possession of me to take my husband with me, and so to keep him from her, and also to have his company when I passed the barriers of life. I told you that my brother was a doctor. In his medical-student days the sort of trick I have been playing on Sir Henry was enacted by some of his fellow-students for his benefit, and almost scared him into fever. One day my brother described the trick to me, and I asked him to show me how it was done. I used a small electric lamp and a very strong reflector.'

'How did you find out the secret door of the wardrobe?' I asked.

'Quite by chance. I was putting some dresses into the wardrobe one day and accidentally touched the secret panel. I saw at once that here was my opportunity.'

'You must have been alarmed at your success,' I said, after a pause. 'And now I have one more question to ask: Why did you summon me to the Grange?'

She made a faint, impatient movement.

'I wanted to be certain that my husband was really very ill,' she said. 'I wanted you to talk to him – I guessed he would confide in you; I thought it most probable that you would tell him that he was a victim of brain hallucinations. This would frighten him and would suit my purpose exactly. I also sent for you as a blind. I felt sure that under these circumstances neither you nor my husband could possibly suspect me.'

She was silent again, panting from exhaustion.

'I have failed,' she said, after a long pause. 'You have discovered the truth. It never occurred to me for a moment that you would go into the room. He will recover now.'

She paused; a fresh attack of haemorrhage came on. Her breath came quickly. Her end was very near. Her dim eyes could scarcely see.

Groping feebly with her hand she took mine.

'Dr Halifax – promise.'

'What?' I asked.

'I have failed, but let me keep his love, what little love he has for me, before he marries that other woman. Promise that you will never tell him.'

'Rest easy,' I answered, 'I will never tell him.'

Sir Henry entered the room.

I made way for him to kneel by his wife's side.

As the grey morning broke Lady Studley died.

Before my departure from the Grange I avoided Sir Henry as much as possible. Once he spoke of the apparition and asked if I had seen it. 'Yes,' I replied.

Before I could say anything further, he continued:-

'I know now why it came; it was to warn me of my unhappy wife's death.' He said no more. I could not enlighten him, and he is unlikely now ever to learn the truth.

The following day I left Studley Grange. I took with me, without asking leave of any-one, a certain long black cloak, a small electric lamp, and a magnifying glass of considerable power.

It may be of interest to explain how Lady Studley in her unhealthy condition of mind and body performed the extraordinary trick by which she hoped to undermine her husband's health, and ultimately cause his death.

I experimented with the materials which I carried away with me, and succeeded, so my friends told me, in producing a most ghastly effect.

I did it in this way. I attached the mirror of a laryngoscope to my forehead in such a manner as to enable it to throw a strong reflection into one of my eyes. In the centre of the bright side of the laryngoscope a small electric lamp was fitted. This was connected with a battery which I carried in my hand. The battery was similar to those used by the ballet girls in Drury Lane Theatre, and could be brought into force by a touch and extinguished by the removal of the pressure. The eye which was thus brilliantly illumined looked through a lens of some power. All the rest of the face and figure was completely covered by the black cloak. Thus the brightest possible light was thrown on the magnified eye, while there was corresponding increased gloom around.

When last I heard of Studley Grange it was let for a term of years and Sir Henry had gone abroad. I have not heard that he has married again, but he probably will, sooner or later.

Father Brown

Created by G. K. Chesterton (1874 – 1936)

ARGUABLY THE MOST widely gifted of the writers featured in this book, Chesterton published dozens of books in his lifetime on subjects ranging from theology to literary criticism. He was also famous as a prolific journalist, able to turn his gift for wit and paradox on a wide array of literary, social, political and religious issues. He wrote a number of novels, including *The Napoleon of Notting Hill*, a fantasy set in a future London, but his best known works of fiction are the Father Brown stories in which an unassuming Roman Catholic priest solves apparently insoluble mysteries through logic and his knowledge of the human heart. Chesterton himself became a Roman Catholic in 1922. 'The Hammer of God' is one of the most memorable of the Father Brown stories. At one point in the narrative, the murderer, confronted by the simple priest's apparent ability to read his mind, asks, 'Are you a devil?' 'I am a man,' Father Brown replies, 'and therefore have all devils in my heart.' His knowledge of the devils inside him and inside others is what enables Father Brown to perform the apparently impossible feats of deduction which enliven Chesterton's stories.

The Hammer of God

THE LITTLE VILLAGE of Bohun Beacon was perched on a hill so steep that the tall spire of its church seemed only like the peak of a small mountain. At the foot of the church stood a smithy, generally red with fires and always littered with hammers and scraps of iron; opposite to this, over a rude cross of cobbled paths, was 'The Blue Boar', the only inn of the place. It was upon this crossway, in the lifting of a leaden and silver daybreak, that two brothers met in the street and spoke; though one was beginning the day and the other finishing it. The Rev. and Hon. Wilfred Bohun was very devout, and was making his way to some austere exercises of prayer or contemplation at dawn. Colonel the Hon. Norman Bohun, his elder brother, was by no means devout, and was sitting in evening dress on the bench outside 'The Blue Boar', drinking what the philosophic observer was free to regard either as his last glass on Tuesday or his first on Wednesday. The colonel was not particular.

The Bohuns were one of the very few aristocratic families really dating from the Middle Ages, and their pennon had actually seen Palestine. But it is a great mistake to suppose that such houses stand high in chivalric tradition. Few except the poor preserve traditions. Aristocrats live not in traditions but in fashions. The Bohuns had been Mohocks under Queen Anne and Mashers under Queen Victoria. But like more than one of the really ancient houses, they had rotted in the last two centuries into mere drunkards and dandy degenerates, till there had even come a whisper of insanity. Certainly there was something hardly human about the colonel's wolfish pursuit of pleasure, and his chronic resolution not to go home till morning had a touch of the hideous clarity of insomnia. He was a tall, fine animal, elderly, but with hair still startlingly yellow. He would have looked merely blonde and leonine, but his blue eyes were sunk so deep in his face that they looked black. They were a little too close together. He had very long yellow moustaches; on each side of them a fold or furrow from nostril to jaw, so that a sneer seemed cut into his face. Over his evening clothes he wore a curious pale yellow coat that looked more like a very light dressing gown than an overcoat, and on the back of his head was stuck an extraordinary broad-brimmed hat of a bright green colour, evidently some oriental curiosity caught up at random. He was proud of appearing in such incongruous attires – proud of the fact that he always made them look congruous.

His brother the curate had also the yellow hair and the elegance, but he was buttoned up to the chin in black, and his face was clean-shaven, cultivated, and a little nervous. He seemed to live for nothing but his religion; but there were some who said (notably the blacksmith, who was a Presbyterian) that it was a love of Gothic architecture rather than of God, and that his haunting of the church like a ghost was only another and purer turn of the almost morbid thirst for beauty which sent his brother raging after women and wine. This charge was doubtful, while the man's practical piety was indubitable. Indeed, the charge was mostly an ignorant misunderstanding of the love of solitude and secret prayer, and was founded on his being often found kneeling, not before the altar, but in peculiar places, in the crypts or gallery, or even in the belfry. He was at the moment about to enter the church through the yard of the smithy, but stopped and frowned a little as he saw his brother's cavernous eyes staring in the same direction. On the hypothesis that the colonel was interested in the church he did not waste any speculations. There only remained the blacksmith's shop, and though the blacksmith was a Puritan and none of his people, Wilfred Bohun had heard some scandals about a beautiful and rather celebrated wife. He flung a suspicious look across the shed, and the colonel stood up laughing to speak to him.

'Good morning, Wilfred,' he said. 'Like a good landlord I am watching sleeplessly over my people. I am going to call on the blacksmith.'

Wilfred looked at the ground, and said: 'The blacksmith is out. He is over at Greenford.'

'I know,' answered the other with silent laughter; 'that is why I am calling on him.'

'Norman,' said the cleric, with his eye on a pebble in the road, 'are you ever afraid of thunderbolts?'

'What do you mean?' asked the colonel. 'Is your hobby meteorology?'

'I mean,' said Wilfred, without looking up, 'do you ever think that God might strike you in the street?'

'I beg your pardon,' said the colonel; 'I see your hobby is folklore.'

'I know your hobby is blasphemy,' retorted the religious man, stung in the one live place of his nature. 'But if you do not fear God, you have good reason to fear man.'

The elder raised his eyebrows politely. 'Fear man?' he said.

'Barnes the blacksmith is the biggest and strongest man for forty miles round,' said the clergyman sternly. 'I know you are no coward or weakling, but he could throw you over the wall.'

This struck home, being true, and the lowering line by mouth and nostril darkened and deepened. For a moment he stood with the heavy sneer on his face. But in an instant Colonel Bohun had recovered his own cruel good humour and laughed, showing two dog-like front teeth under his yellow moustache. 'In that case, my dear Wilfred,' he said quite carelessly, 'it was wise for the last of the Bohuns to come out partially in armour.'

And he took off the queer round hat covered with green, showing that it was lined within with steel. Wilfred recognised it indeed as a light Japanese or Chinese helmet torn down from a trophy that hung in the old family hall.

'It was the first hat to hand,' explained his brother airily; 'always the nearest hat – and the nearest woman.'

'The blacksmith is away at Greenford,' said Wilfred quietly; 'the time of his return is unsettled.'

And with that he turned and went into the church with bowed head, crossing himself like one who wishes to be quit of an unclean spirit. He was anxious to forget such grossness in the cool twilight of his tall Gothic cloisters; but on that morning it was fated that his still round of religious exercises should be everywhere arrested by small shocks. As he entered the church, hitherto always empty at that hour, a kneeling figure rose hastily to its feet and came towards the full daylight of the doorway. When the curate saw it he stood still with surprise. For the early worshipper was none other than the village idiot, a nephew of the blacksmith, one who neither would nor could care for the church or for anything else. He was always called 'Mad Joe' and seemed to have no other name; he was a dark, strong, slouching lad, with a heavy white face, dark straight hair, and a mouth always open. As he passed the priest, his moon-calf countenance gave no hint of what he had been doing or thinking of. He had never been known to pray before. What sort of prayers was he saying now? Extraordinary prayers surely.

Wilfred Bohun stood rooted to the spot long enough to see the idiot go out into the sunshine, and even to see his dissolute brother hail him with a sort of avuncular jocularity. The last thing he saw was the colonel throwing pennies at the open mouth of Joe, with the serious appearance of trying to hit it.

This ugly sunlit picture of the stupidity and cruelty of the earth sent the ascetic finally to his prayers for purification and new thoughts. He went up to a pew in the gallery, which brought him under a coloured window which he loved and always quieted his spirit; a blue window with an angel carrying lilies. There he began to think less about the half-wit, with his livid face and mouth like a fish. He began to think less of his evil brother, pacing like a lean lion in his horrible hunger. He sank deeper and deeper into those cold and sweet colours of silver blossoms and sapphire sky.

In this place half an hour afterwards he was found by Gibbs, the village cobbler, who had been sent for him in some haste. He got to his feet with promptitude, for he knew that no small matter would have brought Gibbs into such a place at all. The cobbler was, as in many villages, an atheist, and his appearance in church was a shade more extraordinary than Mad Joe's. It was a morning of theological enigmas.

'What is it?' asked Wilfred Bohun rather stiffly, but putting out a trembling hand for his hat.

The atheist spoke in a tone that, coming from him, was quite startlingly respectful, and even, as it were, huskily sympathetic.

'You must excuse me, sir,' he said in a hoarse whisper, 'but we didn't think it right not to let you know at once. I'm afraid a rather dreadful thing has happened, sir. I'm afraid your brother – '

Wilfred clenched his frail hands. 'What devilry has he done now?' he cried in voluntary passion.

'Why, sir,' said the cobbler, coughing, 'I'm afraid he's done nothing, and won't do anything. I'm afraid he's done for. You had really better come down, sir.'

The curate followed the cobbler down a short winding stair which brought them out at an entrance rather higher than the street. Bohun saw the tragedy in one glance, flat underneath him like a plan. In the yard of the smithy were standing five or six men mostly in black, one in an inspector's uniform. They included the doctor, the Presbyterian minister, and the priest from the Roman Catholic chapel, to which the blacksmith's wife belonged. The latter was speaking to her, indeed, very rapidly, in an undertone, as she, a magnificent woman with red-gold hair, was sobbing blindly on a bench. Between these two groups, and just clear of the main heap of hammers, lay a man in evening dress, spread-eagled and flat on his face. From the height above Wilfred could have sworn to every item of his costume and appearance, down to the Bohun rings upon his fingers; but the skull was only a hideous splash, like a star of blackness and blood.

Wilfred Bohun gave but one glance, and ran down the steps into the yard. The doctor, who was the family physician, saluted him, but he scarcely took any notice. He could only stammer out: 'My brother is dead. What does it mean? What is this horrible mystery?' There was an unhappy silence; and then the cobbler, the most outspoken man present, answered: 'Plenty of horror, sir,' he said; 'but not much mystery.'

'What do you mean?' asked Wilfred, with a white face.

'It's plain enough,' answered Gibbs. 'There is only one man for forty miles round that could have struck such a blow as that, and he's the man that had most reason to.'

'We must not prejudge anything,' put in the doctor, a tall, black-bearded man, rather nervously; 'but it is competent for me to corroborate what Mr Gibbs says about the nature of the blow, sir; it is an incredible blow. Mr Gibbs says that only one man in this district could have done it. I should have said myself that nobody could have done it.'

A shudder of superstition went through the slight figure of the curate. 'I can hardly understand,' he said.

'Mr Bohun,' said the doctor in a low voice, 'metaphors literally fail me. It is inadequate to say that the skull was smashed to bits like an eggshell. Fragments of bone were driven into the body and the ground like bullets into a mud wall. It was the hand of a giant.'

He was silent a moment, looking grimly through his glasses; then he added: 'The thing has one advantage – that it clears most people of suspicion at one stroke. If you or I or any normally made man in the country were accused of this crime, we should be acquitted as an infant would be acquitted of stealing the Nelson column.'

'That's what I say,' repeated the cobbler obstinately; 'there's only one man that could have done it, and he's the man that would have done it. Where's Simeon Barnes, the blacksmith?'

'He's over at Greenford,' faltered the curate.

'More likely over in France,' muttered the cobbler.

'No; he is in neither of those places,' said a small and colourless voice, which came from the little Roman priest who had joined the group. 'As a matter of fact, he is coming up the road at this moment.'

The little priest was not an interesting man to look at, having stubbly brown hair and a round and stolid face. But if he had been as splendid as Apollo no one would have looked at him at that moment. Everyone turned round and peered at the pathway which wound across the plain below, along which was indeed walking, at his own huge stride and with a hammer on his shoulder, Simeon the smith. He was a bony and gigantic man, with deep, dark, sinister eyes and a dark chin beard. He was walking and talking quietly with two other men; and though he was never specially cheerful, he seemed quite at his ease.

'My God!' cried the atheistic cobbler, 'and there's the hammer he did it with.'

'No,' said the inspector, a sensible-looking man with a sandy moustache, speaking for the first time. 'There's the hammer he did it with over there by the church wall. We have left it and the body exactly as they are.'

All glanced round and the short priest went across and looked down in silence at the tool where it lay. It was one of the smallest and the lightest of the hammers, and would not have caught the eye among the rest; but on the iron edge of it were blood and yellow hair.

After a silence the short priest spoke without looking up, and there was a new note in his dull voice. 'Mr Gibbs was hardly right,' he said, 'in saying that there is no mystery. There is at least the mystery of why so big a man should attempt so big a blow with so little a hammer.'

'Oh, never mind that,' cried Gibbs, in a fever. 'What are we to do with Simeon Barnes?'

'Leave him alone,' said the priest quietly. 'He is coming here of himself. I know those two men with him. They are very good fellows from Greenford, and they have come over about the Presbyterian chapel.'

Even as he spoke the tall smith swung round the corner of the church, and strode into his own yard. Then he stood there quite still, and the hammer fell from his hand. The inspector, who had preserved impenetrable propriety, immediately went up to him.

'I won't ask you, Mr Barnes,' he said, 'whether you know anything about what has happened here. You are not bound to say. I hope you don't know, and that you will be able to prove it. But I must go through the form of arresting you in the King's name for the murder of Colonel Norman Bohun.'

'You are not bound to say anything,' said the cobbler in officious excitement. 'They've got to prove everything. They haven't proved yet that it is Colonel Bohun, with the head all smashed up like that.'

'That won't wash,' said the doctor aside to the priest. 'That's out of the detective stories. I was the colonel's medical man, and I knew his body better than he did. He had very fine hands, but quite peculiar ones. The second and third fingers were the same length. Oh, that's the colonel right enough.'

As he glanced at the brained corpse upon the ground the iron eyes of the motionless blacksmith followed them and rested there also.

'Is Colonel Bohun dead?' said the smith quite calmly. 'Then he's damned.'

'Don't say anything! Oh, don't say anything,' cried the atheist cobbler, dancing about in an ecstasy of admiration of the English legal system. For no man is such a legalist as the good Secularist.

The blacksmith turned on him over his shoulder the august face of a fanatic.

'It's well for you infidels to dodge like foxes because the world's law favours you,' he said; 'but God guards His own in His pocket, as you shall see this day.'

Then he pointed to the colonel and said: 'When did this dog die in his sins?'

'Moderate your language,' said the doctor.

'Moderate the Bible's language, and I'll moderate mine. When did he die?'

'I saw him alive at six o'clock this morning,' stammered Wilfred Bohun.

'God is good,' said the smith. 'Mr Inspector, I have not the slightest objection to being arrested. It is you who may object to arresting me. I don't mind leaving the court without a stain on my character. You do mind perhaps leaving the court with a bad set-back in your career.'

The solid inspector for the first time looked at the blacksmith with a lively eye; as did everybody else, except the short, strange priest, who was still looking down at the little hammer that had dealt the dreadful blow.

'There are two men standing outside this shop,' went on the blacksmith with ponderous lucidity, 'good tradesmen in Greenford whom you all know, who will swear that they saw me from before midnight till daybreak and long after in the committee room of our Revival Mission, which sits all night, we save souls so fast. In Greenford itself twenty people could swear to me for all that time. If I were a heathen, Mr Inspector, I would let you walk on to your downfall. But as a Christian man I feel bound to give you your chance, and ask you whether you will hear my alibi now or in court.'

The inspector seemed for the first time disturbed, and said, 'Of course I should be glad to clear you altogether now.'

The smith walked out of his yard with the same long and easy stride, and returned to his two friends from Greenford, who were indeed friends of nearly everyone present. Each of them said a few words which no one ever thought of disbelieving. When they had spoken, the innocence of Simeon stood up as solid as the great church above them.

One of those silences struck the group which are more strange and insufferable than any speech. Madly, in order to make conversation, the curate said to the Catholic priest:

'You seem very much interested in that hammer, Father Brown.'

'Yes, I am,' said Father Brown; 'why is it such a small hammer?'

The doctor swung round on him.

'By George, that's true,' he cried; 'who would use a little hammer with ten larger hammers lying about?'

Then he lowered his voice in the curate's ear and said: 'Only the kind of person that can't lift a large hammer. It is not a question of force or courage between the sexes. It's a question of lifting power in the shoulders. A bold woman could commit ten murders with a light hammer and never turn a hair. She could not kill a beetle with a heavy one.'

Wilfred Bohun was staring at him with a sort of hypnotised horror, while Father Brown listened with his head a little on one side, really interested and attentive. The doctor went on with more hissing emphasis:

'Why do these idiots always assume that the only person who hates the wife's lover is the wife's husband? Nine times out of ten the person who most hates the wife's lover is the wife. Who knows what insolence or treachery he had shown her – look there!'

He made a momentary gesture towards the red-haired woman on the bench. She had lifted her head at last and the tears were drying on her splendid face. But the eyes were fixed on the corpse with an electric glare that had in it something of idiocy.

The Rev. Wilfred Bohun made a limp gesture as if waving away all desire to know; but Father Brown, dusting off his sleeve some ashes blown from the furnace, spoke in his indifferent way.

'You are like so many doctors,' he said; 'your mental science is really suggestive. It is your physical science that is utterly impossible. I agree that the woman wants to kill the co-respondent much more than the petitioner does. And I agree that a woman will always pick up a small hammer instead of a big one. But the difficulty is one of physical impossibility. No woman ever born could have smashed a man's skull out flat like that.' Then he added reflectively, after a pause: 'These people haven't grasped the whole of it. The man was actually wearing an iron helmet, and the blow scattered it like broken glass. Look at that woman. Look at her arms.'

Silence held them all up again, and then the doctor said rather sulkily: 'Well, I may be wrong; there are objections to everything. But I stick to the main point. No man but an idiot would pick up that little hammer if he could use a big hammer.'

With that the lean and quivering hands of Wilfred Bohun went up to his head and seemed to clutch his scanty yellow hair. After an instant they dropped, and he cried: 'That was the word I wanted; you have said the word.'

Then he continued, mastering his discomposure: 'The words you said were, "No man but an idiot would pick up the small hammer."'

'Yes,' said the doctor. 'Well?'

'Well,' said the curate, 'no man but an idiot did.' The rest stared at him with eyes arrested and riveted, and he went on in a febrile and feminine agitation.

'I am a priest,' he cried unsteadily, 'and a priest should be no shedder of blood. I – I mean that he should bring no one to the gallows. And I thank God that I see the criminal clearly now – because he is a criminal who cannot be brought to the gallows.'

'You will not denounce him?' inquired the doctor.

'He would not be hanged if I did denounce him,' answered Wilfred with a wild but curiously happy smile. 'When I went into the church this morning I found a madman praying there – that poor Joe, who has been wrong all his life. God knows what he prayed; but with such strange folk it is not incredible to suppose that their prayers are all upside down. Very likely a lunatic would pray before killing a man. When I last saw poor Joe he was with my brother. My brother was mocking him.'

'By Jove!' cried the doctor, 'this is talking at last. But how do you explain – '

The Rev. Wilfred was almost trembling with the excitement of his own glimpse of the truth. 'Don't you see; don't you see,' he cried feverishly; 'that is the only theory that covers both the queer things, that answers both the riddles. The two riddles are the little hammer and the big blow. The smith might have struck the big blow, but would not have chosen the little hammer. His wife would have chosen the little hammer, but she could not have struck the big blow. But the madman might have done both. As for the little hammer – why, he was mad and might have picked up anything. And for the big blow, have you never heard, doctor, that a maniac in his paroxysm may have the strength of ten men?'

The doctor drew a deep breath and then said, 'By golly, I believe you've got it.'

Father Brown had fixed his eyes on the speaker so long and steadily as to prove that his large grey, ox-like eyes were not quite so insignificant as the rest of his face. When silence had fallen he said with marked respect: 'Mr Bohun, yours is the only theory yet propounded which holds water every way and is essentially unassailable. I think, therefore, that you deserve to be told, on my positive knowledge, that it is not the true one.' And with that the odd little man walked away and stared again at the hammer.

'That fellow seems to know more than he ought to,' whispered the doctor peevishly to Wilfred. 'Those popish priests are deucedly sly.'

'No, no,' said Bohun, with a sort of wild fatigue. 'It was the lunatic. It was the lunatic.'

The group of the two clerics and the doctor had fallen away from the more official group containing the inspector and the man he had arrested. Now, however, that their own party had broken up, they heard voices from the others. The priest looked up quietly and then looked down again as he heard the blacksmith say in a loud voice:

'I hope I've convinced you, Mr Inspector. I'm a strong man, as you say, but I couldn't have flung my hammer bang here from Greenford. My hammer hasn't got wings that it should come flying half a mile over hedges and fields.'

The inspector laughed amicably and said: 'No, I think you can be considered out of it, though it's one of the rummiest coincidences I ever saw. I can only ask you to give us all the assistance you can in finding a man as big and strong as yourself. By George! you might be useful, if only to hold him! I suppose you yourself have no guess at the man?'

'I may have a guess,' said the pale smith, 'but it is not at a man.' Then, seeing the scared eyes turn towards his wife on the bench, he put his huge hand on her shoulder and said: 'Nor a woman either.'

'What do you mean?' asked the inspector jocularly. 'You don't think cows use hammers, do you?'

'I think no thing of flesh held that hammer,' said the blacksmith in a stifled voice; 'mortally speaking, I think the man died alone.'

Wilfred made a sudden forward movement and peered at him with burning eyes.

'Do you mean to say, Barnes,' came the sharp voice of the cobbler, 'that the hammer jumped up of itself and knocked the man down?'

'Oh, you gentlemen may stare and snigger,' cried Simeon; 'you clergymen who tell us on Sunday in what a stillness the Lord smote Sennacherib. I believe that One who walks invisible in every house defended the honour of mine, and laid the defiler dead before the door of it. I believe the force in that blow was just the force there is in earthquakes, and no force less.'

Wilfred said, with a voice utterly undescribable: 'I told Norman myself to beware of the thunderbolt.'

'That agent is outside my jurisdiction,' said the inspector with a slight smile.

'You are not outside His,' answered the smith; 'see you to it,' and, turning his broad back, he went into the house.

The shaken Wilfred was led away by Father Brown, who had an easy and friendly way with him. 'Let us get out of this horrid place, Mr Bohun,' he said. 'May I look inside your church? I hear it's one of the oldest in England. We take some interest, you know,' he added with a comical grimace, 'in old English churches.'

Wilfred Bohun did not smile, for humour was never his strong point. But he nodded rather eagerly, being only too ready to explain the Gothic splendours to someone more likely to be sympathetic than the Presbyterian blacksmith or the atheist cobbler.

'By all means,' he said; 'let us go in at this side.' And he led the way into the high side entrance at the top of the flight of steps. Father Brown was mounting the first step to follow him when he felt a hand on his shoulder, and turned to behold the dark, thin figure of the doctor, his face darker yet with suspicion.

'Sir,' said the physician harshly, 'you appear to know some secrets in this black business. May I ask if you are going to keep them to yourself?'

'Why, doctor,' answered the priest, smiling quite pleasantly, 'there is one very good reason why a man of my trade should keep things to himself when he is not sure of them, and that is that it is so constantly his duty to keep them to himself when he is sure of them. But if you think I have been discourteously reticent with you or anyone, I will go to the extreme limit of my custom. I will give you two very large hints.'

'Well, sir?' said the doctor gloomily.

'First,' said Father Brown quietly, 'the thing is quite in your own province. It is a matter of physical science. The blacksmith is mistaken, not perhaps in saying that the blow was divine, but certainly in saying that it came by a miracle. It was no miracle, doctor, except in so far as man is himself a miracle, with his strange and wicked and yet half-heroic heart. The force that smashed that skull was a force well known to scientists – one of the most frequently debated of the laws of nature.'

The doctor, who was looking at him with frowning intentness, only said: 'And the other hint?'

'The other hint is this,' said the priest. 'Do you remember the blacksmith, though he believes in miracles, talking scornfully of the impossible fairy tale that his hammer had wings and flew half a mile across country?'

'Yes,' said the doctor, 'I remember that.'

'Well,' added Father Brown, with a broad smile, 'that fairy tale was the nearest thing to the real truth that has been said today.' And with that he turned his back and stumped up the steps after the curate.

The Reverend Wilfred, who had been waiting for him, pale and impatient, as if this little delay were the last straw for his nerves, led him immediately to his favourite corner of the church, that part of the gallery closest to the carved roof and lit by the wonderful window with the angel. The little Latin priest explored and admired everything exhaustively, talking cheerfully but in a low voice all the time. When in the course of his investigation he found the side exit and the winding stair down which Wilfred had rushed to find his brother dead, Father Brown ran not down but up, with the agility of a monkey, and his clear voice came from an outer platform above.

'Come up here, Mr Bohun,' he called. 'The air will do you good.'

Bohun followed him, and came out on a kind of stone gallery or balcony outside the building, from which one could see the illimitable plain in which their small hill stood, wooded away to the purple horizon and dotted with villages and farms. Clear and square, but quite small beneath them, was the blacksmith's yard, where the inspector still stood taking notes and the corpse still lay like a smashed fly.

'Might be the map of the world, mightn't it?' said Father Brown.

'Yes,' said Bohun very gravely, and nodded his head.

Immediately beneath and about them the lines of the Gothic building plunged outwards into the void with a sickening swiftness akin to suicide. There is that element of Titan energy in the architecture of the Middle Ages that, from whatever aspect it be seen, it always seems to be rushing away, like the strong back of some maddened horse. This church was hewn out of ancient and silent stone, bearded with old fungoids and stained with the nests of birds. And yet, when they saw it from below, it sprang like a fountain at the stars; and when they saw it, as now, from above, it poured like a cataract into a voiceless pit. For these two men on the tower were left alone with the most terrible aspect of Gothic; the monstrous foreshortening and disproportion, the dizzy perspectives, the glimpses of great things small and small things great; a topsy-turvydom of stone in the mid-air. Details of stone, enormous by their proximity, were relieved against a pattern of fields and farms, pygmy in their distance. A carved bird or beast at a corner seemed like some vast walking or flying dragon wasting the pastures and villages below. The whole atmosphere was dizzy and dangerous, as if men were upheld in air amid the gyrating wings of colossal genii; and the whole of that old church, as tall and rich as a cathedral, seemed to sit upon the sunlit country like a cloudburst.

'I think there is something rather dangerous about standing on these high places even to pray,' said Father Brown. 'Heights were made to be looked at, not to be looked from.'

'Do you mean that one may fall over,' asked Wilfred.

'I mean that one's soul may fall if one's body doesn't,' said the other priest.

'I scarcely understand you,' remarked Bohun indistinctly.

'Look at that blacksmith, for instance,' went on Father Brown calmly; 'a good man, but not a Christian – hard, imperious, unforgiving. Well, his Scotch religion was made up by men who prayed on hills and high crags, and learnt to look down on the world more than to look up at heaven. Humility is the mother of giants. One sees great things from the valley; only small things from the peak.'

'But he – he didn't do it,' said Bohun tremulously.

'No,' said the other in an odd voice; 'we know he didn't do it.'

After a moment he resumed, looking tranquilly out over the plain with his pale grey eyes. 'I knew a man,' he said, 'who began by worshipping with others before the altar, but who grew fond of high and lonely places to pray from, corners or niches in the belfry or the spire. And once in one of those dizzy places, where the whole world seemed to turn under him like a wheel, his brain turned also, and he fancied he was God. So that, though he was a good man, he committed a great crime.'

Wilfred's face was turned away, but his bony hands turned blue and white as they tightened on the parapet of stone.

'He thought it was given to him to judge the world and strike down the sinner. He would never have had such a thought if he had been kneeling with other men upon a floor. But he saw all men walking about like insects. He saw one especially strutting just below him, insolent and evident by a bright green hat – a poisonous insect.'

Rooks cawed round the corners of the belfry; but there was no other sound till Father Brown went on.

'This also tempted him, that he had in his hand one of the most awful engines of nature; I mean gravitation, that mad and quickening rush by which all earth's creatures fly back to her heart when released. See, the inspector is strutting just below us in the smithy. If I were to toss a pebble over this parapet it would be something like a bullet by the time it struck him. If I were to drop a hammer – even a small hammer – '

Wilfred Bohun threw one leg over the parapet, and Father Brown had him in a minute by the collar.

'Not by that door,' he said quite gently; 'that door leads to hell.'

Bohun staggered back against the wall, and stared at him with frightful eyes.

'How do you know all this?' he cried. 'Are you a devil?'

'I am a man,' answered Father Brown gravely; 'and therefore have all devils in my heart. Listen to me,' he said after a short pause. 'I know what you did – at least, I can guess the great part of it. When you left your brother you were racked with no unrighteous rage, to the extent even that you snatched up a small hammer, half inclined to kill him with his foulness on his mouth. Recoiling, you thrust it under your buttoned coat instead, and rushed into the church. You pray wildly in many places, under the angel window, upon the platform above, and a higher platform still, from which you could see the colonel's Eastern hat like the back of a green beetle crawling about. Then something snapped in your soul, and you let God's thunderbolt fall.'

Wilfred put a weak hand to his head, and asked in a low voice: 'How did you know that his hat looked like a green beetle?'

'Oh, that,' said the other with the shadow of a smile, 'that was common sense. But hear me further. I say I know all this; but no one else shall know it. The next step is for you; I shall take no more steps; I will seal this with the seal of confession. If you ask me why, there are many reasons, and only one that concerns you. I leave things to you because you have not yet gone very far wrong, as assassins go. You did not help to fix the crime on the smith when it was easy; or on his wife, when that was easy. You tried to fix it on the imbecile because you knew that he could not suffer. That was one of the gleams that it is my business to find in assassins. And now come down into the village, and go your own way as free as the wind; for I have said my last word.'

They went down the winding stairs in utter silence, and came out into the sunlight by the smithy. Wilfred Bohun carefully unlatched the wooden gate of the yard, and going up to the inspector, said: 'I wish to give myself up; I have killed my brother.'

Eugène Valmont

Created by Robert Barr (1849 – 1912)

BORN IN SCOTLAND, Robert Barr went with his family to Canada as a small boy and it was there and in the United States that he began his career as a journalist. He returned to the UK in the early 1880s and became a well-known figure in literary London, a prolific writer of novels and short stories. In 1892 he was the co-founder, with Jerome K. Jerome, of *The Idler*. He was a friend of Conan Doyle, who, in the preface to his historical novel *Rodney Stone*, acknowledges Barr's assistance in providing information about the world of prizefighting in which the book is set. Barr was also one of the earliest writers to produce a parody of a Sherlock Holmes story, publishing 'The Pegram Mystery', featuring Sherlaw Kombs, in 1894. His own most succesful ventures into the crime genre were the short stories he wrote about the French detective resident in London, Eugène Valmont, which were published in *The Windsor Magazine* and *Pearson's Magazine* in 1904 and 1905 and later in book form. Like Holmes, Valmont is not a man given to false modesty (despite his earlier, forced resignation from a government position in his native France) and his self-possession and self-confidence are apparent throughout the stories. None of Valmont's cases demands feats of Sherlockian deduction but the wit and energy with which Barr relates them make them entertaining reading.

The Clue of the Silver Spoons

WHEN THE CARD was brought in to me, I looked upon it with some misgiving, for I scented a commercial transaction, and, although such cases are lucrative enough, nevertheless I, Eugène Valmont, formerly high in the service of the French Government, do not care to be connected with them. They usually pertain to sordid business affairs, presenting little that is of interest to a man who, in his time, has dealt with subtle questions of diplomacy upon which the welfare of nations sometimes turned.

The name of Bentham Gibbes is familiar to everyone, connected as it is with the much-advertised pickles, whose glaring announcements in crude crimson and green strike the eye throughout Great Britain, and shock the artistic sense wherever seen. Me! I have never tasted them, and shall not so long as a French restaurant remains open in London. But I doubt not they are as pronounced to the palate as their advertisement is distressing to the eye. If then, this gross pickle manufacturer expected me to track down those who were infringing upon the recipes for making his so-called sauces, chutneys, and the like, he would find himself mistaken, for I was now in a position to pick and choose my cases, and a case of pickles did not allure me. 'Beware of imitations,' said the advertisement; 'none genuine without a facsimile of the signature of Bentham Gibbes.' Ah, well, not for me were either the pickles or the tracking of imitators. A forged cheque! yes, if you like, but the forged signature of Mr Gibbes on a pickle bottle was out of my line. Nevertheless, I said to Armand:-

'Show the gentleman in,' and he did so.

To my astonishment there entered a young man, quite correctly dressed in the dark frock-coat, faultless waistcoat and trousers that proclaimed a Bond Street tailor. When he spoke his voice and language were those of a gentleman.

'Monsieur Valmont?' he inquired.

'At your service,' I replied, bowing and waving my hand as Armand placed a chair for him, and withdrew.

'I am a barrister with chambers in the Temple,' began Mr Gibbes, 'and for some days a matter has been troubling me about which I have now come to seek your advice, your name having been suggested by a friend in whom I confided.'

'Am I acquainted with him?' I asked.

'I think not,' replied Mr Gibbes; 'he also is a barrister with chambers in the same building as my own. Lionel Dacre is his name.'

'I never heard of him.'

'Very likely not. Nevertheless, he recommended you as a man who could keep his own counsel, and if you take up this case I desire the utmost secrecy preserved, whatever may be the outcome.'

I bowed, but made no protestation. Secrecy is a matter of course with me.

The Englishman paused for a few moments as if he expected fervent assurances; then went on with no trace of disappointment on his countenance at not receiving them.

'On the night of the twenty-third, I gave a little dinner to six friends of mine in my own rooms. I may say that so far as I am aware they are all gentlemen of unimpeachable character. On the night of the dinner I was detained later than I expected at a reception, and in driving to the Temple was still further delayed by a block of traffic in Piccadilly, so that when I arrived at my chambers there was barely time for me to dress and receive my guests. My man Johnson had everything laid out ready for me in my dressing-room, and as I passed through to it I hurriedly flung off the coat I was wearing and carelessly left it hanging over the back of a chair in the dining-room, where neither Johnson nor myself noticed it until my attention was called to it after the dinner was over, and everyone rather jolly with wine.

'This coat contains an inside pocket. Usually any frock-coat I wear at an afternoon reception has not an inside pocket, but I had been rather on the rush all day.

'My father is a manufacturer whose name may be familiar to you, and I am on the directors' board of his company. On this occasion I took a cab from the city to the reception I spoke of, and had not time to go and change at my rooms. The reception was a somewhat bohemian affair, extremely interesting, of course, but not too particular as to costume, so I went as I was. In this inside pocket rested a thin package, composed of two pieces of cardboard, and between them rested five twenty-pound Bank of England notes, folded lengthwise, held in place by an elastic rubber band. I had thrown the coat across the chair-back in such a way that the inside pocket was exposed, leaving the ends of the notes plainly recognisable.

'Over the coffee and cigars one of my guests laughingly called attention to what he termed my vulgar display of wealth, and Johnson, in some confusion at having neglected to put away the coat, now picked it up, and took it to the reception-room where the wraps of my guests lay about promiscuously. He should, of course, have hung it up in my wardrobe, but he said afterwards he thought it belonged to the guest who had spoken. You see, Johnson was in my dressing-room when I threw my coat on the chair in the corner while making my way thither, and I suppose he had not noticed the coat in the hurry of arriving guests, otherwise he would have put it where it belonged. After everybody had gone Johnson came to me and said the coat was there, but the package was missing, nor has any trace of it been found since that night.'

'The dinner was fetched in from outside, I suppose?'

'Yes.'

'How many waiters served it?'

'Two. They are men who have often been in my employ on similar occasions, but, apart from that, they had left my chambers before the incident of the coat happened.'

'Neither of them went into the reception-room, I take it?'

'No. I am certain that not even suspicion can attach to either of the waiters.'

'Your man Johnson – ?'

'Has been with me for years. He could easily have stolen much more than the hundred pounds if he had wished to do so, but I have never known him to take a penny that did not belong to him.'

'Will you favour me with the names of your guests, Mr Gibbes?'

'Viscount Stern sat at my right hand, and at my left Lord Templemere; Sir John Sanclere next to him, and Angus McKeller next to Sanclere. After Viscount Stern was Lionel Dacre, and at his right, Vincent Innis.'

On a sheet of paper I had written the names of the guests, and noted their places at the table.

'Which guest drew your attention to the money?'

'Lionel Dacre.'

'Is there a window looking out from the reception-room?'

'Two of them.'

'Were they fastened on the night of the dinner party?'

'I could not be sure; very likely Johnson would know. You are hinting at the possibility of a thief coming in through a reception-room window while we were somewhat noisy over our wine. I think such a solution highly improbable. My rooms are on the third floor, and a thief would scarcely venture to make an entrance when he could not but know there was a company being entertained. Besides this, the coat was there less than an hour, and it appears to me that whoever stole those notes knew where they were.'

'That seems reasonable,' I had to admit. 'Have you spoken to any one of your loss?'

'To no one but Dacre, who recommended me to see you. Oh, yes, and to Johnson, of course.'

I could not help noting that this was the fourth or fifth time Dacre's name had come up during our conversation.

'What of Dacre?' I asked.

'Oh, well, you see, he occupies chambers in the same building on the ground floor. He is a very good fellow, and we are by way of being firm friends. Then it was he who had called attention to the money, so I thought he should know the sequel.'

'How did he take your news?'

'Now that you call attention to the fact, he seemed slightly troubled. I should like to say, however, that you must not be misled by that. Lionel Dacre could no more steal than he could lie.'

'Did he show any surprise when you mentioned the theft?'

Bentham Gibbes paused a moment before replying, knitting his brows in thought.

'No,' he said at last; 'and, come to think of it, it appeared as if he had been expecting my announcement.'

'Doesn't that strike you as rather strange, Mr Gibbes?'

'Really my mind is in such a whirl, I don't know what to think. But it's perfectly absurd to suspect Dacre. If you knew the man you would understand what I mean. He comes of an excellent family, and he is – oh! he is Lionel Dacre, and when you have said that you have made any suspicion absurd.'

'I suppose you caused the rooms to be thoroughly searched. The packet didn't drop out and remain unnoticed in some corner?'

'No; Johnson and myself examined every inch of the premises.'

'Have you the numbers of the notes?'

'Yes; I got them from the Bank next morning. Payment was stopped, and so far not one of the five has been presented. Of course, one or more may have been cashed at some shop, but none have been offered to any of the banks.'

'A twenty-pound note is not accepted without scrutiny, so the chances are the thief may find some difficulty in disposing of them.'

'As I told you, I don't mind the loss of the money at all. It is the uncertainty, the uneasiness caused by the incident which troubles me. You will comprehend how little I care about the notes when I say that if you are good enough to interest yourself in this case, I shall be disappointed if your fee does not exceed the amount I have lost.'

Mr Gibbes rose as he said this, and I accompanied him to the door assuring him that I should do my best to solve the mystery. Whether he sprang from pickles or not, I realised he was a polished and generous gentleman, who estimated the services of a professional expert like myself at their true value.

I shall not set down the details of my researches during the following few days, because the trend of them must be gone over in the account of that remarkable interview in which I took part somewhat later. Suffice it to say that an examination of the rooms and a close cross-questioning of Johnson satisfied me he and the two waiters were innocent. I became certain no thief had made his way through the window, and finally I arrived at the conclusion that the notes were stolen by one of the guests. Further investigation convinced me that the thief was no other than Lionel Dacre, the only one of the six in pressing need of money at this time. I caused Dacre to be shadowed, and during one of his absences made the acquaintance of his man Hopper, a surly, impolite brute, who accepted my golden sovereign quickly enough, but gave me little in exchange for it. While

I conversed with him, there arrived in the passage where we were talking together a huge case of champagne, bearing one of the best-known names in the trade, and branded as being of the vintage of '78. Now I knew that the product of Camelot Frères is not bought as cheaply as British beer, and I also had learned that two short weeks before Mr Lionel Dacre was at his wits' end for money. Yet he was still the same briefless barrister he had ever been.

On the morning after my unsatisfactory conversation with his man Hopper, I was astonished to receive the following note, written on a dainty correspondence card:-

3 and 4 Vellum Buildings,
Inner Temple, E.

Mr Lionel Dacre presents his compliments to Monsieur Eugène Valmont, and would be obliged if Monsieur Valmont could make it convenient to call upon him in his chambers tomorrow morning at eleven.

******

Had the young man become aware that he was being shadowed, or had the surly servant informed him of the inquiries made? I was soon to know. I called punctually at eleven next morning, and was received with charming urbanity by Mr Dacre himself. The taciturn Hopper had evidently been sent away for the occasion.

'My dear Monsieur Valmont, I am delighted to meet you,' began the young man with more of effusiveness than I had ever noticed in an Englishman before, although his very next words supplied an explanation that did not occur to me until afterwards as somewhat far-fetched. 'I believe we are by way of being countrymen, and, therefore, although the hour is early, I hope you will allow me to offer you some of this bottled sunshine of the year '78 from *la belle France*, to whose prosperity and honour we shall drink together. For such a toast any hour is propitious,' and to my amazement he brought forth from the case I had seen arrive two days before, a bottle of that superb Camelot Frères '78.

'Now,' said I to myself, 'it is going to be difficult to keep a clear head if the aroma of this nectar rises to the brain. But tempting as is the cup, I shall drink sparingly, and hope he may not be so judicious.'

Sensitive, I already experienced the charm of his personality, and well understood the friendship Mr Bentham Gibbes felt for him. But I saw the trap spread before me. He expected, under the influence of champagne and courtesy, to extract a promise from me which I must find myself unable to give.

'Sir, you interest me by claiming kinship with France. I had understood that you belonged to one of the oldest families of England.'

'Ah, England!' he cried, with an expressive gesture of outspreading hands truly Parisian in its significance. 'The trunk belongs to England, of course, but the root – ah! the root – Monsieur Valmont, penetrated the soil from which this wine of the gods has been drawn.'

Then filling my glass and his own he cried:-

'To France, which my family left in the year 1066!'

I could not help laughing at his fervent ejaculation.

'1066! With William the Conqueror! That is a long time ago, Mr Dacre.'

'In years perhaps; in feelings but a day. My forefathers came over to steal, and, lord! how well they accomplished it. They stole the whole country – something like a theft, say I – under that prince of robbers whom you have well named the Conqueror. In our secret hearts we all admire a great thief, and if not a great one, then an expert one, who covers his tracks so perfectly that the hounds of justice are baffled in attempting to follow them. Now even you, Monsieur Valmont (I can see you are the most generous of men, with a lively sympathy found to perfection only in France), even you must suffer a pang of regret when you lay a thief by the heels who has done his task deftly.'

'I fear, Mr Dacre, you credit me with a magnanimity to which I dare not lay claim. The criminal is a danger to society.'

'True, true, you are in the right, Monsieur Valmont. Still, admit there are cases that would touch you tenderly. For example, a man, ordinarily honest; a great need; a sudden opportunity. He takes that of which another has abundance, and he, nothing. What then, Monsieur Valmont? Is the man to be sent to perdition for a momentary weakness?'

His words astonished me. Was I on the verge of hearing a confession? It almost amounted to that already.

'Mr Dacre,' I said, 'I cannot enter into the subtleties you pursue. My duty is to find the criminal.'

'Again I say you are in the right, Monsieur Valmont, and I am enchanted to find so sensible a head on French shoulders. Although you are a more recent arrival, if I may say so, than myself, you nevertheless already give utterance to sentiments which do honour to England. It is your duty to hunt down the criminal. Very well. In that I think I can aid you, and thus have taken the liberty of requesting your attendance here this morning. Let me fill your glass again, Monsieur Valmont.'

'No more, I beg of you, Mr Dacre.'

'What, do you think the receiver is as bad as the thief?'

I was so taken aback by this remark that I suppose my face showed the amazement within me. But the young man merely laughed with apparently free-hearted enjoyment, poured some wine into his own glass, and tossed it off. Not knowing what to say, I changed the current of conversation.

'Mr Gibbes said you had been kind enough to recommend me to his attention. May I ask how you came to hear of me?'

'Ah! who has not heard of the renowned Monsieur Valmont,' and as he said this, for the first time, there began to grow a suspicion in my mind that he was chaffing me, as it is called in England – a procedure which I cannot endure. Indeed, if this gentleman practised such a barbarism in my own country he would find himself with a duel on his hands before he had gone far. However, the next instant his voice resumed its original fascination, and I listened to it as to some delicious melody.

'I need only mention my cousin, Lady Gladys Dacre, and you will at once understand why I recommended you to my friend. The case of Lady Gladys, you will remember, required a delicate touch which is not always to be had in this land of England, except when those who possess the gift do us the honour to sojourn with us.'

I noticed that my glass was again filled, and bowing an acknowledgment of his compliment, I indulged in another sip of the delicious wine. I sighed, for I began to realise it was going to be very difficult for me, in spite of my disclaimer, to tell this man's friend he had stolen the money. All this time he had been sitting on the edge of the table, while I occupied a chair at its end. He sat there in careless fashion, swinging a foot to and fro. Now he sprang to the floor, and drew up a chair, placing on the table a blank sheet of paper. Then he took from the mantelshelf a packet of letters, and I was astonished to see they were held together by two bits of cardboard and a rubber band similar to the combination that had contained the folded bank notes. With great nonchalance he slipped off the rubber band, threw it and the pieces of cardboard on the table before me, leaving the documents loose to his hand.

'Now, Monsieur Valmont,' he cried jauntily, 'you have been occupied for several days on this case, the case of my dear friend Bentham Gibbes, who is one of the best fellows in the world.'

'He said the same of you, Mr Dacre.'

'I am gratified to hear it. Would you mind letting me know to what point your researches have led you?'

'They have led me in a direction rather than to a point.'

'Ah! In the direction of a man, of course?'

'Certainly.'

'Who is he?'

'Will you pardon me if I decline to answer this question at the present moment?'

'That means you are not sure.'

'It may mean, Mr Dacre, that I am employed by Mr Gibbes, and do not feel at liberty to disclose the results of my quest without his permission.'

'But Mr Bentham Gibbes and I are entirely at one in this matter. Perhaps you are aware that I am the only person with whom he has discussed the case beside yourself.'

'That is undoubtedly true, Mr Dacre; still, you see the difficulty of my position.'

'Yes, I do, and so shall press you no further. But I also have been studying the problem in a purely amateurish way, of course. You will perhaps express no disinclination to learn whether or not my deductions agree with yours.'

'None in the least. I should be very glad to know the conclusion at which you have arrived. May I ask if you suspect any one in particular?'

'Yes, I do.'

'Will you name him?'

'No; I shall copy the admirable reticence you yourself have shown. And now let us attack this mystery in a sane and businesslike manner. You have already examined the room. Well, here is a rough sketch of it. There is the table; in this corner stood the chair on which the coat was flung. Here sat Gibbes at the head of the table. Those on the left-hand side had their backs to the chair. I, being on the centre to the right, saw the chair, the coat, and the notes, and called attention to them. Now our first duty is to find a motive. If it were a murder, our motive might be hatred, revenge, robbery – what you like. As it is simply the stealing of money, the man must have been either a born thief or else some hitherto innocent person pressed to the crime by great necessity. Do you agree with me, Monsieur Valmont?'

'Perfectly. You follow exactly the line of my own reasoning.'

'Very well. It is unlikely that a born thief was one of Mr Gibbes's guests. Therefore we are reduced to look for a man under the spur of necessity; a man who has no money of his own but who must raise a certain amount, let us say, by a certain date. If we can find such a man in that company, do you not agree with me that he is likely to be the thief?'

'Yes, I do.'

'Then let us start our process of elimination. Out goes Viscount Stern, a lucky individual with twenty thousand acres of land, and God only knows what income. I mark off the name of Lord Templemere, one of His Majesty's judges, entirely above suspicion. Next, Sir John Sanclere; he also is rich, but Vincent Innis is still richer, so the pencil obliterates both names. Now we arrive at Angus McKeller, an author of some note, as you are well aware, deriving a good income from his books and a better one from his plays; a canny Scot, so we may rub his name from our paper and our memory. How do my erasures correspond with yours, Monsieur Valmont?'

'They correspond exactly, Mr Dacre.'

'I am flattered to hear it. There remains one name untouched, Mr Lionel Dacre, the descendant, as I have said, of robbers.'

'I have not said so, Mr Dacre.'

'Ah! my dear Valmont, the politeness of your country asserts itself. Let us not be deluded, but follow our inquiry wherever it leads. I suspect Lionel Dacre. What do you know of his circumstances before the dinner of the twenty-third?'

As I made no reply he looked up at me with his frank, boyish face illumined by a winning smile.

'You know nothing of his circumstances?' he asked.

'It grieves me to state that I do. Mr Lionel Dacre was penniless on the night of the dinner.'

'Oh, don't exaggerate, Monsieur Valmont,' cried Dacre with a gesture of pathetic protest; 'his pocket held one sixpence, two pennies, and a halfpenny. How came you to suspect he was penniless?'

'I knew he ordered a case of champagne from the London representative of Camelot Frères, and was refused unless he paid the money down.'

'Quite right, and then when you were talking to Hopper you saw that case of champagne delivered. Excellent! excellent! Monsieur Valmont. But will a man steal, think you, even to supply himself with so delicious a wine as this we have been tasting? And, by the way, forgive my neglect, allow me to fill your glass, Monsieur Valmont.'

'Not another drop, if you will excuse me, Mr Dacre.'

'Ah, yes, champagne should not be mixed with evidence. When we have finished, perhaps. What further proof have you discovered, monsieur?'

'I hold proof that Mr Dacre was threatened with bankruptcy, if, on the twenty-fourth, he did not pay a bill of seventy-eight pounds that had been long outstanding. I hold proof that this was paid, not on the twenty-fourth, but on the twenty-sixth. Mr Dacre had gone to the solicitor and assured him he would pay the money on that date, whereupon he was given two days' grace.'

'Ah, well, he was entitled to three, you know, in law. Yes, there, Monsieur Valmont, you touch the fatal point. The threat of bankruptcy will drive a man in Dacre's position to almost any crime. Bankruptcy to a barrister means ruin. It means a career blighted; it means a life buried, with little chance of resurrection. I see, you grasp the supreme importance of that bit of evidence. The case of champagne is as nothing compared with it, and this reminds me that in the crisis now upon us I shall take another sip, with your permission. Sure you won't join me?'

'Not at this juncture, Mr Dacre.'

'I envy your moderation. Here's to the success of our search, Monsieur Valmont.'

I felt sorry for the gay young fellow as with smiling face he drank the champagne.

'Now, monsieur,' he went on, 'I am amazed to learn how much you have discovered. Really, I think tradespeople, solicitors, and all such should keep better guard on their tongues than they do. Nevertheless, these documents at my elbow, which I expected would surprise you, are merely the letters and receipts. Here is the communication from the solicitor threatening me with bankruptcy; here is his receipt dated the twenty-sixth; here is the refusal of the wine merchant, and here is his receipt for the money. Here are smaller bills liquidated. With my pencil we will add them up. Seventy-eight pounds – the principal debt – bulks large. We add the smaller items and it reaches a total of ninety-three pounds seven shillings and fourpence. Let us now examine my purse. Here is a five-pound note; there is a golden sovereign. I now count out and place on the table twelve and sixpence in silver and two pence in coppers. The purse thus becomes empty. Let us add the silver and copper to the amount on the paper. Do my eyes deceive me, or is the sum exactly a hundred pounds? There is your money fully accounted for.'

'Pardon me, Mr Dacre,' I said, 'but I observe a sovereign resting on the mantelpiece.'

Dacre threw back his head and laughed with greater heartiness than I had yet known him to indulge in during our short acquaintance.

'By Jove,' he cried, 'you've got me there. I'd forgotten entirely about that pound on the mantelpiece, which belongs to you.'

'To me? Impossible!'

'It does, and cannot interfere in the least with our century calculation. That is the sovereign you gave to my man Hopper, who, knowing me to be hard-pressed, took it and shamefacedly presented it to me, that I might enjoy the spending of it. Hopper belongs to our family, or the family belongs to him. I am never sure which. You must have missed in him the deferential bearing of a man-servant in Paris, yet he is true gold, like the sovereign you bestowed upon him, and he bestowed upon me. Now here, Monsieur, is the evidence of the theft, together with the rubber band and two pieces of cardboard. Ask my friend Gibbes to examine them minutely. They are all at your disposition, Monsieur, and thus you learn how much easier it is to deal with the master than with the servant. All the gold you possess would not have wrung these incriminating documents from old Hopper. I was compelled to send him away to the West End an hour ago, fearing that in his brutal British way he might assault you if he got an inkling of your mission.'

'Mr Dacre,' said I slowly, 'you have thoroughly convinced me – '

'I thought I would,' he interrupted with a laugh.

' – that you did not take the money.'

'Oho, this is a change of wind, surely. Many a man has been hanged on a chain of circumstantial evidence much weaker than this which I have exhibited to you. Don't you see the subtlety of my action? Ninety-nine persons in a hundred would say: "No man could be such a fool as to put Valmont on his own track, and then place in Valmont's hands such striking evidence." But there comes in my craftiness. Of course, the rock you run up against will be Gibbes's incredulity. The first question he will ask you may be this: "Why did not Dacre come and borrow the money from me?" Now there you find a certain weakness in your chain of evidence. I knew perfectly well that Gibbes would lend me the money, and he knew perfectly well that if I were pressed to the wall I should ask him.'

'Mr Dacre,' said I, 'you have been playing with me. I should resent that with most men, but whether it is your own genial manner or the effect of this excellent champagne, or both together, I forgive you. But I am convinced of another thing. You know who took the money.'

'I don't know, but I suspect.'

'Will you tell me whom you suspect?'

'That would not be fair, but I shall now take the liberty of filling your glass with champagne.'

'I am your guest, Mr Dacre.'

'Admirably answered, monsieur,' he replied, pouring out the wine, 'and now I offer you a clue. Find out all about the story of the silver spoons.'

'The story of the silver spoons! What silver spoons?'

'Ah! That is the point. Step out of the Temple into Fleet Street, seize the first man you meet by the shoulder, and ask him to tell you about the silver spoons. There are but two men and two spoons concerned. When you learn who those two men are, you will know that one of them did not take the money, and I give you my assurance that the other did.'

'You speak in mystery, Mr Dacre.'

'But certainly, for I am speaking to Monsieur Eugène Valmont.'

'I echo your words, sir. Admirably answered. You put me on my mettle, and I flatter myself that I see your kindly drift. You wish me to solve the mystery of this stolen money. Sir, you do me honour, and I drink to your health.'

'To yours, monsieur,' said Lionel Dacre, and thus we drank and parted.

On leaving Mr Dacre I took a hansom to a café in Regent Street, which is a passable imitation of similar places of refreshment in Paris. There, calling for a cup of black coffee, I sat down to think. The clue of the silver spoons! He had laughingly suggested that I should take by the shoulders the first man I met, and ask him what the story of the silver spoons was. This course naturally struck me as absurd, and he doubtless intended it to seem absurd. Nevertheless, it contained a hint. I must ask somebody, and that the right person, to tell me the tale of the silver spoons.

Under the influence of the black coffee I reasoned it out in this way. On the night of the twenty-third one of the six guests there present stole a hundred pounds, but Dacre had said that an actor in the silver spoon episode was the actual thief. That person, then, must have been one of Mr Gibbes's guests at the dinner of the twenty-third. Probably two of the guests were the participators in the silver spoon comedy, but, be that as it may, it followed that one at least of the men around Mr Gibbes's table knew the episode of the silver spoons. Perhaps Bentham Gibbes himself was cognisant of it. It followed, therefore, that the easiest plan was to question each of the men who partook of that dinner. Yet if only one knew about the spoons, that one must also have some idea that these spoons formed the clue which attached him to the crime of the twenty-third, in which case he was little likely to divulge what he knew to an entire stranger.

Of course, I might go to Dacre himself and demand the story of the silver spoons, but this would be a confession of failure on my part, and I rather dreaded Lionel Dacre's hearty laughter when I admitted that the mystery was too much for me. Besides this I was very well aware of the young man's kindly intentions towards me. He wished me to unravel the coil myself, and so I determined not to go to him except as a last resource.

I resolved to begin with Mr Gibbes, and, finishing my coffee, I got again into a hansom, and drove back to the Temple. I found Bentham Gibbes in his room, and after greeting me, his first inquiry was about the case.

'How are you getting on?' he asked.

'I think I'm getting on fairly well,' I replied, 'and expect to finish in a day or two, if you will kindly tell me the story of the silver spoons.'

'The silver spoons?' he echoed, quite evidently not understanding me.

'There happened an incident in which two men were engaged, and this incident related to a pair of silver spoons. I want to get the particulars of that.'

'I haven't the slightest idea what you are talking about,' replied Gibbes, thoroughly bewildered. 'You will need to be more definite, I fear, if you are to get any help from me.'

'I cannot be more definite, because I have already told you all I know.'

'What bearing has all this on our own case?'

'I was informed that if I got hold of the clue of the silver spoons I should be in a fair way of settling our case.'

'Who told you that?'

'Mr Lionel Dacre.'

'Oh, does Dacre refer to his own conjuring?'

'I don't know, I'm sure. What was his conjuring?'

'A very clever trick he did one night at dinner here about two months ago.'

'Had it anything to do with silver spoons?'

'Well, it was silver spoons or silver forks, or something of that kind. I had entirely forgotten the incident. So far as I recollect at the moment there was a sleight-of-hand man of great expertness in one of the music halls, and the talk turned upon him. Then Dacre said the tricks he did were easy, and holding up a spoon or a fork, I don't remember which, he professed his ability to make it disappear before our eyes, to be found afterwards in the clothing of some one there present. Several offered to bet that he could do nothing of the kind, but he said he would bet with no one but Innis, who sat opposite him. Innis, with some reluctance, accepted the bet, and then Dacre, with a great show of the usual conjurer's gesticulations, spread forth his empty hands, and said we should find the spoon in Innis's pocket, and there, sure enough, it was. It seemed a proper sleight-of-hand trick, but we were never able to get him to repeat it.'

'Thank you very much, Mr Gibbes; I think I see daylight now.'

'If you do you are cleverer than I by a long chalk,' cried Bentham Gibbes as I took my departure.

I went directly downstairs, and knocked at Mr Dacre's door once more. He opened the door himself, his man not yet having returned.

'Ah, monsieur,' he cried, 'back already? You don't mean to tell me you have so soon got to the bottom of the silver spoon entanglement?'

'I think I have, Mr Dacre. You were sitting at dinner opposite Mr Vincent Innis. You saw him conceal a silver spoon in his pocket. You probably waited for some time to understand what he meant by this, and as he did not return the spoon to its place, you proposed a conjuring trick, made the bet with him, and thus the spoon was returned to the table.'

'Excellent! excellent, monsieur! That is very nearly what occurred, except that I acted at once. I had had experiences with Mr Vincent Innis before. Never did he enter these rooms of mine without my missing some little trinket after he was gone. Although Mr Innis is a very rich person, I am not a man of many possessions, so if anything is taken, I meet little difficulty in coming to a knowledge of my loss. Of course, I never mentioned these abstractions to him. They were all trivial, as I have said, and so far as the silver spoon was concerned, it was of no great value either. But I thought the bet and the recovery of the spoon would teach him a lesson; it apparently has not done so. On the night of the twenty-third he sat at my right hand, as you will see by consulting your diagram of the table and the guests. I asked him a question twice, to which he did not reply, and looking at him I was startled by the expression in his eyes. They were fixed on a distant corner of the room, and following his gaze I saw what he was staring at with such hypnotising concentration. So absorbed was he in contemplation of the packet there so plainly exposed, now my attention was turned to it, that he seemed to be entirely oblivious of what was going on around him. I roused him from his trance by jocularly calling Gibbes's attention to the display of money. I expected in this way to save Innis from committing the act which he seemingly did commit. Imagine then the dilemma in which I was placed when Gibbes confided to me the morning after what had occurred the night before. I was positive Innis had taken the money, yet I possessed no proof of it. I could not tell Gibbes, and I dare not speak to Innis. Of course, monsieur, you do not need to be told that Innis is not a thief in the ordinary sense of the word. He has no need to steal, and yet apparently cannot help doing so. I am sure that no attempt has been made to pass those notes. They are doubtless resting securely in his house at Kensington. He is, in fact, a kleptomaniac, or a maniac of some sort. And now, monsieur, was my hint regarding the silver spoons of any value to you?'

'Of the most infinite value, Mr Dacre.'

'Then let me make another suggestion. I leave it entirely to your bravery; a bravery which, I confess, I do not myself possess. Will you take a hansom, drive to Mr Innis's house on the Cromwell Road, confront him quietly, and ask for the return of the packet? I am anxious to know what will happen. If he hands it to you, as I expect he will, then you must tell Mr Gibbes the whole story.'

'Mr Dacre, your suggestion shall be immediately acted upon, and I thank you for your compliment to my courage.'

I found that Mr Innis inhabited a very grand house. After a time he entered the study on the ground floor, to which I had been conducted. He held my card in his hand, and was looking at it with some surprise.

'I think I have not the pleasure of knowing you, Monsieur Valmont,' he said, courteously enough.

'No. I ventured to call on a matter of business. I was once investigator for the French Government, and now am doing private detective work here in London.'

'Ah! And how is that supposed to interest me? There is nothing that I wish investigated. I did not send for you, did I?'

'No, Mr Innis, I merely took the liberty of calling to ask you to let me have the package you took from Mr Bentham Gibbes's frock-coat pocket on the night of the twenty-third.'

'He wishes it returned, does he?'

'Yes.'

Mr Innis calmly walked to a desk, which he unlocked and opened, displaying a veritable museum of trinkets of one sort and another. Pulling out a small drawer he took from it the packet containing the five twenty-pound notes. Apparently it had never been opened. With a smile he handed it to me.

'You will make my apologies to Mr Gibbes for not returning it before. Tell him I have been unusually busy of late.'

'I shall not fail to do so,' said I, with a bow.

'Thanks so much. Good-morning, Monsieur Valmont.'

'Good-morning, Mr Innis.'

And so I returned the packet to Mr Bentham Gibbes, who pulled the notes from between their pasteboard protection, and begged me to accept them.

Sebastian Zambra

Created by Headon Hill (1857 – 1927)

IN THE 1890s and early 1900s, Francis Edward Grainger wrote a large number of crime stories under the pseudonym of 'Headon Hill' which were published in the monthly magazines of the period and later collected in book form. In many ways his most original creation was Kala Persad, an elderly Hindu sage who is brought to London by a young man named Mark Poignand. This odd couple join forces to solve crimes in the capital. However, Headon Hill's most Sherlockian character is the private detective Sebastian Zambra. Indeed, some of the Zambra stories quite blatantly 'borrow' their plots from Conan Doyle stories. None of Headon Hill's narratives is particularly original and the crimes they describe rarely need a mastermind to solve them. In many ways, however, they are typical of their period and of the crime fiction which filled so many pages of the magazines of the late Victorian and Edwardian era. And who could resist a story which, whatever its other merits, has such a memorably eye-catching title as 'The Sapient Monkey'?

The Sapient Monkey

I WOULD ADVISE every person whose duties take him into the field of 'private enquiry' to go steadily through the daily papers the first thing every morning. Personally I have found the practice most useful, for there are not many *causes célèbres* in which my services are not enlisted on one side or the other, and by this method I am always up in my main facts before I am summoned to assist. When I read the account of the proceedings at Bow Street against Franklin Gale in connection with the Tudways' bank robbery, I remember thinking that on the face of it there never was a clearer case against a misguided young man.

Condensed for the sake of brevity, the police-court report disclosed the following state of things. Franklin Gale, clerk, aged twenty-three, in the employment of Messrs. Tudways, the well-known private bankers of the Strand, was brought up on a warrant charged with stealing the sum of £500 – being the moneys of his employers. Mr James Spruce, assistant cashier at the bank, gave evidence to the effect that he missed the money from his till on the afternoon of July 22nd. On making up his cash for the day he discovered that he was short of £300 worth of notes and £200 in gold. He had no idea how the amount had been abstracted. The prisoner was an assistant bookkeeper at the bank, and had access behind the counter. Detective Sergeant Simmons said that the case had been placed in his hands for the purpose of tracing the stolen notes. He had ascertained that one of them – of the value of £5 – had been paid to Messrs. Crosthwaite & Co., tailors, of New Bond Street, on July 27th, by Franklin Gale. As a result, he had applied for a warrant, and had arrested the prisoner. The latter was remanded for a week, at the end of which period it was expected that further evidence would be forthcoming. I had hardly finished reading the report when a telegram was put into my hands demanding my immediate presence at 'Rosemount', Twickenham. From the address given, and from the name of 'Gale' appended to the despatch, I concluded that the affair at Tudways' Bank was the cause of the summons. I had little doubt that I was to be retained in the interests of the prisoner, and my surmise proved correct.

'Rosemount' was by no means the usual kind of abode from which the ordinary run of bank clerks come gaily trooping into the great City in shoals by the early trains. There was nothing of cheap gentility about the 'pleasant suburban residence standing in its own grounds of an acre', as the house-agent would say – with its lawns sloping down to the river, shaded by mulberry and chestnut trees, and plentifully garnished with the noble flower which gave it half its name. 'Rosemount' was assuredly the home either of some prosperous merchant or of a private gentleman, and when I crossed its threshold I did so quite prepared for the fuller enlightenment which was to follow. Mr Franklin Gale was evidently not one of the struggling genus bank clerk, but must be the son of well-to-do people, and not yet flown from the parent nest. When I left my office I had thought that I was bound on a forlorn hope, but at the sight of 'Rosemount' – my first real 'touch' of the case – my spirits revived. Why should a young man living amid such signs of wealth want to rob his employers? Of course I recognised that the youth of the prisoner precluded the probability of the place being his own. Had he been older, I should have reversed the argument. 'Rosemount' in the actual occupation of a middle-aged bank clerk would have been *prima-facie* evidence of a tendency to outrun the constable. I was shown into a well-appointed library, where I was received by a tall, silver-haired old gentleman of ruddy complexion, who had apparently been pacing the floor in a state of agitation. His warm greeting towards me – a perfect stranger – had the air of one who clutches at a straw.

'I have sent for you to prove my son's innocence, Mr Zambra,' he said. 'Franklin no more stole that money than I did. In the first place, he didn't want it; and, secondly, if he had been ever so pushed for cash, he would rather have cut off his right hand than put it into his employer's till. Besides, if these thick-headed policemen were bound to lock one of us up, it ought to have been me. The five-pound note with which Franklin paid his tailor was one – so he assures me, and I believe him – which I gave him myself.'

'Perhaps you would give me the facts in detail?' I replied.

'As to the robbery, both my son and I are as much in the dark as old Tudway himself,' Mr Gale proceeded. 'Franklin tells me that Spruce, the cashier, is accredited to be a most careful man, and the very last to leave his till to take care of itself. The facts that came out in evidence are perfectly true. Franklin's desk is close to the counter, and the note identified as one of the missing ones was certainly paid by him to Crosthwaite & Co., of New Bond Street, a few days after the robbery. It bears his endorsement, so there can be no doubt about that.

'So much for their side of the case. Ours is, I must confess, from a legal point of view, much weaker, and lies in my son's assertion of innocence, coupled with the knowledge of myself and his mother and his sisters that he is incapable of such a crime. Franklin insists that the note he paid to Crosthwaite & Co., the tailors, was one that I gave him on the morning of the 22nd. I remember perfectly well giving him a five-pound note at breakfast on that day, just before he left for town, so that he must have had it several hours before the robbery was committed. Franklin says that he had no other banknotes between the 22nd and the 27th, and that he cannot, therefore, be mistaken. The note which I gave him I got fresh from my own bankers a day or two before, together with some others; and here is the most unfortunate point in the case. The solicitor whom I have engaged to defend Franklin has made the necessary enquiries at my bankers, and finds that the note paid to the tailors is not one of those which I drew from the bank.'

'Did not your son take notice of the number of the note you gave him?' I asked.

'Unfortunately, no. He is too much worried about the numbers of notes at his business, he says, to note those which are his own property. He simply sticks to it that he knows it must be the same note because he had no other.'

In the slang of the day, Mr Franklin Gale's story seemed a little too thin. There was the evidence of Tudways that the note paid to the tailor was one of those stolen from them, and there was the evidence of Mr Gale, senior's, bankers that it was not one of those handed to their client. What was the use of the prisoner protesting in the face of this that he had paid his tailor with his father's present? The notes stolen from Tudways were, I remembered reading, consecutive ones of a series, so that the possibility of young Gale having at the bank changed his father's gift for another note, which was subsequently stolen, was knocked on the head. Besides, he maintained that it was the same note.

'I should like to know something of your son's circumstances and position,' I said, trying to divest the question of any air of suspicion it might have implied.

'I am glad you asked me that,' returned Mr Gale, 'for it touches the very essence of the whole case. My son's circumstances and position are such that were he the most unprincipled scoundrel in creation he would have been nothing less than an idiot to have done this thing. Franklin is not on the footing of an ordinary bank clerk, Mr Zambra. I am a rich man, and can afford to give him anything in reason, though he is too good a lad ever to have taken advantage of me. Tudway is an old friend of mine, and I got him to take Franklin into the bank with a view to a partnership. Everything was going on swimmingly towards that end; the boy had perfected himself in his duties, and made himself valuable; I was prepared to invest a certain amount of capital on his behalf; and, lastly, Tudway, who lives next door to me here, got so fond of him that he allowed Franklin to become engaged of his daughter Maud. Would any young man in his senses go and steal a paltry £500 under such circumstances as that?'

I thought not, but I did not say so yet.

'What are Mr Tudway's views about the robbery?' I asked.

'Tudway is an old fool,' replied Mr Gale. 'He believes what the police tell him, and the police tell him that Franklin is guilty. I have no patience with him. I ordered him out of this house last night. He had the audacity to come and offer not to press the charge if the boy would confess.'

'And Miss Tudway?'

'Ah! she's a brick. Maud sticks to him like a true woman. But what is the use of our sticking to him against such evidence?', broke down poor Mr Gale, impotently. 'Can you, Mr Zambra, give us a crumb of hope?'

Before I could reply there was a knock at the library door, and a tall, graceful girl entered the room. Her face bore traces of weeping, and she looked anxious and dejected; but I could see that she was naturally quick and intelligent.

'I have just run over to see if there is any fresh news this morning,' she said, with an enquiring glance at me.

'This is Mr Zambra, my dear, come to help us,' said Mr Gale; 'and this,' he continued, turning to me, 'is Miss Maud Tudway. We are all enlisted in the same cause.'

'You will be able to prove Mr Franklin Gale's innocence, sir?' she exclaimed.

'I hope so,' I said; 'and the best way to do it will be to trace the robbery to its real author. Has Mr Franklin any suspicions on that head?'

'He is as much puzzled as we,' said Miss Tudway. 'I went with Mr Gale here to see him in that horrible place yesterday, and he said there was absolutely no one in the bank he cared to suspect. But he must get off the next time he appears. My evidence ought to do that. I saw with my own eyes that he had only one £5 note in his purse on the 25th – that is two days before he paid the tailor, and three days after the robbery.'

'I am afraid that won't help us much,' I said. 'You see, he might easily have had the missing notes elsewhere. But tell me, under what circumstances did you see the £5 note?'

'There was a garden party at our house,' replied Miss Tudway, 'and Franklin was there. During the afternoon a man came to the gate with an accordion and a performing monkey, and asked permission to show the monkey's tricks. We had the man in, and after the monkey had done a lot of clever things the man said that the animal could tell a good banknote from a "flash" one. He was provided with spurious notes for the purpose; would any gentlemen lend him a good note for a minute, just to show the trick? The man was quite close to Franklin, who was sitting next to me. Franklin, seeing the man's hand held out towards him, took out his purse and handed him a note, at the same time calling my attention to the fact that it was his only one, and laughingly saying that he hoped the man was honest. The sham note and the good one were placed before the monkey, who at once tore up the bad note and handed the good one back to Franklin.'

'This is more important than it seems,' I said, after a moment's review of the whole case. 'I must find that man with the monkey, but it bids fair to be difficult. There must be so many of them in that line of business.'

Miss Tudway smiled for the first time during the interview. She said. 'I go in for amateur photography, and I thought that the man and his monkey made such a good "subject" that I insisted on taking him before he left. Shall I fetch the photograph?'

'By all means,' I said. 'Photography is of the greatest use to me in my work. I generally arrange it myself, but if you have chanced to take the right picture for me in this case so much the better.'

Miss Tudway hurried across to her father's house and quickly returned with the photograph. It was a fair effort for an amateur, and portrayed an individual of the usual seedy stamp, equipped with a huge accordion and a small monkey secured by a string. With this in my hand it would only be a matter of time before I found the itinerant juggler who had presented himself at the Tudways' garden party, and I took my leave of old Mr Gale and Miss Maud in a much more hopeful frame of mind. Every circumstance outside the terrible array of actual evidence pointed to my client's innocence, and if this evidence had been manufactured for the purpose, I felt certain that the 'monkey man' had had a hand in it.

On arriving at my office I summoned one of my assistants – a veteran of doubtful antecedents – who owns to no other name than 'Old Jemmy'. Old Jemmy's particular line of business is a thorough knowledge of the slums and the folk who dwell there; and I knew that after an hour or two on Saffron Hill my ferret, armed with the photograph, would bring me the information I wanted. Towards evening Old Jemmy came in with his report, to the effect that the 'party' I was after was to be found in the top attic of 7 Little Didman's Fields, Hatton Garden, just recovering from the effects of a prolonged spree.

'He's been drunk for three or four days, the landlord told me,' Old Jemmy said. 'Had a stroke of luck, it seems, but he is expected to go on tramp tomorrow, now his coin has given out. His name is Pietro Schilizzi.'

I knew I was on the right scent now, and that the 'monkey man' had been made the instrument of changing the note which Franklin Gale had lent him for one of the stolen ones. A quick cab took me to Little Didman's Fields in a quarter of an hour, and I was soon standing inside the doorway of a pestilential apartment on the top floor of No. 7, which had been pointed out to me as the abode of Pietro Schilizzi. A succession of snores from a heap of rags in a corner told me the whereabouts of the occupier. I went over, and shaking him roughly by the shoulder, said in Italian:

'Pietro, I want you to tell me about that little juggle with the banknote at Twickenham the other day. You will be well rewarded.'

The fellow rubbed his eyes in half-drunken astonishment, but there certainly was no guilty fear about him as he replied:

'Certainly, signor; anything for money. There was nothing wrong about the note, was there? Anyhow, I acted innocently in the matter.'

'No one finds fault with you,' I said; 'but see, here is a five-pound note. It shall be yours if you will tell me exactly what happened.'

'I was with my monkey up at Highgate the other evening,' Mr Schilizzi began, 'and was showing Jacko's trick of telling a good note from a bad one. It was a small house in the Napier Road. After I had finished, the gentleman took me into a public house and stood me a drink. He wanted me to do something for him, he said. He had a young friend who was careless, and never took the number of notes, and he wanted to teach him a lesson. He had a bet about the number of a note, he said. Would I go down to Twickenham next day to a house he described, where there was to be a party, and do my trick with the monkey? I was to borrow a note from the young gentleman, and then, instead of giving him back his own note after the performance, I was to substitute one which the Highgate gentleman gave me for the purpose. He met me at Twickenham next day, and came behind the garden wall to point out the young gentleman to me. I managed it just as the Highgate gentleman wanted, and he gave me a couple of pounds for my pains. I have done no wrong; the note I gave back was a good one.'

'Yes,' I said, 'but it happens to have been stolen. Put on your hat and show me where this man lives in Highgate.'

The Napier Road was a shabby street of dingy houses, with a public house at the corner. Pietro stopped about half-way down the row and pointed out No. 21.

'That is where the gentleman lives,' he said.

We retraced our steps to the corner public house.

'Can you tell me who lives at No. 21?' I asked of the landlord, who happened to be in the bar.

'Certainly,' was the answer; 'it is Mr James Spruce – a good customer of mine, and the best billiard player hereabouts. He is a cashier at Messrs. Tudways' bank, in the Strand, I believe.'

It all came out at the trial – not of Franklin Gale, but of James Spruce, the fraudulent cashier. Spruce had himself abstracted the notes and gold entrusted to him, and his guilty conscience telling him that he might be suspected, he had cast about for a means of throwing suspicion on some other person. Chancing to witness the performance of Pietro's monkey, he had grasped the opportunity for foisting one of the stolen notes on Franklin Gale, knowing that sooner or later it would be traced to him. The other notes he had intended to hold over till it was safe to send them out of the country; but the gold was the principal object of his theft.

Mr Tudway, the banker, was, I hear, so cut up about the false accusation that he had made against his favourite that he insisted on Franklin joining him as a partner at once, and the marriage is to take place before very long. I am also told that the photograph of the 'monkey man', handsomely enlarged and mounted, will form one of the mural decorations of the young couple.

Carnacki the Ghost Finder

Created by William Hope Hodgson (1877 – 1918)

REMEMBERED TODAY CHIEFLY for pioneering horror novels such as *The House on the Borderland*, William Hope Hodgson was born in Essex, the son of a clergyman and he had worked as a merchant seaman, as the owner of a School of Physical Culture and as a public lecturer before his first short story appeared in *The Royal Magazine* in 1904. He published dozens of other stories in a variety of genres, as well as several novels, over the next fourteen years. Hope Hodgson served in the Royal Artillery in the First World War and he was killed in action in April 1918. The Carnacki stories, about a Sherlockian investigator of supernatural events, first appeared in magazines such as *The Idler* in the years between 1910 and 1912 and were collected in book form in 1913. Most of the stories are formulaic and depend for their effects on the reader's willingness to accept the existence of entities of unspeakable evil forever lurking in dark corners of old houses and waiting to scare the living daylights out of the ghost finder and his associates. 'The Horse of the Invisible' is different. There is an intriguing ambiguity to this particular story. Is the threat in it really supernatural or is a villain entirely of this world making use of ghostly legends for his own purposes? Are both natural and supernatural forces at work? Hope Hodgson never allows us to be certain one way or the other.

The Horse of the Invisible

I HAD THAT afternoon received an invitation from Carnacki. When I reached his place I found him sitting alone. As I came into the room he rose with a perceptibly stiff movement and extended his left hand. His face seemed to be badly scarred and bruised and his right hand was bandaged. He shook hands and offered me his paper, which I refused. Then he passed me a handful of photographs and returned to his reading.

Now, that is just Carnacki. Not a word had come from him and not a question from me. He would tell us all about it later. I spent about half an hour looking at the photographs which were chiefly 'snaps' (some by flashlight) of an extraordinarily pretty girl; though in some of the photographs it was wonderful that her prettiness was so evident for so frightened and startled was her expression that it was difficult not to believe that she had been photographed in the presence of some imminent and overwhelming danger.

The bulk of the photographs were of interiors of different rooms and passages and in every one the girl might be seen, either full length in the distance or closer, with perhaps little more than a hand or arm or portion of the head or dress included in the photograph. All of these had evidently been taken with some definite aim that did not have for its first purpose the picturing of the girl, but obviously of her surroundings and they made me very curious, as you can imagine.

Near the bottom of the pile, however, I came upon something definitely extraordinary. It was a photograph of the girl standing abrupt and clear in the great blaze of a flashlight, as was plain to be seen. Her face was turned a little upward as if she had been frightened suddenly by some noise. Directly above her, as though half-formed and coming down out of the shadows, was the shape of a single enormous hoof.

I examined this photograph for a long time without understanding it more than that it had probably to do with some queer case in which Carnacki was interested. When Jessop, Arkright and Taylor came in Carnacki quietly held out his hand for the photographs which I returned in the same spirit and afterwards we all went in to dinner. When we had spent a quiet hour at the table we pulled our chairs round and made ourselves snug and Carnacki began:

'I've been North,' he said, speaking slowly and painfully between puffs at his pipe. 'Up to Hisgins of East Lancashire. It has been a pretty strange business all round, as I fancy you chaps will think, when I have finished. I knew before I went, something about the "horse story", as I have heard it called; but I never thought of it coming my way, somehow. Also I know now that I never considered it seriously – in spite of my rule always to keep an open mind. Funny creatures, we humans!

'Well, I got a wire asking for an appointment, which of course told me that there was some trouble. On the date I fixed old Captain Hisgins himself came up to see me. He told me a great many new details about the horse story; though naturally I had always known the main points and understood that if the first child were a girl, that girl would be haunted by the Horse during her courtship.

'It is, as you can see already, an extraordinary story and though I have always known about it, I have never thought it to be anything more than an old-time legend, as I have already hinted. You see, for seven generations the Hisgins family have had men children for their first-born and even the Hisgins themselves have long considered the tale to be little more than a myth.

'To come to the present, the eldest child of the reigning family is a girl and she has been often teased and warned in jest by her friends and relations that she is the first girl to be the eldest for seven generations and that she would have to keep her men friends at arm's length or go into a nunnery if she hoped to escape the haunting. And this, I think, shows us how thoroughly the tale had grown to be considered as nothing worthy of the least serious thought. Don't you think so?

'Two months ago Miss Hisgins became engaged to Beaumont, a young naval officer, and on the evening of the very day of the engagement, before it was even formally announced, a most extraordinary thing happened which resulted in Captain Hisgins making the appointment and my ultimately going down to their place to look into the thing.

'From the old family records and papers that were entrusted to me I found that there could be no possible doubt that prior to something like a hundred and fifty years ago there were some very extraordinary and disagreeable coincidences, to put the thing in the least emotional way. In the whole of the two centuries prior to that date there were five first-born girls out of a total of seven generations of the family. Each of these girls grew up to maidenhood and each became engaged, and each one died during the period of engagement, two by suicide, one by falling from a window, one from a "broken heart" (presumably heart failure, owing to sudden shock through fright). The fifth girl was killed one evening in the park round the house; but just how, there seemed to be no exact knowledge; only that there was an impression that she had been kicked by a horse. She was dead when found.

'Now, you see, all of these deaths might be attributed in a way – even the suicides – to natural causes, I mean as distinct from supernatural. You see? Yet, in every case the maidens had undoubtedly suffered some extraordinary and terrifying experiences during their various courtships for in all of the records there was mention either of the neighing of an unseen horse or of the sounds of an invisible horse galloping, as well as many other peculiar and quite inexplicable manifestations. You begin to understand now, I think, just how extraordinary a business it was that I was asked to look into.

'I gathered from one account that the haunting of the girls was so constant and horrible that two of the girls' lovers fairly ran away from their lady-loves. And I think it was this, more than anything else, that made me feel that there had been something more in it than a mere succession of uncomfortable coincidences.

'I got hold of these facts before I had been many hours in the house and after this I went pretty carefully into the details of the thing that happened on the night of Miss Hisgins' engagement to Beaumont. It seems that as the two of them were going through the big lower corridor, just after dusk and before the lamps had been lighted, there had been a sudden, horrible neighing in the corridor, close to them. Immediately afterward Beaumont received a tremendous blow or kick which broke his right forearm. Then the rest of the family and the servants came running to know what was wrong. Lights were brought and the corridor and, afterwards, the whole house searched, but nothing unusual was found.

'You can imagine the excitement in the house and the half incredulous, half believing talk about the old legend. Then, later, in the middle of the night the old Captain was waked by the sound of a great horse galloping round and round the house.

'Several times after this both Beaumont and the girl said that they had heard the sounds of hoofs near to them after dusk, in several of the rooms and corridors.

'Three nights later Beaumont was waked by a strange neighing in the night-time seeming to come from the direction of his sweetheart's bedroom. He ran hurriedly for her father and the two of them raced to her room. They found her awake and ill with sheer terror, having been awakened by the neighing, seemingly close to her bed.

'The night before I arrived, there had been a fresh happening and they were all in a frightfully nervy state, as you can imagine.

'I spent most of the first day, as I have hinted, in getting hold of details; but after dinner I slacked off and played billiards all the evening with Beaumont and Miss Hisgins. We stopped about ten o'clock and had coffee and I got Beaumont to give me full particulars about the thing that had happened the evening before.

'He and Miss Hisgins had been sitting quietly in her aunt's boudoir whilst the old lady chaperoned them, behind a book. It was growing dusk and the lamp was at her end of the table. The rest of the house was not yet lit as the evening had come earlier than usual.

'Well, it seems that the door into the hall was open and suddenly the girl said: "H'sh! what's that?"

'They both listened and then Beaumont heard it – the sound of a horse outside of the front door.

'"Your father?" he suggested, but she reminded him that her father was not riding.

'Of course they were both ready to feel queer, as you can suppose, but Beaumont made an effort to shake this off and went into the hall to see whether anyone was at the entrance. It was pretty dark in the hall and he could see the glass panels of the inner draught-door, clear-cut in the darkness of the hall. He walked over to the glass and looked through into the drive beyond, but there was nothing in sight.

'He felt nervous and puzzled and opened the inner door and went out on to the carriage-circle. Almost directly afterward the great hall door swung to with a crash behind him. He told me that he had a sudden awful feeling of having been trapped in some way – that is how he put it. He whirled round and gripped the door handle, but something seemed to be holding it with a vast grip on the other side. Then, before he could be fixed in his mind that this was so, he was able to turn the handle and open the door.

'He paused a moment in the doorway and peered into the hall, for he had hardly steadied his mind sufficiently to know whether he was really frightened or not. Then he heard his sweetheart blow him a kiss out of the greyness of the big, unlit hall and he knew that she had followed him from the boudoir. He blew her a kiss back and stepped inside the doorway, meaning to go to her. And then, suddenly, in a flash of sickening knowledge he knew that it was not his sweetheart who had blown him that kiss. He knew that something was trying to tempt him alone into the darkness and that the girl had never left the boudoir. He jumped back and in the same instant of time he heard the kiss again, nearer to him. He called out at the top of his voice: "Mary, stay in the boudoir. Don't move out of the boudoir until I come to you." He heard her call something in reply from the boudoir and then he had struck a clump of a dozen or so matches and was holding them above his head and looking round the hall. There was no one in it, but even as the matches burned out there came the sounds of a great horse galloping down the empty drive.

'Now you see, both he and the girl had heard the sounds of the horse galloping; but when I questioned more closely I found that the aunt had heard nothing, though it is true she is a bit deaf, and she was further back in the room. Of course, both he and Miss Hisgins had been in an extremely nervous state and ready to hear anything. The door might have been slammed by a sudden puff of wind owing to some inner door being opened; and as for the grip on the handle, that may have been nothing more than the sneck catching.

'With regard to the kisses and the sounds of the horse galloping, I pointed out that these might have seemed ordinary enough sounds, if they had been only cool enough to reason. As I told him, and as he knew, the sounds of a horse galloping carry a long way on the wind so that what he had heard might have been nothing more than a horse being ridden some distance away. And as for the kiss, plenty of quiet noises – the rustle of a paper or a leaf – have a somewhat similar sound, especially if one is in an overstrung condition and imagining things.

'I finished preaching this little sermon on common-sense versus hysteria as we put out the lights and left the billiard room. But neither Beaumont nor Miss Hisgins would agree that there had been any fancy on their parts.

'We had come out of the billiard room by this time and were going along the passage and I was still doing my best to make both of them see the ordinary, commonplace possibilities of the happening, when what killed my pig, as the saying goes, was the sound of a hoof in the dark billiard room we had just left.

'I felt the "creep" come on me in a flash, up my spine and over the back of my head. Miss Hisgins whooped like a child with the whooping-cough and ran up the passage, giving little gasping screams. Beaumont, however, ripped round on his heels and jumped back a couple of yards. I gave back too, a bit, as you can understand.

'"There it is," he said in a low, breathless voice. "Perhaps you'll believe now."

'"There's certainly something," I whispered, never taking my gaze off the closed door of the billiard room.

'"H'sh!" he muttered. "There it is again."

'There was a sound like a great horse pacing round and round the billiard room with slow, deliberate steps. A horrible cold fright took me so that it seemed impossible to take a full breath, you know the feeling, and then I saw we must have been walking backwards for we found ourselves suddenly at the opening of the long passage.

'We stopped there and listened. The sounds went on steadily with a horrible sort of deliberateness, as if the brute were taking a sort of malicious gusto in walking about all over the room which we had just occupied. Do you understand just what I mean?

'Then there was a pause and a long time of absolute quiet except for an excited whispering from some of the people down in the big hall. The sound came plainly up the wide stairway. I fancy they were gathered round Miss Hisgins, with some notion of protecting her.

'I should think Beaumont and I stood there, at the end of the passage for about five minutes, listening for any noise in the billiard room. Then I realised what a horrible funk I was in and I said to him: "I'm going to see what's there."

'"So'm I," he answered. He was pretty white, but he had heaps of pluck. I told him to wait one instant and I made a dash into my bedroom and got my camera and flashlight. I slipped my revolver into my right-hand pocket and a knuckle-duster over my left fist, where it was ready and yet would not stop me from being able to work my flashlight.

'Then I ran back to Beaumont. He held out his hand to show me that he had his pistol and I nodded, but whispered to him not to be too quick to shoot, as there might be some silly practical joking at work, after all. He had got a lamp from a bracket in the upper hall which he was holding in the crook of his damaged arm, so that we had a good light. Then we went down the passage towards the billiard room and you can imagine that we were a pretty nervous couple.

'All this time there had not been a sound, but abruptly when we were within perhaps a couple of yards of the door we heard the sudden clumping of a hoof on the solid parquet floor of the billiard room. In the instant afterward it seemed to me that the whole place shook beneath the ponderous hoof falls of some huge thing, coming towards the door. Both Beaumont and I gave back a pace or two, and then realised and hung on to our courage, as you might say, and waited. The great tread came right up to the door and then stopped and there was an instant of absolute silence, except that so far as I was concerned, the pulsing in my throat and temples almost deafened me.

'I dare say we waited quite half a minute and then came the further restless clumping of a great hoof. Immediately afterward the sounds came right on as if some invisible thing passed through the closed door and the ponderous tread was upon us. We jumped, each of us, to our side of the passage and I know that I spread myself stiff against the wall. The clungk clunck, clungk clunck, of the great hoof falls passed right between us and slowly and with deadly deliberateness, down the passage. I heard them through a haze of blood-beats in my ears and temples and my body was extraordinarily rigid and pringling and I was horribly breathless. I stood for a little time like this, my head turned so that I could see up the passage. I was conscious only that there was a hideous danger abroad. Do you understand?

'And then, suddenly, my pluck came back to me. I was aware that the noise of the hoof-beats sounded near the other end of the passage. I twisted quickly and got my camera to bear and snapped off the flashlight. Immediately afterward, Beaumont let fly a storm of shots down the passage and began to run, shouting: "It's after Mary. Run! Run!"

'He rushed down the passage and I after him. We came out on the main landing and heard the sound of a hoof on the stairs and after that, nothing. And from thence onward, nothing.

'Down below us in the big hall I could see a number of the household round Miss Hisgins, who seemed to have fainted and there were several of the servants clumped together a little way off, staring up at the main landing and no one saying a single word. And about some twenty steps up the stairs was old Captain Hisgins with a drawn sword in his hand where he had halted, just below the last hoof-sound. I think I never saw anything finer than the old man standing there between his daughter and that infernal thing.

'I daresay you can understand the queer feeling of horror I had at passing that place on the stairs where the sounds had ceased. It was as if the monster were still standing there, invisible. And the peculiar thing was that we never heard another sound of the hoof, either up or down the stairs.

'After they had taken Miss Hisgins to her room I sent word that I should follow, so soon as they were ready for me. And presently, when a message came to tell me that I could come any time, I asked her father to give me a hand with my instrument box and between us we carried it into the girl's bedroom. I had the bed pulled well out into the middle of the room, after which I erected the electric pentacle round the bed.

'Then I directed that lamps should be placed round the room, but that on no account must any light be made within the pentacle;

neither must anyone pass in or out. The girl's mother I had placed within the pentacle and directed that her maid should sit without, ready to carry any message so as to make sure that Mrs Hisgins did not have to leave the pentacle. I suggested also that the girl's father should stay the night in the room and that he had better be armed.

'When I left the bedroom I found Beaumont waiting outside the door in a miserable state of anxiety. I told him what I had done and explained to him that Miss Hisgins was probably perfectly safe within the "protection"; but that in addition to her father remaining the night in the room, I intended to stand guard at the door. I told him that I should like him to keep me company, for I knew that he could never sleep, feeling as he did, and I should not be sorry to have a companion. Also, I wanted to have him under my own observation, for there was no doubt but that he was actually in greater danger in some ways than the girl. At least, that was my opinion and is still, as I think you will agree later.

'I asked him whether he would object to my drawing a pentacle round him for the night and got him to agree, but I saw that he did not know whether to be superstitious about it or to regard it more as a piece of foolish mumming; but he took it seriously enough when I gave him some particulars about the Black Veil case, when young Aster died. You remember, he said it was a piece of silly superstition and stayed outside. Poor devil!

'The night passed quietly enough until a little while before dawn when we both heard the sounds of a great horse galloping round and round the house just as old Captain Hisgins had described it. You can imagine how queer it made me feel and directly afterward, I heard someone stir within the bedroom. I knocked at the door, for I was uneasy, and the Captain came. I asked whether everything was right; to which he replied yes, and immediately asked me whether I had heard the galloping, so that I knew he had heard them also. I suggested that it might be well to leave the bedroom door open a little until the dawn came in, as there was certainly something abroad. This was done and he went back into the room, to be near his wife and daughter.

'I had better say here that I was doubtful whether there was any value in the "Defense" about Miss Hisgins, for what I term the "personal-sounds" of the manifestation were so extraordinarily material that I was inclined to parallel the case with that one of Harford's where the hand of the child kept materialising within the pentacle and patting the floor. As you will remember, that was a hideous business.

'Yet, as it chanced, nothing further happened and so soon as daylight had fully come we all went off to bed.

'Beaumont knocked me up about midday and I went down and made breakfast into lunch. Miss Hisgins was there and seemed in very fair spirits, considering. She told me that I had made her feel almost safe for the first time for days. She told me also that her cousin, Harry Parsket, was coming down from London and she knew that he would do anything to help fight the ghost. And after that she and Beaumont went out into the grounds to have a little time together.

'I had a walk in the grounds myself and went round the house, but saw no traces of hoof-marks and after that I spent the rest of the day making an examination of the house, but found nothing.

'I made an end of my search before dark and went to my room to dress for dinner. When I got down the cousin had just arrived and I found him one of the nicest men I have met for a long time. A chap with a tremendous amount of pluck, and the particular kind of man I like to have with me in a bad case like the one I was on.

'I could see that what puzzled him most was our belief in the genuineness of the haunting and I found myself almost wanting something to happen, just to show him how true it was. As it chanced, something did happen, with a vengeance.

'Beaumont and Miss Hisgins had gone out for a stroll just before the dusk and Captain Hisgins asked me to come into his study for a short chat whilst Parsket went upstairs with his traps, for he had no man with him.

'I had a long conversation with the old Captain in which I pointed out that the "haunting" had evidently no particular connection with the house, but only with the girl herself and that the sooner she was married, the better as it would give Beaumont a right to be with her at all times and further than this, it might be that the manifestations would cease if the marriage were actually performed.

'The old man nodded agreement to this, especially to the first part and reminded me that three of the girls who were said to have been "haunted" had been sent away from home and met their deaths whilst away. And then in the midst of our talk there came a pretty frightening interruption, for all at once the old butler rushed into the room, most extraordinarily pale:

"'Miss Mary, sir! Miss Mary, sir!" he gasped. "She's screaming...out in the Park, sir! And they say they can hear the Horse – "

'The Captain made one dive for a rack of arms and snatched down his old sword and ran out, drawing it as he ran. I dashed out and up the stairs, snatched my camera-flashlight and a heavy revolver, gave one yell at Parsket's door: "The Horse!" and was down and into the grounds.

'Away in the darkness there was a confused shouting and I caught the sounds of shooting, out among the scattered trees. And then, from a patch of blackness to my left, there burst suddenly an infernal gobbling sort of neighing. Instantly I whipped round and snapped off the flashlight. The great light blazed out momentarily, showing me the leaves of a big tree close at hand, quivering in the night breeze, but I saw nothing else and then the ten-fold blackness came down upon me and I heard Parsket shouting a little way back to know whether I had seen anything.

'The next instant he was beside me and I felt safer for his company, for there was some incredible thing near to us and I was momentarily blind because of the brightness of the flashlight. "What was it? What was it?" he kept repeating in an excited voice. And all the time I was staring into the darkness and answering, mechanically, "I don't know. I don't know."

'There was a burst of shouting somewhere ahead and then a shot. We ran towards the sounds, yelling to the people not to shoot; for in the darkness and panic there was this danger also. Then there came two of the game-keepers racing hard up the drive with their lanterns and guns; and immediately afterward a row of lights dancing towards us from the house, carried by some of the men-servants.

'As the lights came up I saw we had come close to Beaumont. He was standing over Miss Hisgins and he had his revolver in his hand. Then I saw his face and there was a great wound across his forehead. By him was the Captain, turning his naked sword this way and that, and peering into the darkness; a little behind him stood the old butler, a battle-axe from one of the arm-stands in the hall in his hands. Yet there was nothing strange to be seen anywhere.

'We got the girl into the house and left her with her mother and Beaumont, whilst a groom rode for a doctor. And then the rest of us, with four other keepers, all armed with guns and carrying lanterns, searched round the homepark. But we found nothing.

'When we got back we found that the doctor had been. He had bound up Beaumont's wound, which luckily was not deep, and ordered Miss Hisgins straight to bed. I went upstairs with the Captain and found Beaumont on guard outside of the girl's door. I asked him how he felt and then, so soon as the girl and her mother were ready for us, Captain Hisgins and I went into the bedroom and fixed the pentacle again round the bed. They had already got lamps about the room and after I had set the same order of watching as on the previous night, I joined Beaumont outside of the door.

'Parsket had come up while I had been in the bedroom and between us we got some idea from Beaumont as to what had happened out in the Park. It seems that they were coming home after their stroll from the direction of the West Lodge. It had got quite dark and suddenly Miss Hisgins said: "Hush!" and came to a standstill. He stopped and listened, but heard nothing for a little. Then he caught it – the sound of a horse, seemingly a long way off, galloping towards them over the grass. He told the girl that it was nothing and started to hurry her towards the house, but she was not deceived, of course. In less than a minute they heard it quite close to them in the darkness and they started running. Then Miss Hisgins caught her foot and fell. She began to scream and that is what the butler heard. As Beaumont lifted the girl he heard the hoofs come thudding right at him. He stood over her and fired all five chambers of his revolver right at the sounds. He told us that he was sure he saw something that looked like an enormous horse's head, right upon him in the light of the last flash of his pistol. Immediately afterwards he was struck a tremendous blow which knocked him down and then the Captain and the butler came running up, shouting. The rest, of course, we knew.

'About ten o'clock the butler brought us up a tray, for which I was very glad, as the night before I had got rather hungry. I warned Beaumont, however, to be very particular not to drink any spirits and I also made him give me his pipe and matches. At midnight I drew a pentacle round him and Parsket and I sat one on each side of him, outside the pentacle, for I had no fear that there would be any manifestation made against anyone except Beaumont or Miss Hisgins.

'After that we kept pretty quiet. The passage was lit by a big lamp at each end so that we had plenty of light and we were all armed, Beaumont and I with revolvers and Parsket with a shot-gun. In addition to my weapon I had my camera and flashlight.

'Now and again we talked in whispers and twice the Captain came out of the bedroom to have a word with us. About half past one we had all grown very silent and suddenly, about twenty minutes later, I held up my hand, silently, for there seemed to be a sound of galloping out in the night. I knocked on the bedroom door for the Captain to open it and when he came I whispered to him that we thought we heard the Horse. For some time we stayed listening, and both Parsket and the Captain thought they heard it; but now I was not so sure, neither was Beaumont. Yet afterwards, I thought I heard it again.

'I told Captain Hisgins I thought he had better go into the bedroom and leave the door a little open and this he did. But from that time onward we heard nothing and presently the dawn came in and we all went very thankfully to bed.

'When I was called at lunch-time I had a little surprise, for Captain Hisgins told me that they had held a family council and had decided to take my advice and have the marriage without a day's more delay than possible. Beaumont was already on his way to London to get a special license and they hoped to have the wedding next day.

'This pleased me, for it seemed the sanest thing to be done in the extraordinary circumstances and meanwhile I should continue my investigations; but until the marriage was accomplished, my chief thought was to keep Miss Hisgins near to me.

'After lunch I thought I would take a few experimental photographs of Miss Hisgins and her surroundings. Sometimes the camera sees things that would seem very strange to normal human eyesight.

'With this intention and partly to make an excuse to keep her in my company as much as possible, I asked Miss Hisgins to join me in my experiments. She seemed glad to do this and I spent several hours with her, wandering all over the house, from room to room and whenever the impulse came I took a flashlight of her and the room or corridor in which we chanced to be at the moment.

'After we had gone right through the house in this fashion, I asked her whether she felt sufficiently brave to repeat the experiments in the cellars. She said yes, and so I rooted out Captain Hisgins and Parsket, for I was not going to take her even into what you might call artificial darkness without help and companionship at hand.

'When we were ready we went down into the wine cellar, Captain Hisgins carrying a shot-gun and Parsket a specially prepared background and a lantern. I got the girl to stand in the middle of the cellar whilst Parsket and the Captain held out the background behind her. Then I fired off the flashlight, and we went into the next cellar where we repeated the experiment.

'Then in the third cellar, a tremendous, pitch-dark place, something extraordinary and horrible manifested itself. I had stationed Miss Hisgins in the centre of the place, with her father and Parsket holding the background as before. When all was ready and just as I pressed the trigger of the "flash", there came in the cellar that dreadful, gobbling neighing that I had heard out in the Park. It seemed to come from somewhere above the girl and in the glare of the sudden light I saw that she was staring tensely upward, but at no visible thing. And then in the succeeding comparative darkness, I was shouting to the Captain and Parsket to run Miss Hisgins out into the daylight.

'This was done instantly and I shut and locked the door afterwards making the First and Eighth signs of the Saaamaaa Ritual opposite to each post and connecting them across the threshold with a triple line.

'In the meanwhile Parsket and Captain Hisgins carried the girl to her mother and left her there, in a half-fainting condition whilst I stayed on guard outside of the cellar door, feeling pretty horrible for I knew that there was some disgusting thing inside, and along with this feeling there was a sense of half-ashamedness, rather miserable, you know, because I had exposed Miss Hisgins to the danger.

'I had got the Captain's shot-gun and when he and Parsket came down again they were each carrying guns and lanterns. I could not possibly tell you the utter relief of spirit and body that came to me when I heard them coming, but just try to imagine what it was like, standing outside of that cellar. Can you?

'I remember noticing, just before I went to unlock the door, how white and ghastly Parsket looked and the old Captain was grey-looking and I wondered whether my face was like theirs. And this, you know, had its own distinct effect upon my nerves, for it seemed to bring the beastliness of the thing bash down on to me in a fresh way. I know it was only sheer will power that carried me up to the door and made me turn the key.

'I paused one little moment and then with a nervy jerk sent the door wide open and held my lantern over my head. Parsket and the Captain came one on each side of me and held up their lanterns, but the place was absolutely empty. Of course, I did not trust to a casual look of this kind, but spent several hours with the help of the two others in sounding every square foot of the floor, ceiling and walls.

'Yet, in the end I had to admit that the place itself was absolutely normal and so we came away. But I sealed the door and outside, opposite each door-post I made the First and Last signs of the Saaamaaa Ritual, joined them as before, with a triple line. Can you imagine what it was like, searching that cellar?

'When we got upstairs I inquired very anxiously how Miss Hisgins was and the girl came out herself to tell me that she was all right and that I was not to trouble about her, or blame myself, as I told her I had been doing.

'I felt happier then and went off to dress for dinner and after that was done, Parsket and I took one of the bathrooms to develop the negatives that I had been taking. Yet none of the plates had anything to tell us until we came to the one that was taken in the cellar. Parsket was developing and I had taken a batch of the fixed plates out into the lamplight to examine them.

'I had just gone carefully through the lot when I heard a shout from Parsket and when I ran to him he was looking at a partly-developed negative which he was holding up to the red lamp. It showed the girl plainly, looking upward as I had seen her, but the thing that astonished me was the shadow of an enormous hoof, right above her, as if it were coming down upon her out of the shadows. And you know, I had run her bang into that danger. That was the thought that was chief in my mind.

'As soon as the developing was complete I fixed the plate and examined it carefully in a good light. There was no doubt about it at all, the thing above Miss Hisgins was an enormous, shadowy hoof. Yet I was no nearer to coming to any definite knowledge and the only thing I could do was to warn Parsket to say nothing about it to the girl for it would only increase her fright, but I showed the thing to her father for I considered it right that he should know.

'That night we took the same precaution for Miss Hisgins' safety as on the two previous nights and Parsket kept me company; yet the dawn came in without anything unusual having happened and I went off to bed.

'When I got down to lunch I learnt that Beaumont had wired to say that he would be in soon after four; also that a message had been sent to the Rector. And it was generally plain that the ladies of the house were in a tremendous fluster.

'Beaumont's train was late and he did not get home until five, but even then the Rector had not put in an appearance and the butler came in to say that the coachman had returned without him as he had been called away unexpectedly. Twice more during the evening the carriage was sent down, but the clergyman had not returned and we had to delay the marriage until the next day.

'That night I arranged the "Defense" round the girl's bed and the Captain and his wife sat up with her as before. Beaumont, as I expected, insisted on keeping watch with me and he seemed in a curiously frightened mood; not for himself, you know, but for Miss Hisgins. He had a horrible feeling he told me, that there would be a final, dreadful attempt on his sweetheart that night.

'This, of course, I told him was nothing but nerves; yet really, it made me feel very anxious; for I have seen too much not to know that under such circumstances a premonitory conviction of impending danger is not necessarily to be put down entirely to nerves. In fact, Beaumont was so simply and earnestly convinced that the night would bring some extraordinary manifestation that I got Parsket to rig up a long cord from the wire of the butler's bell, to come along the passage handy.

'To the butler himself I gave directions not to undress and to give the same order to two of the footmen. If I rang he was to come instantly, with the footmen, carrying lanterns and the lanterns were to be kept ready lit all night. If for any reason the bell did not ring and I blew my whistle, he was to take that as a signal in the place of the bell.

'After I had arranged all these minor details I drew a pentacle about Beaumont and warned him very particularly to stay within it, whatever happened. And when this was done, there was nothing to do but wait and pray that the night would go as quietly as the night before.

'We scarcely talked at all and by about one a.m. we were all very tense and nervous so that at last Parsket got up and began to walk up and down the corridor to steady himself a bit. Presently I slipped off my pumps and joined him and we walked up and down, whispering occasionally for something over an hour, until in turning I caught my foot in the bell-cord and went down on my face; but without hurting myself or making a noise.

'When I got up Parsket nudged me.

'"Did you notice that the bell never rang?" he whispered.

'"Jove!" I said, "you're right."

'"Wait a minute," he answered. "I'll bet it's only a kink somewhere in the cord." He left his gun and slipped along the passage and taking the top lamp, tiptoed away into the house, carrying Beaumont's revolver ready in his right hand. He was a plucky chap, I remember thinking then, and again, later.

'Just then Beaumont motioned to me for absolute quiet. Directly afterwards I heard the thing for which he listened – the sound of a horse galloping, out in the night. I think that I may say I fairly shivered. The sound died away and left a horrible, desolate, eerie feeling in the air, you know. I put my hand out to the bell-cord, hoping Parsket had got it clear. Then I waited, glancing before and behind.

'Perhaps two minutes passed, full of what seemed like an almost unearthly quiet. And then, suddenly, down the corridor at the lighted end there sounded the clumping of a great hoof and instantly the lamp was thrown with a tremendous crash and we were in the dark. I tugged hard on the cord and blew the whistle; then I raised my snapshot and fired the flashlight. The corridor blazed into brilliant light, but there was nothing, and then the darkness fell like thunder. I heard the Captain at the bedroom-door and shouted to him to bring out a lamp, quick; but instead something started to kick the door and I heard the Captain shouting within the bedroom and then the screaming of the women. I had a sudden horrible fear that the monster had got into the bedroom, but in the same instant from up the corridor there came abruptly the vile, gobbling neighing that we had heard in the park and the cellar. I blew the whistle again and groped blindly for the bell-cord, shouting to Beaumont to stay in the Pentacle, whatever happened. I yelled again to the Captain to bring out a lamp and there came a smashing sound against the bedroom door. Then I had my matches in my hand, to get some light before that incredible, unseen Monster was upon us.

'The match scraped on the box and flared up dully and in the same instant I heard a faint sound behind me. I whipped round in a kind of mad terror and saw something in the light of the match – a monstrous horse-head close to Beaumont.

'"Look out, Beaumont!" I shouted in a sort of scream. "It's behind you!"

'The match went out abruptly and instantly there came the huge bang of Parsket's double-barrel (both barrels at once), fired evidently single-handed by Beaumont close to my ear, as it seemed. I caught a momentary glimpse of the great head in the flash and of an enormous hoof amid the belch of fire and smoke seeming to be descending upon Beaumont. In the same instant I fired three chambers of my revolver. There was the sound of a dull blow and then that horrible, gobbling neigh broke out close to me. I fired twice at the sound. Immediately afterward something struck me and I was knocked backwards. I got on to my knees and shouted for help at the top of my voice. I heard the women screaming behind the closed door of the bedroom and was dully aware that the door was being smashed from the inside, and directly afterwards I knew that Beaumont was struggling with some hideous thing near to me. For an instant I held back, stupidly, paralysed with funk and then, blindly and in a sort of rigid chill of goose-flesh I went to help him, shouting his name. I can tell you, I was nearly sick with the naked fear I had on me. There came a little, choking scream out of the darkness, and at that I jumped forward into the dark. I gripped a vast, furry ear. Then something struck me another great blow knocking me sick. I hit back, weak and blind and gripped with my other hand at the incredible thing. Abruptly I was dimly aware of a tremendous crash behind me and a great burst of light. There were other lights in the passage and a noise of feet and shouting. My hand-grips were torn from the thing they held; I shut my eyes stupidly and heard a loud yell above me and then a heavy blow, like a butcher chopping meat and then something fell upon me.

'I was helped to my knees by the Captain and the butler. On the floor lay an enormous horse-head out of which protruded a man's trunk and legs. On the wrists were fixed great hoofs. It was the monster. The Captain cut something with the sword that he held in his hand and stooped and lifted off the mask, for that is what it was. I saw the face then of the man who had worn it. It was Parsket. He had a bad wound across the forehead where the Captain's sword had bit through the mask. I looked bewilderedly from him to Beaumont, who was sitting up, leaning against the wall of the corridor. Then I stared at Parsket again.

'"By Jove!" I said at last, and then I was quiet for I was so ashamed for the man. You can understand, can't you? And he was opening his eyes. And you know, I had grown so to like him.

'And then, you know, just as Parsket was getting back his wits and looking from one to the other of us and beginning to remember, there happened a strange and incredible thing. For from the end of the corridor there sounded suddenly, the clumping of a great hoof. I looked that way and then instantly at Parsket and saw a horrible fear in his face and eyes. He wrenched himself round, weakly, and stared in mad terror up the corridor to where the sound had been, and the rest of us stared, in a frozen group. I remember vaguely half sobs and whispers from Miss Hisgins' bedroom, all the while that I stared frightenedly up the corridor.

'The silence lasted several seconds and then, abruptly there came again the clumping of the great hoof, away at the end of the corridor. And immediately afterward the clungk, clunck-clungk, clunck of mighty hoofs coming down the passage towards us.

'Even then, you know, most of us thought it was some mechanism of Parsket's still at work and we were in the queerest mixture of fright and doubt. I think everyone looked at Parsket. And suddenly the Captain shouted out:

'"Stop this damned fooling at once. Haven't you done enough?"

'For my part, I was now frightened for I had a sense that there was something horrible and wrong. And then Parsket managed to gasp out:

'"It's not me! My God! It's not me! My God! It's not me."

'And then, you know, it seemed to come home to everyone in an instant that there was really some dreadful thing coming down the passage. There was a mad rush to get away and even old Captain Hisgins gave back with the butler and the footmen. Beaumont fainted outright, as I found afterwards, for he had been badly mauled. I just flattened back against the wall, kneeling as I was, too stupid and dazed even to run. And almost in the same instant the ponderous hoof-falls sounded close to me and seeming to shake the solid floor as they passed. Abruptly the great sounds ceased and I knew in a sort of sick fashion that the thing had halted opposite to the door of the girl's bedroom. And then I was aware that Parsket was standing rocking in the doorway with his arms spread across, so as to fill the doorway with his body. Parsket was extraordinarily pale and the blood was running down his face from the wound in his forehead; and then I noticed that he seemed to be looking at something in the passage with a peculiar, desperate, fixed, incredibly masterful gaze. But there was really nothing to be seen. And suddenly the clungk, clunck-clungk, clunck recommenced and passed onward down the passage. In the same moment Parsket pitched forward out of the doorway on to his face.

'There were shouts from the huddle of men down the passage and the two footmen and the butler simply ran, carrying their lanterns, but the Captain went against the side-wall with his back and put the lamp he was carrying over his head. The dull tread of the Horse went past him, and left him unharmed and I heard the monstrous hoof-falls going away and away through the quiet house and after that a dead silence.

'Then the Captain moved and came towards us, very slow and shaky and with an extraordinarily grey face.

'I crept towards Parsket and the Captain came to help me. We turned him over and, you know, I knew in a moment that he was dead; but you can imagine what a feeling it sent through me.

'I looked at the Captain and suddenly he said:

'"That – That – That – " and I know that he was trying to tell me that Parsket had stood between his daughter and whatever it was that had gone down the passage. I stood up and steadied him, though I was not very steady myself. And suddenly his face began to work and he went down on to his knees by Parsket and cried like some shaken child. Then the women came out of the doorway of the bedroom and I turned away and left him to them, whilst I went over to Beaumont.

'That is practically the whole story and the only thing that is left to me is to try to explain some of the puzzling parts, here and there.

'Perhaps you have seen that Parsket was in love with Miss Hisgins and this fact is the key to a good deal that was extraordinary. He was doubtless responsible for some portions of the "haunting"; in fact I think for nearly everything, but, you know, I can prove nothing and what I have to tell you is chiefly the result of deduction.

'In the first place, it is obvious that Parsket's intention was to frighten Beaumont away and when he found that he could not do this, I think he grew so desperate that he really intended to kill him. I hate to say this, but the facts force me to think so.

'I am quite certain that it was Parsket who broke Beaumont's arm. He knew all the details of the so-called "Horse Legend", and got the idea to work upon the old story for his own end. He evidently had some method of slipping in and out of the house, probably through one of the many French windows, or possibly he had a key to one or two of the garden doors, and when he was supposed to be away, he was really coming down on the quiet and hiding somewhere in the neighbourhood.

'The incident of the kiss in the dark hall I put down to sheer nervous imaginings on the part of Beaumont and Miss Hisgins, yet I must say that the sound of the horse outside of the front door is a little difficult to explain away. But I am still inclined to keep to my first idea on this point, that there was nothing really unnatural about it.

'The hoof sounds in the billiard-room and down the passage were done by Parsket from the floor below by bumping up against the panelled ceiling with a block of wood tied to one of the window-hooks. I proved this by an examination which showed the dents in the woodwork.

'The sounds of the horse galloping round the house were possibly made also by Parsket, who must have had a horse tied up in the plantation near by, unless, indeed, he made the sounds himself, but I do not see how he could have gone fast enough to produce the illusion. In any case, I don't feel perfect certainty on this point. I failed to find any hoof marks, as you remember.

'The gobbling neighing in the park was a ventriloquial achievement on the part of Parsket and the attack out there on Beaumont was also by him, so that when I thought he was in his bedroom, he must have been outside all the time and joined me after I ran out of the front door. This is almost probable. I mean that Parsket was the cause, for if it had been something more serious he would certainly have given up his foolishness, knowing that there was no longer any need for it. I cannot imagine how he escaped being shot, both then and in the last mad action of which I have just told you. He was enormously without fear of any kind for himself as you can see.

'The time when Parsket was with us, when we thought we heard the Horse galloping round the house, we must have been deceived. No one was very sure, except, of course, Parsket, who would naturally encourage the belief.

'The neighing in the cellar is where I consider there came the first suspicion into Parsket's mind that there was something more at work than his sham-haunting. The neighing was done by him in the same way that he did it in the park; but when I remember how ghastly he looked I feel sure that the sounds must have had some infernal quality added to them which frightened the man himself. Yet, later, he would persuade himself that he had been getting fanciful. Of course, I must not forget that the effect upon Miss Hisgins must have made him feel pretty miserable.

'Then, about the clergyman being called away, we found afterwards that it was a bogus errand, or, rather, call and it is apparent that Parsket was at the bottom of this, so as to get a few more hours in which to achieve his end and what that was, a very little imagination will show you; for he had found that Beaumont would not be frightened away. I hate to think this, but I'm bound to. Anyway, it is obvious that the man was temporarily a bit off his normal balance. Love's a queer disease!

'Then, there is no doubt at all but that Parsket left the cord to the butler's bell hitched somewhere so as to give him an excuse to slip away naturally to clear it. This also gave him the opportunity to remove one of the passage lamps. Then he had only to smash the other and the passage was in utter darkness for him to make the attempt on Beaumont.

'In the same way, it was he who locked the door of the bedroom and took the key (it was in his pocket). This prevented the Captain from bringing a light and coming to the rescue. But Captain Hisgins broke down the door with the heavy fender-curb and it was his smashing the door that sounded so confusing and frightening in the darkness of the passage.

'The photograph of the monstrous hoof above Miss Hisgins in the cellar is one of the things that I am less sure about. It might have been faked by Parsket, whilst I was out of the room, and this would have been easy enough, to anyone who knew how. But, you know, it does not look like a fake. Yet, there is as much evidence of probability that it was faked, as against; and the thing is too vague for an examination to help to a definite decision so that I will express no opinion, one way or the other. It is certainly a horrible photograph.

'And now I come to that last, dreadful thing. There has been no further manifestation of anything abnormal so that there is an extraordinary uncertainty in my conclusions. If we had not heard those last sounds and if Parsket had not shown that enormous sense of fear the whole of this case could be explained in the way in which I have shown. And, in fact, as you have seen, I am of the opinion that almost all of it can be cleared up, but I see no way of going past the thing we heard at the last and the fear that Parsket showed.

'His death – no, that proves nothing. At the inquest it was described somewhat untechnically as due to heart-spasm. That is normal enough and leaves us quite in the dark as to whether he died because he stood between the girl and some incredible thing of monstrosity.

'The look on Parsket's face and the thing he called out when he heard the great hoof-sounds coming down the passage seem to show that he had the sudden realization of what before then may have been nothing more than a horrible suspicion. And his fear and appreciation of some tremendous danger approaching was probably more keenly real even than mine. And then he did the one fine, great thing!'

'And the cause?' I said. 'What caused it?'

Carnacki shook his head.

'God knows,' he answered, with a peculiar, sincere reverence. 'If that thing was what it seemed to be one might suggest an explanation which would not offend one's reason, but which may be utterly wrong. Yet I have thought, though it would take a long lecture on Thought Induction to get you to appreciate my reasons, that Parsket had produced what I might term a kind of "induced haunting", a kind of induced simulation of his mental conceptions to his desperate thoughts and broodings. It is impossible to make it clearer in a few words.'

'But the old story!' I said. 'Why may not there have been something in that?'

'There may have been something in it,' said Carnacki. 'But I do not think it had anything to do with this. I have not clearly thought out my reasons, yet; but later I may be able to tell you why I think so.'

'And the marriage? And the cellar – was there anything found there?' asked Taylor.

'Yes, the marriage was performed that day in spite of the tragedy,' Carnacki told us. 'It was the wisest thing to do considering the things that I cannot explain. Yes, I had the floor of that big cellar up, for I had a feeling I might find something there to give me some light. But there was nothing.

'You know, the whole thing is tremendous and extraordinary. I shall never forget the look on Parsket's face. And afterwards the disgusting sounds of those great hoofs going away through the quiet house.'

Carnacki stood up:

'Out you go!' he said in friendly fashion, using the recognised formula.

And we went presently out into the quiet of the Embankment, and so to our homes.

Thorpe Hazell

Created by Victor Whitechurch (1868 – 1933)

A CLERGYMAN WHO wrote both religious books and novels with a Church of England setting, Victor Whitechurch was also a prolific author of crime fiction. His short stories appeared in many of the dozens and dozens of monthly magazines that flourished in the late Victorian and Edwardian eras, including *The Strand*, *Pearson's Magazine* and *The Royal Magazine*. Whitechurch is little known today but he had a long career as a writer which stretched from the 1890s to the 1930s. His last published fiction consisted of two novels which appeared under the famous Collins Crime Club imprint. His most notable creation is Thorpe Hazell, a prosperous eccentric with a taste for vegetarian food and first editions who is also extraordinarily knowledgeable about the railway network and is consequently called upon to investigate many of the crimes that occur on it. Hazell appeared in nine stories published between 1899 and 1905 and later collected, together with six others, in *Thrilling Stories of the Railway* (1912).

The Affair of the Corridor Express

THORPE HAZELL STOOD in his study in his London flat. On the opposite wall he had pinned a bit of paper, about an inch square, at the height of his eye, and was now going through the most extraordinary contortions.

With his eyes fixed on the paper he was craning his neck as far as it would reach and twisting his head about in all directions. This necessitated a fearful rolling of the eyes in order to keep them on the paper, and was supposed to be a means of strengthening the muscles of the eye for angular sight.

Presently there came a tap at the door.

'Come in!' cried Hazell, still whirling his head round.

'A gentleman wishes to see you at once, sir!' said the servant, handing him a card.

Hazell paused in his exercises, took it from the tray, and read:

'Mr F. W. Wingrave, M.A., B.Sc.'

'Oh, show him in,' said Hazell, rather impatiently, for he hated to be interrupted when he was doing his 'eye gymnastics'. There entered a young man of about five-and-twenty, with a look of keen anxiety on his face.

'You are Mr Thorpe Hazell?' he asked.

'I am.'

'You will have seen my name on my card – I am one of the masters at Shillington School – I had heard your name, and they told me at the station that it might be well to consult you – I hope you don't mind – I know you're not an ordinary detective, but – '

'Sit down, Mr Wingrave,' said Hazell, interrupting his nervous flow of language. 'You look quite ill and tired.'

'I have just been through a very trying experience,' replied Wingrave, sinking into a seat. 'A boy I was in charge of has just mysteriously disappeared, and I want you to find him for me, and I want to ask your opinion. They say you know all about railways, but – '

'Now, look here, my dear sir, you just have some hot toast and water before you say another word. I conclude you want to consult me on some railway matter. I'll do what I can, but I won't hear you till you've had some refreshment. Perhaps you prefer whiskey – though I don't advise it.'

Wingrave, however, chose the whiskey, and Hazell poured him out some, adding soda-water.

'Thank you,' he said. 'I hope you'll be able to give me advice. I am afraid the poor boy must be killed; the whole thing is a mystery, and I – '

'Stop a bit, Mr Wingrave. I must ask you to tell me the story from the very beginning. That's the best way.'

'Quite right. The worry of it has made me incoherent, I fear. But I'll try and do what you propose. First of all, do you know the name of Carr-Mathers?'

'Yes, I think so. Very rich, is he not?'

'A millionaire. He has only one child, a boy of about ten, whose mother died at his birth. He is a small boy for his age, and idolised by his father. About three months ago this young Horace Carr-Mathers was sent to our school – Cragsbury House, just outside Shillington. It is not a very large school, but exceedingly select, and the headmaster, Dr Spring, is well known in high-class circles. I may tell you that we have the sons of some of the leading nobility preparing for the public schools. You will readily understand that in such an establishment as ours the most scrupulous care is exercised over the boys, not only as regards their moral and intellectual training, but also to guard against any outside influences.'

'Kidnapping, for example,' interposed Hazell.

'Exactly. There have been such cases known, and Dr Spring has a very high reputation to maintain. The slightest rumour against the school would go ill with him – and with all of us masters.

'Well, this morning the headmaster received a telegram about Horace Carr-Mathers, requesting that he should be sent up to town.'

'Do you know the exact wording?' asked Hazell.

'I have it with me,' replied Wingrave, drawing it from his pocket.

Hazell took it from him, and read as follows:

'Please grant Horace leave of absence for two days. Send him to London by 5.45 express from Shillington, in first-class carriage, giving guard instructions to look after him. We will meet train in town – Carr-Mathers'

'Um,' grunted Hazell, as he handed it back. 'Well, he can afford telegrams.'

'Oh, he's always wiring about something or other,' replied Wingrave; 'he seldom writes a letter. Well, when the doctor received this he called me into his study.

'"I suppose I must let the boy go," he said, "but I'm not at all inclined to allow him to travel by himself. If anything should happen to him his father would hold us responsible as well as the railway company. So you had better take him up to town, Mr Wingrave."

'"Yes, sir."

'"You need do no more than deliver him to his father. If Mr Carr-Mathers is not at the terminus to meet him, take him with you in a cab to his house in Portland Place. You'll probably be able to catch the last train home, but, if not, you can get a bed at an hotel."

'"Very good, sir."

'So, shortly after half-past five, I found myself standing on the platform at Shillington, waiting for the London express.'

'Now, stop a moment,' interrupted Hazell, sipping a glass of filtered water which he had poured out for himself. 'I want to get a clear notion of this journey of yours from the beginning, for, I presume, you will shortly be telling me that something strange happened during it. Was there anything to be noticed before the train started?'

'Nothing at the time. But I remembered afterwards that two men seemed to be watching me rather closely when I took the tickets and I heard one of them say "Confound", beneath his breath. But my suspicions were not aroused at the moment.'

'I see. If there is anything in this it was probably because he was disconcerted when he saw you were going to travel with the boy. Did these two men get into the train?'

'I'm coming to that. The train was in sharp to time, and we took our seats in a first-class compartment.'

'Please describe the exact position.'

'Our carriage was the third from the front. It was a corridor train, with access from carriage to carriage all the way through. Horace and myself were in a compartment alone. I had bought him some illustrated papers for the journey, and for some time he sat quietly enough, looking through them. After a bit he grew fidgety, as you know boys will.'

'Wait a minute. I want to know if the corridor of your carriage was on the left or on the right – supposing you to be seated facing the engine?'

'On the left.'

'Very well, go on.'

'The door leading into the corridor stood open. It was still daylight, but dusk was setting in fast – I should say it was about half-past six, or a little more. Horace had been looking out of the window on the right side of the train when I drew his attention to Rutherham Castle, which we were passing. It stands, as you know, on the left side of the line. In order to get a better view of it he went out into the corridor and stood there. I retained my seat on the right side of the compartment, glancing at him from time to time. He seemed interested in the corridor itself, looking about him, and once or twice shutting and opening the door of our compartment. I can see now that I ought to have kept a sharper eye on him, but I never dreamed that any accident could happen. I was reading a paper myself, and became rather interested in a paragraph. It may have been seven or eight minutes before I looked up. When I did so, Horace had disappeared.

'I didn't think anything of it at first, but only concluded that he had taken a walk along the corridor.'

'You don't know which way he went?' inquired Hazell.

'No. I couldn't say. I waited a minute or two, and then rose and looked out into the corridor. There was no one there. Still my suspicions were not aroused. It was possible that he had gone to the lavatory. So I sat down again, and waited. Then I began to get a little anxious, and determined to have a look for him. I walked to either end of the corridor, and searched the lavatories, but they were both empty. Then I looked in all the other compartments of the carriage, and asked their occupants if they had seen him go by, but none of them had noticed him.'

'Do you remember how these compartments were occupied?'

'Yes. In the first, which was reserved for ladies, there were five ladies. The next was a smoker with three gentlemen in it. Ours came next. Then, going towards the front of the train, were the two men I had noticed at Shillington; the last compartment had a gentleman and lady and their three children.'

'Ah! how about those two men – what were they doing?'

'One of them was reading a book, and the other appeared to be asleep.'

'Tell me. Was the door leading to the corridor from their compartment shut?'

'Yes, it was. I was in a most terrible fright, and I went back to my compartment and pulled the electric communicator. In a few seconds the front guard came along the corridor and asked me what I wanted. I told him I had lost my charge. He suggested that the boy had walked through to another carriage, and I asked him if he would mind my making a thorough search of the train with him. To this he readily agreed. We went back to the first carriage and began to do so. We examined every compartment from end to end of the train; we looked under every seat, in spite of the protestations of some of the passengers; we searched all the lavatories – every corner of the train – and we found absolutely no trace of Horace Carr-Mathers. No one had seen the boy anywhere.'

'Had the train stopped?'

'Not for a second. It was going at full speed all the time. It only slowed down after we had finished the search – but it never quite stopped.'

'Ah! We'll come to that presently. I want to ask you some questions first. Was it still daylight?'

'Dusk, but quite light enough to see plainly – besides which, the train lamps were lit.'

'Exactly. Those two men, now, in the next compartment to yours – tell me precisely what happened when you visited them the second time with the guard.'

'They asked a lot of questions – like many of the other passengers – and seemed very surprised.'

'You looked underneath their seats?'

'Certainly.'

'On the luggage-racks? A small boy like that could be rolled up in a rug and put on the rack.'

'We examined every rack on the train.'

Thorpe Hazell lit a cigarette and smoked furiously, motioning to his companion to keep quiet. He was thinking out the situation. Suddenly he said:

'How about the window in those two men's compartment?'

'It was shut – I particularly noticed it.'

'You are quite sure you searched the whole of the train?'

'Absolutely certain; so was the guard.'

'Ah!' remarked Hazell, 'even guards are mistaken sometimes. It – er – was only the inside of the train you searched, eh?'

'Of course.'

'Very well,' replied Hazell, 'now, before we go any further, I want to ask you this. Would it have been to anyone's interest to have murdered the boy?'

'I don't think so – from what I know. I don't see how it could be.'

'Very well. We will take it as a pure case of kidnapping, and presume that he is alive and well. This ought to console you to begin with.'

'Do you think you can help me?'

'I don't know yet. But go on and tell me all that happened.'

'Well, after we had searched the train I was at my wits' end – and so was the guard. We both agreed, however, that nothing more could be done till we reached London. Somehow, my strongest suspicions concerning those two men were aroused, and I travelled in their compartment for the rest of the journey.'

'Oh! Did anything happen?'

'Nothing. They both wished me good-night, hoped I'd find the boy, got out, and drove off in a hansom.'

'And then?'

'I looked about for Mr Carr-Mathers, but he was nowhere to be seen. Then I saw an inspector, and put the case before him. He promised to make inquiries and to have the line searched on the part where I missed Horace. I took a hansom to Portland Place, only to discover that Mr Carr-Mathers is on the Continent and not expected home for a week. Then I came on to you – the inspector had advised me to do so. And that's the whole story. It's a terrible thing for me, Mr Hazell. What do you think of it?'

'Well,' replied Hazell, 'of course it's very clear that there is a distinct plot. Someone sent that telegram, knowing Mr Carr-Mathers' proclivities. The object was to kidnap the boy. It sounds absurd to talk of brigands and ransoms in this country, but the thing is done over and over again for all that. It is obvious that the boy was expected to travel alone, and that the train was the place chosen for the kidnapping. Hence the elaborate directions. I think you were quite right in suspecting those two men, and it might have been better if you had followed them up without coming to me.'

'But they went off alone!'

'Exactly. It's my belief they had originally intended doing so after disposing of Horace, and that they carried out their original intentions.'

'But what became of the boy? How did they – '

'Stop a bit, I'm not at all clear in my own mind. But you mentioned that while you were concluding your search with the guard the train slackened speed?'

'Yes. It almost came to a stop – and then went very slowly for a minute or so. I asked the guard why, but I didn't understand his reply.'

'What was it?'

'He said it was a P.W. operation.'

Hazell laughed. 'P.W. stands for permanent way,' he explained, 'I know exactly what you mean now. There is a big job going on near Longmoor – they are raising the level of the line, and the up-trains are running on temporary rails. So they have to proceed very slowly. Now it was after this that you went back to the two men whom you suspected?'

'Yes.'

'Very well. Now let me think the thing over. Have some more whiskey? You might also like to glance at the contents of my book-case. If you know anything of first editions and bindings they will interest you.'

Wingrave, it is to be feared, paid but small heed to the books, but watched Hazell anxiously as the latter smoked cigarette after cigarette, his brows knit in deep thought. After a bit he said slowly:

'You will understand that I am going to work upon the theory that the boy has been kidnapped and that the original intention has been carried out, in spite of the accident of your presence in the train. How the boy was disposed of meanwhile is what baffles me; but that is a detail – though it will be interesting to know how it was done. Now, I don't want to raise any false hopes, because I may very likely be wrong, but we are going to take action upon a very feasible assumption, and if I am at all correct, I hope to put you definitely on the track. Mind, I don't promise to do so, and, at best, I don't promise to do more than put you on a track. Let me see – it's just after nine. We have plenty of time. We'll drive first to Scotland Yard, for it will be as well to have a detective with us.'

He filled a flask with milk, put some plasmon biscuits and a banana into a sandwich case, and then ordered his servant to hail a cab.

An hour later, Hazell, Wingrave, and a man from Scotland Yard were closeted together in one of the private offices of the Mid-Eastern Railway with one of the chief officials of the line. The latter was listening attentively to Hazell.

'But I can't understand the boy not being anywhere in the train, Mr Hazell,' he said.

'I can – partly,' replied Hazell, 'but first let me see if my theory is correct.'

'By all means. There's a down-train in a few minutes. I'll go with you, for the matter is very interesting. Come along, gentlemen.'

He walked forward to the engine and gave a few instructions to the driver, and then they took their seats in the train. After a run of half an hour or so they passed a station.

'That's Longmoor,' said the official, 'now we shall soon be on the spot. It's about a mile down that the line is being raised.'

Hazell put his head out of the window. Presently an ominous red light showed itself. The train came almost to a stop, and then proceeded slowly, the man who had shown the red light changing it to green. They could see him as they passed, standing close to a little temporary hut. It was his duty to warn all approaching drivers, and for this purpose he was stationed some three hundred yards in front of the bit of line that was being operated upon. Very soon they were passing this bit. Naphtha lamps shed a weird light over a busy scene, for the work was being continued night and day. A score or so of sturdy navvies were shovelling and picking along the track.

Once more into the darkness. On the other side of the scene of operations, at the same distance, was another little hut, with a guardian for the up-train. Instead of increasing the speed in passing this hut, which would have been usual, the driver brought the train almost to a standstill. As he did so the four men got out of the carriage, jumping from the footboard to the ground. On went the train, leaving them on the left side of the down track, just opposite the little hut. They could see the man standing outside, his back partly turned to them. There was a fire in a brazier close by that dimly outlined his figure.

He started suddenly, as they crossed the line towards him.

'What are you doing here?' he cried. 'You've no business here – you're trespassing.'

He was a big, strong-looking man, and he backed a little towards his hut as he spoke.

'I am Mr Mills, the assistant-superintendent of the line,' replied the official, coming forward.

'Beg pardon, sir; but how was I to know that?' growled the man.

'Quite right. It's your duty to warn off strangers. How long have you been stationed here?'

'I came on at five o'clock; I'm regular nightwatchman, sir.'

'Ah! Pretty comfortable, eh?'

'Yes, thank you, sir,' replied the man, wondering why the question was asked, but thinking, not unnaturally, that the assistant-superintendent had come down with a party of engineers to supervise things.

'Got the hut to yourself?'

'Yes, sir.'

Without another word, Mr Mills walked to the door of the hut. The man, his face suddenly growing pale, moved, and stood with his back to it.

'It's – it's private, sir!' he growled.

Hazell laughed. 'All right, my man,' he said. 'I was right, I think – hullo! – look out! Don't let him go!'

For the man had made a quick rush forward. But the Scotland Yard officer and Hazell were on him in a moment, and a few seconds later the handcuffs clicked on his wrists. Then they flung the door open, and there, lying in the corner, gagged and bound, was Horace Carr-Mathers.

An exclamation of joy broke forth from Wingrave, as he opened his knife to cut the cords. But Hazell stopped him.

'Just half a moment,' he said: 'I want to see how they've tied him up.'

A peculiar method had been adopted in doing this. His wrists were fastened behind his back, a stout cord was round his body just under the armpits, and another cord above the knees. These were connected by a slack bit of rope.

'All right!' went on Hazell; 'let's get the poor lad out of his troubles – there, that's better. How do you feel, my boy?'

'Awfully stiff!' said Horace, 'but I'm not hurt. I say, sir,' he continued to Wingrave, 'how did you know I was here? I am glad you've come.'

'The question is how did you get here?' replied Wingrave. 'Mr Hazell, here, seemed to know where you were, but it's a puzzle to me at present.'

'If you'd come half an hour later you wouldn't have found him,' growled the man who was handcuffed. 'I ain't so much to blame as them as employed me.'

'Oh, is that how the land lies?' exclaimed Hazell. 'I see. You shall tell us presently, my boy, how it happened. Meanwhile, Mr Mills, I think we can prepare a little trap – eh?'

In five minutes all was arranged. A couple of the navvies were brought up from the line, one stationed outside to guard against trains, and with certain other instructions, the other being inside the hut with the rest of them. A third navvy was also dispatched for the police.

'How are they coming?' asked Hazell of the handcuffed man.

'They were going to take a train down from London to Rockhampstead on the East-Northern, and drive over. It's about ten miles off.'

'Good! They ought soon to be here,' replied Hazell, as he munched some biscuits and washed them down with a draught of milk, after which he astonished them all by solemnly going through one of his 'digestive exercises'.

A little later they heard the sound of wheels on a road beside the line. Then the man on watch said, in gruff tones:

'The boy's inside!'

But they found more than the boy inside, and an hour later all three conspirators were safely lodged in Longmoor gaol.

'Oh, it was awfully nasty, I can tell you,' said Horace Carr-Mathers, as he explained matters afterwards. 'I went into the corridor, you know, and was looking about at things, when all of a sudden I felt my coat-collar grasped behind, and a hand was laid over my mouth. I tried to kick and shout, but it was no go. They got me into the compartment, stuffed a handkerchief into my mouth, and tied it in. It was just beastly. Then they bound me hand and foot, and opened the window on the right-hand side – opposite the corridor. I was in a funk, for I thought they were going to throw me out, but one of them told me to keep my pecker up, as they weren't going to hurt me. Then they let me down out of the window by that slack rope, and made it fast to the handle of the door outside. It was pretty bad. There was I, hanging from the door-handle in a sort of doubled-up position, my back resting on the foot-board of the carriage, and the train rushing along like mad. I felt sick and awful, and I had to shut my eyes. I seemed to hang there for ages.'

'I told you you only examined the inside of the train,' said Thorpe Hazell to Wingrave. 'I had my suspicions that he was somewhere on the outside all the time, but I was puzzled to know where. It was a clever trick.'

'Well,' went on the boy, 'I heard the window open above me after a bit. I looked up and saw one of the men taking the rope off the handle. The train was just beginning to slow down. Then he hung out of the window, dangling me with one hand. It was horrible. I was hanging below the footboard now. Then the train came almost to a stop, and someone caught me round the waist. I lost my senses for a minute or two, and then I found myself lying in the hut.'

'Well, Mr Hazell,' said the assistant-superintendent, 'you were perfectly right, and we all owe you a debt of gratitude.'

'Oh,' said Hazell, 'it was only a guess at the best. I presumed it was simply kidnapping, and the problem to be solved was how and where the boy was got off the train without injury. It was obvious that he had been disposed of before the train reached London. There was only one other inference. The man on duty was evidently the confederate, for, if not, his presence would have stopped the whole plan of action. I'm very glad to have been of any use. There are interesting points about the case, and it has been a pleasure to me to undertake it.'

A little while afterwards Mr Carr-Mathers himself called on Hazell to thank him.

'I should like,' he said, 'to express my deep gratitude substantially; but I understand you are not an ordinary detective. But is there any way in which I can serve you, Mr Hazell?'

'Yes – two ways.'

'Please name them.'

'I should be sorry for Mr Wingrave to get into trouble through this affair – or Dr Spring either.'

'I understand you, Mr Hazell. They were both to blame, in a way. But I will see that Dr Spring's reputation does not suffer, and that Wingrave comes out of it harmlessly.'

'Thank you very much.'

'You said there was a second way in which I could serve you.'

'So there is. At Dunn's sale last month you were the purchaser of two first editions of *The New Bath Guide*. If you cared to dispose of one, I – '

'Say no more, Mr Hazell. I shall be glad to give you one for your collection.'

Hazell stiffened.

'You misunderstand me!' he exclaimed icily. 'I was about to add that if you cared to dispose of a copy I would write you out a cheque.'

'Oh, certainly,' replied Mr Carr-Mathers with a smile, 'I shall be extremely pleased.'

Whereupon the transaction was concluded.

Mr Barnes and Mr Mitchel

Created by Rodrigues Ottolengui (1861 – 1937)

BORN IN CHARLESTON, South Carolina in the year the American Civil War began, Ottolengui moved to New York in his teens to study dentistry and remained there for the rest of his life. When he died in 1937, most of his obituaries concentrated on his career as a pioneering dentist (he was one of the first practitioners in America to make use of X-rays) and on his status as an amateur entomologist who had become one of the world's leading experts on a particular family of moths. Few made much of the crime fiction he had published in the 1890s but Ottolengui's novels and (particularly) short stories featuring the professional detective Mr Barnes and the wealthy amateur Mr Mitchel are well worth reading. 'The Azteck Opal', originally published in *The Idler* in April 1895, is probably the best of them all.

The Azteck Opal

'MR MITCHEL,' BEGAN Mr Barnes, the detective, after exchanging greetings, 'I have called to see you upon a subject which I am sure will enlist your keenest interest, for several reasons. It relates to a magnificent jewel; it concerns your intimate friends; and it is a problem requiring the most analytical qualities of the mind in its solution.'

'Ah! Then you have solved it?' asked Mr Mitchel.

'I think so. You shall judge. I have today been called in to investigate one of the most singular cases that has fallen in my way. It is one in which the usual detective methods would be utterly valueless. The facts were presented to me, and the solution of the mystery could only be reached by analytical deduction.'

'That is to say, by using your brains?'

'Precisely! Now, you have admitted that you consider yourself more expert in this direction than the ordinary detective. I wish to place you for once in the position of a detective, and then see you prove your ability.

'Early this morning I was summoned, by a messenger, to go aboard of the steam yacht *Idler*, which lay at anchor in the lower bay.'

'Why, the *Idler* belongs to my friend Mortimer Gray,' exclaimed Mr Mitchel.

'Yes!' replied Mr Barnes. 'I told you that your friends are interested. I went immediately with the man who had come to my office, and in due season I was aboard of the yacht. Mr Gray received me very politely, and took me to his private room adjoining the cabin. Here he explained to me that he had been off on a cruise for a few weeks, and was approaching the harbour last night, when, in accordance with his plans, a sumptuous dinner was served, as a sort of farewell feast, the party expecting to separate today.'

'What guests were on the yacht?'

'I will tell you everything in order, as the facts were presented to me. Mr Gray enumerated the party as follows. Besides himself and his wife, there were his wife's sister, Mrs Eugene Cortlandt, and her husband, a Wall Street broker. Also, Mr Arthur Livingstone, and his sister, and a Mr Dermett Moore, a young man supposed to be devoting himself to Miss Livingstone.'

'That makes seven persons, three of whom are women. I ought to say, Mr Barnes, that, though Mr Gray is a club friend, I am not personally acquainted with his wife, nor with the others. So I have no advantage over you.'

'I will come at once to the curious incident which made my presence desirable. According to Mr Gray's story, the dinner had proceeded as far as the roast, when suddenly there was a slight shock as the yacht touched, and at the same time the lamps spluttered and then went out, leaving the room totally dark. A second later the vessel righted herself and sped on, so that before any panic ensued, it was evident to all that the danger had passed. The gentlemen begged the ladies to resume their seats, and remain quiet until the lamps were lighted; this, however, the attendants were unable to do, and they were ordered to bring fresh lamps. Thus there was almost total darkness for several minutes.'

'During which, I presume, the person who planned the affair readily consummated his design?'

'So you think that the whole series of events was pre-arranged? Be that as it may, something did happen in that dark room. The women had started from their seats when the yacht touched, and when they groped their way back in the darkness some of them found the wrong places, as was seen when the fresh lamps were brought. This was considered a good joke, and there was some laughter, which was suddenly checked by an exclamation from Mr Gray, who quickly asked his wife, "Where is your opal?"'

'Her opal?' asked Mr Mitchel, in tones which showed that his greatest interest was now aroused. 'Do you mean, Mr Barnes, that she was wearing the Azteck opal?'

'Oh! You know the gem?'

'I know nearly all gems of great value; but what of this one?'

'Mrs Gray and her sister, Mrs Cortlandt, had both donned décolleté costumes for this occasion, and Mrs Gray had worn this opal as a pendant to a thin gold chain which hung round her neck. At Mr Gray's question, all looked towards his wife, and it was noted that the clasp was open, and the opal missing. Of course it was supposed that it had merely fallen to the floor, and a search was immediately instituted. But the opal could not be found.'

'That is certainly a very significant fact,' said Mr Mitchel. 'But was the search thorough?'

'I should say extremely thorough, when we consider it was not conducted by a detective, who is supposed to be an expert in such matters. Mr Gray described to me what was done, and he seems to have taken every precaution. He sent the attendants out of the salon, and he and his guests systematically examined every part of the room.'

'Except the place where the opal really was concealed, you mean.'

'With that exception, of course, since they did not find the jewel. Not satisfied with this search by lamplight, Mr Gray locked the salon, so that no one could enter it during the night, and another investigation was made in the morning.'

'The pockets of the seven persons present were not examined, I presume?'

'No! I asked Mr Gray why this had been omitted, and he said that it was an indignity which he could not possibly show to a guest. As you have asked this question, Mr Mitchel, it is only fair for me to tell you that when I spoke to Mr Gray on the subject he seemed very much confused. Nevertheless, however unwilling he may have been to search those of his guests who are innocent, he emphatically told me that if I had reasonable proof that any one present had purloined the opal, he wished that individual to be treated as any other thief, without regard to sex or social position.'

'One can scarcely blame him, because that opal was worth a fabulous sum. I have myself offered Gray twenty-five thousand dollars for it, which was refused. This opal is one of the eyes of an Azteck Idol, and if the other could be found, the two would be as interesting as any jewels in the world.'

'That is the story which I was asked to unravel,' continued Mr Barnes, 'and I must now relate to you what steps I have taken towards that end. It appears that, because of the loss of the jewels, no person has left the yacht, although no restraint was placed upon any one by Mr Gray. All knew, however, that he had sent for a detective, and it was natural that no one should offer to go until formally dismissed by the host. My plan, then, was to have a private interview with each of the seven persons who had been present at the dinner.'

'Then you exempted the attendants from your suspicions?'

'I did. There was but one way by which one of the servants could have stolen the opal, and this was prevented by Mr Gray. It was possible that the opal had fallen on the floor, and, though not found at night, a servant might have discovered and have appropriated it on the following morning, had he been able to enter the salon. But Mr Gray had locked the doors. No servant, however bold, would have been able to take the opal from the lady's neck.'

'I think your reasoning is good, and we will confine ourselves to the original seven.'

'After my interview with Mr Gray, I asked to have Mrs Gray sent in to me. She came in, and at once I noted that she placed herself on the defensive. Women frequently adopt that manner with a detective. Her story was very brief. The main point was that she was aware of the theft before the lamps were relighted. In fact, she felt some one's arms steal around her neck, and knew when the opal was taken. I asked why she had made no outcry, and whether she suspected any special person. To these questions she replied that she supposed it was merely a joke perpetrated in the darkness, and therefore had made no resistance. She would not name any one as suspected by her, but she was willing to tell me that the arms were bare, as she detected when they touched her neck. I must say here, that although Miss Livingstone's dress was not cut low in the neck, it was, practically, sleeveless; and Mrs Cortlandt's dress had no sleeves at all. One other significant statement made by this lady was that her husband had mentioned to her your offer of twenty-five thousand dollars for the opal, and had urged her to permit him to sell it, but she had refused.'

'So! It was Madam that would not sell. The plot thickens!'

'You will observe, of course, the point about the naked arms of the thief. I therefore sent for Mrs Cortlandt next. She had a curious story to tell. Unlike her sister, she was quite willing to express her suspicions. Indeed, she plainly intimated that she supposed that Mr Gray himself had taken the jewel. I will endeavour to repeat her words:

'"Mr Barnes," said she, "the affair is very simple. Gray is a miserable old skinflint. A Mr Mitchel, a crank who collects gems, offered to buy that opal, and he has been bothering my sister for it ever since. When the lamps went out, he took the opportunity to steal it. I do not think this, I know it. How? Well, on account of the confusion and darkness, I sat in my sister's seat when I returned to the table. This explains his mistake, but he put his arms round my neck, and deliberately felt for the opal. I did not understand his purpose at the time, but now it is very evident."

'"Yes, madam," said I, "but how do you know it was Mr Gray?"

'"Why, I grabbed his hand, and before he could pull it away I felt the large cameo ring on his little finger. Oh! there is no doubt whatever."

'I asked her whether Mr Gray had his sleeves rolled up, and though she could not understand the purport of the question, she said "No". Next I had Miss Livingstone come in. She is a slight, tremulous young lady, who cries at the slightest provocation. During the interview, brief as it was, it was only by the greatest diplomacy that I avoided a scene of hysterics. She tried very hard to convince me that she knew absolutely nothing. She had not left her seat during the disturbance; of that she was sure. So how could she know anything about it? I asked her to name the one whom she thought might have taken the opal, and at this her agitation reached such a climax that I was obliged to let her go.'

'You gained very little from her I should say.'

'In a case of this kind, Mr Mitchel, where the criminal is surely one of a very few persons, we cannot fail to gain something from each person's story. A significant feature here was that though Miss Livingstone assures us that she did not leave her seat, she was sitting in a different place when the lamps were lighted again.'

'That might mean anything or nothing.'

'Exactly! but we are not deducing values yet. Mr Dermett Moore came to me next, and he is a straightforward, honest man if I ever saw one. He declared that the whole affair was a great mystery to him, and that, while ordinarily he would not care anything about it, he could not but be somewhat interested because he thought that one of the ladies, he would not say which one, suspected him. Mr Livingstone also impressed me favourably in spite of the fact that he did not remove his cigarette from his mouth throughout the whole of my interview with him. He declined to name the person suspected by him, though he admitted that he could do so. He made this significant remark:

'"You are a detective of experience, Mr Barnes, and ought to be able to decide which man amongst us could place his arms around Mrs Gray's neck without causing her to cry out. But if your imagination fails you, suppose you enquire into the financial standing of all of us, and see which one would be most likely to profit by thieving? Ask Mr Cortlandt."'

'Evidently Mr Livingstone knows more than he tells.'

'Yet he told enough for one to guess his suspicions, and to understand the delicacy which prompted him to say no more. He, however, gave me a good point upon which to question Mr Cortlandt. When I asked that gentleman if any of the men happened to be in pecuniary difficulties, he became grave at once. I will give you his answer.

'"Mr Livingstone and Mr Moore are both exceedingly wealthy men, and I am a millionaire, in very satisfactory business circumstances at present. But I am very sorry to say, that though our host, Mr Gray, is also a distinctly rich man, he has met with some reverses recently, and I can conceive that ready money would be useful to him. But for all that, it is preposterous to believe what your question evidently indicates. None of the persons in this party is a thief, and least of all could we suspect Mr Gray. I am sure that if he wished his wife's opal, she would give it to him cheerily. No, Mr Barnes, the opal is in some crack, or crevice, which we have overlooked. It is lost, not stolen."'

'That ended the interviews with the several persons present, but I made one or two other enquiries, from which I elicited at least two significant facts. First, it was Mr Gray himself who had indicated the course by which the yacht was steered last night, and which ran her over a sand-bar. Second, someone had nearly emptied the oil from the lamps, so that they would have burned out in a short time, even though the yacht had not touched.'

'These, then, are your facts? And from these you have solved the problem? Well, Mr Barnes, who stole the opal?'

'Mr Mitchel, I have told you all I know, but I wish you to work out a solution before I reveal my own opinion.'

'I have already done so, Mr Barnes. Here! I will write my suspicion on a bit of paper. So! Now tell me yours, and you shall know mine afterwards.'

'Why, to my mind it is very simple. Mr Gray, failing to obtain the opal from his wife by fair means, resorted to a trick. He removed the oil from the lamps, and charted out a course for his yacht which would take her over a sand-bar, and when the opportune moment came he stole the jewel. His actions since then have been merely to cover his crime, by shrouding the affair with mystery. By insisting upon a thorough search, and even sending for a detective, he makes it impossible for those who were present to accuse him hereafter. Undoubtedly Mr Cortlandt's opinion will be the one generally adopted. Now what do you think?'

'I think I will go with you at once, and board the yacht *Idler*.'

'But you have not told me whom you suspect,' said Mr Barnes, somewhat irritated.

'Oh! That's immaterial,' said Mr Mitchel, calmly preparing for the street. 'I do not suspect Mr Gray, so if you are correct you will have shown better ability than I. Come! Let us hurry!'

On their way to the dock, from which they were to take the little steam launch which was waiting to carry the detective back to the yacht, Mr Barnes asked Mr Mitchel the following questions:

'Mr Mitchel,' said he, 'you will note that Mrs Cortlandt alluded to you as a "crank who collects gems". I must admit that I have myself harboured a great curiosity as to your reasons for purchasing jewels, which are valued beyond a mere conservative commercial price. Would you mind explaining why you began your collection?'

'I seldom explain my motives to others, especially when they relate to my more important pursuits in life. But in view of all that has passed between us, I think your curiosity justifiable, and I will gratify it. To begin with, I am a very wealthy man. I inherited great riches, and I have made a fortune myself. Have you any conception of the difficulties which harass a man of means?'

'Perhaps not in minute detail, though I can guess that the lot of the rich is not as free from care as the pauper thinks it is.'

'The point is this: the difficulty with a poor man is to get rich, while with the rich man the greatest trouble is to prevent the increase of his wealth. Some men, of course, make no effort in that direction, and those men are a menace to society. My own idea of the proper use of a fortune is to manage it for the benefit of others, as well as one's self, and especially to prevent its increase.'

'And is it so difficult to do this? Cannot money be spent without limit?'

'Yes; but unlimited evil follows such a course. This is sufficient to indicate to you that I am ever in search of a legitimate means of spending my income, provided that I may do good thereby. If I can do this, and at the same time afford myself pleasure, I claim that I am making the best use of my money. Now I happen to be so constructed, that the most interesting studies to me are social problems, and of these I am most entertained with the causes and environments of crime. Such a problem as the one you brought to me today is of immense attractiveness to me, because the environment is one which is commonly supposed to preclude rather than to invite crime. Yet we have seen that despite the wealth of all concerned, someone has stooped to the commonest of crimes – theft.'

'But what has this to do with your collection of jewels?'

'Everything! Jewels – especially those of great magnitude – seem to be a special cause of crime. A hundred-carat diamond will tempt a man to theft, as surely as the false beacon on a rocky shore entices the mariner to wreck and ruin. All the great jewels of the world have murder and crime woven into their histories. My attention was first called to this by accidentally overhearing a plot in a ballroom to rob the lady of the house of a large ruby which she wore on her breast. I went to her, taking the privilege of an intimate friend, and told her enough to persuade her to sell the stone to me. I fastened it into my scarf, and then sought the presence of the plotters, allowing them to see what had occurred. No words passed between us, but by my act I prevented a crime that night.'

'Then am I to understand that you buy jewels with that end in view?'

'After that night I conceived this idea. If all the great jewels in the world could be collected together, and put in a place of safety, hundreds of crimes would be prevented, even before they had been conceived. Moreover, the search for, and acquirement of, these jewels would necessarily afford me abundant opportunity for studying the crimes which are perpetrated in order to gain possession of them. Thus you understand more thoroughly why I am anxious to pursue this problem of the Azteck opal.'

Several hours later Mr Mitchel and Mr Barnes were sitting at a quiet table in the corner of the dining-room at Mr Mitchel's club. On board the yacht Mr Mitchel had acted rather mysteriously. He had been closeted a while with Mr Gray, after which he had had an interview with two or three of the others. Then when Mr Barnes had begun to feel neglected, and tired of waiting alone on deck, Mr Mitchel had come towards him, arm-in-arm with Mr Gray, and the latter said:

'I am very much obliged to you, Mr Barnes, for your services in this affair, and I trust the enclosed cheque will remunerate you for your trouble.'

Mr Barnes, not quite comprehending it all, had attempted to protest, but Mr Mitchel had taken him by the arm, and hurried him off. In the cab which bore them to the club the detective asked for an explanation, but Mr Mitchel only replied:

'I am too hungry to talk now. We will have dinner first.'

The dinner was over at last, and nuts and coffee were before them, when Mr Mitchel took a small parcel from his pocket, and handed it to Mr Barnes, saying:

'It is a beauty, is it not?'

Mr Barnes removed the tissue paper, and a large opal fell on the tablecloth, where it sparkled with a thousand colours under the electric lamps.

'Do you mean that this is – ,' cried the detective.

'The Azteck opal, and the finest harlequin I ever saw,' interrupted Mr Mitchel. 'But you wish to know how it came into my possession? Principally so that it may join the collection and cease to be a temptation to this world of wickedness.'

'Then Mr Gray did not steal it?' asked Mr Barnes, with a touch of chagrin in his voice.

'No, Mr Barnes! Mr Gray did not steal it. But you are not to consider yourself very much at fault. Mr Gray tried to steal it, only he failed. That was not your fault, of course. You read his actions aright, but you did not give enough weight to the stories of the others.'

'What important point did I omit from my calculation?'

'I might mention the bare arms which Mrs Gray said she felt round her neck. It was evidently Mr Gray who looked for the opal on the neck of his sister-in-law, but as he did not bare his arms, he would not have done so later.'

'Do you mean that Miss Livingstone was the thief?'

'No! Miss Livingstone being hysterical, she changed her seat without realizing it, but that does not make her a thief. Her excitement when with you was due to her suspicions, which, by the way, were correct. But let us return for a moment to the bare arms. That was the clue from which I worked. It was evident to me that the thief was a man, and it was equally plain that in the hurry of the few moments of darkness, no man would have rolled up his sleeves, risking the return of the attendants with lamps, and the consequent discovery of himself in such a singular disarrangement of costume.'

'How do you account for the bare arms?'

'The lady did not tell the truth, that is all. The arms which encircled her neck were not bare. Neither were they unknown to her. She told you that lie to shield the thief. She also told you that her husband wished to sell the Azteck opal to me, but that she had refused. Thus she deftly led you to suspect him. Now, if she wished to shield the thief, yet was willing to accuse her husband, it followed that the husband was not the thief.'

'Very well reasoned, Mr Mitchel. I see now where you are tending, but I shall not get ahead of your story.'

'So much I had deduced, before we went on board the yacht. When I found myself alone with Gray I candidly told him of your suspicions, and your reasons for harbouring them. He was very much disturbed, and pleadingly asked me what I thought. As frankly I told him that I believed that he had tried to take the opal from his wife – we can scarcely call it stealing since the law does not – but that I believed he had failed. He then confessed; admitted emptying the lamps, but denied running the boat on the sand-bar. But he assured me that he had not reached his wife's chair when the lamps were brought in. He was, therefore, much astonished at missing the gem. I promised him to find the jewel upon condition that he would sell it to me. To this he most willingly acceded.'

'But how could you be sure that you would recover the opal?'

'Partly by my knowledge of human nature, and partly because of my inherent faith in my own abilities. I sent for Mrs Gray, and noted her attitude of defence, which, however, only satisfied me the more that I was right in my suspicions. I began by asking her if she knew the origin of the superstition that an opal brings bad luck to its owner. She did not, of course, comprehend my tactics, but she added that she "had heard the stupid superstition, but took no interest in such nonsense". I then gravely explained to her that the opal is the engagement stone of the Orient. The lover gives it to his sweetheart, and the belief is that should she deceive him even in the most trifling manner, the opal will lose its brilliancy and become cloudy. I then suddenly asked her if she had ever noted a change in her opal. "What do you mean to insinuate?" she cried out angrily. "I mean," said I, sternly, "that if an opal has changed colour in accordance with the superstition this one should have done so. I mean that though your husband greatly needs the money which I have offered him you have refused to allow him to sell it, and yet you have permitted another to take it from you tonight. By this act you might have seriously injured if not ruined Mr Gray. Why have you done it?"'

'How did she receive it?' asked Mr Barnes, admiring the ingenuity of Mr Mitchel.

'She began to sob, and between her tears she admitted that the opal had been taken by the man I suspected, but she earnestly declared that she had harboured no idea of injuring her husband. Indeed, she was so agitated in speaking upon this point, that I believe that Gray never thoroughly explained to her why he wished to sell the gem. She urged me to recover the opal if possible, and purchase it, so that her husband might be relieved from his pecuniary embarrassment. I then sent for the thief, Mrs Gray told me his name; but would you not like to hear how I had picked him out before we went aboard? I still have that bit of paper upon which I wrote his name, in confirmation of what I say.'

'Of course, I know now that you mean Mr Livingstone, but would like to hear your reasons for suspecting him.'

'From your account Miss Livingstone suspected some one, and this caused her to be so agitated that she was unaware of the fact that she had changed her seat. Women are shrewd in these affairs, and I was confident that the girl had good reason for her conduct. It was evident that the person in her mind was either her brother or her sweetheart. I decided between these two men from your account of your interviews with them. Moore impressed you as being honest, and he told you that one of the ladies suspected him. In this he was mistaken, but his speaking to you of it was not the act of a thief. Mr Livingstone, on the other hand, tried to throw suspicion upon Mr Gray.'

'Of course that was sound reasoning after you had concluded that Mrs Gray was lying. Now tell me how you recovered the jewel?'

'That was easier than I expected. I simply told Mr Livingstone when I got him alone, what I knew, and asked him to hand me the opal. With a perfectly imperturbable manner, understanding that I promised secrecy, he quietly took it from his pocket and gave it to me, saying:

'"Women are very poor conspirators. They are too weak."'

'What story did you tell Mr Gray?'

'Oh, he would not be likely to enquire too closely into what I should tell him. My cheque was what he most cared for. I told him nothing definitely, but I inferred that his wife had secreted the gem during the darkness, that he might not ask her for it again; and that she had intended to find it again at a future time, just as he had meant to pawn it and then pretend to recover it from the thief by offering a reward.'

'One more question. Why did Mr Livingstone steal it?'

'Ah! The truth about that is another mystery worth probing, and one which I shall make it my business to unravel. I will venture two prophecies. First – Mr Livingstone did not steal it at all. Mrs Gray simply handed it to him in the darkness. There must have been some powerful motive to lead her to such an act; something which she was weighing, and decided impulsively. This brings me to the second point. Livingstone used the word conspirator, which is a clue. You will recall what I told you that this gem is one of a pair of opals, and that with the other, the two would be as interesting as any jewels in the world. I am confident now that Mr Livingstone knows where that other opal is, and that he has been urging Mrs Gray to give or lend him hers, as a means of obtaining the other. If she hoped to do this, it would be easy to understand why she refused to permit the sale of the one she had. This, of course, is guesswork, but I'll promise that if any one ever owns both it shall be your humble servant, Leroy Mitchel, jewel collector.'

Klimo

Created by Guy Boothby (1867 – 1905)

GUY BOOTHBY WAS born in South Australia, came to England with his mother and brothers to attend school in the West Country and then returned to his native land to work as a clerk in Adelaide. His earliest ambitions were directed towards the theatre and he wrote plays and opera libretti which were performed but attracted little attention. His first successes came with a travel book, about his journeys in South-East Asia and Australia, and with his debut novel, *In Strange Company*, published in 1894. Moving back to England, Boothby became one of the most productive and most financially successful novelists of his time. In the decade before his death of pneumonia at the age of only thirty-seven, he published nearly fifty books. His most popular creation was Dr Nikola, a Mephistophelean supercriminal who appeared in five books, but he also wrote stories featuring an array of other rogues, detectives and private investigators. Klimo, likened to Sherlock Holmes in the first paragraph of 'The Duchess of Wiltshire's Diamonds', has been described as an 'anti-detective'. Certainly the story, first published in *Pearson's Magazine* in February 1897, is one of the most unusual crime tales of its period and Klimo one of the most memorable characters.

The Duchess of Wiltshire's Diamonds

To THE REFLECTIVE mind the rapidity with which the inhabitants of the world's greatest city seize upon a new name or idea and familiarise themselves with it, can scarcely prove otherwise than astonishing. As an illustration of my meaning let me take the case of Klimo – the now famous private detective, who has won for himself the right to be considered as great as Lecocq, or even the late lamented Sherlock Holmes.

Up to a certain morning London had never even heard his name, nor had it the remotest notion as to who or what he might be. It was as sublimely ignorant and careless on the subject as the inhabitants of Kamtchaika or Peru. Within twenty-four hours, however, the whole aspect of the case was changed. The man, woman, or child who had not seen his posters, or heard his name, was counted an ignoramus unworthy of intercourse with human beings.

Princes became familiar with it as their trains tore them to Windsor to luncheon with the Queen; the nobility noticed and commented upon it as they drove about the town: merchants, and business men generally, read it as they made their ways by omnibus and Underground, to their various shops and counting-houses; street boys called each other by it as a nickname; music hall artistes introduced it into their patter, while it was even rumoured that the Stock Exchange itself had paused in the full flood tide of business to manufacture a riddle on the subject.

That Klimo made his profession pay him well was certain, first from the fact that his advertisements must have cost a good round sum, and, second, because he had taken a mansion in Belverton Street, Park Lane, next door to Porchester House, where, to the dismay of that aristocratic neighbourhood, he advertised that he was prepared to receive and be consulted by his clients. The invitation was responded to with alacrity, and from that day forward, between the hours of twelve and two, the pavement upon the north side of the street was lined with carriages, every one containing some person desirous of testing the great man's skill.

I must here explain that I have narrated all this in order to show the state of affairs existing in Belverton Street and Park Lane when Simon Carne arrived, or was supposed to arrive in England. If my memory serves me correctly, it was on Wednesday, the 3rd of May, that the Earl of Amberley drove to Victoria to meet and welcome the man whose acquaintance he had made in India under such peculiar circumstances, and under the spell of whose fascination he and his family had fallen so completely.

Reaching the station, his lordship descended from his carriage, and made his way to the platform set apart for the reception of the Continental express. He walked with a jaunty air, and seemed to be on the best of terms with himself and the world in general. How little he suspected the existence of the noose into which he was so innocently running his head!

As if out of compliment to his arrival, the train put in an appearance within a few moments of his reaching the platform. He immediately placed himself in such a position that he could make sure of seeing the man he wanted, and waited patiently until he should come in sight. Carne, however, was not among the first batch, indeed, the majority of passengers had passed before his lordship caught sight of him.

One thing was very certain, however great the crush might have been, it would have been difficult to mistake Carne's figure. The man's infirmity and the peculiar beauty of his face rendered him easily recognisable. Possibly, after his long sojourn in India, he found the morning cold, for he wore a long fur coat, the collar of which he had turned up round his ears, thus making a fitting frame for his delicate face. On seeing Lord Amberley he hastened forward to greet him.

'This is most kind and friendly of you,' he said as he shook the other by the hand. 'A fine day and Lord Amberley to meet me. One could scarcely imagine a better welcome.'

As he spoke, one of his Indian servants approached and salaamed before him. He gave him an order, and received an answer in Hindustani, whereupon he turned again to Lord Amberley.

'You may imagine how anxious I am to see my new dwelling,' he said. 'My servant tells me that my carriage is here, so may I hope that you will drive back with me and see for yourself how I am likely to be lodged.'

'I shall be delighted,' said Lord Amberley, who was longing for the opportunity, and they accordingly went out into the station yard together to discover a brougham, drawn by two magnificent horses, and with Nur Ali, in all the glory of white raiment and crested turban, on the box, waiting to receive them. His lordship dismissed his Victoria, and when Jowur Singh had taken his place beside his fellow servant upon the box, the carriage rolled out of the station yard in the direction of Hyde Park.

'I trust her ladyship is quite well,' said Simon Carne politely, as they turned into Gloucester Place.

'Excellently well, thank you,' replied his lordship. 'She bade me welcome you to England in her name as well as my own, and I was to say that she is looking forward to seeing you.'

'She is most kind, and I shall do myself the honour of calling upon her as soon as circumstances will permit,' answered Carne. 'I beg you will convey my best thanks to her for her thought of me.'

While these polite speeches were passing between them they were rapidly approaching a large hoarding on which was displayed a poster setting forth the name of the now famous detective, Klimo.

Simon Carne, leaning forward, studied it, and when they had passed, turned to his friend again.

'At Victoria and on all the hoardings we meet I see an enormous placard, bearing the word "Klimo". Pray, what does it mean?'

His lordship laughed.

'You are asking a question which, a month ago, was on the lips of nine out of every ten Londoners. It is only within the last fortnight that we have learned who and what "Klimo" is.'

'And pray what is he?'

'Well, the explanation is very simple. He is neither more nor less than a remarkably astute private detective, who has succeeded in attracting notice in such a way that half London has been induced to patronise him. I have had no dealings with the man myself. But a friend of mine, Lord Orpington, has been the victim of a most audacious burglary, and, the police having failed to solve the mystery, he has called Klimo in. We shall therefore see what he can do before many days are past. But, there, I expect you will soon know more about him than any of us.'

'Indeed! And why?'

'For the simple reason that he has taken No. 1, Belverton Terrace, the house adjoining your own, and sees his clients there.'

Simon Carne pursed up his lips, and appeared to be considering something.

'I trust he will not prove a nuisance,' he said at last. 'The agents who found me the house should have acquainted me with the fact. Private detectives, on however large a scale, scarcely strike one as the most desirable of neighbours – particularly for a man who is so fond of quiet as myself.'

At this moment they were approaching their destination. As the carriage passed Belverton Street and pulled up, Lord Amberley pointed to a long line of vehicles standing before the detective's door.

'You can see for yourself something of the business he does,' he said. 'Those are the carriages of his clients, and it is probable that twice as many have arrived on foot.'

'I shall certainly speak to the agent on the subject,' said Carne, with a shadow of annoyance upon his face. 'I consider the fact of this man's being so close to me a serious drawback to the house.'

Jowur Singh here descended from the box and opened the door in order that his master and his guest might alight, while portly Ram Gafur, the butler, came down the steps and salaamed before them with Oriental obsequiousness. Carne greeted his domestics with kindly condescension, and then, accompanied by the ex-Viceroy, entered his new abode.

'I think you may congratulate yourself upon having secured one of the most desirable residences in London,' said his lordship ten minutes or so later, when they had explored the principal rooms.

'I am very glad to hear you say so,' said Carne. 'I trust your lordship will remember that you will always be welcome in the house as long as I am its owner.'

'It is very kind of you to say so,' returned Lord Amberley warmly. 'I shall look forward to some months of pleasant intercourse. And now I must be going. To-morrow, perhaps, if you have nothing better to do, you will give us the pleasure of your company at dinner. Your fame has already gone abroad, and we shall ask one or two nice people to meet you, including my brother and sister-in-law. Lord and Lady Gelpington, Lord and Lady Orpington, and my cousin, the Duchess of Wiltshire, whose interest in china and Indian Art, as perhaps you know, is only second to your own.'

'I shall be most glad to come.'

'We may count on seeing you in Eaton Square, then, at eight o'clock?'

'If I am alive you may be sure I shall be there. Must you really go? Then good-bye, and many thanks for meeting me.'

His lordship having left the house Simon Carne went upstairs to his dressing room, which it was to be noticed he found without inquiry, and rang the electric bell, beside the fireplace, three times. While he was waiting for it to be answered he stood looking out of the window at the long line of carriages in the street below.

'Everything is progressing admirably,' he said to himself. 'Amberley does not suspect any more than the world in general. As a proof he asks me to dinner tomorrow evening to meet his brother and sister-in-law, two of his particular friends, and above all Her Grace of Wiltshire. Of course I shall go, and when I bid Her Grace good-bye it will be strange if I am not one step nearer the interest on Liz's money.'

At this moment the door opened, and his valet, the grave and respectable Belton, entered the room. Carne turned to greet him impatiently.

'Come, come, Belton,' he said, 'we must be quick. It is twenty minutes to twelve and if we don't hurry, the folk next door will become impatient. Have you succeeded in doing what I spoke to you about last night?'

'I have done everything, sir.'

'I am glad to hear it. Now lock that door and let us get to work. You can let me have your news while I am dressing.'

Opening one side of a massive wardrobe that completely filled one end of the room, Belton took from it a number of garments. They included a well worn velvet coat, a baggy pair of trousers – so old that only a notorious pauper or a millionaire could have afforded to wear them – a flannel waistcoat, a Gladstone collar, a soft silk tie, and a pair of embroidered carpet slippers upon which no old clothes man in the most reckless way of business in Petticoat Lane would have advanced a single halfpenny. Into these he assisted his master to change.

'Now give me the wig, and unfasten the straps of this hump,' said Carne, as the other placed the garments just referred to upon a neighbouring chair.

Belton did as he was ordered, and then there happened a thing the like of which no one would have believed. Having unbuckled a strap on either shoulder, and slipped his hand beneath the waistcoat, he withdrew a large papier-mâché hump, which he carried away and carefully placed in a drawer of the bureau. Relieved of his burden, Simon Carne stood up as straight and well-made a man as any in Her Majesty's dominions. The malformation, for which so many, including the Earl and Countess of Amberley, had often pitied him, was nothing but a hoax intended to produce an effect which would permit him additional facilities of disguise.

The hump discarded, and the grey wig fitted carefully to his head in such a manner that not even a pinch of his own curly locks could be seen beneath it, he adorned his cheeks with a pair of crépu-hair whiskers, donned the flannel vest and the velvet coat previously mentioned, slipped his feet into the carpet slippers, placed a pair of smoked glasses upon his nose, and declared himself ready to proceed about his business. The man who would have known him for Simon Carne would have been as astute as, well, shall we say, as the private detective – Klimo himself.

'It's on the stroke of twelve,' he said, as he gave a final glance at himself in the pier-glass above the dressing-table, and arranged his tie to his satisfaction. 'Should anyone call, instruct Ram Gafur to tell them that I have gone out on business, and shall not be back until three o'clock.'

'Very good, sir.'

'Now undo the door and let me go in.' Thus commanded, Belton went across to the large wardrobe which, as I have already said, covered the whole of one side of the room, and opened the middle door. Two or three garments were seen inside suspended on pegs, and these he removed, at the same time pushing towards the right the panel at the rear. When this was done a large aperture in the wall between the two houses was disclosed. Through this door Carne passed, drawing it behind him.

In No. 1, Belverton Terrace, the house occupied by the detective, whose presence in the street Carne seemed to find so objectionable, the entrance thus constructed was covered by the peculiar kind of confessional box in which Klimo invariably sat to receive his clients, the rearmost panels of which opened in the same fashion as those in the wardrobe in the dressing-room. These being pulled aside, he had but to draw them to again after him, take his seat, ring the electric bell to inform his housekeeper that he was ready, and then welcome his clients as quickly as they cared to come.

Punctually at two o'clock the interviews ceased, and Klimo, having reaped an excellent harvest of fees, returned to Porchester House to become Simon Carne once more.

Possibly it was due to the fact that the Earl and Countess of Amberley were brimming over with his praise, it may have been the rumour that he was worth as many millions as you have fingers upon your hand that did it; one thing, however, was self evident, within twenty-four hours of the noble Earl's meeting him at Victoria Station, Simon Carne was the talk, not only of fashionable, but also of unfashionable, London.

That his household were, with one exception, natives of India, that he had paid a rental for Porchester House which ran into five figures, that he was the greatest living authority upon china and Indian art generally, and that he had come over to England in search of a wife, were among the smallest of the canards set afloat concerning him.

During dinner next evening Carne put forth every effort to please. He was placed on the right hand of his hostess and next to the Duchess of Wiltshire. To the latter he paid particular attention, and to such good purpose that when the ladies returned to the drawing-room afterwards Her Grace was full of his praises. They had discussed

THE

china of all sorts, Carne had pror
longed for all her life, but had ne
she had promised to show hin
which the famous necklace, of
most of its time. She would be
own ball in a week's time, she
see the case when it came fron
only too pleased to show it to him.

He also took wit
before. She re
into the usu
her by me
to includ
book,
the

As Simon Carne drove home in his luxur
he smiled to himself as he thought of the success w
his first endeavour. Two of the guests, who were stew
Jockey Club, had heard with delight his idea of purchasing a hor
order to have an interest in the Derby. While another, on hearing that
he desired to become the possessor of a yacht, had offered to propose
him for the R.C.Y.C. To crown it all, however, and much better than
all, the Duchess of Wiltshire had promised to show him her famous
diamonds.

'By this time next week,' he said to himself, 'Liz's interest should be
considerably closer. But satisfactory as my progress has been hitherto
it is difficult to see how I am to get possession of the stones. From
what I have been able to discover they are only brought from the
bank on the day the Duchess intends to wear them, and they are
taken back by His Grace the morning following.

'While she has got them on her person it would be manifestly
impossible to get them from her. And as, when she takes them off,
they are returned to their box and placed in a safe, constructed in the
wall of the bedroom adjoining, and which for the occasion is occupied
by the butler and one of the under footmen, the only key being in the
possession of the Duke himself, it would be equally foolish to hope
to appropriate them. In what manner therefore I am to become their
possessor passes my comprehension. However, one thing is certain,
obtained they must be, and the attempt must be made on the night
of the ball if possible. In the meantime I'll set my wits to work upon
a plan.'

Next day Simon Carne was the recipient of an invitation to the
ball in question, and two days later he called upon the Duchess of
Wiltshire at her residence in Belgrave Square with a plan prepared.

him the small vase he had promised her four nights
eived him most graciously, and their talk fell at once
channel. Having examined her collection and charmed
ns of one or two judicious criticisms, he asked permission
photographs of certain of her treasures in his forthcoming
hen little by little he skilfully guided the conversation on to
bject of jewels.

since we are discussing gems, Mr Carne,' she said, 'perhaps it
would interest you to see my famous necklace. By good fortune I
have it in the house now, for the reason that an alteration is being
made to one of the clasps by my jewellers.'

'I should like to see it immensely,' answered Carne. 'At one time
and another I have had the good fortune to examine the jewels of the
leading Indian Princes, and I should like to be able to say that I had
seen the famous Wiltshire necklace.'

'Then you shall certainly have that honour,' she answered with a
smile. 'If you will ring that bell I will send for it.'

Carne rang the bell as requested, and when the butler entered he
was given the key of the safe and ordered to bring the case to the
drawing-room.

'We must not keep it very long,' she observed while the man was
absent. 'It is to be returned to the bank in an hour's time.'

'I am indeed fortunate,' Carne replied, and turned to the
description of some curious Indian wood carving, of which he
was making a special feature in his book. As he explained, he had
collected his illustrations from the doors of Indian temples, from
the gateways of palaces, from old brass work, and even from carved
chairs and boxes he had picked up in all sorts of odd corners. Her
Grace was most interested.

'How strange that you should have mentioned it,' she said. 'If carved
boxes have any interest for you, it is possible my jewel case itself may
be of use to you. As I think I told you during Lady Amberley's dinner,
it came from Benares, and has carved upon it the portraits of nearly
every god in the Hindu Pantheon.'

'You raise my curiosity to fever heat,' said Carne.

A few moments later the servant returned, bringing with him a
wooden box, about sixteen inches long, by twelve wide, and eight

deep, which he placed upon a table beside his mistress, after which he retired.

'This is the case to which I have just been referring,' said the Duchess, placing her hand on the article in question. 'If you glance at it you will see how exquisitely it is carved.'

Concealing his eagerness with an effort, Simon Carne drew his chair up to the table, and examined the box.

It was with justice she had described it as a work of art. What the wood was of which it was constructed Carne was unable to tell. It was dark and heavy, and, though it was not teak, closely resembled it. It was literally covered with quaint carving, and of its kind was a unique work of art.

'It is most curious and beautiful,' said Carne when he had finished his examination. 'In all my experience I can safely say I have never seen its equal. If you will permit me I should very much like to include a description and an illustration of it in my book.'

'Of course you may do so; I shall be only too delighted,' answered Her Grace. 'If it will help you in your work I shall be glad to lend it to you for a few hours in order that you may have the illustration made.'

This was exactly what Carne had been waiting for, and he accepted the offer with alacrity.

'Very well, then,' she said. 'On the day of my ball, when it will be brought from the bank again, I will take the necklace out and send the case to you. I must make one proviso however, and that is that you let me have it back the same day.'

'I will certainly promise to do that,' replied Carne.

'And now let us look inside,' said his hostess.

Choosing a key from a bunch she carried in her pocket, she unlocked the casket, and lifted the lid. Accustomed as Carne had all his life been to the sight of gems, what he saw before him then almost took his breath away. The inside of the box, both sides and bottom, was quilted with the softest Russia leather, and on this luxurious couch reposed the famous necklace. The fire of the stones when the light caught them was sufficient to dazzle the eyes, so fierce was it.

As Carne could see, every gem was perfect of its kind, and there were no fewer than three hundred of them. The setting was a fine example of the jeweller's art, and last, but not least, the value of the whole affair was fifty thousand pounds, a mere fleabite to the man who had given it to his wife, but a fortune to any humbler person.

'And now that you have seen my property, what do you think of it?' asked the Duchess as she watched her visitor's face.

'It is very beautiful,' he answered, 'and I do not wonder that you are proud of it. Yes, the diamonds are very fine, but I think it is their abiding place that fascinates me more. Have you any objection to my measuring it?'

'Pray do so, if it is likely to be of any assistance to you,' replied Her Grace.

Carne thereupon produced a small ivory rule, ran it over the box, and the figures he thus obtained he jotted down in his pocket book.

Ten minutes later, when the case had been returned to the safe, he thanked the Duchess for her kindness and took his departure, promising to call in person for the empty case on the morning of the ball.

Reaching home he passed into his study, and, seating himself at his writing table, pulled a sheet of note paper towards him and began to sketch, as well as he could remember it, the box he had seen. Then he leant back in his chair and closed his eyes.

'I have cracked a good many hard nuts in my time,' he said reflectively, 'but never one that seemed so difficult at first sight as this. As far as I see at present, the case stands as follows: the box will be brought from the bank where it usually reposes to Wiltshire House on the morning of the dance. I shall be allowed to have possession of it, without the stones of course, for a period possibly extending from eleven o'clock in the morning to four or five, at any rate not later than seven, in the evening. After the ball the necklace will be returned to it, when it will be locked up in the safe, over which the butler and a footman will mount guard.

'To get into the room during the night is not only too risky, but physically out of the question; while to rob Her Grace of her treasure during the progress of the dance would be equally impossible. The Duke fetches the casket and takes it back to the bank himself, so that to all intents and purposes I am almost as far off the solution as ever.'

Half-an-hour went by and found him still seated at his desk, staring at the drawing on the paper, then an hour. The traffic of the streets rolled past the house unheeded. Finally Jowur Singh announced his carriage, and, feeling that an idea might come to him with a change of scene, he set off for a drive in the park.

By this time his elegant mail phaeton, with its magnificent horses and Indian servant on the seat behind, was as well-known as Her Majesty's state equipage, and attracted almost as much attention. To-day, however, the fashionable world noticed that Simon Carne looked preoccupied. He was still working out his problem, but so far without much success. Suddenly something, no one will ever be able to say what, put an idea into his head. The notion was no sooner born in his brain than he left the park and drove quickly home. Ten minutes had scarcely elapsed before he was back in his study again, and had ordered that Wajib Baksh should be sent to him.

When the man he wanted put in an appearance, Carne handed him the paper upon which he had made the drawing of the jewel case.

'Look at that,' he said, 'and tell me what thou seest there.'

'I see a box,' answered the man, who by this time was well accustomed to his master's ways.

'As thou say'st, it is a box,' said Carne. 'The wood is heavy and thick, though what wood it is I do not know. The measurements are upon the paper below. Within, both the sides and bottom are quilted with soft leather as I have also shown. Think now, Wajib Baksh, for in this case thou wilt need to have all thy wits about thee. Tell me is it in thy power, oh most cunning of all craftsmen, to insert such extra sides within this box that they, being held by a spring, shall lie so snug as not to be noticeable to the ordinary eye? Can it be so arranged that, when the box is locked, they shall fall flat upon the bottom thus covering and holding fast what lies beneath them, and yet making the box appear to the eye as if it were empty. Is it possible for thee to do such a thing?'

Wajib Baksh did not reply for a few moments. His instinct told him what his master wanted, and he was not disposed to answer hastily, for he also saw that his reputation as the most cunning craftsman in India was at stake.

'If the Heaven-born will permit me the night for thought,' he said at last, 'I will come to him when he rises from his bed and tell him what I can do, and he can then give his orders as it pleases him.'

'Very good,' said Carne. 'Then tomorrow morning I shall expect thy report. Let the work be good and there will be many rupees for thee to touch in return. As to the lock and the way it shall act, let that be the concern of Hiram Singh.'

Wajib Baksh salaamed and withdrew, and Simon Carne for the time being dismissed the matter from his mind.

Next morning, while he was dressing, Belton reported that the two artificers desired an interview with him. He ordered them to be admitted, and forthwith they entered the room. It was noticeable that Wajib Baksh carried in his hand a heavy box, which, upon Carne's motioning him to do so, he placed upon the table.

'Have ye thought over the matter?' he asked, seeing that the men waited for him to speak.

'We have thought of it,' replied Hiram Singh, who always acted as spokesman for the pair. 'If the Presence will deign to look he will see that we have made a box of the size and shape such as he drew upon the paper.'

'Yes, it is certainly a good copy,' said Carne condescendingly, after he had examined it.

Wajib Baksh showed his white teeth in appreciation of the compliment, and Hiram Singh drew closer to the table.

'And now, if the Sahib will open it, he will in his wisdom be able to tell if it resembles the other that he has in his mind.'

Carne opened the box as requested, and discovered that the interior was an exact counterfeit of the Duchess of Wiltshire's jewel case, even to the extent of the quilted leather lining which had been the other's principal feature. He admitted that the likeness was all that could be desired.

'As he is satisfied,' said Hiram Singh, 'it may be that the Protector of the Poor will deign to try an experiment with it. See, here is a comb. Let it be placed in the box, so – now he will see what he will see.'

The broad, silver-backed comb, lying upon his dressing-table, was placed on the bottom of the box, the lid was closed, and the key turned in the lock. The case being securely fastened, Hiram Singh laid it before his master.

'I am to open it, I suppose?' said Carne, taking the key and replacing it in the lock.

'If my master pleases,' replied the other.

Carne accordingly turned it in the lock, and, having done so, raised the lid and looked inside. His astonishment was complete. To all intents and purposes the box was empty. The comb was not to be seen, and yet the quilted sides and bottom were, to all appearances, just the same as when he had first looked inside.

'This is most wonderful,' he said. And indeed it was as clever a conjuring trick as any he had ever seen.

'Nay, it is very simple,' Wajib Baksh replied. 'The Heaven-born told me that there must be no risk of detection.'

He took the box in his own hands and, running his nails down the centre of the quilting, divided the false bottom into two pieces; these he lifted out, revealing the comb lying upon the real bottom beneath.

'The sides, as my lord will see,' said Hiram Singh, taking a step forward, 'are held in their appointed places by these two springs. Thus, when the key is turned the springs relax, and the sides are driven by others into their places on the bottom, where the seams in the quilting mask the join. There is but one disadvantage. It is as follows: When the pieces which form the bottom are lifted out in order that my lord may get at whatever lies concealed beneath, the springs must of necessity stand revealed. However, to anyone who knows sufficient of the working of the box to lift out the false bottom, it will be an easy matter to withdraw the springs and conceal them about his person.'

'As you say that is an easy matter,' said Carne, 'and I shall not be likely to forget. Now one other question. Presuming I am in a position to put the real box into your hands for say eight hours, do you think that in that time you can fit it up so that detection will be impossible?'

'Assuredly, my lord,' replied Hiram Singh with conviction. 'There is but the lock and the fitting of the springs to be done. Three hours at most would suffice for that.'

'I am pleased with you,' said Carne. 'As a proof of my satisfaction, when the work is finished you will each receive five hundred rupees. Now you can go.'

According to his promise, ten o'clock on the Friday following found him in his hansom driving towards Belgrave Square. He was a little anxious, though the casual observer would scarcely have been able to tell it. The magnitude of the stake for which he was playing was enough to try the nerve of even such a past master in his profession as Simon Carne.

Arriving at the house he discovered some workmen erecting an awning across the footway in preparation for the ball that was to take place at night. It was not long, however, before he found himself in the boudoir, reminding Her Grace of her promise to permit him an opportunity of making a drawing of the famous jewel case. The Duchess was naturally busy, and within a quarter of an hour he was on his way home with the box placed on the seat of the carriage beside him.

'Now,' he said, as he patted it good-humouredly, 'if only the notion worked out by Hiram Singh and Wajib Baksh holds good, the famous Wiltshire diamonds will become my property before very many hours are passed. By this time to-morrow, I suppose, London will be all agog concerning the burglary.'

On reaching his house he left his carriage and himself carried the box into his study. Once there he rang his bell and ordered Hiram Singh and Wajib Baksh to be sent to him. When they arrived he showed them the box upon which they were to exercise their ingenuity.

'Bring your tools in here,' he said, 'and do the work under my own eyes. You have but nine hours before you, so you must make the most of them.'

The men went for their implements, and as soon as they were ready set to work. All through the day they were kept hard at it, with the result that by five o'clock the alterations had been effected and the case stood ready. By the time Carne returned from his afternoon drive in the Park it was quite prepared for the part it was to play in his scheme. Having praised the men, he turned them out and locked the door, then went across the room and unlocked a drawer in his writing table. From it he took a flat leather jewel case which he opened. It contained a necklace of counterfeit diamonds, if anything a little larger than the one he intended to try to obtain. He had purchased it that morning in the Burlington Arcade for the purpose of testing the apparatus his servants had made, and this he now proceeded to do.

Laying it carefully upon the bottom he closed the lid and turned the key. When he opened it again the necklace was gone, and even though he knew the secret he could not for the life of him see where the false bottom began and ended. After that he reset the trap and tossed the necklace carelessly in. To his delight it acted as well as on the previous occasion. He could scarcely contain his satisfaction. His conscience was sufficiently elastic to give him no trouble. To him it was scarcely a robbery he was planning, but an artistic trial of skill, in which he pitted his wits and cunning against the forces of society in general.

At half-past seven he dined and afterwards smoked a meditative cigar over the evening paper in the billiard room. The invitations to the ball were for ten o'clock, and at nine-thirty he went to his dressing-room.

'Make me tidy as quickly as you can,' he said to Belton when the latter appeared, 'and while you are doing so listen to my final instructions.

'To-night, as you know, I am endeavouring to secure the Duchess of Wiltshire's necklace. To-morrow morning all London will resound with the hubbub, and I have been making my plans in such a way as to arrange that Klimo shall be the first person consulted. When the messenger calls, if call he does, see that the old woman next door bids him tell the Duke to come personally at twelve o'clock. Do you understand?'

'Perfectly, sir.'

'Very good. Now give me the jewel case, and let me be on. You need not sit up for me.'

Precisely as the clocks in the neighbourhood were striking ten Simon Carne reached Belgrave Square, and, as he hoped, found himself the first guest.

His hostess and her husband received him in the ante-room of the drawing-room.

'I come laden with a thousand apologies,' he said as he took Her Grace's hand, and bent over it with that ceremonious politeness which was one of the man's chief characteristics. 'I am most unconscionably early, I know, but I hastened here in order that I might personally return the jewel case you so kindly lent me. I must trust to your generosity to forgive me. The drawings took longer than I expected.'

'Please do not apologise,' answered Her Grace. 'It is very kind of you to have brought the case yourself. I hope the illustrations have proved successful. I shall look forward to seeing them as soon as they are ready. But I am keeping you holding the box. One of my servants will take it to my room.'

She called a footman to her and bade him take the box and place it upon her dressing-table.

'Before it goes I must let you see that I have not damaged it either externally or internally,' said Carne with a laugh. 'It is such a valuable case that I should never forgive myself if it had even received a scratch during the time it has been in my possession.'

So saying he lifted the lid and allowed her to look inside. To all appearance it was exactly the same as when she had lent it to him earlier in the day.

'You have been most careful,' she said. And then, with an air of banter, she continued: 'If you desire it I shall be pleased to give you a certificate to that effect.'

They jested in this fashion for a few moments after the servant's departure, during which time Carne promised to call upon her the following morning at eleven o'clock, and to bring with him the illustrations he had made and a queer little piece of china he had had the good fortune to pick up in a dealer's shop the previous afternoon. By this time fashionable London was making its way up the grand staircase, and with its appearance further conversation became impossible.

Shortly after midnight Carne bade his hostess good night and slipped away. He was perfectly satisfied with his evening's entertainment, and if the key of the jewel case were not turned before the jewels were placed in it, he was convinced they would become his property. It speaks well for his strength of nerve when I record the fact that on going to bed his slumbers were as peaceful and untroubled as those of a little child.

Breakfast was scarcely over next morning before a hansom drew up at his front door and Lord Amberley alighted. He was ushered into Carne's presence forthwith, and on seeing that the latter was surprised at his early visit, hastened to explain.

'My dear fellow,' he said as he took possession of the chair the other offered him, 'I have come round to see you on most important business. As I told you last night at the dance, when you so kindly asked me to come and see the steam yacht you have purchased, I had an appointment with Wiltshire at half-past nine this morning. On reaching Belgrave Square, I found the whole house in confusion. Servants were running hither and thither with scared faces, the butler was on the borders of lunacy, the Duchess was well-nigh hysterical in her boudoir, while her husband was in his study vowing vengeance against all the world.'

'You alarm me,' said Carne, lighting a cigarette with a hand that was as steady as a rock. 'What on earth has happened?'

'I think I might safely allow you fifty guesses and then wager a hundred pounds you'd not hit the mark; and yet in a certain measure it concerns you.'

'Concerns me? Good gracious. What have I done to bring all this about?'

'Pray do not look so alarmed,' said Amberley. 'Personally you have done nothing. Indeed, on second thoughts, I don't know that I am right in saying that it concerns you at all. The fact of the matter is, Carne, a burglary took place last night at Wiltshire House, and the famous necklace has disappeared.'

'Good Heavens! You don't say so?'

'But I do. The circumstances of the case are as follows: When my cousin retired to her room last night after the ball, she unclasped the necklace, and, in her husband's presence, placed it carefully in her jewel case, which she locked. That having been done, Wiltshire took the box to the room which contained the safe, and himself placed it there, locking the iron door with his own key. The room was occupied that night, according to custom, by the butler and one of the footmen, both of whom have been in the family since they were boys.

'Next morning, after breakfast, the Duke unlocked the safe and took out the box, intending to convey it to the Bank as usual. Before leaving, however, he placed it on his study-table and went upstairs to speak to his wife. He cannot remember exactly how long he was absent, but he feels convinced that he was not gone more than a quarter of an hour at the very utmost.

'Their conversation finished, she accompanied him downstairs, where she saw him take up the case to carry it to his carriage. Before he left the house, however, she said: "I suppose you have looked to see that the necklace is all right?" "How could I do so?" was his reply. "You know you possess the only key that will fit it."

'She felt in her pockets, but to her surprise the key was not there.'

'If I were a detective I should say that that is a point to be remembered,' said Carne with a smile. 'Pray, where did she find her keys?'

'Upon her dressing-table,' said Amberley. 'Though she has not the slightest recollection of leaving them there.'

'Well, when she had procured the keys, what happened?'

'Why, they opened the box, and to their astonishment and dismay, found it empty. The jewels were gone!'

'Good gracious. What a terrible loss! It seems almost impossible that it can be true. And pray, what did they do?'

'At first they stood staring into the empty box, hardly believing the evidence of their own eyes. Stare how they would, however, they could not bring them back. The jewels had without doubt disappeared, but when and where the robbery had taken place it was impossible to say. After that they had up all the servants and questioned them, but the result was what they might have foreseen, no one from the butler to the kitchenmaid could throw any light upon the subject. To this minute it remains as great a mystery as when they first discovered it.'

'I am more concerned than I can tell you,' said Carne. 'How thankful I ought to be that I returned the case to Her Grace last night. But in thinking of myself I am forgetting to ask what has brought you to me. If I can be of any assistance I hope you will command me.'

'Well, I'll tell you why I have come,' replied Lord Amberley. 'Naturally they are most anxious to have the mystery solved and the jewels recovered as soon as possible. Wiltshire wanted to send to Scotland Yard there and then, but his wife and I eventually persuaded him to consult Klimo. As you know, if the police authorities are called in first he refuses the business altogether. Now, we thought, as you are his next door neighbour, you might possibly be able to assist us.'

'You may be very sure, my lord, I will do everything that lies in my power. Let us go in and see him at once.'

As he spoke he rose and threw what remained of his cigarette into the fireplace. His visitor having imitated his example, they procured their hats and walked round from Park Lane into Belverton Street to bring up at No. 1. After they had rung the bell the door was opened to them by the old woman who invariably received the detective's clients.

'Is Mr Klimo at home?' asked Carne. 'And, if so, can we see him?'

The old lady was a little deaf, and the question had to be repeated before she could be made to understand what was wanted. As soon, however, as she realised their desire she informed them that her master was absent from town, but would be back as usual at twelve o'clock to meet his clients.

'What on earth's to be done?' said the Earl, looking at his companion in dismay. 'I am afraid I can't come back again, as I have a most important appointment at that hour.'

'Do you think you could intrust the business to me?' asked Carne. 'If so, I will make a point of seeing him at twelve o'clock, and could call at Wiltshire House afterwards and tell the Duke what I have done.'

'That's very good of you,' replied Amberley. 'If you are sure it would not put you to too much trouble, that would be quite the best thing to be done.'

'I will do it with pleasure,' Carne replied. 'I feel it my duty to help in whatever way I can.'

'You are very kind,' said the other. 'Then, as I understand it, you are to call upon Klimo at twelve o'clock, and afterwards to let my cousins know what you have succeeded in doing. I only hope he will help us to secure the thief. We are having too many of these burglaries just now. I must catch this hansom and be off. Goodbye, and many thanks.'

'Goodbye,' said Carne, and shook him by the hand.

The hansom having rolled away, Carne retraced his steps to his own abode.

'It is really very strange,' he muttered as he walked along, 'how often chance condescends to lend her assistance to my little schemes. The mere fact that His Grace left the box unwatched in his study for a quarter of an hour may serve to throw the police off on quite another scent. I am also glad that they decided to open the case in the house, for if it had gone to the bankers' and had been placed in the strong room unexamined, I should never have been able to get possession of the jewels at all.'

Three hours later he drove to Wiltshire House and saw the Duke. The Duchess was far too much upset by the catastrophe to see anyone.

'This is really most kind of you, Mr Carne,' said His Grace when the other had supplied an elaborate account of his interview with Klimo. 'We are extremely indebted to you. I am sorry he cannot come before ten o'clock to-night, and that he makes this stipulation of my seeing him alone, for I must confess I should like to have had someone else present to ask any questions that might escape me. But if that's his usual hour and custom, well, we must abide by it, that's all. I hope he will do some good, for this is the greatest calamity that has ever befallen me. As I told you just now, it has made my wife quite ill. She is confined to her bedroom and quite hysterical.'

'You do not suspect anyone, I suppose,' inquired Carne.

'Not a soul,' the other answered. 'The thing is such a mystery that we do not know what to think. I feel convinced, however, that my servants are as innocent as I am. Nothing will ever make me think them otherwise. I wish I could catch the fellow, that's all. I'd make him suffer for the trick he's played me.'

Carne offered an appropriate reply, and after a little further conversation upon the subject, bade the irate nobleman goodbye and left the house. From Belgrave Square he drove to one of the clubs of which he had been elected a member, in search of Lord Orpington, with whom he had promised to lunch, and afterwards took him to a ship-builder's yard near Greenwich in order to show him the steam yacht he had lately purchased.

It was close upon dinner time before he returned to his own residence. He brought Lord Orpington with him, and they dined in state together. At nine the latter bade him good-bye, and at ten Carne retired to his dressing-room and rang for Belton.

'What have you to report,' he asked, 'with regard to what I bade you do in Belgrave Square?'

'I followed your instructions to the letter,' Belton replied. 'Yesterday morning I wrote to Messrs. Horniblow and Jimson, the house agents in Piccadilly, in the name of Colonel Braithwaite, and asked for an order to view the residence to the right of Wiltshire House. I asked that the order might be sent direct to the house, where the Colonel would get it upon his arrival. This letter I posted myself in Basingstoke, as you desired me to do.

'At nine o'clock yesterday morning I dressed myself as much like an elderly army officer as possible, and took a cab to Belgrave Square. The caretaker, an old fellow of close upon seventy years of age, admitted me immediately upon hearing my name, and proposed that he should show me over the house. This, however, I told him was quite unnecessary, backing my speech with a present of half-a-crown, whereupon he returned to his breakfast perfectly satisfied, while I wandered about the house at my own leisure.

'Reaching the same floor as that upon which is situated the room in which the Duke's safe is kept, I discovered that your supposition was quite correct, and that it would be possible for a man, by opening the window, to make his way along the coping from one house to the other, without being seen. I made certain that there was no one in the bedroom in which the butler slept, and then arranged the long telescope walking stick you gave me, and fixed one of my boots to it by means of the screw in the end. With this I was able to make a regular succession of footsteps in the dust along the ledge, between one window and the other.

'That done, I went downstairs again, bade the caretaker good morning, and got into my cab. From Belgrave Square I drove to the shop of the pawnbroker whom you told me you had discovered was out of town. His assistant inquired my business and was anxious to do what he could for me. I told him, however, that I must see his master personally as it was about the sale of some diamonds I had had left me. I pretended to be annoyed that he was not at home, and muttered to myself, so that the man could hear, something about its meaning a journey to Amsterdam.

'Then I limped out of the shop, paid off my cab, and, walking down a bystreet, removed my moustache, and altered my appearance by taking off my great coat and muffler. A few streets further on I purchased a bowler hat in place of the old-fashioned topper I had hitherto been wearing, and then took a cab from Piccadilly and came home.'

'You have fulfilled my instructions admirably,' said Carne. 'And if the business comes off, as I expect it will, you shall receive your usual percentage. Now I must be turned into Klimo and be off to Belgrave Square to put His Grace of Wiltshire upon the track of this burglar.'

Before he retired to rest that night Simon Carne took something, wrapped in a red silk handkerchief, from the capacious pocket of the coat Klimo had been wearing a few moments before. Having unrolled the covering, he held up to the light the magnificent necklace which for so many years had been the joy and pride of the ducal house of Wiltshire. The electric light played upon it, and touched it with a thousand different hues.

'Where so many have failed,' he said to himself, as he wrapped it in the handkerchief again and locked it in his safe, 'it is pleasant to be able to congratulate oneself on having succeeded. It is without its equal, and I don't think I shall be overstepping the mark if I say that I think when she receives it Liz will be glad she lent me the money.'

Next morning all London was astonished by the news that the famous Wiltshire diamonds had been stolen, and a few hours later Carne learnt from an evening paper that the detectives who had taken up the case, upon the supposed retirement from it of Klimo, were still completely at fault.

That evening he was to entertain several friends to dinner. They included Lord Amberley, Lord Orpington, and a prominent member of the Privy Council. Lord Amberley arrived late, but filled to overflowing with importance. His friends noticed his state, and questioned him.

'Well, gentlemen,' he answered, as he took up a commanding position upon the drawing-room hearthrug, 'I am in a position to inform you that Klimo has reported upon the case, and the upshot of it is that the Wiltshire Diamond Mystery is a mystery no longer.'

'What do you mean?' asked the others in a chorus.

'I mean that he sent in his report to Wiltshire this afternoon, as arranged. From what he said the other night, after being alone in the room with the empty jewel case and a magnifying glass for two minutes or so, he was in a position to describe the modus operandi, and what is more to put the police on the scent of the burglar.'

'And how was it worked?' asked Carne.

'From the empty house next door,' replied the other. 'On the morning of the burglary a man, purporting to be a retired army officer, called with an order to view, got the caretaker out of the way, clambered along to Wiltshire House by means of the parapet outside, reached the room during the time the servants were at breakfast, opened the safe, and abstracted the jewels.'

'But how did Klimo find all this out?' asked Lord Orpington.

'By his own inimitable cleverness,' replied Lord Amberley. 'At any rate it has been proved that he was correct. The man did make his way from next door, and the police have since discovered that an individual, answering to the description given, visited a pawnbroker's shop in the city about an hour later and stated that he had diamonds to sell.'

'If that is so it turns out to be a very simple mystery after all,' said Lord Orpington as they began their meal.

'Thanks to the ingenuity of the cleverest detective in the world,' remarked Amberley.

'In that case here's a good health to Klimo,' said the Privy Councillor, raising his glass.

'I will join you in that,' said Simon Carne. 'Here's a very good health to Klimo and his connection with the Duchess of Wiltshire's diamonds. May he always be equally successful!'

'Hear, hear to that,' replied his guests.

Hagar of the Pawn Shop

Created by Fergus Hume (1859 – 1932)

ONE OF THE most popular crime novels of the Victorian era was *The Mystery of a Hansom Cab*, first published in 1886 and still kept in print today. Its author was Fergus Hume, a young barrister's clerk in Melbourne, Australia. Hume, born in England, had been taken to New Zealand as a young child and had been educated there. After taking a law degree at the University of Otago, he had moved to Australia where he had striven unsuccessfully to make a name for himself as a dramatist. *The Mystery of a Hansom Cab* was his very deliberate attempt to copy the style of the French novelist Émile Gaboriau, then a worldwide bestseller. Two years after the publication of his first and most famous novel, Hume moved back to the England he had left as a small child and he lived and worked in a village in the Essex countryside for the rest of his life. He wrote well over 100 novels and volumes of short stories in his career, nearly all of them in the crime and mystery genre. Hagar, the gypsy woman who inherits a Lambeth pawn shop and is drawn into the lives of her customers, appeared in a collection of stories published in 1898. Lively and resourceful, she is one of the most unusual female detectives of the era and the stories in which she appears are all very readable. 'The Ninth Customer and the Casket' not only shows Hagar at her most forceful but also ends with a neatly comic and surprising twist.

The Ninth Customer
and the Casket

HAGAR HAD ALMOST a genius for reading people's characters in their faces. The curve of the mouth, the glance of the eyes – she could interpret these truly; for to her feminine instinct she added a logical judgment masculine in its discretion. She was rarely wrong when she exercised this faculty; and in the many customers who entered the Lambeth pawn-shop she had ample opportunities to use her talent. To the sleek, white-faced creature who brought for pawning the Renaissance casket of silver she took an instant and violent dislike. Subsequent events proved that she was right in doing so. The ninth customer – as she called him – was an oily scoundrel. In appearance he was a respectable servant – a valet or a butler – and wore an immaculate suit of black broad-cloth. His face was as white as that of a corpse, and almost as expressionless. Two tufts of whisker adorned his lean cheeks, but his thin mouth and receding chin were uncovered with hair. On his badly-shaped head and off his low narrow forehead the scanty hair of iron-gray was brushed smoothly. He dropped his shifty grey eyes when he addressed Hagar, and talked softly in a most deferential manner. Hagar guessed him to be a West-end servant; and by his physiognomy she knew him to be a scoundrel.

This 'gentleman's gentleman' – as Hagar guessed him rightly to be – gave the name of Julian Peters, and the address 42, Mount Street, Mayfair. As certainly as though she had been in the creature's confidence, Hagar knew that name and address were false. Also, she was not quite sure whether he had come honestly by the casket which he wished to pawn, although the story he told was a very fair and, apparently, candid one.

'My late master, miss, left me this box as a legacy,' he said deferentially, 'and I have kept it by me for some time. Unfortunately, I am now out of a situation, and to keep myself going until I obtain a new one I need money. You will understand, miss, that it is only necessity which makes me pawn this box. I want fifteen pounds on it.'

'You can have thirteen,' said Hagar, pricing the box at a glance.

'Oh, indeed, miss, I am sure it is worth fifteen,' said Mr Peters (so-called): 'if you look at the workmanship – '

'I have looked at everything,' replied Hagar, promptly – 'at the silver, the workmanship, the date, and all the rest of it.'

'The date, miss?' asked the man, in a puzzled tone.

'Yes; the casket is Cinque Cento, Florentine work. I dare say if you took it to a West-end jeweler you could get more on it than I am prepared to lend. Thirteen pounds is my limit.'

'I'll take it,' said Peters, promptly. 'I don't care about pawning it in the West-end, where I am known.'

'As a scoundrel, no doubt,' thought Hagar, cynically. However, it was not her place to spoil a good bargain – and getting the Renaissance casket for thirteen pounds was a very good one – so she made out the ticket in the false name of Julian Peters, and handed it to him, together with a ten-pound note and three sovereigns. The man counted the money, with a greedy look in his eyes, and turned to depart with a cringing bow. At the door of the shop he paused, however, to address a last word to Hagar.

'I can redeem that casket whenever I like, miss?' he asked, anxiously.

'To-morrow, if it pleases you,' replied Hagar, coldly, 'so long as you pay me a month's interest for the loan of the money.'

'Thank you, miss; I shall take back the box in a month's time. In the meantime I leave it in your charge, miss, and wish you a very good day.'

Hagar gave a shudder of disgust as he left the shop; for the man to her was a noxious thing, like a snake or a toad. If instinct were worth anything, she felt that this valet was a thief and a scoundrel, who was abusing the trust his employer placed in him. The casket was far more likely to have been thieved than to have come to Mr Peters by will. It is not usual for gentlemen to leave their servants legacies of Cinque Cento caskets.

The box, as Peters called it, was very beautiful; an exquisite example of goldsmith's art, worthy of Benvenuto Cellini himself. Probably it was by one of his pupils. Renaissance work certainly, for in its ornamentation there was visible that mingling of Christianity and paganism which is so striking a characteristic of the re-birth of the Arts in the Italy of Dante and the Medici. On the sides of the casket in relief there were figures of dancing nymph and piping satyr; flower-wreathed altar and vine-crowned priest. On the lid a full-length figure of the Virgin with upraised hands; below clouds and the turrets of a castle; overhead the glory of the Holy Ghost in the form of a wide-winged Dove, and fluttering cherubs and grave saints. Within the casket was lined with dead gold, smooth and lusterless; but this receptacle contained nothing.

Without doubt this tiny gem of goldsmith's art had been the jewel-case of some Florentine lady in that dead and gone century. Perhaps for her some lover had ordered it to be made, with its odd mingling of cross and thyrsus; its hints of asceticism and joyous life. But the Florentine beauty was now dust; all her days of love and vanity and sin were over; and the casket in which she had stored her jewels lay in a dingy London pawn-shop. There was something ironic in the fate meted out by Time and Chance to this dainty trifle of luxury.

While examining the box, Hagar noticed that the gold plate of the case within was raised some little distance above the outside portion. There appeared to her shrewd eyes to be a space between the base of the casket and the inner box of gold. Ever on the alert to discover mysteries, Hagar believed that in this toy there was a secret drawer, which no doubt opened by a concealed spring. At once she set to work searching for this spring.

'It is very cleverly hidden,' she murmured, having been baffled for a long time; ' but a secret recess there is, and I intend to find it. Who knows but what I may stumble on the evidence of some old Florentine tragedy, like that of the Crucifix of Fiesole?'

Her fingers were slender and nimble, and had a wonderfully delicate sense of feeling in their narrow tips. She ran them lightly over the raised work of beaten silver, pressing the laughing heads of the fauns and nymphs. For some time she was unsuccessful, until by chance she touched a delicately-modeled rose, which was carven on the central altar of one side. At once there was a slight click, and the silver slab with its sculptured figures fell downward on a hinge. As she had surmised, the box was divided within into two unequal portions; the upper one, visible when the ordinary lid was lifted, was empty, as has been said; but in the narrowness of the lower receptacle, between the false and the real bottoms of the box, there was a slim packet. Pleased with her discovery – which certainly did credit to her acute intelligence – Hagar drew out the papers. 'Here is my Florentine tragedy!' said she, with glee, and proceeded to examine her treasure-trove.

It did not take her long to discover that the letters – for they were letters, five or six, tied up with rose-hued ribbon – were not fifteenth century, but very late nineteenth; that they were not written in Italian, but in English. Penned in graceful female handwriting upon scented paper – a perfume of violets clung to them still – these letters were full of passionate and undisciplined love. Hagar only read one, but it was sufficient to see that she had stumbled upon an intrigue between a married woman and a man. No address was given, as each letter began unexpectedly with words of fire and adoration, continuing in such style from beginning to end, where the signature appended was 'Beatrice'. In the first one, which Hagar read – and which was a sample of the rest – the writer lamented her marriage, raged that she was bound to a dull husband, and called upon her dearest Paul – evidently the inamorato's name – to deliver her. The passion, the fierce sensual love which burnt in every line of this married woman's epistles, disgusted Hagar not a little. Her pure and virginal soul shrank back from the abyss revealed by this lustful adoration; trembled at the glimpse it obtained of a hidden life. There was, indeed, no tragedy in these letters as yet, but it might be – with such a woman as she who had penned them – that they would become the prelude to one. In every line there was divorce.

'What a liar that valet is!' thought Hagar, as she tied the letters up again. 'This casket was left to him as a legacy, was it? As if a man would entrust such compromising letters to the discretion of a scoundrel like

Peters! No, no; I am sure he doesn't know of this secret place, or of the existence of these letters. He stole this casket from his master, and did not know that it was used to hide these epistles from a married woman. I'll keep the casket safely, and see what comes of it when Mr Peters returns.'

But she did not put the letters back in their secret recess. It might be that the valet would return before the conclusion of the month; and if she were out of the shop at the time, her assistant would give back the casket. Hagar felt that it would be wrong to let the letters get into the hands of so unscrupulous a scoundrel as she believed Peters to be. Did he find out the secret of the hiding-place, and the letters were within, he was quite capable of making capital out of them at the expense of the unhappy woman or his own master. He had the face of a blackmailer; so Hagar reclosed the casket, and put away the letters in the big safe in the parlor.

'She is a light woman – a bad woman,' she thought, thinking of that Beatrice who had written those glowing letters – 'and deserves punishment for having deceived her husband. But I won't give her into the power of that reptile; he would only fatten on her agony. If he comes back for the casket, he shall have it, but without those letters.'

Hagar did not think for a moment that Peters knew of the existence of these epistles, else in place of pawning the box he would have levied blackmail on the wretched Beatrice or her lover. But when in two weeks – long before the conclusion of the month – the valet again appeared, he showed Hagar very plainly that he had learnt the secret in the meantime. How and from whom he had learnt it Hagar forced him to explain. She was able to do this, as he wanted back the casket, yet had not the money to redeem it. This circumstance gave her a power over the man which she exercised mercilessly: and for some time – playing with him in cat-and-mouse fashion – she pretended to misunderstand his errand. But at first sight she saw from his greedy eyes and the triumphant look on his face that he was bent on some knavery.

'I wish to look at my box, if you please, miss,' said he, on first entering the shop. 'I cannot redeem it as yet, but if you would permit me to examine it I – '

'Certainly!' said Hagar, cutting him short; she had no patience with his flowery periods. 'Here is the box. Look at it as long as you please.'

Peters seized the casket eagerly, opened it, and looked into the empty space within; then he shook it, and turned it upside down, as though he expected the inner box to fall out. In a moment Hagar guessed that he had become aware, since pawning the casket, that it contained a secret receptacle, and was looking for the same. With an ironic smile she watched him fingering the delicate carvings with his clumsy hands, and saw that with such coarse handling the casket would never yield up its secret. She therefore revealed it to him, not for his satisfaction, but because she wanted to know the history of the love-letters. For these, without doubt, the creature was looking, and Hagar congratulated herself that she had obeyed her instinct, and had placed the letters beyond his reach.

'You can't find it, I see,' she observed, as Peters put down the casket in disgust.

'Find what?' he asked, with a certain challenge in his regard.

'The secret drawer for which you are looking.'

'How do you know that I look for a secret drawer, miss?'

'I can guess as much from the persistent way in which you press the sides of that box. Your late master, who left you the casket as a legacy, evidently did not explain its secrets. But if you wish to know, look here?' Hagar picked up the box deftly, touched the altar rose with a light finger, and revealed to Mr Peters the secret recess. His face fell, as she knew it would, at the sight of the vacant space.

'Why, it's empty!' he said aloud in a chagrined tone. 'I thought – I thought – '

'That you would find some letters within,' interrupted Hagar, smartly. 'No doubt; but you see, Mr Peters – if that is your name – I happen to have anticipated you.'

'What? You have found the letters?'

'Yes; a neat little bundle of them, which lies in my safe.'

'Please give them to me,' said the man, with tremulous eagerness.

'Give them to you!' repeated Hagar, contemptuously. 'Not I; it is not my business to encourage blackmailing.'

'But they are my letters!' cried Peters getting red, but not denying the imputation of blackmailing. 'You cannot keep my letters!'

'Yes, I can,' retorted Hagar, putting the box on the shelf behind her; 'in the same way that I can keep this casket if I so choose.'

'How dare you!' said the man, losing all his suavity. 'The box is mine!'

'It is your master's, you mean; and the letters also. You stole the casket to get money, and now you would steal the letters, if you could, to extort money from a woman. Do you know what you are, Mr Peters? You are a scoundrel.'

Peters could hardly speak for rage; but when he did find his voice, it was to threaten Hagar with the police. At this she laughed contemptuously.

'The police!' she echoed. 'Are you out of your mind? Call a policeman if you dare, and I give you in charge for thieving that box.'

'You cannot; you do not know my master's name.'

'Do I not?' retorted Hagar, playing a game of bluff. 'You forget that the name and address of your master are in those letters.'

Seeing that he was baffled in this direction, the man changed his high tone for one of diplomacy. He became cringing and wheedling, and infinitely more obnoxious than before. Hagar could hardly listen to his vile propositions with calmness; but she did so advisedly, as she wished to know the story of the letters, the name of the woman who had written them, and that of the man – Peters' master – to whom they had been sent. But the task was disagreeable, and required a great deal of self-restraint.

'Why not share the money with me?' said Peters, in silky tones; 'those letters are worth a great deal. If you let me have them, I can sell them at a high price either to my master or to the lady who wrote them.'

'No doubt,' replied Hagar, with apparent acquiescence; 'but before I agree to your proposal I must know the story.'

'Certainly, miss. I shall tell it to you. I – '

'One moment,' interrupted Hagar. 'Is Peters your real name?'

'Yes, miss; but the address I gave was false; also the Christian name I gave you. I am John Peters, of Duke Street, St. James's, in the employment of Lord Averley.'

'You are his valet?'

'Yes; I have been with him for a long time; but I lost some money at cards a week or two ago, so I – I – '

'So you stole this casket,' finished Hagar, sharply.

'No, miss, I didn't,' replied Peters, with great dignity. 'I borrowed it from my lord's room for a few weeks to get money on it. I intended to redeem and replace it within the month. I shall certainly do so, if our scheme with these letters turns out successful.'

Hagar could scarcely restrain herself from an outbreak when she heard this wretch so coolly discuss the use he intended to make of the profits to be derived from his villainy. However, she kept herself calm, and proceeded to ask further questions with a view to gaining his entire confidence.

'Well, Mr Peters, we will say you borrowed it,' she remarked, ironically; 'but don't you think that was rather a dangerous proceeding?'

'I didn't at the time,' said Peters, ruefully, 'as I didn't know my lord kept letters in it. I did not fancy he would ask after it. However, he did ask two days ago, and found that it was lost.'

'Did he think you had taken it?'

'Lor' bless you, no!' grinned the valet. 'I ain't quite such a fool as to be caught like that. My lord's rooms have been done up lately, so he thought as perhaps the paper-hangers or some of that low lot stole the box.'

'In that case you are safe enough,' said Hagar, enraged at the ingenious villainy of the creature. 'But how did you come to learn that there were letters hidden in this box? You didn't know of them when you pawned it.'

'No, miss, I didn't,' confessed Peters, regretfully; 'but yesterday I heard my lord say to a friend of his that there were letters to him from a married lady in the secret place of the box, so I thought – '

'That you would find the secret place, and use the letters to get money out of the married lady.'

'Yes, I did. That's what we are going to do, ain't it?'

'Is the married lady rich?' asked Hagar, answering the question by asking another.

'Lor', miss, her husband, Mr Delamere, has no end of money! She'd give anything to get those letters back. Why, if her husband saw them he would divorce her for sure! He's a proud man, is Delamere.'

'Has he any suspicion of an intrigue between his wife and Lord Averley?'

'Not he, miss; he'd stop it if he had. Oh, you may be sure she'll give a long price for those letters.'

'No doubt,' assented Hagar. 'Well, Mr Peters, as I am your partner in this very admirable scheme, you had better let me see Mrs Delamere. I'll get more out of her than you would.'

'I daresay, miss. You're a sharp one, you are! But you'll go shares fair?'

'Oh, yes; if I get a good sum, you shall have half,' replied Hagar, ambiguously. 'But where does Mrs Delamere live?'

'In Curzon Street, miss; the house painted a light red. You'll always find her in now about seven. Squeeze her for all she is worth, miss. We've got a good thing on in this business.'

'It would seem so,' replied Hagar, coolly. 'But if I were you, Mr Peters, I would redeem this casket as soon as I could. You may get into trouble else.'

'I'll take the money out of my share of the cash,' said the scoundrel. 'Don't you take less than five hundred, miss; those letters are worth it.'

'Be content; I'll see to all that. To-morrow I shall interview Mrs Delamere; so if you come and see me the day after, I will tell you the result of my visit.'

'Oh, there can only be one result with a sharp one like you,' grinned Peters. 'You squeeze Mrs Delamere like an orange, miss. Say you'll tell her husband, and she'll pay anything. Good day, miss. My stars, you're a sharp girl! Good day.'

Mr Peters departed with this compliment, just in time to stop Hagar from an unholy desire to throw the casket at his head. The man was a greater scoundrel even than she had thought; and she trembled to think of how he would have extorted money from Mrs Delamere had he obtained the letters. Luckily for that lady, her foolish epistles were in the hands of a woman far more honorable than herself.

Although untitled, Mrs Delamere was a very great lady. Certainly she was a beautiful one, and many years younger than her lord and master. Mr Delamere was a wealthy commoner, with a long pedigree, and an over-weening pride. Immersed in politics and Blue-books, he permitted his frivolous and youthful wife to do as she pleased, provided she did not drag his name in the mud. He would have forgiven her anything but that. She could be as extravagant as she pleased; gratify all her costly whims; and flirt – if she so chose, and she did choose – with fifty men; but if once the name of Delamere was whispered about in connection with a scandal, she knew well that her husband would seek either a separation or a divorce. Yet, with all this knowledge, pretty, silly Mrs Delamere was foolish enough to intrigue with Lord Averley, and to write him compromising letters.

She never thought of danger. Averley was a gentleman, a man of honour, and he had told her a dozen times that he always burnt the letters she wrote him. It was therefore a matter of amazement to Mrs Delamere when a gipsy-like girl called to see her with a sealed envelope, and mentioned that such envelope contained her letters to Averley.

'Letters! letters!' said Mrs Delamere, brushing her fluffy yellow curls off her forehead. 'What do you mean?'

'I mean that your letters to Lord Averley are in this envelope,' replied Hagar, looking coldly at the dainty doll before her. 'I mean also that did your husband see them he would divorce you!'

Mrs Delamere turned pale under her rouge. 'Who are you?' she gasped, her blue eyes dilating with terror.

'My name is Hagar Stanley. I am a gipsy girl, and I keep a pawn-shop in Lambeth.'

'A pawn-shop! How – how did you get my – my letters?'

'The valet of Lord Averley pawned a silver box in which they were concealed,' explained Hagar. 'He intended to use them as a means to extort money from you. However, I obtained the letters before he did, and I came instead of him.'

'To extort money also, I suppose?'

For the life of her, Mrs Delamere could not help making the remark. She knew that she was speaking falsely; that this girl with the grave, dark, poetic face was not the kind of woman to blackmail an erring sister. Still, the guilty little creature saw that Hagar – this girl from a pawnshop of the slums – was sitting in judgment upon her, and already, in her own mind, condemned her frivolous conduct. Proud and haughty Mrs Delamere writhed at the look on the face of her visitor, and terrified as she was at the abyss which she saw opening at her feet, she could not help making a slighting remark to gall the woman who came to save her. She said it on the impulse of the moment; and impulse had cost her dearly many a time. But that Hagar was a noble woman it would have cost the frivolous beauty dearly now.

'No, Mrs Delamere,' replied Hagar, keeping her temper – for really this weak little creature was not worth anger – 'I do not wish for money. I came to return you these letters, and I should advise you to destroy them.'

'I shall certainly do that!' said the fashionable lady, seizing the envelope held out to her; 'but you must let me reward you.'

'As you would reward any one who returned you a lost jewel!' retorted the gipsy, with curling lip. 'No, thank you; what I have done for you, Mrs Delamere, is above any reward.'

'Above any reward!' stammered the other wondering if she heard aright.

'I think so,' responded Hagar, gravely. 'I have saved your honour.'

'Saved my honour!' cried Mrs Delamere, furiously. 'How dare you! How dare you!'

'I dare, because I happen to have read one of those letters; I read only one, but I have no doubt that it is a sample of the others. If Mr Delamere read what I did, I am afraid you would have to go through the Divorce Court with Lord Averley as co-respondent.'

'You – you are mistaken,' stammered Mrs Delamere, drawn into defending herself. 'There is nothing wrong between us, I – I swear.'

'It is no use to lie to me,' said Hagar, curtly. 'I have seen what you said to the man; that is enough. However, I have no call to judge you. I came to give you the letters; you hold them in your hand; so I go.'

'Wait! wait! You have been very good. Surely a little money – '

'I am no blackmailer!' cried Hagar, wrathfully; 'but I have saved you from one. Had Lord Averley's valet become possessed of those letters, you would have had to pay thousands of pounds for them.'

'I know, I know,' whimpered the foolish little woman. 'You have been good and kind; you have saved me. Take this ring as – '

'No, I want no gifts from you,' said Hagar, going to the door.

'Why not – why not?'

Hagar looked back with a glance of immeasurable contempt. 'I take nothing from a woman who betrays her husband,' she said, tranquilly. 'Good-night, Mrs Delamere – and be careful how you write letters to your next lover. He may have a valet also,' and Hagar left the magnificent room, with Mrs Delamere standing in it, white with rage and terror and humiliation. In those few contemptuous words of the poor gipsy girl, her sin had come home to her.

Hagar had come to the West-end to see the woman who had written the letters; now she walked back to her Lambeth pawn-shop to interview the man to whom they had been sent. She was not a girl who did things by halves; and, bent upon thwarting in every way the scoundrelism of John Peters, she had sent a message to his master. In reply Lord Averley had informed her that he would call on her at the time and place mentioned in her letter. The time was nine o'clock; the place, the dingy parlor of the pawn-shop; and here Hagar intended to inform Lord Averley of the way in which she had saved Mrs Delamere from the greed of the valet. Also, she intended to make him take back the casket and repay the money lent on it. In all her dabblings in romance, Hagar never forgot that she was a woman of business, and was bound to get as much money as possible for the heir of the old miser who had fed and sheltered her when she had come a fugitive to London. Hagar's ethics would have been quite incomprehensible to the majority of mankind.

True to the hour, Lord Averley made his appearance in Carby's Crescent, and was admitted by Hagar to the back parlor. He was a tall slender, fair man, no longer in his first youth, with a colourless face, which was marked by a somewhat tired expression. He looked a trifle surprised at the sight of Hagar's rich beauty, having expected to find an old hag in charge of a pawn-shop. However, he made no comment but bowed gravely to the girl, and took the seat she offered to him. In the light of the lamp Hagar looked long and earnestly at his handsome face. There was a look of intellect on it which made her wonder how he could have found satisfaction in the love of a frivolous doll like Mrs Delamere. But Hagar quite forgot for the moment that the fullest delight of life lies in contrast.

'I have no doubt you wondered at receiving a letter from a pawn-shop,' she said, abruptly.

'I confess I did,' he replied, quietly: 'but because you mentioned that you had my casket I came. It is here, you say?'

Hagar took the silver box off a near shelf, and placed it on the table before him. 'It was pawned here two weeks ago,' she said, quietly. 'I lent thirteen pounds; so, if you give me that sum and the month's interest, you can have it.'

Without a word Lord Averley counted out the thirteen pounds, but he had to ask her what the interest was. Hagar told him, and in a few moments the transaction was concluded. Then Averley spoke.

'How did you know it was my casket?'

'The man who pawned it told me so.'

'That was strange.'

'Not at all, my lord. I made him tell me.'

'H'm! you look clever,' said Averley, looking at her with interest. 'May I ask the name of the man who pawned this?'

'Certainly. He was your valet, John Peters.'

'Peters!' echoed her visitor. 'Oh, you must be mistaken! Peters is an honest man!'

'He is a scoundrel and a thief, Lord Averley; and but for me he would have been a blackmailer.'

'A blackmailer?'

'Yes. There were letters in that casket.'

'Were letters!' said Averley, hurriedly, and drew the box towards him. 'Do you know the secret?'

'Yes; I found the secret recess and the letters. It was lucky for you that I did so. Your indiscreet speech to a friend informed Peters that compromising letters were hidden in the casket. He came here to find them; but I had already removed them.'

'And where are they now?'

'I gave them back to the married woman who wrote them.'

'How did you know who wrote them?' asked Lord Averley, raising his eyebrows.

'I read one of the letters, and then Peters told me the name of the lady. He proposed to me to blackmail her. I ostensibly agreed, and went to see the lady, to whom I gave back the letters. I asked you here to-night to return the casket; also to put you on your guard against John Peters. He is coming to see me to-morrow, to get – as he thinks – the money obtained by means of the letters. That is the whole story.'

'It's a queer one,' replied Averley, smiling. 'I shall certainly discharge Peters, but I won't prosecute him for thieving. He knows about the letters, and they are far too dangerous to be brought into court.'

'They are not dangerous now, my lord. I have given them back to the woman who wrote them.'

'That was very good of you,' said Averley, satirically. 'May I ask the name of the lady?'

'Surely you know! Mrs Delamere.'

Averley looked aghast for a moment, and then began to laugh quietly. 'My dear young lady,' he said, as soon as he could bring his mirth within bounds, 'would it not have been better to have consulted me before giving back those letters?'

'No,' said Hagar, boldly, 'for you might not have handed them over.'

'Certainly I should not have handed them to Mrs Delamere!' said Averley, with a fresh burst of laughter.

'Why not?'

'Because she never wrote them. My dear lady, I burnt all the letters I got from Mrs Delamere, and I told her I had done so. The letters in this casket signed "Beatrice" were from a different lady altogether. I shall have to see Mrs Delamere. She'll never forgive me. Oh, what a comedy!' and he began laughing again.

Hagar was annoyed. She had acted for the best, no doubt; but she had given the letters to the wrong woman. Shortly the humour of the mistake struck her also, and she laughed in concert with Lord Averley.

'I'm sorry I made a mistake,' she said, at length.

'You couldn't help it,' replied Averley rising. 'It was that scoundrel Peters who put you wrong. But I'll discharge him to-morrow, and get those letters of Beatrice back from Mrs Delamere.'

'And you'll leave that poor little woman alone,' said Hagar, as she escorted him to the door.

'My dear lady, now that Mrs Delamere has read those letters she'll leave me alone – severely. She'll never forgive me. Good-night. Oh, me, what a comedy!'

Lord Averley went off, casket and all. Peters never came back to get his share of the blackmail, so Hagar supposed he had learnt from his master what she had done. As to Mrs Delamere, Hagar often wondered what she said when she read those letters signed 'Beatrice'. But only Lord Averley could have told her that and Hagar never saw him again; nor did she ever see Peters the blackmailer. Finally, she never set eyes again on the Cinque Cento Florentine casket which had contained the love-letters of – the wrong woman.

November Joe

Created by Hesketh Prichard (1876 – 1922)

HESKETH VERNON HESKETH-PRICHARD (wisely, he abbreviated his name when it appeared on his books) led a life at least as eventful as those of his fictional creations. Born in India, the son of a soldier, he became an explorer, adventurer and big-game hunter who travelled around the world from Patagonia to Newfoundland and Haiti to Norway. He also found time to take the field regularly as a county cricketer, playing for Hampshire from the late 1890s to the outbreak of the First World War. During that war Hesketh Prichard, reputedly one of the best shots in the world, was given the task of training men to become snipers on the Western Front. Prichard published several books about his travels and also wrote fiction, often in collaboration with his mother, throughout his adult life. His stories about an aristocratic Spanish bandit, Don Q, later formed the basis for a Hollywood movie starring Douglas Fairbanks. Prichard was a friend of Conan Doyle and it is entirely unsurprising that he should venture into the field of crime fiction. The Flaxman Low stories, written with his mother, are about an occult detective and predate Hope Hodgson's Carnacki stories by a decade. The November Joe stories cleverly transfer Sherlockian skills to a setting – the Canadian wilderness – where they are eminently practical and, indeed, necessary. As one of the characters in the stories remarks, 'the speciality of a Sherlock Holmes is the everyday routine of a woodsman. Observation and deduction are part and parcel of his daily existence.'

The Black Fox Skin

YOU MUST UNDERSTAND that from this time on, my association with November Joe was not continuous but fitful, and that after the events I have just written down I went back to Quebec, where I became once more immersed in my business. Of Joe I heard from time to time, generally by means of smudged letters obviously written from camp and usually smelling of wood smoke. It was such a letter, which, in the following year, caused me once more to seek November. It ran as follows:

'Mr Quaritch, Sir, last week I was up to Widdeney Pond and I see a wonderful red deer buck. I guess he come out of the thick Maine woods to take the place o' that fella you shot there last fall. This great fella has had a accident to his horns or something for they come of his head thick and stunted-like and all over little points. Them horns would look fine at the top of the stairs in your house to Quebec, so come and try for them. I'll be down to Mrs Harding's Friday morning so as I can meet you if you can come. There's only three moose using round here, two cows, and a mean little fella of a bull.'

This was the letter which caused me to seek Mrs Harding's, but owing to a slight accident to the rig I was driven up in, I arrived late to find that November had gone up to a neighbouring farm on some business, leaving word that should I arrive I was to start for his shack and that he would catch me up on the way.

I walked forward during the greater part of the afternoon when, in trying a short cut through the woods, I lost my bearings and I was glad enough to hear Joe's hail behind me.

'Struck your trail 'way back,' said he, 'and followed it up as quick as I could.'

'Have you been to Harding's?'

'No. I struck straight across from Simmons's. O' course I guessed it were probably you, but even if I hadn't known you was coming I'd 'a been certain you didn't know the country and was town-bred.'

'How?'

'You paused wherever there were crossroads, and had a look at your compass.'

'How do you know I did that?' I demanded again; for I had consulted my compass several times, though I could not see what had made Joe aware of the fact.

'You stood it on a log once at Smith's Clearing and again on that spruce stump at the Old Lumber Camp. And each time you shifted your direction.'

I laughed. 'Did you know anything else about me?' I asked.

'Knew you carried a gun, and was wonderful fresh from the city.'

In answer to my laugh Joe continued:

'Twice you went off the road after them two deer you saw, your tracks told me that. And you stepped in under that pine when that little drop o' rain fell. There wasn't enough of it to send a man who'd been a day in the woods into shelter. But I have always noticed how wonderful scared the city makes a man o' a drop o' clean rain-water.'

'Anything else?'

'Used five matches to light your pipe. Struck 'em on a wore-out box. Heads come off, too. That don't happen when you have a new scraper to your box.'

'I say, Joe, I shouldn't like to have you on my trail if I'd committed a crime.'

Joe smiled a singularly pleasant smile. 'I guess I'd catch you all right,' said he.

It was long after dark when we reached November's shack that evening. As he opened the door he displaced something white which lay just inside it. He stooped.

'It's a letter,' he said in surprise as he handed it to me. 'What does it say, Mr Quaritch?'

I read it aloud. It ran:

I am in trouble, Joe. Somebody is robbing my traps. When you get hor.
I pray will be soon, come right over.
  S. Rone

'The skunk!' cried November.

I had never seen him so moved. He had been away hunting for three days and returned to find this message.

'The darned skunk,' he repeated, 'to rob her traps!'

'Her? A woman?'

'S. Rone stands for Sally Rone. You've sure heard of her?'

'No, who is she?'

'I'll tell you,' said Joe. 'Sal's a mighty brave girl – that is, she's a widow. She was married on Rone four years ago last Christmas, and the autumn after he got his back broke to the Red Star Lumber Camp. Didn't hump himself quick enough from under a falling tree. Anyway, he died all right, leaving Sally just enough dollars to carry her over the birth of her son. To make a long story short, there was lots of the boys ready to fill dead man Rone's place when they knew her money must be giving out, and the neighbours were wonderful interested to know which Sal would take. But it soon come out that Sal wasn't taking any of them, but had decided to try what she could do with the trapping herself.'

'Herself?'

'Just that. Rone worked a line o' traps, and Sal was fixed to make her living and the boy's that way. Said a woman was liable to be as successful a trapper as a man. She's at it near three year now, and she's made good. Lives with her boy about four hours' walk nor'west of here, with not another house within five miles of her. She's got a young sister, Ruby, with her on account of the kid, as she has to be out such a lot.'

'A lonely life for a woman.'

'Yes,' agreed November. 'And now some skunk's robbing her and getting her frightened, curse him! How long ago was that paper written?'

I looked again at the letter. 'There's no date.'

'Nothing about who brought it?'

'No.'

November rose, lighted a lantern, and without a word stepped out into the darkness. In five minutes he returned.

'She brought it herself,' he announced. 'Little feet – running – rustling to get home to the little chap. She was here afore Thursday morning's rain, some time Wednesday, not long after I started, I guess.... I'm off soon as ever I can stoke in some grub. You coming?'

'Yes.'

Not much later I was following November's nimbly moving figure upon as hard a woods march as I ever care to try. I was not sorry when a thong of my moccasin gave way and Joe allowed me a minute to tie it up and to get my wind.

'There's Tom Carroll, Phil Gort, and Injin Sylvester,' began November abruptly, 'those three. They're Sally's nearest neighbours, them and Val Black. Val's a good man, but...'

'But what?' said I absently.

'Him and Tom Carroll's cut the top notches for Sally's favour so far.'

'But what's that got to do with...'

'Come on,' snapped November, and hurried forward.

I need say no more about the rest of the journey, it was like a dozen others I had made behind November. Deep in the night I could just make out that we were passing round the lower escarpments of a great wooded mountain, when we saw a light above glimmering through the trees. Soon we reached the lonely cabin in its clearing; the trees closed about it, and the night wind whined overhead through the bareness of the twigs.

Joe knocked at the door, calling at the same time: 'It's me. Are you there, Sally?'

The door opened an inch or two. 'Is it you, Joe?'

November thrust his right hand with its deep scar across the back through the aperture. 'You should know that cut, Sal, you tended it.'

'Come in! Come in!'

I followed Joe into the house, and turned to look at Sally. Already I had made a mental picture of her as a strapping young woman, well

equipped to take her place in the race of life, but I saw a slim g___
gentle red-brown eyes that matched the red-brown of her rebel__
hair, a small face, pale under its weather-tan, but showing a line o_
milk-white skin above her brows. She was in fact extremely pretty,
with a kind of good looks I had not expected, and ten seconds later, I,
too, had fallen under the spell of that charm which was all the more
powerful because Sally herself was unconscious of it.

'You've been long in coming, Joe,' she said with a sudden smile.
'You were away, of course?'

'Aye, just got back 'fore we started for here.' He looked round.
'Where's young Dan?'

'I've just got him off to sleep on the bed there'; she pointed to a
deerskin curtain in the corner.

'What? They been frightening him?'

Mrs Rone looked oddly at November. 'No, but if he heard us
talking he might get scared, for the man who's been robbing me was
in this room not six hours ago and Danny saw him.'

November raised his eyebrows. 'Huh! That's fierce!' he said.
'Danny's rising three, ain't he? He could tell.'

'Nothing at all. It was after dark and the man had his face muffled.
Danny said he was a real good man, he gave him sugar from the
cupboard!' said Sally.

'His hands ... what like was his hands? ... He gave the sugar.'

'I thought of that, but Danny says he had mitts on.'

November drew a chair to the table. 'Tell us all from the first of it...
robbing the traps and to-night.'

In a few minutes we were drinking our tea while our hostess told
us the story.

'It's more'n three weeks now since I found out the traps were being
meddled with. It was done very cunning, but I have my own way
of baiting them and the thief, though he's a clever woodsman and
knows a heap, never dropped to that. Sometimes he'd set 'em and bait
'em like as if they were never touched at all, and other times he'd just
make it appear as if the animal had got itself out. I wouldn't believe
it at first, for I thought there was no one hereabouts would want to
starve me and Danny, but it happened time after time.'

'He must have left tracks,' said Joe.

'Some, yes. But he mostly worked when snow was falling. He's cunning.'

'Did any one ever see his tracks but you?'

'Sylvester did.'

'How was that?' said Joe with sudden interest.

'I came on Sylvester one evening when I was trailing the robber.'

'Perhaps Sylvester himself was the robber.'

Mrs Rone shook her head.

'It wasn't him, Joe. He couldn't 'a' known I was comin' on him, and his tracks was quite different.'

'Well, but to-night? You say the thief come here to-night? What did he do that for?' said Joe, pushing the tobacco firmly into his pipe-bowl.

'He had a good reason,' replied Sally with bitterness. 'Last Thursday when I was on my way back from putting my letter under your door, I come home around by a line of traps which I have on the far side of the mountain. It wasn't anything like my usual time to visit them, not but what I've varied my hours lately to try and catch the villain. I had gone about halfway to Low's Corner when I heard something rustling through the scrub ahead of me, it might have been a lynx or it might have been a dog, but when I come to the trap I saw the thief had made off that minute, for he'd been trying to force open the trap, and when he heard me he wrenched hard, you bet, but he was bound to take care not to be too rough.'

'Good fur, you mean?'

'Good?' Sally's face flushed a soft crimson. 'Good? Why I've never seen one to match it. It was a black fox, lying dead there, but still warm, for it had but just been killed. The pelt was fair in its prime, long and silky and glossy. You can guess, November, what that meant for Danny and me next winter, that I've been worrying about a lot. The whooping-cough's weakened him down bad, and I thought of the things I could get for him while I was skinning out the pelt.' Sally's voice shook, and her eyes filled with tears. 'Oh, Joe, it's hard, hard!'

November sat with his hands upon the table in front of him, and I saw his knuckles whiten as he gripped it.

'Let's hear the end of it!' he said shortly, man-like showing irr.
when his heart was full of pity.

'The skin was worth eight hundred dollars anywhere, and I come
home just singing. I fixed it at once, and, then being scared-like, I hid
it in the cupboard over there behind those old magazines. I'd have
locked it up, but I've nothing that locks. Who has on this section?
Once or twice, being kind of proud of it, I looked at the skin, the last
time was this morning before I went out. I was proud of it. No one
but Ruby knew that I had got it. I left Ruby here, but Mrs Scats had
her seventh yesterday morning, and Ruby ran over to help for a while
after she put Danny to bed. The thief must have been on the watch
and seen her go, and he knew I was due to visit the north line o' traps
and I'd be late anyway. He laid his plan good and clever . . . '

She stopped for a moment to pour out another cup for Joe.

'Where's Ruby now?' he inquired.

'She's stopping the night; they sent over to tell me,' replied Sally.
'Well, to go on, I had a lynx in one of my traps which got dragged
right down by Deerhom Pond, so I was more than special late. Danny
began at once to tell me about the man that came in. I rushed across
and looked in the cupboard; the black fox pelt was gone, of course!'

'What did Danny say about the man?'

'Said he had on a big hat and a neckerchief. He didn't speak a word;
gave Danny sugar, as I have said. He must 'a been here some time,
for he's ransacked the place high and low, and took near every pelt I
got this season.'

Joe looked up. 'Those pelts marked?'

'Yes, my mark's on some, seven pricks of a needle.'

'You've looked around the house to see if he left anything?'

'Sure!' Sally put her hand in her pocket.

'What?'

'Only this.' She opened her hand and disclosed a rifle cartridge.

Joe examined it. 'Soft-nosed bullet for one of them fancy English
guns. Where did you find it?'

'On the floor by the table.'

'Huh!' said Joe, and, picking up the lamp, he began carefully and
methodically to examine every inch of the room.

'Any one but me been using tobacco in here lately?' he asked.

'Not that I know of,' replied Sally.

He made no comment, but continued his search. At last he put down the lamp and resumed his chair, shaking a shred or two of something from his fingers.

'Well?' questioned Mrs Rone.

'A cool hand,' said November. 'When he'd got the skin, he stopped to fill his pipe. It was then he dropped the cartridge; it came out of his pocket with the pipe, I expect. All that I can tell you about him is that he smokes "Gold Nugget" – he pointed to the shreds – 'and carries a small-bore make of English rifle. . . . Hello! where's the old bitch?'

'Old Rizpah? I dunno, less she's gone along to Scats's place. Ruby'd take her if she could, she's that scairt of the woods; but Rizpah's never left Danny before.'

Joe drained his cup. 'We've not found much inside the house,' said he. 'As soon as the sun is up, we'll try our luck outside. Till then I guess we'd best put in a doze.'

Mrs Rone made up a shake-down of skins near the stove, and disappeared behind the deerskin curtain. Before sleep visited me I had time to pass in review the curious circumstances which the last few hours had disclosed. Here was a woman making a noble and plucky struggle to wring a living from Nature. In my fancy I saw her working and toiling early and late in the snow and gloom. And then over the horizon of her life appeared the dastardly thief who was always waiting, always watching to defeat her efforts.

When I woke next morning it was to see, with some astonishment, that a new personage had been drawn into our little drama of the woods. A dark-bearded man in the uniform of a game warden was sitting on the other side of the stove. He was a straightforward-looking chap getting on for middle age, but there was a certain doggedness in his aspect. Mrs Rone, who was preparing breakfast, made haste to introduce him.

'This is Game Warden Evans, Mr Quaritch,' she said. 'He was at Scats's last night. There he heard about me losing fur from the traps, and come right over to see if he couldn't help me.'

Having exchanged the usual salutations, Evans remarked good-humouredly:

'November's out trailing the robber. Him and me's been ta... about the black fox pelt. Joe's wasting his time all right.'

'How's that?' I asked, rather nettled, for wasting his time was about the last accusation I should ever have brought against my comrade.

'Because I can tell him who the thief is.'

'You know!' I exclaimed.

Evans nodded. 'I can find out any time.'

'How?'

'Care to see?' He rose and went to the door.

I followed. It was a clear bright morning, and the snow that had fallen on the previous day was not yet melted. We stepped out into it, but had not left the threshold when Evans touched my shoulder.

'Guess Joe missed it,' he said, pointing with his finger.

I turned in the direction indicated, and saw that upon one of the nails which had been driven into the door of the cabin, doubtless for the purpose of exposing skins to the warmth of the sun, some bright-coloured threads were hanging. Going nearer, I found them to be strands of pink and grey worsted, twisted together.

'What d' you think of that?' asked Evans, with a heavy wink.

Before I could answer, Joe came into sight round a clump of bush on the edge of the clearing.

'Well,' called the game warden, 'any luck?'

November walked up to us, and I waited for his answer with all the eagerness of a partisan. 'Not just exactly,' he said.

'What do you make of that?' asked Evans again, pointing at the fluttering worsted, with a glance of suppressed triumph at Joe.

'Huh!' said November. 'What do you?'

'Pretty clear evidence that, ain't it? The robber caught his necker on those nails as he slipped out. We're getting closer. English rifle, "Gold Nugget" in his pipe, and a pink and grey necker. Find a chap that owns all three. It can't be difficult. Wardens have eyes in their heads as well as you, November.'

'Sure!' agreed Joe politely but with an abstracted look as he examined the door. 'You say you found it here?'

'Yes.'

'Huh!' said Joe again.

'Anything else on the trail?' asked Evans.

November looked at him. 'He shot Rizpah.'

'The old dog? I suppose she attacked him and he shot her.'

'Yes, he shot her first.'

'First? What then?'

'He cut her nigh in pieces with his knife.'

Without more words Joe turned back into the woods and we went after him. Hidden in a low, marshy spot, about half a mile from the house, we came upon the body of the dog. It was evident she had been shot – more than that, the carcass was hacked about in a horrible manner.

'What do you say now, Mr Evans?' inquired Joe.

'What do I say? I say this. When we find the thief we'll likely find the marks of Rizpah's teeth on him. That's what made him mad with rage, and...' Evans waved his hand.

We returned to breakfast at Mrs Rone's cabin. While we were eating, Evans casually brought out a scrap of the worsted he had detached from the nail outside.

'Seen any one with a necker like that, Mrs Rone?' he asked.

The young woman glanced at the bit of wool, then bent over Danny as she fed him. When she raised her head I noticed that she looked very white.

'There's more'n one of that colour hereabouts likely,' she replied, with another glance of studied indifference.

'It's not a common pattern of wool,' said Evans. 'Well, you're all witnesses where I got it. I'm off.'

'Where are you going?' I asked.

'It's my business to find the man with the pink necker.'

Evans nodded and swung off through the door.

November looked at Sally. 'Who is he, Sally?'

Mrs Rone's pretty forehead puckered into a frown. 'Who?'

'Pink and grey necker,' said Joe gently.

A rush of tears filled her red-brown eyes.

'Val Black has one like that. I made it for him myself long ago.'

'And he has a rifle of some English make,' added November.

Mrs Rone started. 'So he has, but I never remembered that till this minute!' She looked back into Joe's grey eyes with indignation. 'And

he smokes "Nugget" all right, too. I know it. All the same, it isn't Val!'
The last words were more than an appeal; they were a statement of faith.

'It's queer them bits of worsted on the doornails,' observed Joe
judicially.

Her colour flamed for a moment. 'Why queer? He's been here to
see m' – us more'n once this time back; the nails might have caught
his necker any day,' she retorted.

'It's just possible,' agreed November in an unconvinced voice.

'It can't be Val!' repeated Mrs Rone steadily.

We walked away, leaving her standing in the doorway looking
after us. When we were out of sight and of earshot I turned to
November.

'The evidence against Black is pretty strong. What's your notion?'

'Can't say yet. I think we'd best join Evans; he'll be trailing the thief.'

We made straight through the woods towards the spot where the
dog's body lay. As we walked I tried again to find out Joe's opinion.

'But the motive? Haven't Mrs Rone and Black always been on good
terms?' I persisted.

Joe allowed that was so, and added: 'Val wanted to marry her years
ago, afore Joe Rone came to these parts at all, but Rone was a mighty
taking kind of chap, laughing and that, and she married him.'

'But surely Black wouldn't rob her, especially now that he has his
chance again.'

'Think not?' said Joe. 'I wonder!' After a pause he went on. 'But it
ain't hard to see what'll be Evans's views on that. He'll say Val's scared
of her growing too independent, for she's made good so far with
her traps, and so he just naturally took a hand to frighten her into
marriage. His case ag'in' Val won't break down for want of motive.'

'One question more, Joe. Do you really think Val Black is the guilty
man?'

November Joe looked up with his quick, sudden smile. 'It'll be a
shock to Evans if he ain't,' said he.

Very soon we struck the robber's trail, and saw from a second line
of tracks that Evans was ahead of us following it.

'Here the thief goes,' said Joe. 'See, he's covered his moccasins with
deerskin, and here we have Evans's tracks. He's hurrying, Evans is
– he's feeling good and sure of the man he's after!'

Twice November pointed out faint signs that meant nothing to me. 'Here's where the robber stopped to light his pipe – see, there's the mark of the butt of his gun between those roots – the snow's thin there. Must 'a' had a match, that chap,' he said after a minute, and standing with his back to the wind, he made a slight movement of his hand.

'What are you doing?' I asked.

'Saving myself trouble,' he turned at right angles and began searching through the trees.

'Here it is. Hung up in a snag.... Seadog match he used.' Then, catching my eye, he went on: 'Unless he was a fool, he'd light his match with his face to the wind, wouldn't he? And most right-handed men 'ud throw the match thereabouts where I hunted for it.'

Well on in the afternoon the trail led out to the banks of a wide and shallow stream, into the waters of which they disappeared. Here we overtook Evans. He was standing by the ashes of a fire almost on the bank.

He looked up as we appeared. 'That you, Joe? Chap's took to the water,' said the game warden, 'but he'll have to do more than that to shake me off.'

'Chap made this too?' inquired November with a glance at the dead fire.

Evans nodded. 'Walked steady till he came here. Dunno what he lit the fire for. Carried grub, I s'pose.'

'No, to cook that partridge,' said Joe.

I glanced at Evans, his face darkened, clearly this did not please him.

'Oh, he shot a partridge?'

'No,' said Joe; 'he noosed it back in the spruces there. The track of the wire noose is plain, and there was some feathers. But look here, Evans, he didn't wear no pink necker.'

Evans's annoyance passed off suddenly. 'That's funny!' said he, 'for he left more than a feather and the scrape of a wire.' The game warden pulled out a pocketbook and showed us wedged between its pages another strand of the pink and grey wool. 'I found it where he passed through those dead spruces. How's that?'

I looked at Joe. To my surprise he threw back his head, and gave one of his rare laughs.

'Well,' cried Evans, 'are you still sure that he didn't wear a pink necker?'

'Surer than ever,' said Joe, and began to poke in the ashes.

Evans eyed him for a moment, transferred his glance to me, and winked. Before long he left us, his last words being that he would have his hands on 'Pink Necker' by night. Joe sat in silence for some ten minutes after he had gone, then he rose and began to lead away southeast.

'Evans'll hear Val Black's the owner of the pink necker at Lavette Village. It's an otter's to a muskrat's pelt that then he'll head straight for Val's. We've got to be there afore him.'

We were. This was the first time I had experience of Joe's activities on behalf of a woman, and, to begin with, I guessed that he himself had a tender feeling for Sally Rone. So he had, but it was not the kind of feeling I had surmised. It was not love, but just an instinct of downright chivalry, such as one sometimes finds deepset in the natures of the men of the woods. Some day later I may tell you what November was like when he fell head over ears in love, but that time is not yet.

The afternoon was yet young when we arrived at Val Black's. At that period he was living in a deserted hut which had once been used by a bygone generation of lumbermen.

It so happened that Val Black was not at home, but Joe entered the hut and searched it thoroughly. I asked him what he was seeking.

'Those skins of Sally's.'

'Then you do think Black . . .'

'I think nothing yet. And here's the man himself anyway.'

He turned to the door as Val Black came swinging up the trail. He was of middle height, strongly built, with quick eyes and dark hair which, though cropped close, still betrayed its tendency to curl. He greeted November warmly; November was, I thought, even more slow-spoken than usual.

'Val,' he said, after some talk, 'have you still got that pinky necker Sally knitted for you?'

'Why d'you ask that?'

'Because I want to be put wise, Val.'

'Yes, I've got her.'

'Where?'

'Right here,' and Black pulled the muffler out of his pocket.

'Huh!' said Joe.

There was a silence, rather a strained silence, between the two. Then November continued. 'Where was you last night?'

Val looked narrowly at Joe, Joe returned his stare.

'Got any reason fer asking?'

'Sure.'

'Got any reason why I should tell you?'

'Yes to that.'

'Say, November Joe, are you searching for trouble?' asked Black in an ominously quiet voice.

'Seems as if trouble was searching for me,' replied November.

There was another silence, then Val jerked out, 'I call your hand.'

'I show it,' said Joe. 'You're suspected of robbing Sally's traps this month back. And you're suspected of entering Sally's house last evening and stealing pelts . . .'

Val fell back against the doorpost.

'Stealin' pelts... Sally's?' he repeated. 'Is that all I'm suspected of?'

'That's all.'

'Then look out!' With a shout of rage he made at Joe.

November stood quite still under the grip of the other's furious hands.

'You act innocent; don't you, you old coyote!' he grinned ironically.

'I never said I suspected you.'

Black drew off, looking a little foolish, but he flared up again.

'Who is it suspects me?'

'Just Evans. And he's got good evidence. Where was you between six and seven last night?'

'In the woods. I come back and slep' here.'

'Was you alone?'

'Yes.'

'Then you can't prove no alibi.' Joe paused.

It was at this moment that Evans, accompanied by two other forest rangers, appeared upon the scene. He had not followed the track, but had come through a patch of standing wood to the north of the hut. Quick as lightning he covered Black with his shotgun.

'Up with your hands,' he cried, 'or I'll put this load of bird-shot into your face.'

Black scowled, but his hands went up. The man was so mad with rage that, I think, had Evans carried a rifle he would not have submitted, but the thought of the blinding charge in Evans's gun cowed him. He stood panting. At a sign, one of the rangers sidled up, and the click of handcuffs followed.

'What am I charged with?' cried Black.

'Robbery.'

'You'll pay me for this, Simon Evans!'

'It won't be for a while – not till they let you out again,' retorted the warden easily. 'Take him off up the trail, Bill.'

The rangers walked away with their prisoner, and Evans turned to Joe.

'Guess I have the laugh of you, November,' he said.

'Looks that way. Where you takin' him?'

'To Lavette. I've sent word to Mrs Rone to come there to-morrow. And now,' continued Evans, 'I'm going to search Black's shack.'

'What for?'

'The stolen pelts.'

'Got a warrant?'

'I'm a warden – don't need one.'

'You'll not search without it,' said November, moving in front of the door.

'Who'll stop me?' Evans's chin shot out doggedly.

'I might,' said Joe in his most gentle manner.

Evans glared at him. 'You?'

'I'm in the right, for it's ag'in' the law, and you know it, Mr Evans.'

Evans hesitated. 'What's your game?' he asked.

Joe made a slight gesture of disclaimer.

Evans turned on his heel.

'Have it your way, but I'll be back with my warrant before sun up to-morrow, and I'm warden, and maybe you'll find it's better to have me for a friend than... '

'Huh! Say, Mr Quaritch, have you a fill of that light baccy o' yours? I want soothin'.'

As soon as Evans was out of sight, Joe beckoned me to a thick piece of scrub not far from the hut.

'Stay right here till I come back. Everything depends on that,' he whispered.

I lay down at my ease in a sheltered spot, and then Joe also took the road for Lavette.

During the hours through which I waited for his return I must acknowledge I was at my wits' end to understand the situation. Everything appeared to be against Black, the cartridge which fitted his rifle, the strands of the telltale neckerchief, the man's own furious behaviour, his manifest passion for Mrs Rone, and the suggested motive for the thefts – all these things pointed, conclusively it seemed to me, in one direction. And yet I knew that almost from the beginning of the inquiry November had decided that Black was innocent. Frankly, I could make neither head nor tail of it.

The evening turned raw, and the thin snow was softening, and though I was weary of my watch I was still dreaming when I started under a hand that touched my shoulder. Joe was crouching at my side. He warned me to caution, but I could not refrain from a question as to where he had been.

'Down to the store at Lavette,' he whispered. 'I was talking about that search-warrant – pretty high-handed I said it was, and the boys agreed to that.'

Then commenced a second vigil. The sun went down behind the tree roots, and was succeeded by the little cold wind that often blows at that hour. Yet we lay in our ambush as the dusk closed quickly about us, nor did we move until a slight young moon was sending level rays between clouds that were piling swiftly in the sky.

After a while Joe touched me to wakefulness, and I saw something moving on the trail below us. A second or two of moonlight gave me a glimpse of the approaching figure of a man, a humped figure that moved swiftly. If ever I saw craft and caution inform an advance, I saw it then.

The clouds swept over, and when next the glint of light came, the dark figure stood before the hut. A whistle, no answer, and its hand went to the latch. I heard Joe sigh as he covered the man with his rifle. Then came his voice in its quiet tones.

'Guess the game's off, Sylvester. Don't turn! Hands up!'

The man stood still as we came behind him. At a word he faced round. I saw the high cheekbones and gleaming eyes of an Indian, his savage face was contracted with animosity.

'Now, Mr Quaritch,' said November suggestively.

I flatter myself I made a neat job of tying up our prisoner.

'Thank you. What's in that bundle on his back?'

I opened it. Several skins dropped out. Joe examined them. 'All got Sally's mark on,' he said. 'Say, Mr Quaritch, let me introduce you to a pretty mean thief.'

★★★★★★

I noticed that Joe took our prisoner along at a good pace towards Lavette. After a mile or two, however, he asked me to go ahead, and if I met with Mrs Rone to make her wait his arrival, but he added, in an aside, 'Tell her nothing about Sylvester.'

I reached the village soon after dawn, but already the people were gathered at the store, where every one was discussing the case. Evans sat complacently listening to the opinions of the neighbours. It was clear to me that the public verdict was dead against Black. Some critics gave the rein to venomous comments which made me realize that, good fellow as Val was, his hot temper had had its effect on his popularity.

As I heard nothing of Mrs Rone, I set out towards her house. When I met her I noticed that her gentle face wore a changed expression. I delivered my message.

'I'll never speak to November again as long as I live!' she said with deep vindictiveness.

I feebly attempted remonstrance. She cut me short.

'That's enough. November's played double with me. I'll show him!'

I walked beside her in silence and, just before we came in sight of the houses, we met with Joe alone. He had evidently left Sylvester in safe custody. Joe glanced from Sally to me. I read understanding in his eyes.

'We've got him trapped safe, Sally. Not a hole for him to slip out by.'

Sally's rage broke from her control. 'You're just too cute, November Joe,' she blazed, 'with your tracking and finding out things, and putting Val in jail! What do you say to it that I've been fooling you all the time? I never lost no pelts! I only said it to get the laugh against ye. Ye was beginning to believe ye could hear the muskrats sneezing!'

'Is that so?' inquired Joe gently.

'Yes, and I'm going into Lavette this minute to tell them!'

Joe stepped in front of her. 'Just as you like, Sally. But how'll ye explain these?' He flung open the bundle of skins he carried.

Mrs Rone turned colour. 'Where did you find them?' she gasped.

'On his back!'

She hesitated a moment, then, 'I gave Val that lot,' she said carelessly.

'That's queer, now,' said Joe, ''cos it was on Injin Sylvester I found them.'

Sally stared at Joe, then laughed suddenly, excitedly. 'Oh, Joe! you're sure the cutest man ever made in this world!' And with that she flung her arms round his neck and kissed him.

'I'd best pass that on to Val Black!' said Joe calmly.

And Sally's blushes were prettier than you could believe.

There is no need for me to tell how Black was liberated from the hands of the crest-fallen Evans, who was as nonplussed as I myself had been at the breakdown of the case, which up to the last moment had on the face of it seemed indestructible.

I have never looked forward to any explanation, more than that which November gave to Mrs Rone, Black, and myself the same evening.

'It was the carcass of Rizpah give me the first start,' said Joe. 'As soon as I saw that I knew it weren't Val.'

'Why?' asked Sally.

'You remember it was hacked up? Now here was the case up to that. A thief had robbed Sally and all the sign he left behind was a few threads of his necker and an English-made cartridge. The thief goes out and old Rizpah attacks him. He shoots her. Then he cuts her body nigh to pieces. Why?' We all shook our heads.

'Because he wants to get his bullet out of her. And why does he want to get his bullet? Only one possible reason. Because it's different to the bullet he dropped on purpose in the house.'

'By Jove!' I cried.

'From that it all fits in. It seems funny that the thief should drop a cartridge, funnier still 'at he shouldn't notice he'd left a bit of his necker stuck to the nails on the door. Still, I'd allow them two things might happen. But when it came to his having more bits of his necker torn off by the spruces where Evans found them, it looked like as if the thief was a mighty poor woodsman. Which he wasn't. He hid his tracks good and cunning. After that I guessed I was on the right scent, but I wasn't plumb sure till I come up to the place where he killed the partridge. While he was snaring it he rested his rifle ag'in' a tree. I saw the mark of the butt on the ground, and the scratch from the foresight upon the bark. Then I knew he didn't carry no English rifle.'

'How did you know?' asked Sally.

'I could measure its length ag'in' the tree. It was nigh a foot shorter than an English rifle.'

Val's fist came down on the table. 'Bully for you, Joe!'

'Well, now, there was one more thing. Besides that black fox Sally here missed other marked pelts. They wasn't much value. Why did the thief take them? Again, only one reason. He wanted 'em for making more false evidence ag'in' Val.'

He paused. 'Go on, Joe,' cried Mrs Rone impatiently.

'When Mr Quaritch and I came to Val's shack we searched it. Nothing there. Why? 'Cos Val had been home all night and Sylvester couldn't get in without wakin' him.'

'But,' said I, 'wasn't there a good case against Black without that?'

'Yes, there was a case, but his conviction wasn't an absolute cinch. On the other hand, if the stolen skins was found hid in his shack ... That's why you had to lie in that brush so long, Mr Quaritch, while

I went in to Lavette and spread it around that the shack hadn't been searched by Evans. Sylvester was at the store and he fell into the trap right enough. We waited for him and we got him.'

'O' course,' continued Joe, 'revenge on Val weren't Sylvester's only game. He meant robbin' Sally, too, and had his plan laid. He must 'a' first gone to Val's and stole a cartridge and the bits of necker before he robbed Sally's house. Last night he started out to leave a few cheap pelts at Val's, but he had the black fox skin separate in his pack with a bit o' tea and flour and tobacco, so if we hadn't took him he'd have lit out into Maine an' sold the black fox pelt there.'

'But, Joe,' said Sally, 'when I came on Sylvester that evening I told you of when I was trailing the robber, how was it that his tracks and the robber's was quite different?'

'Had Sylvester a pack on his back?'

'Yes. Now I think of it, he had.'

'Then I dare bet that if you'd been able to look in that pack you'd 'a' found a second pair o' moccasins in it. Sylvester'd just took them off, I expect. It was snowing, weren't it?'

'Yes.'

'And he held you in talk?'

'He did.'

'Till the snow covered his tracks?'

'It's wonderful clear, Joe,' said Mrs Rone. 'But why should Sylvester have such a down on Val?'

Joe laughed. 'Ask Val!'

'Ten years ago,' said Val, 'when we was both rising twenty year, I gave Sylvester a thrashing he'd likely remember. He had a dog what weren't no use and he decided to shoot it. So he did, but he didn't kill it. He shot it far back and left it in the woods... and I come along... '

'The brute!' exclaimed Sally.

'He's a dangerous Injin,' said November, 'and he's of a breed that never forgets.'

'When he gets out of prison, you'll have to keep awake, Joe,' said Val.

'When he gets out, I'll have the snow in my hair all right, and you and Sally'll be old married folks,' retorted Joe. 'You'll sure be tired of each other by then.'

Sally looked at Val and Joe caught the look.

'Leastways,' he added, 'you'll pretend you are better'n you do now.'

We all laughed.

Craig Kennedy

Created by Arthur B. Reeve (1880 – 1936)

BORN IN NEW YORK STATE, Arthur B. Reeve was educated at Princeton and trained as a lawyer but never practised. Instead he turned to writing fiction and, in 1910, he created his most successful character, the 'scientific detective' Craig Kennedy who went on to appear in dozens of short stories and more than twenty novels. A professor of chemistry, Kennedy applied his knowledge of science and his mastery of scientific gadgets to the solution of apparently baffling crimes. His adventures were narrated by his own Watson-like companion, the journalist Walter Jameson, and were enormously popular in America for several decades. Film versions of Reeve's works were made throughout the 1910s and 1920s and a TV series based on Craig Kennedy's cases was produced as late as 1952. Today Reeve's stories often seem clumsy and stilted but they have a particular charm as reminders of a time when things that are now commonplace (like the X-rays and microphone in 'The Deadly Tube') were seen as miracles of cutting-edge technology.

The Deadly Tube

'FOR HEAVEN'S SAKE, Gregory, what is the matter?' asked Craig Kennedy as a tall, nervous man stalked into our apartment one evening. 'Jameson, shake hands with Dr Gregory. What's the matter, Doctor? Surely your X-ray work hasn't knocked you out like this?'

The doctor shook hands with me mechanically. His hand was icy. 'The blow has fallen,' he exclaimed, as he sank limply into a chair and tossed an evening paper over to Kennedy.

In red ink on the first page, in the little square headed 'Latest News', Kennedy read the caption, 'Society Woman Crippled for Life by X-Ray Treatment'.

'A terrible tragedy was revealed in the suit begun today,' continued the article, 'by Mrs Huntington Close against Dr James Gregory, an X-ray specialist with offices at Madison Avenue, to recover damages for injuries which Mrs Close alleges she received while under his care. Several months ago she began a course of X-ray treatment to remove a birthmark on her neck. In her complaint Mrs Close alleges that Dr Gregory has carelessly caused X-ray dermatitis, a skin disease of cancerous nature, and that she has also been rendered a nervous wreck through the effects of the rays. Simultaneously with filing the suit she left home and entered a private hospital. Mrs Close is one of the most popular hostesses in the smart set, and her loss will be keenly felt.'

'What am I to do, Kennedy?' asked the doctor imploringly. 'You remember I told you the other day about this case – that there was something queer about it, that after a few treatments I was afraid to carry on any more and refused to do so? She really has dermatitis and nervous prostration, exactly as she alleges in her complaint. But, before Heaven, Kennedy, I can't see how she could possibly have been so affected by the few treatments I gave her. And to-night, just as I was leaving the office, I received a telephone call from her husband's attorney, Lawrence, very kindly informing me that the case would be pushed to the limit. I tell you, it looks black for me.'

'What can they do?'

'Do? Do you suppose any jury is going to take enough expert testimony to outweigh the tragedy of a beautiful woman? Do? Why, they can ruin me, even if I get a verdict of acquittal. They can leave me with a reputation for carelessness that no mere court decision can ever overcome.'

'Gregory, you can rely on me,' said Kennedy. 'Anything I can do to help you I will gladly do. Jameson and I were on the point of going out to dinner. Join us, and after that we will go down to your office and talk things over.'

'You are really too kind,' murmured the doctor. The air of relief that was written on his face was pathetically eloquent.

'Now, not a word about the case till we have had dinner,' commanded Craig. 'I see very plainly that you have been worrying about the blow for a long time. Well, it has fallen. The neat thing to do is to look over the situation and see where we stand.'

Dinner over, we rode down-town in the subway, and Gregory ushered us into an office-building on Madison Avenue, where he had a very handsome suite of several rooms. We sat down in his waiting-room to discuss the affair.

'It is indeed a very tragic case,' began Kennedy, 'almost more tragic than if the victim had been killed outright. Mrs Huntington Close is – or rather I suppose I should say was – one of the famous beauties of the city. From what the paper says, her beauty has been hopelessly ruined by this dermatitis, which, I understand, Doctor, is practically incurable.'

Dr Gregory nodded, and I could not help following his eyes as he looked at his own rough and scarred hands.

'Also,' continued Craig, with his eyes half closed and his finger-tips together, as if he were taking a mental inventory of the facts in the case, 'her nerves are so shattered that she will be years in recovering, if she ever recovers.'

'Yes,' said the doctor simply. 'I myself, for instance, am subject to the most unexpected attacks of neuritis. But, of course, I am under the influence of the rays fifty or sixty times a day, while she had only a few treatments at intervals of many days.'

'Now, on the other hand,' resumed Craig, 'I know you, Gregory, very well. Only the other day, before any of this came out, you told me the whole story with your fears as to the outcome. I know that that lawyer of Close's has been keeping this thing hanging over your head for a long time. And I also know that you are one of the most careful X-ray operators in the city. If this suit goes against you, one of the most brilliant men of science in America will be ruined. Now, having said this much, let me ask you to describe just exactly what treatments you gave Mrs Close.'

The doctor led us into his X-ray room adjoining. A number of X-ray tubes were neatly put away in a great glass case, and at one end of the room was an operating-table with an X-ray apparatus suspended over it. A glance at the room showed that Kennedy's praise was not exaggerated.

'How many treatments did you give Mrs Close?' asked Kennedy.

'Not over a dozen, I should say,' replied Gregory. 'I have a record of them and the dates, which I will give you presently. Certainly they were not numerous enough or frequent enough to have caused a dermatitis such as she has. Besides, look here. I have an apparatus which, for safety to the patient, has few equals in the country. This big lead-glass bowl, which is placed over my X-ray tube when in use, cuts off the rays at every point except exactly where they are needed.'

He switched on the electric current, and the apparatus began to sputter. The pungent odour of ozone from the electric discharge filled the room. Through the lead-glass bowl I could see the X-ray tube inside suffused with its peculiar, yellowish-green light, divided into two hemispheres of different shades. That, I knew, was the cathode ray, not the X-ray, for the X-ray itself, which streams outside the tube, is invisible to the human eye. The doctor placed in our hands a couple of fluoroscopes, an apparatus by which X-rays can be detected. It consists simply of a closed box with an opening to which the eyes are placed. The opposite end of the box is a piece of board coated with a salt such as platino-barium cyanide. When the X-ray strikes this salt it makes it glow, or fluoresce, and objects held between the X-ray tube and the fluoroscope cast shadows according to the density of the parts which the X-rays penetrate.

With the lead-glass bowl removed, the X-ray tube sent forth its wonderful invisible radiation and made the back of the fluoroscope glow with light. I could see the bones of my fingers as I held them up between the X-ray tube and the fluoroscope. But with the lead-glass bowl in position over the tube, the fluoroscope was simply a black box into which I looked and saw nothing. So very little of the radiation escaped from the bowl that it was negligible – except at one point where there was an opening in the bottom of the bowl to allow the rays to pass freely through exactly on the spot on the patient where they were to be used.

'The dermatitis, they say, has appeared all over her body, particularly on her head and shoulders,' added Dr Gregory. 'Now I have shown you my apparatus to impress on you how really impossible it would have been for her to contract it from her treatments here. I've made thousands of exposures with never an X-ray burn before – except to myself. As for myself, I'm as careful as I can be, but you can see I am under the rays very often, while the patient is only under them once in a while.'

To illustrate his care he pointed out to us a cabinet directly back of the operating-table, lined with thick sheets of lead. From this cabinet he conducted most of his treatments as far as possible. A little peephole enabled him to see the patient and the X-ray apparatus, while an arrangement of mirrors and a fluorescent screen enabled him to see exactly what the X-rays were disclosing, without his leaving the lead-lined cabinet.

'I can think of no more perfect protection for either patient or operator,' said Kennedy admiringly. 'By the way, did Mrs Close come alone?'

'No, the first time Mr Close came with her. After that, she came with her French maid.'

The next day we paid a visit to Mrs Close herself at the private hospital. Kennedy had been casting about in his mind for an excuse to see her, and I had suggested that we go as reporters from the *Star*. Fortunately after sending up my card on which I had written Craig's name we were at length allowed to go up to her room.

We found the patient reclining in an easy chair, swathed in bandages, a wreck of her former self. I felt the tragedy keenly. All that social position and beauty had meant to her had been suddenly blasted.

'You will pardon my presumption,' began Craig, 'but, Mrs Close, I assure you that I am actuated by the best of motives. We represent the *New York Star* – '

'Isn't it terrible enough that I should suffer so,' she interrupted, 'but must the newspapers hound me, too?'

'I beg your pardon, Mrs Close,' said Craig, 'but you must be aware that the news of your suit of Dr Gregory has now become public property. I couldn't stop the *Star*, much less the other papers, from talking about it. But I can and will do this, Mrs Close. I will see that justice is done to you and all others concerned. Believe me, I am not here as a yellow journalist to make newspaper copy out of your misfortune. I am here to get at the truth sympathetically. Incidentally, I may be able to render you a service, too.'

'You can render me no service except to expedite the suit against that careless doctor – I hate him.'

'Perhaps,' said Craig. 'But suppose someone else should be proved to have been really responsible? Would you still want to press the suit and let the guilty person escape?'

She bit her lip. 'What is it you want of me?' she asked.

'I merely want permission to visit your rooms at your home and to talk with your maid. I do not mean to spy on you, far from it; but consider, Mrs Close, if I should be able to get at the bottom of this thing, find out the real cause of your misfortune, perhaps show that you are the victim of a cruel wrong rather than of carelessness, would you not be willing to let me go ahead? I am frank to tell you that I suspect there is more to this affair than you yourself have any idea of.'

'No, you are mistaken, Mr Kennedy. I know the cause of it. It was my love of beauty. I couldn't resist the temptation to get rid of even a slight defect. If I had left well enough alone I should not be here now. A friend recommended Dr Gregory to my husband, who took me there. My husband wishes me to remain at home, but I tell him I feel more comfortable here in the hospital. I shall never go to that house again – the memory of the torture of sleepless nights in my room there when I felt my good looks going, going' – she shuddered – 'is such that I can never forget it. He says I would be better off there, but no, I cannot go. Still,' she continued wearily, 'there can be no harm in your talking to my maid.'

Kennedy noted attentively what she was saying. 'I thank you, Mrs Close,' he replied. 'I am sure you will not regret your permission. Would you be so kind as to give me a note to her?'

She rang, dictated a short note to a nurse, signed it, and languidly dismissed us.

I don't know that I ever felt as depressed as I did after that interview with one who had entered a living death to ambition, for while Craig had done all the talking I had absorbed nothing but depression. I vowed that if Gregory or anybody else was responsible I would do my share toward bringing on him retribution.

The Closes lived in a splendid big house in the Murray Hill section. The presentation of the note quickly brought Mrs Close's maid down to us. She had not gone to the hospital because Mrs Close had considered the services of the trained nurses quite sufficient.

Yes, the maid had noticed how her mistress had been failing, had noticed it long ago, in fact almost at the time when she had begun the X-ray treatment. She had seemed to improve once when she went away for a few days, but that was at the start, and directly after her return she grew worse again, until she was no longer herself.

'Did Dr Gregory, the X-ray specialist, ever attend Mrs Close at her home, in her room?' asked Craig.

'Yes, once, twice, he call, but he do no good,' she said with her French accent.

'Did Mrs Close have other callers?'

'But, m'sieur, everyone in society has many. What does m'sieur mean?'

'Frequent callers – a Mr Lawrence, for instance?'

'Oh, yes, Mr Lawrence frequently.'

'When Mr Close was at home?'

'Yes, on business and on business, too, when he was not at home. He is the attorney, m'sieur.'

'How did Mrs Close receive him?'

'He is the attorney, m'sieur,' Marie repeated persistently.

'And he, did he always call on business?'

'Oh, yes, always on business, but well, madame, she was a very beautiful woman. Perhaps he like beautiful women – *eh bien*? That was before the Doctor Gregory treated madame. After the doctor treated madame M'sieur Lawrence do not call so often. That's all.'

'Are you thoroughly devoted to Mrs Close? Would you do a favour for her?' asked Craig point-blank.

'Sir, I would give my life, almost, for madame. She was always so good to me.'

'I don't ask you to give your life for her, Marie,' said Craig, 'but you can do her a great service, a very great service.'

'I will do it.'

'To-night,' said Craig, 'I want you to sleep in Mrs Close's room. You can do so, for I know that Mr Close is living at the St. Francis Club until his wife returns from the sanitarium. To-morrow morning come to my laboratory' – Craig handed her his card – 'and I will tell you what to do next. By the way, don't say anything to anyone in the house about it, and keep a sharp watch on the actions of any of the servants who may go into Mrs Close's room.'

'Well,' said Craig, 'there is nothing more to be done immediately.' We had once more regained the street and were walking up-town. We walked in silence for several blocks.

'Yes,' mused Craig, 'there is something you can do, after all, Walter. I would like you to look up Gregory and Close and Lawrence. I already know something about them. But you can find out a good deal with your newspaper connections. I would like to have every bit of scandal that has ever been connected with them, or with Mrs Close, or,' he added significantly, 'with any other woman. It isn't necessary to say that not a breath of it must be published – yet.'

I found a good deal of gossip, but very little of it, indeed, seemed to me at the time to be of importance. Dropping in at the St. Francis Club, where I had some friends, I casually mentioned the troubles of the Huntington Closes. I was surprised to learn that Close spent little of his time at the Club, none at home, and only dropped into the hospital to make formal inquiries as to his wife's condition. It then occurred to me to drop into the office of *Society Squibs*, whose editor I had long known. The editor told me, with that nameless look of the cynical scandalmonger, that if I wanted to learn anything about Huntington Close I had best watch Mrs Frances Tulkington, a very wealthy Western divorcee about whom the smart set were much excited, particularly those whose wealth made it difficult to stand the pace of society as it was going at present.

'And before the tragedy,' said the editor with another nameless look, as if he were imparting a most valuable piece of gossip, 'it was the talk of the town, the attention that Close's lawyer was paying to Mrs Close. But to her credit let me say that she never gave us a chance to hint at anything, and – well, you know us; we don't need much to make snappy society news.'

The editor then waged even more confidential, for if I am anything at all, I am a good listener, and I have found that often by sitting tight and listening I can get more than if I were a too-eager questioner.

'It really was a shame – the way that man Lawrence played his game,' he went on. 'I understand that it was he who introduced Close to Mrs T. They were both his clients. Lawrence had fought her case in the courts when she sued old Tulkington for divorce, and a handsome settlement he got for her, too. They say his fee ran up into the hundred thousands – contingent, you know. I don't know what his game was' – here he lowered his voice to a whisper – 'but they say Close owes him a good deal of money. You can figure it out for yourself as you like. Now, I've told you all I know. Come in again, Jameson, when you want some more scandal, and remember me to the boys down on the *Star*.'

The following day the maid visited Kennedy at his laboratory while I was reporting to him on the result of my investigations.

She looked worn and haggard. She had spent a sleepless night and begged that Kennedy would not ask her to repeat the experiment.

'I can promise you, Marie,' he said, 'that you will rest better to-night. But you must spend one more night in Mrs Close's room. By the way, can you arrange for me to go through the room this morning when you go back?'

Marie said she could, and an hour or so later Craig and I quietly slipped into the Close residence under her guidance. He was carrying something that looked like a miniature barrel, and I had another package which he had given me, both carefully wrapped up. The butler eyed us suspiciously, but Marie spoke a few words to him and I think showed him Mrs Close's note. Anyhow he said nothing.

Within the room that the unfortunate woman had occupied Kennedy took the coverings off the packages. It was nothing but a portable electric vacuum cleaner, which he quickly attached and set running. Up and down the floor, around and under the bed he pushed the cleaner. He used the various attachments to clean the curtains, the walls, and even the furniture. Particularly did he pay attention to the base board on the wall back of the bed. Then he carefully removed the dust from the cleaner and sealed it up in a leaden box.

He was about to detach and pack up the cleaner when another idea seemed to occur to him. 'Might as well make a thorough job of it, Walter,' he said, adjusting the apparatus again. 'I've cleaned everything but the mattress and the brass bars behind the mattress on the bed. Now I'll tackle them. I think we ought to go into the suction-cleaning business – more money in it than in being a detective, I'll bet.'

The cleaner was run over and under the mattress and along every crack and cranny of the brass bed. This done and this dust also carefully stowed away, we departed, very much to the mystification of Marie and, I could not help feeling, of other eyes that peered in through keyholes or cracks in doors.

'At any rate,' said Kennedy exultingly, 'I think we have stolen a march on them. I don't believe they were prepared for this, not at least at this stage in the game. Don't ask me any questions, Walter. Then you will have no secrets to keep if anyone should try to pry them loose. Only remember that this man Lawrence is a shrewd character.'

The next day Marie came, looking even more careworn than before.

'What's the matter, mademoiselle?' asked Craig. 'Didn't you pass a better night?'

'Oh, *mon Dieu*, I rest well, yes. But this morning, while I am at breakfast, Mr Close send for me. He say that I am discharged. Some servant tell of your visit and he verry angr-ry. And now what is to become of me – will madame his wife give a recommendation now?'

'Walter, we have been discovered,' exclaimed Craig with considerable vexation. Then he remembered the poor girl who had been an involuntary sacrifice to our investigation. Turning to her he said: 'Marie, I know several very good families, and I am sure you will not suffer for what you have done by being faithful to your mistress. Only be patient a few days. Go live with some of your folks. I will see that you are placed again.'

The girl was profuse in her thanks as she dried her tears and departed.

'I hadn't anticipated having my hand forced so soon,' said Craig after she had gone, leaving her address. 'However, we are on the right track. What was it that you were going to tell me when Marie came in?'

'Something that may be very important, Craig,' I said, 'though I don't understand it myself. Pressure is being brought to bear on the *Star* to keep this thing out of the papers, or at least to minimise it.'

'I'm not surprised,' commented Craig. 'What do you mean by pressure being brought?'

'Why, Close's lawyer, Lawrence, called up the editor this morning – I don't suppose that you know, but he has some connection with the interests which control the *Star* – and said that the activity of one of the reporters from the *Star*, Jameson by name, was very distasteful to Mr Close and that this reporter was employing a man named Kennedy to assist him.'

'I don't understand it, Craig,' I confessed, 'but here one day they give the news to the papers, and two days later they almost threaten us with suit if we don't stop publishing it.'

'It is perplexing,' said Craig, with the air of one who was not a bit perplexed, but rather enlightened.

He pulled down the district telegraph messenger lever three times, and we sat in silence for a while.

'However,' he resumed, 'I shall be ready for them to-night.'

I said nothing. Several minutes elapsed. Then the messenger rapped on the door.

'I want these two notes delivered right away,' said Craig to the boy; 'here's a quarter for you. Now mind you don't get interested in a detective story and forget the notes. If you are back here quickly with the receipts I'll give you another quarter. Now scurry along.'

Then, after the boy had gone, he said casually to me: 'Two notes to Close and Gregory, asking them to be present with their attorneys to-night. Close will bring Lawrence, and Gregory will bring a young lawyer named Asche, a very clever fellow. The notes are so worded that they can hardly refuse the invitation.'

Meanwhile I carried out an assignment for the *Star*, and telephoned my story in so as to be sure of being with Craig at the crucial moment. For I was thoroughly curious about his next move in the game. I found him still in his laboratory attaching two coils of thin wire to the connections on the outside of a queer-looking little black box.

'What's that?' I asked, eyeing the sinister looking little box suspiciously. 'An infernal machine? You're not going to blow the culprit into eternity, I hope.'

'Never mind what it is, Walter. You'll find that out in due time. It may or it may not be an infernal machine of a different sort than any you have probably ever heard of. The less you know now the less likely you are to give anything away by a look or an act. Come now, make yourself useful as well as ornamental. Take these wires and lay them in the cracks of the floor, and be careful not to let them show. A little dust over them will conceal them beautifully.'

Craig now placed the black box back of one of the chairs well down toward the floor, where it could hardly have been perceived unless one were suspecting something of the sort. While he was doing so I ran the wires across the floor, and around the edge of the room to the door.

'There,' he said, taking the wires from me. 'Now I'll complete the job by carrying them into the next room. And while I'm doing it, go over the wires again and make sure they are absolutely concealed.'

That night six men gathered in Kennedy's laboratory. In my utter ignorance of what was about to happen I was perfectly calm, and so were all the rest, except Gregory. He was easily the most nervous of us all, though his lawyer Asche tried repeatedly to reassure him.

'Mr Close,' began Kennedy, 'if you and Mr Lawrence will sit over here on this side of the room while Dr Gregory and Mr Asche sit on the opposite side with Mr Jameson in the middle, I think both of you opposing parties will be better suited. For I apprehend that at various stages in what I am about to say both you, Mr Close, and you, Dr Gregory, will want to consult your attorneys. That, of course, would be embarrassing, if not impossible, should you be sitting near each other. Now, if we are ready, I shall begin.'

Kennedy placed a small leaden casket on the table of his lecture hall. 'In this casket,' he commenced solemnly, 'there is a certain substance which I have recovered from the dust swept up by a vacuum cleaner in the room of Mrs Close.'

One could feel the very air of the room surcharged with excitement. Craig drew on a pair of gloves and carefully opened the casket. With his thumb and forefinger he lifted out a glass tube and held it gingerly at arm's length. My eyes were riveted on it, for the bottom of the tube glowed with a dazzling point of light.

Both Gregory and his attorney and Close and Lawrence whispered to each other when the tube was displayed, as indeed they did throughout the whole exhibition of Kennedy's evidence.

'No infernal machine was ever more subtle,' said Craig, 'than the tube which I hold in my hand. The imagination of the most sensational writer of fiction might well be thrilled with the mysteries of this fatal tube and its power to work fearful deeds. A larger quantity of this substance in the tube would produce on me, as I now hold it, incurable burns, just as it did on its discoverer before his death. A smaller amount, of course, would not act so quickly. The amount in this tube, if distributed about, would produce the burns inevitably, providing I remained near enough for a long-enough time.'

Craig paused a moment to emphasise his remarks.

'Here in my hand, gentlemen, I hold the price of a woman's beauty.'

He stopped again for several moments, then resumed.

'And now, having shown it to you, for my own safety I will place it back in its leaden casket.'

Drawing off his gloves, he proceeded.

'I have found out by a cablegram to-day that seven weeks ago an order for one hundred milligrams of radium bromide at thirty-five dollars a milligram from a certain person in America was filled by a corporation dealing in this substance.'

Kennedy said this with measured words, and I felt a thrill run through me as he developed his case.

'At that same time, Mrs Close began a series of treatments with an X-ray specialist in New York,' pursued Kennedy. 'Now, it is not generally known outside scientific circles, but the fact is that in their physiological effects the X-ray and radium are quite one and the same. Radium possesses this advantage, however, that no elaborate apparatus is necessary for its use. And, in addition, the emanation from radium is steady and constant, whereas the X-ray at best varies slightly with changing conditions of the current and vacuum in the X-ray tube. Still, the effects on the body are much the same.

'A few days before this order was placed I recall the following despatch which appeared in the New York papers. I will read it.

'Liege, Belgium, Oct. –, 1910. What is believed to be the first criminal case in which radium figures as a death-dealing agent is engaging public attention at this university town. A wealthy old bachelor, Pailin by name, was found dead in his flat. A stroke of apoplexy was at first believed to have caused his death, but a close examination revealed a curious discolouration of his skin. A specialist called in to view the body gave as his opinion that the old man had been exposed for a long time to the emanations of X-ray or radium. The police theory is that M. Pailin was done to death by a systematic application of either X-rays or radium by a student in the university who roomed next to him. The student has disappeared.

'Now here, I believe, was the suggestion which this American criminal followed, for I cut it out of the paper rather expecting sooner or later that some clever person would act on it. I have thoroughly examined the room of Mrs Close. She herself told me she never wanted to return to it, that her memory of sleepless nights in it was too vivid. That served to fix the impression that I had already formed from reading this clipping. Either the X-ray or radium had caused her dermatitis and nervousness. Which was it? I wished to be sure that I would make no mistake. Of course I knew it was useless to look for an X-ray machine in or near Mrs Close's room. Such a thing could never have been concealed. The alternative? Radium! Ah! that was different. I determined on an experiment. Mrs Close's maid was prevailed on to sleep in her mistress's room. Of course radiations of brief duration would do her no permanent harm, although they would produce their effect, nevertheless. In one night the maid became extremely nervous. If she had stayed under them several nights no doubt the beginning of a dermatitis would have affected her, if not more serious trouble. A systematic application, covering weeks and months, might in the end even have led to death.

'The next day I managed, as I have said, to go over the room thoroughly with a vacuum cleaner – a new one of my own which I had bought myself. But tests of the dust which I got from the floors, curtains, and furniture showed nothing at all. As a last thought I had, however, cleaned the mattress of the bed and the cracks and crevices in the brass bars. Tests of that dust showed it to be extremely radioactive. I had the dust dissolved, by a chemist who understands that sort of thing, recrystallised, and the radium salts were extracted from the refuse. Thus I found that I had recovered all but a very few milligrams of the radium that had been originally purchased in London. Here it is in this deadly tube in the leaden casket.

'It is needless to add that the night after I had cleaned out this deadly element the maid slept the sleep of the just – and would have been all right when next I saw her but for the interference of the unjust on whom I had stolen a march.'

Craig paused while the lawyers whispered again to their clients. Then he continued: 'Now three persons in this room had an opportunity to secrete the contents of this deadly tube in the crevices of the metal work of Mrs Close's bed. One of these persons must have placed an order through a confidential agent in London to purchase the radium from the English Radium Corporation. One of these persons had a compelling motive, something to gain by using this deadly element. The radium in this tube in the casket was secreted, as I have said, in the metal work of Mrs Close's bed, not in large enough quantities to be immediately fatal, but mixed with dust so as to produce the result more slowly but no less surely, and thus avoid suspicion. At the same time Mrs Close was persuaded – I will not say by whom – through her natural pride, to take a course of X-ray treatment for a slight defect. That would further serve to divert suspicion. The fact is that a more horrible plot could hardly have been planned or executed. This person sought to ruin her beauty to gain a most selfish and despicable end.'

Again Craig paused to let his words sink into our minds.

'Now I wish to state that anything you gentlemen may say will be used against you. That is why I have asked you to bring your attorneys. You may consult with them, of course, while I am getting ready my next disclosure.'

As Kennedy had developed his points in the case I had been more and more amazed. But I had not failed to notice how keenly Lawrence was following him.

With half a sneer on his astute face, Lawrence drawled: 'I cannot see that you have accomplished anything by this rather extraordinary summoning of us to your laboratory. The evidence is just as black against Dr Gregory as before. You may think you're clever, Kennedy, but on the very statement of facts as you have brought them out there is plenty of circumstantial evidence against Gregory – more than there was before. As for anyone else in the room, I can't see that you have anything on us – unless perhaps this new evidence you speak of may implicate Asche, or Jameson,' he added, including me in a wave of his hand, as if he were already addressing a jury. 'It's my opinion that twelve of our peers would be quite as likely to bring in a verdict of guilty against them as against anyone else even remotely connected with this case, except Gregory. No, you'll have to do better than this in your next case, if you expect to maintain that so-called reputation of yours for being a professor of criminal science.'

As for Close, taking his cue from his attorney, he scornfully added: 'I came to find out some new evidence against the wretch who wrecked the beauty of my wife. All I've got is a tiresome lecture on X-rays and radium. I suppose what you say is true.

'Well, it only bears out what I thought before. Gregory treated my wife at home, after he saw the damage his office treatments had done. I guess he was capable of making a complete job out of it – covering up his carelessness by getting rid of the woman who was such a damning piece of evidence against his professional skill.'

Never a shade passed Craig's face as he listened to this tirade. 'Excuse me a moment,' was all he said, opening the door to leave the room. 'I have just one more fact to disclose. I will be back directly.'

Kennedy was gone several minutes, during which Close and Lawrence fell to whispering behind their hands, with the assurance of those who believed that this was only Kennedy's method of admitting a defeat. Gregory and Asche exchanged a few words similarly, and it was plain that Asche was endeavouring to put a better interpretation on something than Gregory himself dared hope.

As Kennedy re-entered, Close was buttoning up his coat preparatory to leaving, and Lawrence was lighting a fresh cigar.

In his hand Kennedy held a notebook. 'My stenographer writes a very legible shorthand; at least I find it so – from long practice, I suppose. As I glance over her notes I find many facts which will interest you later – at the trial. But – ah, here at the end – let me read:

'"Well, he's very clever, but he has nothing against me, has he?"

'"No, not unless he can produce the agent who bought the radium for you."

'"But he can't do that. No one could ever have recognised you on your flying trip to London disguised as a diamond merchant who had just learned that he could make his faulty diamonds good by applications of radium and who wanted a good stock of the stuff."

'"Still, we'll have to drop the suit against Gregory after all, in spite of what I said. That part is hopelessly spoiled."

'"Yes, I suppose so. Oh, well, I'm free now. She can hardly help but consent to a divorce now, and a quiet settlement. She brought it on herself – we tried every other way to do it, but she – she was too good to fall into it. She forced us to it."

'"Yes, you'll get a good divorce now. But can't we shut up this man Kennedy? Even if he can't prove anything against us, the mere rumour of such a thing coming to the ears of Mrs Tulkington would be unpleasant."

'"Go as far as you like, Lawrence. You know what the marriage will mean to me. It will settle my debts to you and all the rest."

'"I'll see what I can do, Close. He'll be back in a moment."'

Close's face was livid. 'It's a pack of lies!' he shouted, advancing toward Kennedy, 'a pack of lies! You are a fakir and a blackmailer. I'll have you in jail for this, by God – and you too, Gregory.'

'One moment, please,' said Kennedy calmly. 'Mr Lawrence, will you be so kind as to reach behind your chair? What do you find?'

Lawrence lifted up the plain black box and with it he pulled up the wires which I had so carefully concealed in the cracks of the floor.

'That,' said Kennedy, 'is a little instrument called the microphone. Its chief merit lies in the fact that it will magnify a sound sixteen hundred times, and carry it to any given point where you wish to place the receiver. Originally this device was invented for the aid of the deaf, but I see no reason why it should not be used to aid the law. One needn't eavesdrop at the keyhole with this little instrument about. Inside that box there is nothing but a series of plugs from which wires, much finer than a thread, are stretched taut. Yet a fly walking near it will make a noise as loud as a draft-horse. If the microphone is placed in any part of the room, especially if near the persons talking – even if they are talking in a whisper – a whisper such as occurred several times during the evening and particularly while I was in the next room getting the notes made by my stenographer – a whisper, I say, is like shouting your guilt from the housetops.

'You two men, Close and Lawrence, may consider yourselves under arrest for conspiracy and whatever other indictments will lie against such creatures as you. The police will be here in a moment. No, Close, violence won't do now. The doors are locked – and see, we are four to two.'

Cecil Thorold

Created by Arnold Bennett (1867 – 1931)

BENNETT WAS BORN in Hanley in the heart of the Staffordshire Potteries, the setting for much of his best fiction, and moved to London in 1888. During the 1890s he gradually established a reputation as a writer and *Anna of the Five Towns* became his first major critical success in 1902. Other novels set in the Potteries followed (most notably *The Old Wives' Tale* and *Clayhanger*) but Bennett himself had by then become a metropolitan figure who lived in London and Paris for the rest of his life. He died of typhoid, allegedly contracted in France, where he had drunk a glass of suspiciously murky liquid from a tap in order to demonstrate the perfect safety of that nation's water supply. Bennett's crime fiction has been almost completely overshadowed by his other writing but it deserves rescuing from oblivion. The debonair millionaire Cecil Thorold appears in a series of stories, first published in *The Windsor Magazine* in 1905 and then collected in a volume entitled *The Loot of the Cities*. Thorold, who travels elegantly through Edwardian Europe, staying at the best hotels and dining at the best restaurants, is not always a conventional detective hero. Indeed, in some of the stories, he is the perpetrator of the crime rather than the solver of it. However, all the stories demonstrate Bennett's skill and versatility as a writer and remain well worth reading.

A Bracelet at Bruges

I

THE BRACELET HAD fallen into the canal.

And the fact that the canal was the most picturesque canal in the old Flemish city of Bruges, and that the ripples caused by the splash of the bracelet had disturbed reflections of wondrous belfries, towers, steeples, and other unique examples of Gothic architecture, did nothing whatever to assuage the sudden agony of that disappearance. For the bracelet had been given to Kitty Sartorius by her grateful and lordly manager, Lionel Belmont (U.S.A.), upon the completion of the unexampled run of 'The Delmonico Doll', at the Regency Theatre, London. And its diamonds were worth five hundred pounds, to say nothing of the gold.

The beautiful Kitty, and her friend Eve Fincastle, the journalist, having exhausted Ostend, had duly arrived at Bruges in the course of their holiday tour. The question of Kitty's jewellery had arisen at the start. Kitty had insisted that she must travel with all her jewels, according to the custom of theatrical stars of great magnitude. Eve had equally insisted that Kitty must travel without jewels, and had exhorted her to remember the days of her simplicity. They compromised. Kitty was allowed to bring the bracelet, but nothing else save the usual half-dozen rings. The ravishing creature could not have persuaded herself to leave the bracelet behind, because it was so recent a gift and still new and strange and heavenly to her. But, since prudence forbade even Kitty to let the trifle lie about in hotel bedrooms, she was obliged always to wear it. And she had been wearing it this bright afternoon in early October, when the girls, during a stroll, had met one of their new friends, Madame Lawrence, on the world-famous Quai du Rosaire, just at the back of the Hôtel de Ville and the Halles.

Madame Lawrence resided permanently in Bruges. She was between twenty-five and forty-five, dark, with the air of continually subduing a natural instinct to dash, and well dressed in black. Equally interested in the peerage and in the poor, she had made the acquaintance of Eve and Kitty at the Hôtel de la Grande Place, where she called from time to time to induce English travellers to buy genuine Bruges lace, wrought under her own supervision by her own paupers. She was Belgian by birth, and when complimented on her fluent and correct English, she gave all the praise to her deceased husband, an English barrister. She had settled in Bruges like many people settle there, because Bruges is inexpensive, picturesque, and inordinately respectable. Besides an English church and chaplain, it has two cathedrals and an episcopal palace, with a real bishop in it.

'What an exquisite bracelet! May I look at it?' It was these simple but ecstatic words, spoken with Madame Lawrence's charming foreign accent, which had begun the tragedy. The three women had stopped to admire the always admirable view from the little quay, and they were leaning over the rails when Kitty unclasped the bracelet for the inspection of the widow. The next instant there was a plop, an affrighted exclamation from Madame Lawrence in her native tongue, and the bracelet was engulfed before the very eyes of all three.

The three looked at each other nonplussed. Then they looked around, but not a single person was in sight. Then, for some reason which, doubtless, psychology can explain, they stared hard at the water, though the water there was just as black and foul as it is everywhere else in the canal system of Bruges.

'Surely you've not dropped it!' Eve Fincastle exclaimed in a voice of horror. Yet she knew positively that Madame Lawrence had.

The delinquent took a handkerchief from her muff and sobbed into it. And between her sobs she murmured: 'We must inform the police.'

'Yes, of course,' said Kitty, with the lightness of one to whom a five-hundred-pound bracelet is a bagatelle. 'They'll fish it up in no time.'

'Well,' Eve decided, 'you go to the police at once, Kitty; and Madame Lawrence will go with you, because she speaks French, and I'll stay here to mark the exact spot.'

The other two started, but Madame Lawrence, after a few steps, put her hand to her side. 'I can't,' she sighed, pale. 'I am too upset. I cannot walk. You go with Miss Sartorius,' she said to Eve, 'and I will stay,' and she leaned heavily against the railings.

Eve and Kitty ran off, just as if it was an affair of seconds, and the bracelet had to be saved from drowning. But they had scarcely turned the corner, thirty yards away, when they reappeared in company with a high official of police, whom, by the most lucky chance in the world, they had encountered in the covered passage leading to the Place du Bourg. This official, instantly enslaved by Kitty's beauty, proved to be the very mirror of politeness and optimism. He took their names and addresses, and a full description of the bracelet, and informed them that at that place the canal was nine feet deep. He said that the bracelet should undoubtedly be recovered on the morrow, but that, as dusk was imminent, it would be futile to commence angling that night. In the meantime the loss should be kept secret; and to make all sure, a succession of gendarmes should guard the spot during the night.

Kitty grew radiant, and rewarded the gallant officer with smiles; Eve was satisfied, and the face of Madame Lawrence wore a less mournful hue.

'And now,' said Kitty to Madame, when everything had been arranged, and the first of the gendarmes was duly installed at the exact spot against the railings, 'you must come and take tea with us in our winter garden; and be gay! Smile: I insist. And I insist that you don't worry.'

Madame Lawrence tried feebly to smile.

'You are very good-natured,' she stammered.

Which was decidedly true.

II

The winter-garden of the Hôtel de la Grande Place, referred to in all the hotel's advertisements, was merely the inner court of the hotel, roofed in by glass at the height of the first storey. Cane flourished there, in the shape of lounge-chairs, but no other plant. One of the lounge chairs was occupied when, just as the carillon in the belfry at the other end of the Place began to play Gounod's 'Nazareth', indicating the hour of five o'clock, the three ladies entered the winter-garden. Apparently the toilettes of two of them had been adjusted and embellished as for a somewhat ceremonious occasion.

'Lo!' cried Kitty Sartorius, when she perceived the occupant of the chair, 'the millionaire! Mr Thorold, how charming of you to reappear like this! I invite you to tea.'

Cecil Thorold rose with appropriate eagerness.

'Delighted!' he said, smiling, and then explained that he had arrived from Ostend about two hours before and had taken rooms in the hotel.

'You knew we were staying here?' Eve asked as he shook hands with her.

'No,' he replied; 'but I am very glad to find you again.'

'Are you?' She spoke languidly, but her colour heightened and those eyes of hers sparkled.

'Madame Lawrence,' Kitty chirruped, 'let me present Mr Cecil Thorold. He is appallingly rich, but we mustn't let that frighten us.'

From a mouth less adorable than the mouth of Miss Sartorius such an introduction might have been judged lacking in the elements of good form, but for more than two years now Kitty had known that whatever she did or said was perfectly correct because she did or said it. The new acquaintances laughed amiably and a certain intimacy was at once established.

'Shall I order tea, dear?' Eve suggested.

'No, dear,' said Kitty quietly. 'We will wait for the Count.'

'The Count?' demanded Cecil Thorold.

'The Comte d'Avrec,' Kitty explained. 'He is staying here.'

'A French nobleman, doubtless?'

'Yes,' said Kitty; and she added, 'you will like him. He is an archaeologist, and a musician – oh, and lots of things!'

'If I am one minute late, I entreat pardon,' said a fine tenor voice at the door.

It was the Count. After he had been introduced to Madame Lawrence, and Cecil Thorold had been introduced to him, tea was served.

Now, the Comte d'Avrec was everything that a French count ought to be. As dark as Cecil Thorold, and even handsomer, he was a little older and a little taller than the millionaire, and a short, pointed, black beard, exquisitely trimmed, gave him an appearance of staid reliability which Cecil lacked. His bow was a vertebrate poem, his smile a consolation for all misfortunes, and he managed his hat, stick, gloves, and cup with the dazzling assurance of a conjurer. To observe him at afternoon tea was to be convinced that he had been specially created to shine gloriously in drawing-rooms, winter-gardens, and tables d'hôte. He was one of those men who always do the right thing at the right moment, who are capable of speaking an indefinite number of languages with absolute purity of accent (he spoke English much better than Madame Lawrence), and who can and do discourse with verve and accuracy on all sciences, arts, sports, and religions. In short, he was a phoenix of a count; and this was certainly the opinion of Miss Kitty Sartorius and of Miss Eve Fincastle, both of whom reckoned that what they did not know about men might be ignored. Kitty and the Count, it soon became evident, were mutually attracted; their souls were approaching each other with a velocity which increased inversely as the square of the lessening distance between them. And Eve was watching this approximation with undisguised interest and relish.

Nothing of the least importance occurred, save the Count's marvellous exhibition of how to behave at afternoon tea, until the refection was nearly over; and then, during a brief pause in the talk, Cecil, who was sitting to the left of Madame Lawrence, looked sharply round at the right shoulder of his tweed coat; he repeated the gesture a second and yet a third time.

'What is the matter with the man?' asked Eve Fincastle. Both she and Kitty were extremely bright, animated, and even excited.

'Nothing. I thought I saw something on my shoulder, that's all,' said Cecil. 'Ah! It's only a bit of thread.' And he picked off the thread with his left hand and held it before Madame Lawrence. 'See! It's a piece of thin black silk, knotted. At first I took it for an insect – you know how queer things look out of the corner of your eye. Pardon!' He had dropped the fragment on to Madame Lawrence's black silk dress. 'Now it's lost.'

'If you will excuse me, kind friends,' said Madame Lawrence, 'I will go.' She spoke hurriedly, and as though in mental distress.

'Poor thing!' Kitty Sartorius exclaimed when the widow had gone. 'She's still dreadfully upset'; and Kitty and Eve proceeded jointly to relate the story of the diamond bracelet, upon which hitherto they had kept silence (though with difficulty), out of regard for Madame Lawrence's feelings.

Cecil made almost no comment.

The Count, with the sympathetic excitability of his race, walked up and down the winter-garden, asseverating earnestly that such clumsiness amounted to a crime; then he grew calm and confessed that he shared the optimism of the police as to the recovery of the bracelet; lastly he complimented Kitty on her equable demeanour under this affliction.

'Do you know, Count,' said Cecil Thorold, later, after they had all four ascended to the drawing-room overlooking the Grande Place, 'I was quite surprised when I saw at tea that you had to be introduced to Madame Lawrence.'

'Why so, my dear Mr Thorold?' the Count inquired suavely.

'I thought I had seen you together in Ostend a few days ago.'

The Count shook his wonderful head.

'Perhaps you have a brother?' Cecil paused.

'No,' said the Count. 'But it is a favourite theory of mine that everyone has his double somewhere in the world.' Previously the Count had been discussing Planchette – he was a great authority on the supernatural, the sub-conscious, and the subliminal. He now deviated gracefully to the discussion of the theory of doubles.

'I suppose you aren't going out for a walk, dear, before dinner?' said Eve to Kitty.

'No, dear,' said Kitty, positively.

'I think I shall,' said Eve.

And her glance at Cecil Thorold intimated in the plainest possible manner that she wished not only to have a companion for a stroll, but to leave Kitty and the Count in dual solitude.

'I shouldn't, if I were you, Miss Fincastle,' Cecil remarked, with calm and studied blindness. 'It's risky here in the evenings – with these canals exhaling miasma and mosquitoes and bracelets and all sorts of things.'

'I will take the risk, thank you,' said Eve, in an icy tone, and she haughtily departed; she would not cower before Cecil's millions. As for Cecil, he joined in the discussion of the theory of doubles.

III

On the next afternoon but one, policemen were still fishing, without success, for the bracelet, and raising from the ancient duct long-buried odours which threatened to destroy the inhabitants of the quay. (When Kitty Sartorius had hinted that perhaps the authorities might see their way to drawing off the water from the canal, the authorities had intimated that the death-rate of Bruges was already as high as convenient.) Nevertheless, though nothing had happened, the situation had somehow developed, and in such a manner that the bracelet itself was in danger of being partially forgotten; and of all places in Bruges, the situation had developed on the top of the renowned Belfry which dominates the Grande Place in particular and the city in general.

The summit of the Belfry is three hundred and fifty feet high, and it is reached by four hundred and two winding stone steps, each a separate menace to life and limb. Eve Fincastle had climbed those steps alone, perhaps in quest of the view at the top, perhaps in quest of spiritual calm. She had not been leaning over the parapet more than a minute before Cecil Thorold had appeared, his field-glasses slung over his shoulder. They had begun to talk a little, but nervously and only in snatches. The wind blew free up there among the forty-eight bells, but the social atmosphere was oppressive.

'The Count is a most charming man,' Eve was saying, as if in defence of the Count.

'He is,' said Cecil; 'I agree with you.'

'Oh, no, you don't, Mr Thorold! Oh, no, you don't!'

Then there was a pause, and the twain looked down upon Bruges, with its venerable streets, its grass-grown squares, its waterways, and its innumerable monuments, spread out maplike beneath them in the mellow October sunshine. Citizens passed along the thoroughfare in the semblance of tiny dwarfs.

'If you didn't hate him,' said Eve, 'you wouldn't behave as you do.'

'How do I behave, then?'

Eve schooled her voice to an imitation of jocularity:

'All Tuesday evening, and all day yesterday, you couldn't leave them alone. You know you couldn't.'

Five minutes later the conversation had shifted.

'You actually saw the bracelet fall into the canal?' said Cecil.

'I actually saw the bracelet fall into the canal. And no one could have got it out while Kitty and I were away, because we weren't away half a minute.'

But they could not dismiss the subject of the Count, and presently he was again the topic.

'Naturally it would be a good match for the Count – for any man,' said Eve; 'but then it would also be a good match for Kitty. Of course, he is not so rich as some people, but he is rich.'

Cecil examined the horizon with his glasses, and then the streets near the Grand Place.

'Rich, is he? I'm glad of it. By the by, he's gone to Ghent for the day, hasn't he?'

'Yes, he went by the 9.27, and returns by the 4.38.'

Another pause.

'Well,' said Cecil at length, handing the glasses to Eve Fincastle, 'kindly glance down there. Follow the line of the Rue St. Nicolas. You see the cream-coloured house with the enclosed courtyard? Now, do you see two figures standing together near a door – a man and a woman, the woman on the steps? Who are they?'

'I can't see very well,' said Eve.

'Oh, yes, my dear lady, you can,' said Cecil. 'These glasses are the very best. Try again.'

'They look like the Comte d'Avrec and Madame Lawrence,' Eve murmured.

'But the Count is on his way from Ghent! I see the steam of the 4.38 over there. The curious thing is that the Count entered the house of Madame Lawrence, to whom he was introduced for the first time the day before yesterday, at ten o'clock this morning. Yes, it would be a very good match for the Count. When one comes to think of it, it usually is that sort of man that contrives to marry a brilliant and successful actress. There! He's just leaving, isn't he? Now let us descend and listen to the recital of his day's doings in Ghent – shall we?'

'You mean to insinuate,' Eve burst out in sudden wrath, 'that the Count is an – an adventurer, and that Madame Lawrence – Oh! Mr Thorold!' She laughed condescendingly. 'This jealousy is too absurd.

Do you suppose I haven't noticed how impressed you were with Kitty at the Devonshire Mansion that night, and again at Ostend, and again here? You're simply carried away by jealousy; and you think because you are a millionaire you must have all you want. I haven't the slightest doubt that the Count – '

'Anyhow,' said Cecil, 'let us go down and hear about Ghent.'

His eyes made a number of remarks (indulgent, angry, amused, protective, admiring, perspicacious, puzzled), too subtle for the medium of words.

They groped their way down to earth in silence, and it was in silence that they crossed the Grande Place. The Count was seated on the terrasse in front of the hotel, with a liqueur glass before him, and he was making graceful and expressive signs to Kitty Sartorius, who leaned her marvellous beauty out of a first-storey window. He greeted Cecil Thorold and Eve with an equal grace.

'And how is Ghent?' Cecil inquired.

'Did you go to Ghent, after all, Count?' Eve put in. The Comte d'Avrec looked from one to another, and then, instead of replying, he sipped at his glass. 'No,' he said, 'I didn't go. The rather curious fact is that I happened to meet Madame Lawrence, who offered to show me her collection of lace. I have been an amateur of lace for some years, and really Madame Lawrence's collection is amazing. You have seen it? No? You should do so. I'm afraid I have spent most of the day there.'

When the Count had gone to join Kitty in the drawing-room, Eve Fincastle looked victoriously at Cecil, as if to demand of him: 'Will you apologise?'

'My dear journalist,' Cecil remarked simply, 'you gave the show away.'

* * * * * *

That evening the continued obstinacy of the bracelet, which still refused to be caught, began at last to disturb the birdlike mind of Kitty Sartorius. Moreover, the secret was out, and the whole town of Bruges was discussing the episode and the chances of success.

'Let us consult Planchette,' said the Count. The proposal was received with enthusiasm by Kitty. Eve had disappeared.

Planchette was produced; and when asked if the bracelet would be recovered, it wrote, under the hands of Kitty and the Count, a trembling 'Yes'. When asked: 'By whom?' it wrote a word which faintly resembled 'Avrec'.

The Count stated that he should personally commence dragging operations at sunrise. 'You will see,' he said, 'I shall succeed.'

'Let me try this toy, may I?' Cecil asked blandly, and, upon Kitty agreeing, he addressed Planchette in a clear voice: 'Now, Planchette, who will restore the bracelet to its owner?'

And Planchette wrote 'Thorold', but in characters as firm and regular as those of a copy-book.

'Mr Thorold is laughing at us,' observed the Count, imperturbably bland.

'How horrid you are, Mr Thorold!' Kitty exclaimed.

IV

Of the four persons more or less interested in the affair, three were secretly active that night, in and out of the hotel. Only Kitty Sartorius, chief mourner for the bracelet, slept placidly in her bed. It was towards three o'clock in the morning that a sort of preliminary crisis was reached.

From the multiplicity of doors which ventilate its rooms, one would imagine that the average foreign hotel must have been designed immediately after its architect had been to see a Palais Royal farce, in which every room opens into every other room in every act. The Hôtel de la Grande Place was not peculiar in this respect; it abounded in doors. All the chambers on the second storey, over the public rooms, fronting the Place, communicated one with the next, but naturally most of the communicating doors were locked. Cecil Thorold and the Comte d'Avrec had each a bedroom and a sitting-room on that floor. The Count's sitting-room adjoined Cecil's; and the door between was locked, and the key in the possession of the landlord.

Nevertheless, at three a.m. this particular door opened noiselessly from Cecil's side, and Cecil entered the domain of the Count. The moon shone, and Cecil could plainly see not only the silhouette of the Belfry across the Place, but also the principal objects within the room. He noticed the table in the middle, the large easy-chair turned towards the hearth, the old-fashioned sofa; but not a single article did he perceive which might have been the personal property of the Count. He cautiously passed across the room through the moonlight to the door of the Count's bedroom, which apparently, to his immense surprise, was not only shut, but locked, and the key in the lock on the sitting-room side. Silently unlocking it, he entered the bedroom and disappeared...

In less than five minutes he crept back into the Count's sitting-room, closed the door and locked it.

'Odd!' he murmured reflectively; but he seemed quite happy.

There was a sudden movement in the region of the hearth, and a form rose from the armchair. Cecil rushed to the switch and turned on the electric light. Eve Fincastle stood before him. They faced each other.

'What are you doing here at this time, Miss Fincastle?' he asked, sternly. 'You can talk freely; the Count will not waken.'

'I may ask you the same question,' Eve replied, with cold bitterness.

'Excuse me. You may not. You are a woman. This is the Count's room – '

'You are in error,' she interrupted him. 'It is not the Count's room. It is mine. Last night I told the Count I had some important writing to do, and I asked him as a favour to relinquish this room to me for twenty-four hours. He very kindly consented. He removed his belongings, handed me the key of that door, and the transfer was made in the hotel books. And now,' she added, 'may I inquire, Mr Thorold, what you are doing in my room?'

'I – I thought it was the Count's,' Cecil faltered, decidedly at a loss for a moment. 'In offering my humblest apologies, permit me to say that I admire you, Miss Fincastle.'

'I wish I could return the compliment,' Eve exclaimed, and she repeated with almost plaintive sincerity: 'I do wish I could.'

Cecil raised his arms and let them fall to his side.

'You meant to catch me,' he said. 'You suspected something, then? The "important writing" was an invention.' And he added, with a faint smile: 'You really ought not to have fallen asleep. Suppose I had not wakened you?'

'Please don't laugh, Mr Thorold. Yes, I did suspect. There was something in the demeanour of your servant Lecky that gave me the idea. . . . I did mean to catch you. Why you, a millionaire, should be a burglar, I cannot understand. I never understood that incident at the Devonshire Mansion; it was beyond me. I am by no means sure that you didn't have a great deal to do with the Rainshore affair at Ostend. But that you should have stooped to slander is the worst. I confess you are a mystery. I confess that I can make no guess at the nature of your present scheme. And what I shall do, now that I have caught you, I don't know. I can't decide; I must think. If, however, anything is missing to-morrow morning, I shall be bound in any case to denounce you. You grasp that?'

'I grasp it perfectly, my dear journalist,' Cecil replied. 'And something will not improbably be missing. But take the advice of a burglar and a mystery, and go to bed, it is half past three.'

And Eve went. And Cecil bowed her out and then retired to his own rooms. And the Count's apartment was left to the moonlight.

V

'Planchette is a very safe prophet,' said Cecil to Kitty Sartorius the next morning, 'provided it has firm guidance.'

They were at breakfast.

'What do you mean?'

'I mean that Planchette prophesied last night that I should restore to you your bracelet. I do.'

He took the lovely gewgaw from his pocket and handed it to Kitty.

'Ho-ow did you find it, you dear thing?' Kitty stammered, trembling under the shock of joy.

'I fished it up out – out of the mire by a contrivance of my own.'

'But when?'

'Oh! Very early. At three o'clock a.m. You see, I was determined to be first.'

'In the dark, then?'

'I had a light. Don't you think I'm rather clever?'

Kitty's scene of ecstatic gratitude does not come into the story. Suffice it to say that not until the moment of its restoration did she realise how precious the bracelet was to her.

It was ten o'clock before Eve descended. She had breakfasted in her room, and Kitty had already exhibited to her the prodigal bracelet.

'I particularly want you to go up the Belfry with me, Miss Fincastle,' Cecil greeted her; and his tone was so serious and so urgent that she consented. They left Kitty playing waltzes on the piano in the drawing-room.

'And now, O man of mystery?' Eve questioned, when they had toiled to the summit, and saw the city and its dwarfs beneath them.

'We are in no danger of being disturbed here,' Cecil began; 'but I will make my explanation – the explanation which I certainly owe you – as brief as possible. Your Comte d'Avrec is an adventurer (please don't be angry), and your Madame Lawrence is an adventuress. I knew that I had seen them together. They work in concert; and for the most part make a living on the gaming-tables of Europe. Madame Lawrence was expelled from Monte Carlo last year for being too intimate with a croupier. You may be aware that at a roulette-table one can do a great deal with the aid of the croupier. Madame Lawrence appropriated the bracelet "on her own", as it were. The Count (he may be a real Count, for anything I know) heard first of that enterprise from the lips of Miss Sartorius. He was annoyed, angry – because he was really a little in love with your friend, and he saw golden prospects. It is just this fact – the Count's genuine passion for Miss Sartorius – that renders the case psychologically interesting. To proceed, Madame Lawrence became jealous. The Count spent six hours yesterday in trying to get the bracelet from her, and failed. He tried again last night, and succeeded, but not too easily, for he did not re-enter the hotel till after one o'clock. At first I thought he had succeeded in the daytime, and I had arranged accordingly, for I did not see why he should have the honour and glory of restoring the bracelet to its owner. Lecky and I fixed up a sleeping-draught for him. The minor details were simple. When you caught me this morning, the bracelet was in my pocket, and in its stead I had left a brief note for the perusal of the

Count, which has had the singular effect of inducing him to decamp; probably he has not gone alone. But isn't it amusing that, since you so elaborately took his sitting-room, he will be convinced that you are a party to his undoing – you, his staunchest defender?'

Eve's face gradually broke into an embarrassed smile.

'You haven't explained,' she said, 'how Madame Lawrence got the bracelet.'

'Come over here,' Cecil answered. 'Take these glasses and look down at the Quai du Rosaire. You see everything plainly?' Eve could, in fact, see on the quay the little mounds of mud which had been extracted from the canal in the quest of the bracelet. Cecil continued: 'On my arrival in Bruges on Monday, I had a fancy to climb the Belfry at once. I witnessed the whole scene between you and Miss Sartorius and Madame Lawrence, through my glasses. Immediately your backs were turned, Madame Lawrence, her hands behind her, and her back against the railing, began to make a sort of rapid, drawing up motion with her forearms. Then I saw a momentary glitter... Considerably mystified, I visited the spot after you had left it, chatted with the gendarme on duty and got round him, and then it dawned on me that a robbery had been planned, prepared, and executed with extraordinary originality and ingenuity. A long, thin thread of black silk must have been ready tied to the railing, with perhaps a hook at the other end. As soon as Madame Lawrence held the bracelet, she attached the hook to it and dropped it. The silk, especially as it was the last thing in the world you would look for, would be as good as invisible. When you went for the police, Madame retrieved the bracelet, hid it in her muff, and broke off the silk. Only, in her haste, she left a bit of silk tied to the railing. That fragment I carried to the hotel. All along she must have been a little uneasy about me... And that's all. Except that I wonder you thought I was jealous of the Count's attentions to your friend.' He gazed at her admiringly.

'I'm glad you are not a thief, Mr Thorold,' said Eve.

'Well,' Cecil smiled, 'as for that, I left him a couple of louis for fares, and I shall pay his hotel bill.'

'Why?'

'There were notes for nearly ten thousand francs with the bracelet. Ill-gotten gains, I am sure. A trifle, but the only reward I shall have for my trouble. I shall put them to good use.' He laughed, serenely gay.

Miss Lois Cayley

Created by Grant Allen (1848 – 1899)

SOME OF THE best female detectives of the late Victorian period were actually created by male writers. Lois Cayley, who appeared in a series of stories published in *The Strand* before being collected in volume form, is a Cambridge-educated 'New Woman' of the 1890s. Travelling Europe in search of adventure and a means of earning money, Miss Cayley becomes involved in a series of crimes which require all her wit and intelligence to solve. Her creator was Grant Allen, a popular and versatile writer whose other works ranged from science fiction to botany. Born in Canada, Allen had been a professor at a college in the West Indies before arriving in London in the late 1870s to pursue a career as a writer. His best-known and best-selling book was *The Woman Who Did*, published in 1895, which gained notoriety for its portrayal of an independent woman who defies convention to live as a single mother. Allen's feminist sympathies are clearly in evidence in the Lois Cayley stories and in the creation of Hilda Wade, another female detective whose adventures are recorded in an episodic novel that was finished, after Allen's death, by his friend Arthur Conan Doyle.

The Adventure of the Cantankerous Old Lady

ON THE DAY when I found myself with twopence in my pocket, I naturally made up my mind to go round the world.

It was my stepfather's death that drove me to it. I had never seen my stepfather. Indeed, I never even thought of him as anything more than Colonel Watts-Morgan. I owed him nothing, except my poverty. He married my dear mother when I was a girl at school in Switzerland; and he proceeded to spend her little fortune, left at her sole disposal by my father's will, in paying his gambling debts. After that, he carried my dear mother off to Burma; and when he and the climate between them had succeeded in killing her, he made up for his appropriations at the cheapest rate by allowing me just enough to send me to Girton. So, when the Colonel died, in the year I was leaving college, I did not think it necessary to go into mourning for him. Especially as he chose the precise moment when my allowance was due, and bequeathed me nothing but his consolidated liabilities.

'Of course you will teach,' said Elsie Petheridge, when I explained my affairs to her. 'There is a good demand just now for high-school teachers.'

I looked at her, aghast. 'Teach! Elsie,' I cried (I had come up to town to settle her in at her unfurnished lodgings.) 'Did you say teach? That's just like you dear good schoolmistresses! You go to Cambridge, and get examined till the heart and life have been examined out of you; then you say to yourselves at the end of it all, "Let me see; what am I good for now? I'm just about fit to go away and examine other people!" That's what our Principal would call "a vicious circle" – if one could ever admit there was anything vicious at all about you, dear. No, Elsie, I do not propose to teach. Nature did not cut me out for a high-school teacher. I couldn't swallow a poker if I tried for weeks. Pokers don't agree with me. Between ourselves, I am a bit of a rebel.'

'You are, Brownie,' she answered, pausing in her papering, with her sleeves rolled up – they called me 'Brownie,' partly because of my dark complexion, but partly because they could never understand me. 'We all knew that long ago.'

I laid down the paste-brush and mused.

'Do you remember, Elsie,' I said, staring hard at the paper-board, 'when I first went to Girton, how all you girls wore your hair quite straight, in neat smooth coils, plaited up at the back about the size of a pancake; and how of a sudden I burst in upon you, like a tropical hurricane, and demoralised you; and how, after three days of me, some of the dear innocents began with awe to cut themselves artless fringes, while others went out in fear and trembling and surreptitiously purchased a pair of curling-tongs? I was a bomb-shell in your midst in those days; why, you yourself were almost afraid at first to speak to me.'

'You see, you had a bicycle,' Elsie put in, smoothing the half-papered wall; 'and in those days, of course, ladies didn't bicycle. You must admit, Brownie, dear, it was a startling innovation. You terrified us so. And yet, after all, there isn't much harm in you.'

'I hope not,' I said devoutly. 'I was before my time that was all; at present, even a curate's wife may blamelessly bicycle.'

'But if you don't teach,' Elsie went on, gazing at me with those wondering big blue eyes of hers, 'whatever will you do, Brownie?' Her horizon was bounded by the scholastic circle.

'I haven't the faintest idea,' I answered, continuing to paste. 'Only, as I can't trespass upon your elegant hospitality for life, whatever I mean to do, I must begin doing this morning, when we've finished the papering. I couldn't teach' (teaching, like mauve, is the refuge of the incompetent); 'and I don't, if possible, want to sell bonnets.'

'As a milliner's girl?' Elsie asked, with a face of red horror.

'As a milliner's girl; why not? 'Tis an honest calling. Earls' daughters do it now. But you needn't look so shocked. I tell you, just at present, I am not contemplating it.'

'Then what do you contemplate?'

I paused and reflected. 'I am here in London,' I answered, gazing rapt at the ceiling, 'London, whose streets are paved with gold though it looks at first sight like flagstones; London, the greatest and richest city in the world, where an adventurous soul ought surely to find some loophole for an adventure. (That piece is hung crooked, dear; we shall have to take it down again.) I devise a Plan, therefore. I submit myself to fate; or, if you prefer it, I leave my future in the hands of Providence. I shall stroll out this morning, as soon as I've "cleaned myself", and embrace the first stray enterprise that offers. Our Bagdad teems with enchanted carpets. Let one but float my way, and, hi, presto, I seize it. I go where glory or a modest competence waits me. I snatch at the first offer, the first hint of an opening.'

Elsie stared at me, more aghast and more puzzled than ever. 'But, how?' she asked. 'Where? When? You are so strange! What will you do to find one?'

'Put on my hat and walk out,' I answered. 'Nothing could be simpler. This city bursts with enterprises and surprises. Strangers from east and west hurry through it in all directions. Omnibuses traverse it from end to end – even, I am told, to Islington and Putney; within, folk sit face to face who never saw one another before in their lives, and who may never see one another again, or, on the contrary, may pass the rest of their days together.'

I had a lovely harangue all pat in my head, in much the same strain, on the infinite possibilities of entertaining angels unawares, in cabs, on the Underground, in the aerated bread shops; but Elsie's widening eyes of horror pulled me up short like a hansom in Piccadilly when the inexorable upturned hand of the policeman checks it. 'Oh, Brownie,' she cried, drawing back, 'you don't mean to tell me you're going to ask the first young man you meet in an omnibus to marry you?'

I shrieked with laughter, 'Elsie,' I cried, kissing her dear yellow little head, 'you are *impayable*. You never will learn what I mean. You don't understand the language. No, no; I am going out, simply in search of adventure. What adventure may come, I have not at this moment the faintest conception. The fun lies in the search, the uncertainty, the toss-up of it. What is the good of being penniless – with the trifling exception of twopence – unless you are prepared to accept your position in the spirit of a masked ball at Covent Garden?'

'I have never been to one,' Elsie put in.

'Gracious heavens, neither have I! What on earth do you take me for? But I mean to see where fate will lead me.'

'I may go with you?' Elsie pleaded.

'Certainly not, my child,' I answered – she was three years older than I, so I had the right to patronise her. 'That would spoil all. Your dear little face would be quite enough to scare away a timid adventure.' She knew what I meant. It was gentle and pensive, but it lacked initiative.

So, when we had finished that wall, I popped on my best hat, and popped out by myself into Kensington Gardens.

I am told I ought to have been terribly alarmed at the straits in which I found myself – a girl of twenty-one, alone in the world, and only twopence short of penniless, without a friend to protect, a relation to counsel her. (I don't count Aunt Susan, who lurked in ladylike indigence at Blackheath, and whose counsel, like her tracts, was given away too profusely to everybody to allow of one's placing any very high value upon it.) But, as a matter of fact, I must admit I was not in the least alarmed. Nature had endowed me with a profusion of crisp black hair, and plenty of high spirits. If my eyes had been like Elsie's – that liquid blue which looks out upon life with mingled pity and amazement – I might have felt as a girl ought to feel under such conditions; but having large dark eyes, with a bit of a twinkle in them, and being as well able to pilot a bicycle as any girl of my acquaintance, I have inherited or acquired an outlook on the world which distinctly leans rather towards cheeriness than despondency. I croak with difficulty. So I accepted my plight as an amusing experience, affording full scope for the congenial exercise of courage and ingenuity.

How boundless are the opportunities of Kensington Gardens – the Round Pond, the winding Serpentine, the mysterious seclusion of the Dutch brick Palace! Genii swarm there. One jostles possibilities. It is a land of romance, bounded on the north by the Abyss of Bayswater, and on the south by the Amphitheatre of the Albert Hall.

But for a centre of adventure I choose the Long Walk; it beckoned me somewhat as the North-West Passage beckoned my seafaring ancestors – the buccaneering mariners of Elizabethan Devon. I sat down on a chair at the foot of an old elm with a poetic hollow, prosaically filled by a utilitarian plate of galvanised iron. Two ancient ladies were seated on the other side already – very grand-looking dames, with the haughty and exclusive ugliness of the English aristocracy in its later stages. For frank hideousness, commend me to the noble dowager. They were talking confidentially as I sat down; the trifling episode of my approach did not suffice to stem the full stream of their conversation. The great ignore the intrusion of their inferiors.

'Yes, it's a terrible nuisance,' the eldest and ugliest of the two observed – she was a high-born lady, with a distinctly cantankerous cast of countenance. She had a Roman nose, and her skin was wrinkled like a wilted apple; she wore coffee-coloured point-lace in her bonnet, with a complexion to match. 'But what could I do, my dear? I simply couldn't put up with such insolence. So I looked her straight back in the face – oh, she quailed, I can tell you; and I said to her, in my iciest voice – you know how icy I can be when occasion demands it' – the second old lady nodded an ungrudging assent, as if perfectly prepared to admit her friend's rare gift of iciness – 'I said to her, "Celestine, you can take your month's wages, and half an hour to get out of this house." And she dropped me a deep reverence, and she answered: "Oui, madame, merci beaucoup, madame; je ne desire pas mieux, madame." And out she flounced. So there was the end of it.'

'Still, you go to Schlangenbad on Monday?'

'That's the point. On Monday. If it weren't for the journey, I should have been glad enough to be rid of minx. I'm glad as it is, indeed; for a more insolent upstanding, independent, answer-you-back-again young woman, with a sneer of her own, I never saw, Amelia – but I must get to Schlangenbad. Now, there the difficulty comes in. On the one hand, if I engage a maid in London, I have the choice of two evils. Either I must take a traipsing English girl – and I know by experience that an English girl on the Continent is a vast deal worse than no maid at all: you have to wait upon her, instead of her waiting upon you; she gets seasick on the crossing, and when she reaches France or Germany, she hates the meals, and she detests the hotel servants, and she can't speak the language, so that she's always calling you in to interpret for her in her private differences with the *fille-de-chambre* and the landlord; or else I must pick up a

French maid in London, and I know equally by experience that the French maids one engages in London are invariably dishonest – more dishonest than the rest even; they've come here because they have no character to speak of elsewhere, and they think you aren't likely to write and enquire of their last mistress in Toulouse or St. Petersburg. Then, again, on the other hand, I can't wait to get a Gretchen, an unsophisticated little Gretchen of the Taunus at Schlangenbad – I suppose there are unsophisticated girls in Germany still – made in Germany – they don't make 'em any longer in England, I'm sure – like everything else, the trade in rustic innocence has been driven from the country. I can't wait to get a Gretchen, as I should like to do, of course, because I simply daren't undertake to cross the Channel alone and go all that long journey by Ostend or Calais, Brussels and Cologne, to Schlangenbad.'

'You could get a temporary maid,' her friend suggested, in a lull of the tornado.

The Cantankerous Old Lady flared up. 'Yes, and have my jewel-case stolen! Or find she was an English girl without one word of German. Or nurse her on the boat when I want to give my undivided attention to my own misfortunes. No, Amelia, I call it positively unkind of you to suggest such a thing. You're so unsympathetic! I put my foot down there. I will not take any temporary person.'

I saw my chance. This was a delightful idea. Why not start for Schlangenbad with the Cantankerous Old Lady?

Of course, I had not the slightest intention of taking a lady's-maid's place for a permanency. Nor even, if it comes to that, as a passing expedient. But if I wanted to go round the world, how could I do better than set out by Rhine country? The Rhine leads you on to the Danube, the Danube to the Black Sea, the Black Sea to Asia; and so, by way of India, China and Japan, you reach the Pacific and San Francisco; whence one returns quite easily by New York and the White Star Liners. I began to feel like a globe-trotter already; the Cantankerous Old Lady was the thin end of the wedge – the first rung of the ladder! I proceeded to put my foot on it.

I leaned around the corner of the tree and spoke. 'Excuse me,' I said, in my suavest voice, 'but I think I see a way out of your difficulty.'

My first impression was that the Cantankerous Old Lady would go off in a fit of apoplexy. She grew purple in the face with indignation and astonishment, that a casual outsider should venture to address her; so much so, indeed, that for a second I almost regretted my well-meant interposition. Then she scanned me up and down, as if I were a girl in a mantle shop, and she contemplated buying either me or the mantle. At last, catching my eye, she thought better of it, and burst out laughing.

'What do you mean by this eavesdropping?' she asked.

I flushed up in turn. 'This is a public place,' I replied, with dignity; 'and you spoke in a tone which was hardly designed for the strictest privacy. If you don't wish to be overheard, you oughtn't to shout. Besides, I desired to do you a service.'

The Cantankerous Old Lady regarded me once more from head to foot. I did not quail. Then she turned to her companion. 'The girl has spirit,' she remarked, in an encouraging tone, as if she were discussing some absent person. 'Upon my word, Amelia, I rather like the look of her. Well, my good woman, what do you want to suggest to me?'

'Merely this,' I replied, bridling up and crushing her. 'I am a Girton girl, an officer's daughter, no more a good woman than most others of my class; and I have nothing in particular to do for the moment. I don't object to going to Schlangenbad. I would convoy you over, as companion, or a lady-help, or anything else you choose to call it; I would remain with you there for a week, till you could arrange with your Gretchen, presumably unsophisticated; and then would leave you. Salary is unimportant; my fare suffices. I accept the chance as a cheap opportunity of attaining Schlangenbad.'

The yellow-faced old lady put up her long-handled tortoise-shell eyeglasses and inspected me all over again. 'Well, I declare,' she murmured. 'What are girls coming to, I wonder? Girton, you say; Girton! That place at Cambridge! You speak Greek, of course; but how about German?'

'Like a native,' I answered, with cheerful promptitude. 'I was at school in Canton Berne; it is a mother tongue to me.'

'No, no,' the old lady went on, fixing her keen small eyes on my mouth. 'Those little lips could never frame themselves to "schlecht" or "wunderschon"; they were not cut out for it.'

'Pardon me,' I answered, in German. 'What I say, that I mean. The never-to-be-forgotten music of the Fatherland's-speech has on my infant ear from the first-beginning impressed itself.'

The old lady laughed aloud.

'Don't jabber it to me, child,' she cried. 'I hate the lingo. It's the one tongue on earth that even a pretty girl's lips fail to render attractive. You yourself make faces over it. What's your name, young woman?'

'Lois Cayley.'

'Lois! What a name! I never heard of any Lois in my life before, except Timothy's grandmother. You're not anybody's grandmother, are you?'

'Not to my knowledge,' I answered, gravely.

She burst out laughing again.

'Well, you'll do, I think,' she said, catching my arm. 'That big mill down yonder hasn't ground the originality altogether out of you. I adore originality. It was clever of you to catch at the suggestion of this arrangement. Lois Cayley, you say; any relation of a madcap Captain Cayley whom I used once to know, in the Forty-second Highlanders?'

'His daughter,' I answered, flushing. For I was proud of my father.

'Ha! I remember; he died, poor fellow; he was a good soldier – and his' – I felt she was going to say 'his fool of a widow,' but a glance from me quelled her – 'his widow went and married that good-looking scapegrace, Jack Watts-Morgan. Never marry a man, my dear, with a double-barrelled name and no visible means of subsistence; above all, if he's generally known by a nickname. So you're poor Tom Cayley's daughter, are you? Well, well, we can settle this little matter between us. Mind, I'm a person who always expects to have my own way. If you come with me to Schlangenbad, you must do as I tell you.'

'I think I could manage it – for a week,' I answered, demurely.

She smiled at my audacity. We passed on to terms. They were quite satisfactory. She wanted no references. 'Do I look like a woman who cares about a reference? What are called characters are usually essays in how not to say it. You take my fancy; that's the point! And poor Tom Cayley! But, mind, I will not be contradicted.'

'I will not contradict your wildest misstatement,' I answered, smiling.

'And your name and address?' I asked, after we had settled preliminaries.

A faint red spot rose quaintly in the centre of the Cantankerous Old Lady's sallow cheek. 'My dear,' she murmured 'my name is the one thing on earth I'm really ashamed of. My parents chose to inflict upon me the most odious label that human ingenuity ever devised for a Christian soul; and I've not had courage enough to burst out and change it.'

A gleam of intuition flashed across me, 'You don't mean to say,' I exclaimed, 'that you're called Georgina?'

The Cantankerous Old Lady gripped my arm hard. 'What an unusually intelligent girl!' she broke in. 'How on earth did you guess? It is Georgina.'

'Fellow-feeling,' I answered. 'So is mine, Georgina Lois. But as I quite agree with you as to the atrocity of such conduct, I have suppressed the Georgina. It ought to be made penal to send innocent girls into the world so burdened.'

'My opinion to a T! You are really an exceptionally sensible young woman. There's my name and address; I start on Monday.'

I glanced at her card. The very copperplate was noisy. 'Lady Georgina Fawley, 49 Fortescue Crescent, W.'

It had taken us twenty minutes to arrange our protocols. As I walked off, well pleased, Lady Georgina's friend ran after me quickly.

'You must take care,' she said, in a warning voice. 'You've caught a Tartar.'

'So I suspect,' I answered. 'But a week in Tartary will be at least an experience.'

'She has an awful temper.'

'That's nothing. So have I. Appalling, I assure you. And if it comes to blows, I'm bigger and younger and stronger than she is.'

'Well, I wish you well out of it.'

'Thank you. It is kind of you to give me this warning. But I think I can take care of myself. I come, you see, of a military family.'

I nodded my thanks, and strolled back to Elsie's. Dear little Elsie was in transports of surprise when I related my adventure.

'Will you really go? And what will you do, my dear, when you get there?'

'I haven't a notion,' I answered; 'that's where the fun comes in. But, anyhow, I shall have got there.'

'Oh, Brownie, you might starve!'

307

'And I might starve in London. In either place, I have only two hands and one head to help me.'

'But, then, here you are among friends. You might stop with me for ever.'

I kissed her fluffy forehead. 'You good, generous little Elsie,' I cried; 'I won't stop here one moment after I have finished the painting and papering. I came here to help you. I couldn't go on eating your hard-earned bread and doing nothing. I know how sweet you are; but the last thing I want is to add to your burdens. Now let us roll up our sleeves again and hurry on with the dado.'

'But, Brownie, you'll want to be getting your own things ready. Remember, you're off to Germany on Monday.'

I shrugged my shoulders. 'Tis a foreign trick I picked up in Switzerland. 'What have I got to get ready?' I asked. 'I can't go out and buy a complete summer outfit in Bond Street for twopence. Now, don't look at me like that: be practical, Elsie, and let me help you paint the dado.' For unless I helped her, poor Elsie could never have finished it herself. I cut out half her clothes for her; her own ideas were almost entirely limited to differential calculus. And cutting out a blouse by differential calculus is weary, uphill work for a high-school teacher.

By Monday I had papered and furnished the rooms, and was ready to start on my voyage of exploration. I met the Cantankerous Old Lady at Charing Cross, by appointment, and proceeded to take charge of her luggage and tickets.

Oh my, how fussy she was! 'You will drop that basket! I hope you have got through tickets, via Malines, not by Brussels – I won't go by Brussels. You have to change there. Now, mind you notice how much the luggage weighs in English pounds, and make the man at the office give you a note of it to check those horrid Belgian porters. They'll charge you for double the weight, unless you reduce it at once to kilogrammes. I know their ways. Foreigners have no consciences. They just go to the priest and confess, you know, and wipe it all out, and start fresh again on a career of crime next morning. I'm sure I don't know why I ever go abroad. The only country in the world fit to live in is England. No mosquitoes, no passports, no – goodness gracious, child, don't let that odious man bang about my hat-box!

Have you no immortal soul, porter, that you crush other people's property as if it was blackbeetles? No, I will not let you take this, Lois; this is my jewel-box – it contains all that remains of the Fawley family jewels. I positively decline to appear at Schlangenbad without a diamond to my back. This never leaves my hands. It's hard enough nowadays to keep body and skirt together. Have you secured that coupe at Ostend?'

We got into our first-class carriage. It was clean and comfortable; but the Cantankerous Old Lady made the porter mop the floor, and fidgeted and worried till we slid out of the station. Fortunately, the only other occupant of the compartment was a most urbane and obliging Continental gentleman – I say Continental, because I couldn't quite make out whether he was French, German, or Austrian – who was anxious in every way to meet Lady Georgina's wishes. Did madame desire to have the window open? Oh, certainly, with pleasure; the day was so sultry. Closed a little more? *Parfaitement*, there was a current of air, *il faut l'admettre*. Madame would prefer the corner? No? then perhaps she would like this valise for a footstool? *Permettez* – just thus. A cold draught runs so often along the floor in railway carriages. This is Kent that we traverse; ah, the garden of England! As a diplomat, he knew every nook of Europe, and he echoed the *mot* he had accidentally heard drop from madame's lips on the platform: no country in the world so delightful as England!

'Monsieur is attached to the Embassy in London?' Lady Georgina inquired, growing affable.

He twirled his grey moustache: a waxed moustache of some distinction. 'No, madame; I have quitted the diplomatic service; I inhabit London now *pour mon agrément*. Some of my compatriots call it *triste*; for me, I find it the most fascinating capital in Europe. What gaiety! What movement! What poetry! What mystery!'

'If mystery means fog, it challenges the world,' I interposed.

He gazed at me with fixed eyes. 'Yes, mademoiselle,' he answered in quite a different and markedly chilly voice. 'Whatever your great country attempts – were it only a fog – it achieves consummately.'

I have quick intuitions. I felt the foreign gentleman took an instinctive dislike to me.

To make up for it, he talked much, and with animation, to Lady Georgina. They ferreted out friends in common, and were as much surprised at it as people always are at that inevitable experience.

'Ah yes, Madame, I recollect him well in Vienna. I was there at the time, attached to our Legation. He was a charming man; you read his masterly paper on the Central Problem of the Dual Empire?'

'You were in Vienna then!' the Cantankerous Old Lady mused back. 'Lois, my child, don't stare' – she had covenanted from the first to call me Lois, as my father's daughter, and I confess I preferred it to being Miss Cayley'd. 'We must surely have met. Dare I ask your name, monsieur?'

I could see the foreign gentleman was delighted at this turn. He had played for it, and carried his point. He meant her to ask him. He had a card in his pocket, conveniently close; and he handed it across to her. She read it, and passed it on: 'M. le Comte de Laroche-sur-Loiret.' 'Oh, I remember your name well,' the Cantankerous Old Lady broke in. 'I think you knew my husband, Sir Evelyn Fawley, and my father, Lord Kynaston.'

The Count looked profoundly surprised and delighted. 'What! you are then Lady Georgina Fawley!' he cried striking an attitude. 'Indeed, miladi, your admirable husband was one of the very first to exert his influence in my favour at Vienna. Do I recall him, *ce cher* Sir Evelyn? If I recall him! What a fortunate encounter! I must have seen you some years ago at Vienna, miladi, though I had not then the great pleasure of making your acquaintance. But your face had impressed itself on my sub-conscious self!' (I did not learn till later that the esoteric doctrine of the sub-conscious self was Lady Georgina's favourite hobby.) 'The moment chance led me to this carriage this morning, I said to myself, "That face, those features: so vivid, so striking: I have seen them somewhere. With what do I connect them in the recesses of my memory? A high-born family; genius; rank; the diplomatic service; some unnameable charm; some faint touch of eccentricity. Ha! I have it. Vienna, a carriage with footmen in red livery, a noble presence, a crowd of wits – poets, artists, politicians – pressing eagerly round the landau." That was my mental picture as I sat and confronted you: I understand it all now; this is Lady Georgina Fawley!'

I thought the Cantankerous Old Lady, who was a shrewd person in her way, must surely see through this obvious patter; but I had under-estimated the average human capacity for swallowing flattery. Instead of dismissing his fulsome nonsense with a contemptuous smile, Lady Georgina perked herself up with a conscious air of coquetry, and asked for more. 'Yes, they were delightful days in Vienna,' she said simpering; 'I was young then, Count; I enjoyed life with a zest.'

'Persons of miladi's temperament are always young,' the Count retorted, glibly, leaning forward and gazing at her. 'Growing old is a foolish habit of the stupid and the vacant. Men and women of *esprit* are never older. One learns as one goes on in life to admire, not the obvious beauty of mere youth and health' – he glanced across at me disdainfully – 'but the profounder beauty of deep character in a face – that calm and serene beauty which is imprinted on the brow by experience of the emotions.'

'I have had my moments,' Lady Georgina murmured, with her head on one side.

'I believe it, miladi,' the Count answered, and ogled her.

Thenceforward to Dover, they talked together with ceaseless animation. The Cantankerous Old Lady was capital company. She had a tang in her tongue, and in the course of ninety minutes she had flayed alive the greater part of London society, with keen wit and sprightliness. I laughed against my will at her ill-tempered sallies; they were too funny not to amuse, in spite of their vitriol. As for the Count, he was charmed. He talked well himself, too, and between them I almost forgot the time till we arrived at Dover.

It was a very rough passage. The Count helped us to carry our nineteen hand-packages and four rugs on board; but I noticed that, fascinated as she was with him, Lady Georgina resisted his ingenious efforts to gain possession of her precious jewel-case as she descended the gangway. She clung to it like grim death, even in the chops of the Channel. Fortunately I am a good sailor, and when Lady Georgina's sallow cheeks began to grow pale, I was steady enough to supply her with her shawl and her smelling-bottle. She fidgeted and worried the whole way over. She would be treated like a vertebrate animal. Those horrid Belgians had no right to stick their deck-chairs just in front of her. The impertinence of the hussies with the bright red hair – a grocer's daughters, she felt sure – in venturing to come and sit on the same bench with her – the bench 'for ladies only', under the lee of the funnel! 'Ladies only', indeed! Did the baggages pretend they considered themselves ladies? Oh, that placid old gentleman in the episcopal gaiters was their father, was he? Well, a bishop should bring up his daughters better, having his children in subjection with all gravity. Instead of which – 'Lois, my smelling-salts!' This was a beastly boat; such an odour of machinery; they had no decent boats nowadays; with all our boasted improvements, she could remember well when the cross-Channel service was much better conducted than it was at present. But that was before we had compulsory education. The working classes were driving trade out of the country, and the consequence was, we couldn't build a boat which didn't reek like an oil-shop. Even the sailors on oar were French – jabbering idiots; not an honest British Jacktar among the lot of them; though the stewards were English, and very inferior Cockney English at that, with their off-hand ways, and their School Board airs and graces. She'd School Board them if they were her servants; she'd show them the sort of respect that was due to people of birth and education. But the children of the lower classes never learnt their catechism nowadays; they were too much occupied with literatoor, jography, and free-'and drawrin'. Happily for my nerves, a good lurch to leeward put a stop for a while to the course of her thoughts on the present distresses.

At Ostend the Count made a second gallant attempt to capture the jewel-case, which Lady Georgina automatically repulsed. She had a fixed habit, I believe, of sticking fast to that jewel-case; for she was too overpowered by the Count's urbanity, I feel sure, to suspect for a moment his honesty of purpose. But whenever she travelled, I fancy, she clung to her case as if her life depended upon it; it contained the whole of her valuable diamonds.

We had twenty minutes for refreshments at Ostend during which interval my old lady declared with warmth that I must look after her registered luggage; though, as it was booked through to Cologne, I could not even see it till we crossed the German frontier; for the Belgian *douaniers* seal up the van as soon as the through baggage for Germany is unloaded. To satisfy her, however, I went through the formality of pretending to inspect it, and rendered myself hateful to the head of the *douane* by asking various foolish and inept questions, on which Lady Georgina insisted. When I had finished this silly and uncongenial task – for I am not by nature fussy, and it is hard to assume fussiness as another person's proxy – I returned to our coupe which I had arranged for in London. To my great amazement, I found the Cantankerous Old Lady and the egregious Count comfortably seated there. 'Monsieur has been good enough to accept a place in our carriage,' she observed, as I entered.

He bowed and smiled. 'Or, rather, madame has been so kind as to offer me one,' he corrected.

'Would you like some lunch, Lady Georgina?' I asked, in my chilliest voice. 'There are ten minutes to spare, and the buffet is excellent.'

'An admirable inspiration,' the Count murmured. 'Permit me to escort you, miladi.'

'You will come, Lois?' Lady Georgina asked.

'No, thank you,' I answered, for I had an idea. 'I am a capital sailor, but the sea takes away my appetite.'

'Then you'll keep our places,' she said, turning to me. 'I hope you won't allow them to stick in any horrid foreigners! They will try to force them on you unless you insist. I know their tricky ways. You have the tickets, I trust? And the bulletin for the coupe? Well, mind you don't lose the paper for the registered luggage. Don't let those dreadful porters touch my cloaks. And if anybody attempts to get in, be sure you stand in front of the door as they mount to prevent them.'

The Count handed her out; he was all high courtly politeness. As Lady Georgina descended, he made yet another dexterous effort to relieve her of the jewel-case.

I don't think she noticed it, but automatically once more she waved him aside. Then she turned to me. 'You'd better take care of it. If I lay it down in the buffet while I am eating my soup; some rogue may run away with it. But mind, don't let it out of your hands on any account. Hold it so, on your knee; and, for Heaven's sake, don't part with it.'

By this time my suspicions of the Count were profound. From the first I had doubted him; he was so blandly plausible. But as we landed at Ostend I had accidentally overheard a low whispered conversation when he passed a shabby-looking man, who had travelled in a second-class carriage from London. 'That succeeds?' the shabby-looking man had muttered under his breath in French, as the haughty nobleman with the waxed moustache brushed by him.

'That succeeds admirably,' the Count had answered, in the same soft undertone. *'Ça reussit à merveille.'*

I understood him to mean that he had prospered in his attempt to impose on Lady Georgina.

They had been gone five minutes at the buffet, when the Count came back hurriedly to the door of the coupé with a nonchalant air. 'Oh, mademoiselle,' he said, in an off-hand tone, 'Lady Georgina has sent me to fetch her jewel-case.'

I gripped it hard with both hands. 'Pardon, M. le Comte,' I answered; 'Lady Georgina entrusted it to my safe keeping, and, without her leave, I cannot give it up to any one.'

'You mistrust me?' he cried, looking black. 'You doubt my honour? You doubt my word when I say that miladi has sent me?'

'Du tout,' I answered, calmly. 'But I have Lady Georgina's orders to stick to this case; and till Lady Georgina returns I stick to it.'

He murmured some indignant remark below his breath, and walked off. The shabby-looking passenger was pacing up and down the platform outside in a badly-made dust-coat. As they passed their lips moved. The Count's seemed to mutter, *'C'est un coup manque.'*

However, he did not desist even so. I saw he meant to go on with his dangerous little game. He returned to the buffet and rejoined Lady Georgina. I felt sure it would be useless to warn her, so completely had the Count succeeded in gulling her; but I took my own steps. I examined the jewel-case closely. It had a leather outer covering; within was a strong steel box, with stout bands of metal to bind it. I took my cue at once, and acted for the best on my own responsibility.

When Lady Georgina and the Count returned, they were like old friends together. The quails in aspic and the sparkling hock had evidently opened their hearts to one another. As far as Malines they laughed and talked without ceasing. Lady Georgina was now in her finest vein of spleen: her acid wit grew sharper and more caustic each moment. Not a reputation in Europe had a rag left to cover it as we steamed in beneath the huge iron roof of the main central junction.

I had observed all the way from Ostend that the Count had been anxious lest we might have to give up our coupe at Malines. I assured him more than once that his fears were groundless, for I had arranged at Charing Cross that it should run right through to the German frontier. But he waved me aside, with one lordly hand. I had not told Lady Georgina of his vain attempt to take possession of her jewel-case; and the bare fact of my silence made him increasingly suspicious of me.

'Pardon me, mademoiselle,' he said, coldly; 'you do not understand these lines as well as I do. Nothing is more common than for those rascals of railway clerks to sell one a place in a coupe or a *wagon-lit*, and then never reserve it, or turn one out half way. It is very possible miladi may have to descend at Malines.'

Lady Georgina bore him out by a large variety of selected stories concerning the various atrocities of the rival companies which had stolen her luggage on her way to Italy. As for *trains de luxe*, they were dens of robbers.

So when we reached Malines, just to satisfy Lady Georgina, I put out my head and inquired of a porter. As I anticipated, he replied that there was no change; we went through to Verviers.

The Count, however, was still unsatisfied. He descended, and made some remarks a little farther down the platform to an official in the gold-banded cap of a *chef-de-gare*, or some such functionary. Then he returned to us, all fuming. 'It is as I said,' he exclaimed, flinging open the door. 'These rogues have deceived us. The coupe goes no farther. You must dismount at once, miladi, and take the train just opposite.'

I felt sure he was wrong, and I ventured to say so. But Lady Georgina cried, 'Nonsense, child! The *chef-de-gare* must know. Get out at once! Bring my bag and the rugs. Mind that cloak! Don't forget the sandwich-tin! Thanks Count; will you kindly take charge of my umbrellas? Hurry up, Lois; hurry up! the train is just starting!'

I scrambled after her, with my fourteen bundles, keeping a quiet eye meanwhile on the jewel-case.

We took our seats in the opposite train, which I noticed was marked 'Amsterdam, Bruxelles, Paris'. But I said nothing. The Count jumped in, jumped about, arranged our parcels, jumped out again. He spoke to a porter; then he rushed back excitedly. '*Mille pardons*, miladi,' he cried. 'I find the *chef-de-gare* has cruelly deceived me. You were right, after all, mademoiselle! We must return to the coupé!'

With singular magnanimity, I refrained from saying, 'I told you so.'

Lady Georgina, very flustered and hot by this time, tumbled out once more, and bolted back to the coupé. Both trains were just starting. In her hurry, at last, she let the Count take possession of her jewel-case. I rather fancy that as he passed one window he handed it in to the shabby-looking passenger; but I am not certain. At any rate, when we were comfortably seated in our own compartment once more, and he stood on the footboard just about to enter, of a sudden he made an unexpected dash back, and flung himself wildly into a Paris carriage. At the self-same moment, with a piercing shriek, both trains started.

Lady Georgina threw up her hands in a frenzy of horror. 'My diamonds!' she cried aloud. 'Oh, Lois, my diamonds!'

'Don't distress yourself,' I answered, holding her back, for I verily believe she would have leapt from the train. 'He has only taken the outer shell, with the sandwich-case inside it. Here is the steel box!' And I produced it, triumphantly.

She seized it, overjoyed. 'How did this happen?' she cried, hugging it, for she loved those diamonds.

'Very simply,' I answered. 'I saw the man was a rogue, and that he had a confederate with him in another carriage. So, while you were gone to the buffet at Ostend, I slipped the box out of the case, and put in the sandwich-tin, that he might carry it off, and we might have proofs against him. All you have to do now is to inform the conductor, who will telegraph to stop the train to Paris. I spoke to him about that at Ostend, so that everything is ready.'

She positively hugged me. 'My dear,' she cried, 'you are the cleverest little woman I ever met in my life! Who on earth could have suspected such a polished gentleman? Why, you're worth your weight in gold. What the dickens shall I do without you at Schlangenbad?'

PETER MARK ROGET

The Man Who Became A Book

Every day thousands of people worldwide consult *Roget's Thesaurus*. How many stop to consider why that endlessly useful reference book is so called? Of those who know that it owes its name to the man who first devised it, how many know anything more about him?

Yet Peter Mark Roget was one of the most remarkable men of the nineteenth century and he achieved much in his long life. He did not even begin the great work of classification which bears his name until he was 70. Before that, the polymathic Roget had already made his own contributions to knowledge in a dozen different fields from optics and anatomy to mathematics and education. He would probably have been surprised that his posthumous reputation rests on his thesaurus. No doubt he would have expected that it would be his involvement in the foundation of the University of London that would be his lasting legacy. Or his books on magnetism, galvanism and physiology. Or his scientific papers on persistence of vision, with their later impact on the development of motion pictures. Or his association with major thinkers such as the computer pioneer Charles Babbage and the philosopher Jeremy Bentham. The range of his interests was astonishing and, for sixty years, he was at the centre of the intellectual revolution of his times.

Nick Rennison's biography reveals the full story of Roget's involvement with the great issues and the great personalities of the nineteenth century and recounts the forgotten life behind one of the most famous of all reference books.

To order your copy:

£9.99 including free postage and packing
(UK and Republic of Ireland only)
£11.99 for overseas orders

For credit card orders phone 0207 430 1021 (ref RS)

For orders by post – cheques payable to
Oldcastle Books, 21 Great Ormond Street, London WC1N 3JB
www.noexit.co.uk

SHERLOCK HOLMES

Mark Campbell

Who is Holmes? The world's most famous detective? A drug addict with a heart as cold as ice? A millstone around the neck of his creator? He's all of these things and much, much more.

Sherlock Holmes was the brainchild of Portsmouth GP Arthur Conan Doyle. A writer of historical romantic fiction, Doyle became unhappy that the detective's enormous success eclipsed his more serious offerings. But after attempting to wipe him out at the Reichenbach Falls in Switzerland, Doyle was faced with a vociferous backlash from the general public and eventually he had no choice but to bring his sleuth back from the grave to face more puzzling mysteries.

While not strictly speaking 'canonical', Holmes' deerstalker, curved pipe and cries of 'Elementary, my dear Watson!' have been immortalised in countless stage, film, television and radio productions. An iconic fictional creation, inseparable from his partner-in-crime Dr John Watson, Sherlock Holmes has charmed and fascinated millions of people around the world since his first appearance over a century ago. He is one of English literature's finest creations.

Mark Campbell writes for *The Independent*, *Midweek* and *Crime Time* and has produced Pocket Essentials on *Doctor Who*, *Agatha Christie* and *Carry On Films*. He lives in South East London, near the 'melancholy Plumstead Marshes' of *The Sign of Four*.

To order your copy:

£9.99 including free postage and packing
(UK and Republic of Ireland only)
£11.99 for overseas orders

For credit card orders phone 0207 430 1021 (ref RS)

For orders by post – cheques payable to
Oldcastle Books, 21 Great Ormond Street, London WC1N 3JB
www.noexit.co.uk